Queen of Sheba

Queen of Sheba

Ewa Kassala

Paperback: ISBN: 978-1-7342857-5-8
ePub: ISBN: 978-1-3936995-0-7

***

Written by Ewa Kassala
Published by Royal Hawaiian Press
Cover art by Tyrone Roshantha
Translated by Wieslawa Mentzen
Publishing Assistance: Balasubramanian Nambi

***

For more works by this author, please visit:
www.royalhawaiianpress.com

***

Version Number 1.00

For my Dad, Husband, and Son

When was it?

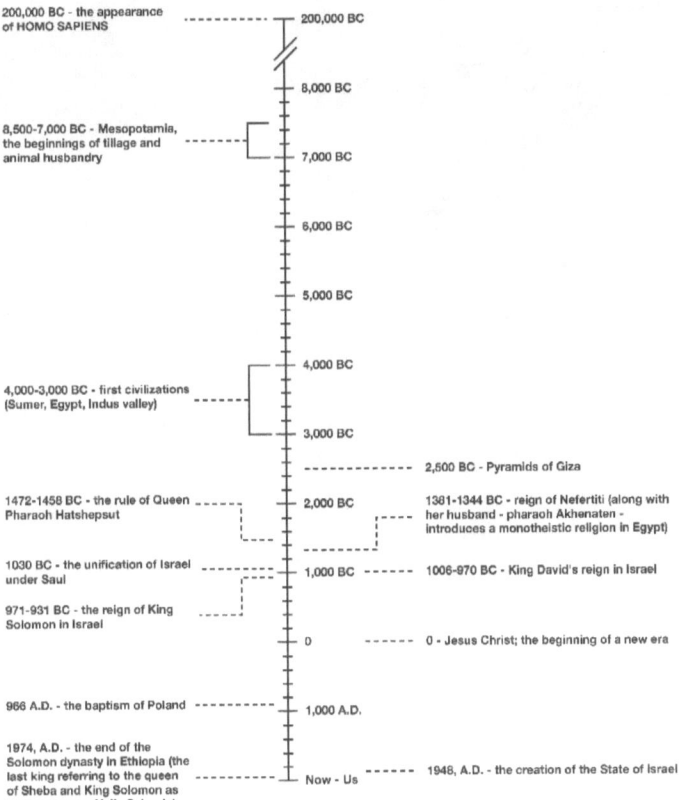

200,000 BC - the appearance of HOMO SAPIENS ---------- 200,000 BC

8,000 BC

8,500-7,000 BC - Mesopotamia, the beginnings of tillage and animal husbandry ------- 7,000 BC

6,000 BC

5,000 BC

4,000 BC

4,000-3,000 BC - first civilizations (Sumer, Egypt, Indus valley) ------- 3,000 BC

----------- 2,500 BC - Pyramids of Giza

1472-1458 BC - the rule of Queen Pharaoh Hatshepsut ----- 2,000 BC   1381-1344 BC - reign of Nefertiti (along with her husband - pharaoh Akhenaten - introduces a monotheistic religion in Egypt)

1030 BC - the unification of Israel under Saul --------- 1,000 BC ------ 1006-970 BC - King David's reign in Israel

971-931 BC - the reign of King Solomon in Israel -----

0 ------- 0 - Jesus Christ; the beginning of a new era

966 A.D. - the baptism of Poland ---------- 1,000 A.D.

1974, A.D. - the end of the Solomon dynasty in Ethiopia (the last king referring to the queen of Sheba and King Solomon as ancestors, was Haile Selassie) ---------- Now - Us ------ 1948, A.D. - the creation of the State of Israel

TABLE OF CONTENTS

PROLOGUE

I saw her for the first time when she was five years old. That I would be her companion and guardian was decided by the gods, speaking to me through the voice of her father, King Nikal. When information came to him that I had the ability to see the future, and that one day when I opened the curtains of time, I saw his daughter sitting on the throne of Sheba, he ordered me to come to the palace. On the day I turned twenty-one, I left the walls of the temple in which I was raised. This is the age at which the Silver Mother finally decided what the fate of each of her charges will be – I was one of them. I was a priestess of the Lady of the Moon.

Since then, I have been accompanying the princess constantly. I did not leave her side as she was growing up, when she became a woman, and when she sat on the throne. Together, we read Egyptian papyri and scrolls from Assyria, studied maps, looked at the stars, and explored the secrets of the world of gods, people, and animals. I was with her in battles and at the time when bloody executions were carried out on her orders. I bowed with her when she offered sacrifices to the gods in their temples, and like her, I asked the most powerful of them, Illumkuh, for his support. I traveled through the desert sands with her when she was going to the kingdom of Israel to meet Solomon. I watched the trust with which she gave him her heart and body. I trembled in fear when she abandoned our eternal faith and entrusted herself and the kingdom to the new god. I saw the signs of pain when she gave birth to her son and happiness in her eyes when she first took him in her arms. I shared her pride when Menelik sat on the throne. I hugged her when she was in despair after Solomon's death.

Now that so many years have passed since I saw her for the first time, I was opening the curtain of time again. I wanted to know what awaited us. I had done this so many times over the course of my long life. I looked into the future, but what I saw was not entirely understandable to me. I saw images, but I could only guess what they meant.

The ability to see the future is beautiful; only few are able to. Only, the powerful gift of revelation is greater, and it was received by the wisest woman in the world, Great Kandake, Queen of Sheba, Makeda.

Chapter 1

DREAMS OF THE THRONE
PRINCESS MAKEDA IS FIVE YEARS OLD

The Kingdom of Sheba

Mariba[1]

"You will be her companion and guardian," said King Nikal. "From now on your life, your whole life, all your skills and knowledge, everything that Lady of the Moon in her mercy has provided you with, you will sacrifice to the princess. You have an obligation to protect her and take care of her. She is the greatest treasure of our kingdom. From today on, you will be with her until the end of your days. Only me, she herself, or death can release you from this obligation. No one else and nothing else."

We were in the royal chamber. Nikal was sitting on a wide, wooden chair, padded with a lamb's skin. I was kneeling three, maybe four cubits away from him, my forehead almost touched the smooth stone floor.

"King, it's an honor for me," I whispered so quietly that he probably did not hear me.

---

[1] J. Klinkowski, the Ark of the Covenant. From Sinai to Aksum, Wrocław 2010 (he writes about Mariba, the capital of the kingdom of Sheba, as well as the gods worshiped there - author's note).

My larynx was tight from nervousness. I have never seen the king or visited a palace before. I felt stunned by what was happening around me. However, a thought restoring my senses appeared in my head that I could not tremble in front of anyone, not even the king, after all I was supposed to be the hemet of princess Makeda. That's what the Lady of the Moon decided, and nobody dared to argue with her will. Although I was the bravest of the brave, and at the same time the Seer, for a short while I lost the confidence, which I did not lack in everyday life, before the powerful Nikal, famous for his heavy hand. I swallowed quickly and I repeated louder and more confidently, raising my head, "It is an honor and a great privilege for me, mukarrib[2]."

"You will receive everything you need," words that fell from my mouth were obvious to him, so he accepted them without a questioning comment. "You'll live with the princess in her room. From now on you will not only be her main guardian, but also her shadow."

"King, everything will be done according to your wishes," my voice had fully regained its strength. "This is also the will of the Lady of the Moon."

"The Great Priestess sent you to me, assuring that you are perfect for the role your Lady gave you. And as the gods always know better than us, it remains for me to accept her decision humbly, but also with joy. I know that you will fulfill your duties perfectly. You have a skin that is noble black and ebony, you are strong and predatory. You have teeth in the shape of sharp arrowheads, so if you need to, you will kill. And at the same time, you are smart. You were born to be a priestess and a warrior. Your supervisor assured me that I can entrust you with the full care of Makeda. I believe her," he patted his thigh, acknowledging that we already had this part of the conversation behind us.

---

[2] The title of the rulers of the kingdom of Sheba meaning "priest-prince" or "king"

In the days that followed, I quickly noticed that this was how he signaled settling the matter and his willingness to move to the next topic.

"Everything is clear then," he said. "Now get up, sit closer to me, because from now on, you are one of us," he pointed his hand at the low stool near the throne, "and tell me what you saw exactly."

I thought that it was in this very place that Makeda used to sit when she was talking to her father. I wondered how she felt, having his powerful feet shod in soldierly leather sandals on thick soles, massive calves, and knees covered with a cloth of a simple tunic before her eyes. Was she afraid? I did not lift my head. The king was famous for his impetuosity. The priestess ordered me to obey him unconditionally. I did not know how he would react if I dared to look him in the eye.

"Look at me!" he ordered, as if he sensed my fears.

I looked up. I looked at him confidently and without fear. He guessed that I had not done it earlier because of my temple upbringing, which taught me to never look directly at the person higher in status, especially at the king.

"You will be close to my daughter and also to me," he explained calmly. "I allow you more familiarity when we are alone. Then, you can stand and sit in my presence, and even look me in the eyes."

"Thank you, mukarrib," I appreciated the award.

"What's your name?"

"I was given the name Seshep-dua[3], which means the Light of Tomorrow, but the priestesses always called me Seshep, or just hemet."

"In Egyptian, hemet means a priest or a craftsman, doesn't it?"

---

[3] The translation from Egyptian hieroglyphs by prof. Andrzej Ćwiek from the A. Mickiewicz University in Poznań.

"Yes, these are words from the land of the pharaohs. They are similar, for both the priest and the craftsman, as sanctified by spiritual power, are tools in the hands of the gods. Like every one of us."

"You must know what you're talking about," he said. "How do you want us to address you?"

"Hemet Seshep, mukarrib."

"Let it be so." He slapped his thigh again. "So, Hemet Seshep, tell me about your vision. Everything, with details. I want to know everything."

I closed my eyes and went back to that day.

"I was sitting by the eternal source, lord. I looked at it for a long time. When I was ready, I opened the curtain of time..."

"How?"

I knelt down in front of him the same way as on that day in front of the spring. I leaned forward as I had done then, and then slowly and gently made a gesture, as if I were sliding open the still surface of the water with my hands.

The king nodded.

"What did you see?"

"I saw Makeda sitting on the throne, standing in the great hall filled to the brim with people. It was golden, powerful, impressive. Low stairs led to it, and huge golden lions stood on its sides. The Great Priest of Illumkuh and the Great Priestess the Lady of the Moon were standing next to Makeda. I also saw myself there."

"And my sons? What about Sirah and Tomay?"

"They were not there."

"I guess I was not there either?"

"Makeda became the queen because you, mukarrib, passed the govern on to her, when dying."

"Say something more."

"What?"

"When was it?"

"You have long years of reign awaiting you. Your daughter will sit on the throne as an adult woman. I told you that I also saw myself there. I had a lot of gray hair."

"Why will not any of my sons become king? What is going to happen? Will they die, perish in a battle? Leave?"

"I do not know, sir. I did not see them behind the curtain of time."

The king fell silent and closed his eyes. He tried to think about what I had told him. I did not know how much he succeeded in this. He paused for a moment, then straightened up and clapped his hands.

"Time for you to get to know each other. Bring the princess!" he ordered, as the maid appeared almost immediately in the doorway.

After a moment, I saw her. It seemed as if the sun had appeared in person in the room. Makeda had so much light in her that I squinted my eyes. She did not enter the room, but she ran into it, along with her joy, childish chirping and freshness. I knew she was five years old. She was slender, flexible, and lively. She had a much lighter skin than her father. Her long, dark, slightly curly hair gathered at the nape of her neck in a knot. Beautiful, black, very expressive eyes looked intelligent. She was beautiful.

She stood in the doorway, nodded regally to her father with a disarming childish dignity, and then greeted me. At the same time, she smiled delightfully, watching the room. When she found that there was nobody there besides the king and I, she jumped up happily, ran to her father, and jumped on his knees.

When I looked at her long, slim arms and legs, at her agile and quick movements, the leopardesses of the High Priestess stood before my eyes. Makeda had their grace, still some awkwardness of movements, but also dormant strength and predatoriness.

"How great that you are here!" she exclaimed, hugging her father.

It was clear to me that such scenes happened often between them. Surely, she was not afraid of him, as it seemed to me before. While during the conversation with the ruler, I had doubts about the type of emotions that he aroused in me. But at that moment, I got to like him. Someone who treated his daughter like that had to be a good man.

He did not seem surprised by her behavior. He embraced her tightly, and she settled in his arms comfortably.

"It's good that you too are already with us, Hemet Seshep," she turned her head towards me.

As soon as she entered the room, I got up from the chair and stood near the throne.

"I did not tell you the name of your new guardian," Nikal said, surprised. "We talked that the messenger of the Lady of the Moon would come to become your companion and guardian. I told you that she was a priestess who had the gift of seeing, but I certainly did not give you her name. I did not even know it myself."

"Father, I saw Hemet in my dreams. I know that we will love each other," Makeda stretched out her hand to me.

"From now on, we will always be together. For good and for bad," she said happily.

When I knelt down in front of her and kissed her little hand, she added, "We have lots of hard times awaiting us. Well... actually really a lot," she said, as if remembering what she knew, but seeing my face, she quickly added to comfort me that there would be much more of the good ones.

Israel

Jerusalem

It was late in the evening. A dark blue sky stretched above the palatial terrace, the moon shone brightly, and the stars twinkled.

Solomon stood next to the sofa where the queen was resting. At this time of the year, she liked to rest in this place in the evenings.

"Mother, I came to your call."

"Your father is getting weaker," she did not look up.

Bathsheba just turned fifty years old, but she was still a beautiful woman. Even though the time had silvered her dark hair, wrinkles marked her forehead and the sides of her mouth, her eyes still had a youthful glow. Also, her figure had hardly changed since the day she was allowed to stand before King David for the first time.

She did not hide her sadness. Her husband, the King of Israel, had been so weak for several months that he almost never left his bed. She shared this weakness; it made her reflective and inclined to memories.

"Do you know that it is from this terrace that he saw me for the first time?" she pointed a chair to her son and waited for him to sit down. "I was taking an evening bath. I did not think anyone could see me," she justified herself. "Over there," she pointed to the house with a flat roof, perfectly visible from the palace terrace. "I lived there then."

Solomon knew the story, like every man in Jerusalem. But he had never heard it from his mother's mouth until now.

"I was Uriah's wife then. He was a devoted soldier and a good man. David considered him one of the most valiant and deserving. I was married to him very young. People were delighted with my beauty and said that Uriah was lucky. I was docile and submissive to him," she sighed, recalling her memories. "A wife should listen to her husband; I have learned this from my family home."

Solomon loved his mother very much. He knew perfectly well that she was not only beautiful, but also, and perhaps even above all, wise and good. She was the greatest woman he had ever known. He compared the princesses he met and every other girl in his surroundings to her. None of them was able to measure up to her, even to the slightest extent.

"Uriah was at war against the Ammonites. Joab was at the head of the army then. They besieged Rabba. I was at home with just servants." Bathsheba closed her eyes. When she opened them after a while, they shone strongly. "I remember that evening really well. After all, it changed my whole life. The air was trembling from the smells of flowers and ripe fruit. An aura of mystery hovered above the city. I felt disturbing vibrations. I knew something unusual was going to happen. Women sense these things... The servants helped me with the evening bath. They washed my body, then anointed it, and combed my hair. Of course, as in a bath, I was naked apart from a headband."

Solomon listened, not daring to move or disturb the story with even the slightest gesture.

"I was in the inner yard of the house. We were just finishing the treatments, when there was a loud knock on the gate. The scared doorman let the royal messengers inside, bowing low to the guests. When the servants told me, who was in our home, I could not believe it. It thought I was dreaming, but it was really happening. I quickly put on the proper outfit and let them come in. At that time, I did not know what was waiting for me," she again accepted the tone, as if excusing herself for what had happened next. "I heard from them that I should go to the palace immediately. At first, I thought that something bad had happened to Uriah. However, I thought that even if it did, I would be informed about it in a different way. I knew one thing: the king called for me. So, I should not delay for a single moment. I threw the most beautiful shawl I had on my head and went to the palace, surrounded by David's servants."

"Mother, it was God's plan the way things went." Solomon understood her anxiety. He knew, after all, what happened next, because more or less amazing sounding stories about the meeting of his parents had been circulating throughout the country for years. "Nothing happens on earth without divine approval."

She nodded, acknowledging him.

"When I entered, he was standing here," she indicated a place by the wall separating the terrace from the city.

It was high enough to cover a standing man freely. Its openwork construction made it possible to observe what was happening outside and at the same time not being noticed.

"You could not even suspect you were being watched." Solomon wanted to calm her down and assure her that whatever his mother said, he was always on her side.

"Yes, that's true. I could not…"

"And besides, if my father did not invite you to the palace, I would not be here in this world," he laughed, making a pensive face. "I am grateful to God for letting you meet."

Prince Solomon was twenty-five years old. He was tall, handsome, though some people found him maybe a little too slim, but his build was proportional and harmonious. His head was adorned by a lush raven hair, and his face by a thick, short, carefully trimmed beard. His nose was straight and his lips not very prominent. His big, dark eyes were the most visible features in his face. Wherever he appeared, he compelled gazes. He possessed something that made people feel safe with him. They wanted to be as close to him as possible, because he spread around himself this kind of radiance which made people feel that there is someone who is just and wise, who carries with him peace and knowledge inherited with the blood of his ancestors.

"I do not know how it happened, but from the first moment I saw him, I knew he was a man of my life. I loved him before he spoke his first words. It was a moment, a small moment, like a flare of a star in the sky. I understood from the very beginning that I loved him forever and that I was created to be with him, look after him and give him happiness, and that this was my destiny. It was love at first sight! I never felt something like that with Uriah."

"You were, and you are the best wife and mother one can imagine."

"Solomon," she leaned close enough to be able to put her hand on his. "You are a great son, my pride. I love you very much. Thank you for supporting me."

He leaned over and kissed the tips of her fingers. She smiled sadly and sighed. She stroked his hair.

"Dear, I say it with a pain in my heart, because I know how difficult it is for you, but soon your father will go to Yahweh. When this happens, you will sit on the throne."

"May this time never come," he accented his words with a decisive stamp of his foot. "You know that Israel has not had and will not have a better king than David."

"As the books say, everything has its place and time. Your father, guided by the will of the Most High, has appointed you as his successor. And so, it will happen," she straightened up to emphasize the inevitability of what was to come.

"Maybe Adonijah would be a better ruler than me?"

He cocked his head in a perverse way, waiting for her reaction. It was stronger than he could have expected. She got upset, as if she did not notice that he was joking.

"Adonijah?" His words stirred her so much that she stood up. "Of course, he would like that. I am sure that if he only could, he would now sit on the throne. But the crown of Israel is not meant for him; you know it well! God has predestined it for you," she pointed to him. "You, understand? David promised it to me personally," she added more calmly.

As the upbringing and customs demanded, when the woman got up, the man also rose. So as soon as she got up, Solomon did the same.

"Mother, you often say that everything happens according to the God's will. I agree with you. It will be then as it should be," he replied philosophically, wanting to calm her down, and at the same time, strongly believing in what he said.

"He looked at the sky, shows us the paths, but we choose which one we will take. We have free will," she announced loudly, as if she wanted to communicate it to the whole world. "It is difficult for me to admit that Adonijah may have a stronger desire to become a king than you, but reason and experience tell me that it is unfortunately possible. That's why we should be vigilant."

"Mother, God watches over everything," he reassured her. "Many years ago, he directed your steps so that you became a queen and gave birth to me. If I am to be a ruler, it will be so, regardless of Adonijah's intentions."

The Kingdom of Sheba

Aksum

Sheba comprised the lands lying on the eastern and western part of the narrowest isthmus of the Red Sea. Palace of King Nikal, as well as the most important temples, stood in the eastern part. The west included numerous duchies, including Kush, Punt and Aksum, the largest and richest of all, managed by Prince Seth.

In order to keep the subordinate areas obedient to himself, Seth needed Nikal's soldiers and authority. But above all, he needed his brokerage in trade. He maintained very good contacts with Egypt, but he did not have direct access to countries on the eastern side of the Red Sea, which were the largest recipients of goods from the Black Continent. For Nikal, Aksum and other principalities to the south and the interior of the continent were the territories captured by his ancestors, so they belonged to the kingdom of Sheba. Because they were rich in gold, frankincense, and myrrh, like no other countries in the world, he could not imagine to lose them.

Nikal had a daughter, Makeda, who was famous for her beauty and intelligence, and two sons. 14-year-old Sirah was being prepared to be his successor. Tomaj was two years younger than his older brother.

Prince Seth had only one son, named Den. Seth believed that Nikal was a weak king. He did not like his way of exercising power and friendly politics towards the princes of the western lands. He was convinced that if he were the king of Sheba, he would very quickly multiply the proceeds to the treasury and make Sheba such a powerful kingdom, that it could even stand up to Egypt.

He had been trying for a long time to drag the rulers of Kush and Punt, and lesser ones, to his side. He knew that if he succeeded, he could openly oppose Nikal. However, none of the princes was willing to make an alliance with him against the king. He was thus left with waiting for a convenient opportunity that would present itself sooner or later and taking covert actions that might weaken Nikal.

"No one can know about it, do you understand?"

Seth handed a bundle with gold to a tall man with a deep scar on his cheek. "And do it without leaving any traces. None!"

"It will be according to your will, sir," the man bowed low. "It should not be a problem, after all, he's still a child!"

"I hope so!"

Prince Seth dismissed the assassin who had been on his services for a long time. He did not want anyone to see them together; that's why he did not call him to the palace but told him to appear in his house on the seafront, which hardly anyone visited. He had a house built on stilts, among lush vegetation. He liked to meet other princes there, organize meetings, or stay alone. He often took his beloved son there. So, it was also this time.

When the man with the scar left, Seth called Den.

"You're only eight years old, you have whole life ahead of you," he said, ordering him to sit in front of himself. "But you are a wise boy, so I will tell you something that no one but you and me can know. Are you ready for it?"

"Yes, father," he nodded.

He was smart and tough. He had his father's character. From an early age, he tried to get his way in every case, and he was convinced that he was better and wiser than everyone around him, which he thought meant that he deserved to get the best out of life. That's what his father taught him.

His mother was almost absent in his life. From the moment she gave birth to a boy and the priestesses said that she would not be able to have more children, Seth hardly maintained any relations with her, although he did not send her to her family home. He gave her the part of the palace most distant from his chambers, and limited her opportunity to see Den.

Seth took his son by the wrist.

"I believe you but let us additionally swear by blood!" he said, pulling a large knife from behind his belt.

Den's eyes widened because he did not know what to expect. His father was unpredictable and cruel. More than once, he had seen him personally kill defiant subjects or soldiers who dared disagree with his opinion. He was afraid, but he did not move.

"My blood," Seth thought proudly, and cut the skin at his wrist.

He did the same to his son.

"You and I are one. In your and my veins, flows the blood of our ancestors, the great warriors. From now on, we are connected not only by blood, but a common secret and the pursuit of winning the Sheba throne."

He put a bleeding hand to the son's wound.

"Our goal is power. Know that the purpose of everything I do is for you to become my successor one day. I want us to reign not only in Aksum, but in the whole kingdom. We will be the kings of all Sheba! Everything I do is meant to lead to it. Almakah will help us!"

Israel

Jerusalem

"Let's sit down, please," said the queen, returning to the sofa, "I will tell you the rest of the story of my relationship with your father. I want you to finally hear it from me."

Bathsheba resumed her story.

"I spent that extraordinary night in the royal bedroom. And the following ones too. We looked at the stars, we talked, we were as close to each other as a woman and a man can be. I went back home and slept off the tiredness. You could think it was a difficult time for me? I am ashamed, but it was not. At least, I cannot say that I would think so at the time. I was so fascinated by what was going on that I forgot about the whole world. Only David counted. I loved him above all else. And I was sure that God led me to him. After all, nothing happens without his consent, right?"

Solomon nodded.

"It soon turned out that I was pregnant. This news made David very happy. He took me in his arms and danced. He sang all the time. He was happy. We both were.

"And when my whole world was spinning with joy, all of sudden, a sobering came. I realized that I belonged to another man. Uriah was my husband. I swore to him before God, and I broke my promise. Furthermore, I was not only an unfaithful wife, but I betrayed the man who was in the battle. As you know, the custom demands that the fighting soldiers did not enjoy a pleasure with any women during the war, giving all their strength to victory. At this time, it is the duty and obligation of their wives to remain faithful to them. They should not err only by deeds, but not even with their eyes, nor with a thought! And I? I broke the law that the Supreme had given us in his goodness and wisdom. Oh, unworthy! I told David about my worries."

She fell silent and did not pick up the tale for a long moment. Finally, she spoke again; her voice was much quieter now, "David ordered me to go home and wait. I did according to his wishes. I was afraid of what would happen next, but I believed that God was with us because he has seen our great love. Love is what is the most important in life, isn't it?" she asked and continued without waiting for an answer. "The king called Uriah to Jerusalem. My husband learned about everything before he got to the palace. People told him what was going on in his absence. Our city is like a tiny village: everyone knows everything."

She hung her voice again. It was clear that those events caused strong emotions in her.

"I understood Uriah's pain and indignation, and at the same time, I was constantly praying that God would forgive both me and David for our sins," she wrung her hands. "It was awful, but the king wanted Uriah to think that he had called him to ask what was going on in the war. However, he immediately discovered that David wanted him to come into the house and lay down with me in bed. Then the child who would be born and would have a father. I did not like the king's behavior. I would prefer him to choose a different way of solving this matter, but I was very young then. I could not fight for myself. I did not even know I could do that. I lived as if what was going on was not about me, but about someone else."

Solomon was sitting with his eyes down. He did not speak. He listened.

"David commanded Uriah to stay at home. But he was honorable; he could not tolerate an insult. Feeling respect for the king, he did not tell him that he knew what had happened, he just said, 'The Ark, the whole Israel and Judah live in tents, my master

Joab and his servants are camping in the middle of nowhere, and I would go home to eat and drink there, and sleep with my wife? God, I cannot do anything like that.'[4] He bowed and left. He did not cross the doorway of his house, just as he planned. He put his weapon down by the entrance, laid down on the blanket and spent the night there. I did not go to him. I did not have courage."

Solomon imagined the pain, despair, and humiliation of that man. At the same time, he knew that if things went differently, he would not be sitting with his mother on the terrace of the royal palace now, because he probably would not have been given a chance from God to come to existence. *"So, is it really so, that everything that happens, has been written somewhere earlier? Do we really have no effect on what concerns us? Does the path we follow depend on God or on ourselves?"* he thought, looking at the hands of his subtly gesticulating mother.

"I did not sleep. I prayed and I cried. What did I count on? That he will come home, spend the night with me and everything will be fine? That I will give birth to the king's child and my husband will consider it his own? I really did not know. I fell asleep at dawn, exhausted by despair, and when I woke up, the sun was high in the sky."

Uriah was already gone. The next days I also cried, praying more fervently than ever in my life. At the same time, completely outside of me, something horrible happened. Something God really punished your father and me for. It was a sin next to which our previous intercourse was nothing. Believe me!" she rubbed her hands nervously. She had long wanted to tell her son about it. She knew that he had undoubtedly heard different versions of the events from years ago, but she had never been able to tell him about them personally and in accordance with her own conscience. Now, when Solomon was soon to become the

---

[4] Old Testament, 2 Sm, David and Bathsheba 11, 1-7.

successor of David, she wanted him to know the story from her own mouth. So that, sitting on the throne, he could avoid his father's mistakes; so that he would know how terrible the wrath of Yahweh could be and how big a punishment he sends on people for breaking the commandments.

"What happened next was terrible! Although I would like to forget it, this matter will be with me until the end of my days. I learned how ruthless your father was only when it was already too late to do anything. I think he wanted me to never know the truth," she hung up her voice again because the next words would not leave her mouth.

They sat in silence. Above them, the moon was shining with not a single cloud to cover it.

Finally, the queen's voice resounded, "At dawn, David's servants handed Uriah a letter that he was supposed to pass to his commander Joab. It was stated in it that Joab should send Uriah to the toughest and most dangerous part of the battle. So, Uriah unknowingly, gave his commanding officer a death sentence for himself, stamped and signed by the king. Now, I think maybe he felt so disgraced that he wanted to die then? Maybe he put himself on the swords of enemies himself? To this day, for this reason, I have a ragged heart." The queen gave a quiet moan, "Uriah died in a battle. Other soldiers returned home, and I became a widow. I did not know that my husband died because of David. In my naiveté, I thought that it was God's will. I must admit that at that time, I felt a kind of relief, because everything seemed to have worked out on its own. To this day, I feel ashamed because of it. When I received a message about my husband's death, I cried for a long time. I wore mourning clothes and put ashes on my head, as custom dictate. I suffered, but mainly because of the sin that I committed with David, because I was sure that it contributed to the death of a really good man like my husband. It was only later that I found out that his death was not accidental."

The queen fell silent again. She was sad but letting go for the first time of something that had been stuck inside her and tormenting her for years, brought her relief.

"When the period of mourning was over, I began to live in the palace. It seemed to me that I left the past behind forever. David surrounded me with love and royal abundance. When the day was coming when our child was to come into the world, I accidentally witnessed a conversation that changed my attitude to everything that happened later...I was sitting here on this terrace. It was morning. I waited for David who had been personally looking after one of the construction in the city since the dawn. I thought that I would give him a pleasant surprise by meeting him. When the time came for the childbirth, and I felt worse and worse, the king honored me with giving the chambers, that still belong to me, to my exclusive use. In this way, he officially recognized me as his lady. There were servants with me ready to call a midwife at any moment. That morning I felt so good that I decided to meet him. I waited, and he still was not coming. When he finally appeared, the prophet Nathan was with him. They went into the room, not knowing that I was on the terrace. I heard the whole conversation very well."

Bathsheba got up, walked a few steps and put her hands on the terrace balustrade. She was looking at the city that was sleeping at that time. Then she raised her head higher, towards the starry sky, and sighed deeply.

"There were two people in one city: one rich and the other poor, Nathan said then. Rich one had many sheep and oxen, and the poor one had nothing but the one little lamb he had bought. He nursed her, and she grew up with his children: she ate his bread, drank from his cup, and slept on his bosom. She was like one of his daughters to him. It happened that someone visited this rich man. But the rich man did not sacrifice any of his sheep or an ox to prepare a meal for the man who came to him. Instead, he took the only sheep from this poor man and prepared a meal for the man who came to him[5]. Nathan was nervous, and David began to share his mood. 'What a vile thing!' he cried. 'From Yahweh, the man who did this deserved the highest punishment!' And then Nathan shouted that David was this bad man! That he did not respect the law, took Uriah's wife and what was the worst, sent him to death. 'You killed him with the sword of the enemies! You! He died on your order! You deliberately sent him where the death was certain! You will be punished for this.' David replied, 'I have sinned. But I love Bathsheba like no one else in the world. Those who sin because of love are justified. I will humbly subject myself to the punishment because I know that I deserved it. My life belongs to God, he owns me.' Then there was silence. I did not know what happened. After a while, I heard Nathan again, 'God forgave you your sin. You will not die. However, the son who will be born soon, will die.' I heard only that much, actually too much. After these words, I fainted."

Solomon approached his mother and embraced her tightly. She hugged him gratefully. She put her head on his shoulder.

"When I regained my senses, your father was with me. The servants were bustling around. The childbirth began. I gave birth to a boy. He died after seven days. It was the punishment that God gave us."

Solomon caressed her hair.

"Your father spent almost all this time in the temple. He thought that he would appease God with his prayers and sacrifices, and that our son, the fruit of love, would survive. However, the deeds we committed were shameful, and they required punishment. We both received it. We suffered, but it was at that time that we became even closer to each other. When the days of mourning and well-deserved penance finally passed,

---

[5] Old Testament, 2 Samuel 11, 1-27 God's punishment sent to David (David and Nathan's statements are literal quotes from the Old Testament - author's footnote).

marriage took place. Soon God heard our prayers and gave us the most wonderful gift we could expect - you. You are a child of great love, Solomon, a gift from God who loved you and gave you important tasks on earth. By sending us to you, he also gave David a sign that his guilt had been forgiven."

The kingdom of Sheba, Mariba

Three months later

It happened just as the princess announced. We fell in love at the first meeting. Already then, I felt as if we had always known each other. I lived in a room next to her room, and from that day on we were inseparable.

One night, I was awakened by her cry. I immediately jumped to my feet and was at her bedside in one moment. She was kneeling, sitting on her heels. She was rocking. The wide-open eyes shone with unearthly light. I was sure she could not see me. I approached carefully. She spoke quietly, but clearly,

"I'm coming to you, I'm coming. Wait for me," I heard. "We'll meet when the time comes. I come..."

She repeated the same words many times, among which "I come" and "wait" appeared most often.

Finally, she raised her hands up, as though in a gesture of prayer. She bowed her head in a distinguished move, as she did many times during the holidays and ceremonies in which she accompanied her father, and then she stretched, smiled with satisfaction and laid down on her side to sleep peacefully till morning.

Unlike her, I could not sleep anymore that night. I wondered where she wandered in her dreams. Who was she meeting with, what was she talking about, and finally - to whom was she coming, and when the time she was talking about in her dreams would come?

Everything cleared up the next day. She woke up happy and rested, when the sun was high already. I was sitting in a chair by her bed.

"Have you been here all night?" she asked, her smile lighting up the room.

"Yes. I ran, because I wanted to be with my lady during her journey," I said truthfully, as always.

"I was at the king from the distant land again," she confessed quietly, sitting down on the edge of the bed.

I sat even closer to her.

"I am, and I will always be with you," I assured.

"I know and thank you for that," she hugged her cheek to mine. I felt the warmth of a skin of the child, not quite awake from sleep yet. "I'll tell you something," she whispered straight into my ear, "but you have to keep it secret. This is my father's wish. I know that you will not say anything, but I promised my dad that I would not tell anyone what you are about to hear. I'm sure of you more than of myself. I have seen in my dreams that you will always be faithful to me."

I embraced her small body. She seemed so helpless!

"I will always be with you," I assured her in a whisper. She embraced me, and after a moment I heard, "It wasn't the first time already, that I saw in my dreams a ruler from a distant country to which I will go when I become a queen. However, before this happens, there must be a lot of water flowing in the rivers, and I should learn a lot during this time. A lot will happen before I meet him. I do not know yet where he is or which direction I should go, but I can be sure that he is already waiting for me, even though he does not even know about my existence. Our meeting will change the fate of the world. I have no idea how. I do not know when and I do not know what will happen, but I am sure it will happen."

She sighed as if she were an adult woman.

"First, however, I will become the Queen of Sheba," she assured. "My father knows that. I told him. He asked me not to tell anyone that I have visions, because that will hurt alliances and peace in Sheba. The princes quietly think that one of their sons will at the right time take me as a wife and we will rule together in his duchy, or that one of their sons has a chance for a crown. That is why they are obedient to my father. As if they did not remember that I have two brothers, each of whom is a more important heir than me," she said to herself. "I saw in my dreams that none of the princes will be my husband. A ruler from a distant land is destined for me. However, I cannot talk about it to anyone, because it's just the dreams of a little girl, as my father says. He would like to think that, but I'm sure that what I happen to see at nights are prophecies. I know that they will come true. When they come to me, it is as if the sky was breaking open. Brightness flows on me. I see everything clearly. And each time more and more."

I listened carefully. Everything was starting to come together. Behold, I had the honor of guarding the princess who I knew would sit on the throne of Sheba someday. I learned about it by opening the curtain of time. Nikal called me, knowing about my vision and the dreams of his daughter. Two different, independent sources, that is both Makeda and I, had similar visions. It could not have been just the dreams of a child or visions of a priestess who was looking behind the veil of time. Nikal was an experienced ruler. He knew that if something was going to happen by the will of the gods, even if we do not like it, we should give up the hope that things will be different from what they would like.

"Have you had such dreams for a long time?"

"When I was little, I did not distinguish between a dream and reality. At that time, my mother often visited me at nights. As you know, she died just after giving birth. However, I still feel that she has not left me. Recently, since the time you have appeared, she visits me less frequently. She says I'm in good hands now."

I was tough, but when I heard that, tears rolled down my cheeks, surprising even myself.

"Mom is glad you're with me. You will look after me better than she does because you can fight, and in the future this skill may be useful more than both of us think today. I do not know that, but she says so, and she is very wise."

"Makeda, you are an extraordinary girl," I whispered, knowing that what we were saying would stay between us. "You will be a great queen someday. But before that happens, we should be careful. Your father is right: do not tell anyone about your visions. It could be dangerous for the country and for you."

"I will not tell anyone, I swear," she promised.

That's how I got to know the secret of Princess Makeda.

The Kingdom of Israel, Jerusalem

At the same time

King David was already old. He was cold even when covered with layers. His servants said, "We will have to look for a young girl, let her be always with the king, take care of him, let her sleep next to him, if necessary, warming him up in this way." They looked all over Israel for one that would be beautiful enough. Finally, a Shunammite woman named Abishtag was found and brought to the palace. She was really beautiful. She cared for the king and served him. However, he did not approach her[6].

Queen Bathsheba liked Abishtag. Every day she saw her efforts, kindness, and patience. The girl was quiet, modest, smiling gently, and at the same time, she behaved as if she was

[6] The Millennium Bible - Holy Scriptures of the Old and New Testament, Old Testament, 1 Kings 1.1-27, the history of Solomon. Poznań 2000.

born only to serve David. Looking at her face, one could think that taking care of the king was her joy, destiny, and the greatest thing that could happen to her in life. At the same time, she was completely unaware of her unusual beauty and grace. She did not seem to notice glances admiring her. She focused on taking care of the king and moved around with her head low.

When the queen saw her modesty, she ordered her to become an inseparable companion of the king, not only during the day. The girl spent also her nights with her master, warming him with her body and watching him constantly.

At that time also, Solomon was often by his sick father's bed. They had long conversations, and on the days when the king was worse, the son read old scrolls to him. Sometimes they both were silent or slept: the king in his bed, and Solomon in the chair next to him. In such moments, Abishtag, exhausted by constant vigil, most often also fell asleep, lying down somewhere nearby.

One morning, when the three of them had just fallen asleep after a light breakfast, Bathsheba quietly entered the room. Abishtag immediately raised her head, and when she saw the queen, she got up in panic, adjusted her outfit and bowed low. Hearing the movement, Solomon also opened his eyes. Fortunately, the queen's entrance did not wake David up.

"Solomon, come with me," whispered Bathsheba. "Immediately!" She stressed her demand with gesture.

"You stay with the King and do not step away from him." She looked at Abishtag. "Do not let anything be given to the king without my permission. No drinks, food or gifts. The guard in front of the door will be reinforced. Do not be surprised when more soldiers come here."

The girl nodded without saying a word. She understood that something extraordinary had happened, which in consequence could be a threat to the king's life.

"What happened, mother?" Solomon waited until they were behind the door of the chamber.

The queen did not even break her stride.

"We must hurry! Nathan and Zadok will be here soon, I have already sent for them. Let's go, I will tell you everything in my room."

"What happened? I want to know now. Nathan and Zadok can wait."

"Son," she stopped, took his hands and looked into his eyes. "Son," she repeated, and her voice betrayed an outrage and fear. "Adonijah proclaimed himself king!"

"What?" At first, he did not believe what he had heard. "How come!?"

"Exactly!" She was upset. "Let's go, we have to act! We will wonder later," she turned and quickly walked towards her chamber.

Solomon stood still for a moment, then shook his head in disbelief and followed her.

He was primarily a thinker. He wasn't fond of disputes and fighting, and palace intrigues repelled him. Adonijah was the eldest son of David. Solomon understood therefore that his older half-brother's dream of the throne was justified. However, succession to the throne in Israel was not as obvious as in neighboring countries. The reigning king appointed the heir, guided by the divine order. So, it was in David's case. A few months earlier, the prophet Nathan gave the king the will of Yahweh, who according to the will of the Supreme, chose Solomon, not Adonijah, to govern Israel.

David often said that the will of the Lord is sacred for him, and so Solomon will inherit the throne. But he never announced it publicly, and now he was terminally ill. Most probably, this was the reason of Adonijah's audacity. He intended to take advantage of the king's weakness and proclaimed himself the successor; believing that once he puts the crown onto his head, Solomon will not have the courage to oppose him.

The prophet Nathan and the priest Zadok were already waiting in Bathsheba's chamber.

"Queen," they greeted the ruler first.

"Solomon," they bowed their heads in front of her son.

"What are the news?" Bathsheba sat down, indicating the place for them.

In the situation they found themselves, she was not going to waste time on ceremonial greeting.

"Speak up," she urged.

"Adonijah indeed proclaimed himself king. It's a fact," began Zadok, "He made a sacrifice of sheep, calves and bulls by the Zoheleth stone, summoning his brothers, friends, supporters, and part of the army there."

"By making the sacrifice in a holy place, he told the gathered people that as the eldest son of David, he shall be king," added the prophet Nathan. "The priest Abiathar blessed him, and Joab, as the commander of the royal army, testified with the presence of the troops that everything is done according to David's will."

"People gathered in the valley dared not even think that Adonijah would declare himself king without agreeing on this beforehand with his father. After all, it would be an insult to Yahweh," Solomon remarked with calmness that was unusual in this situation. "It's not the fault of the people that they cheered him. They could not know that he lied to them."

"You're right," the queen admitted, noting the balanced reaction of her son with satisfaction. "Could our people imagine that one could be so bold as to proclaim oneself a king against Yahweh's will? Maybe Adonijah simply lost his mind?"

"We are all human. We submit to the rulers, believing that they are wise, and we should trust them," Solomon explained the behavior of crowds. "And Adonijah is not crazy," he added. "He just takes advantage of the situation. He is a soldier; he judged that it was time to act. I think he also thought that when he puts on the crown, Father will decide that apparently, it's God's will.

In doing so, he thought the ill king will not have the strength nor the desire to change what's already happened."

"Solomon is right," Zadok agreed. "I don't know how the king will react when he finds out. Because he doesn't know yet, right?" He looked questioningly at Bathsheba and Solomon, and when they both confirmed his suspicions, he continued, "The party is going on in the valley right now. A boisterous celebration began on Adonijah's orders."

"What to do in this situation? Haven't things gone too far?" The queen lost confidence for a moment.

"What's your advice?"

"Maybe it happened so by the Lord's will?" Solomon expressed his opinion quietly, but firmly. "Adonijah can surely be a good king. He is brave; he will quickly conquer another territory, strengthen our borders; he will rule with a tough, firm hand. Yahweh could have changed his mind. He saw me on the throne once, and now he prefers Adonijah?"

"Prince, forgive me, but I have a different opinion," Nathan protested, "your father united Israel by the will of Yahweh. We are strong as ever. Now is the time to strengthen and stabilize what we have. The time of war has passed, we need peace and wise governance. You have to build, create, develop. A warrior will not do this. Israel needs a wise ruler of a peaceful nature now. You have known for long time that Yahweh has chosen you. Your father talked about this many times. Your task will be to build, including the erection of the temple for the Ark of the Covenant. Adonijah will not do it!"

"We all know the fact that Solomon is destined to govern Israel," the queen regained her self-assurance.

"Let us think how to reverse the course of events. And fast!"

"I agree that you need to act without delay," Zadok nodded. "Let's hurry and pray; hopefully it's not too late!"

"Lady, let's talk with the king as soon as possible. Yahweh will give you both clear thinking and the right words," Nathan assured.

"Father is sleeping, he is weak," worried Solomon.

"I assure you that he will be grateful to be awakened," said Nathan.

"I've known David for years. I also suppose that the need for rapid action will add him strength," Zadok backed the prophet.

***

After a while, the queen was bending over her sleeping spouse in his chamber.

"My lord," she whispered, and when he opened his eyes, kissed his hand, kneeling. "In the name of God, you promised that our son Solomon will be the king after you."

"So, it will be," he said in a calm voice, awakened.

"So, you do not know, my beloved, that Adonijah declared himself king? He did it without your knowledge?"

David got up on the bed. Just as Zadok predicted, the news shocked him, but paradoxically, also gave him strength.

"What!?" His voice, very weak recently, sounded so loud now that the prophet Nathan, listening behind the door of the chamber, was sure that Bathsheba just gave her husband the disturbing news, and he decided to come in.

"Lord," he bowed, approaching the bed. "I hear that the latest information has already reached you."

"What is what I have just heard supposed to mean? Speak!" David was sitting upright, a blush appearing on his cheeks.

"King, my lord, Adonijah made a sacrifice of many cattle, fat calves, and lambs by the Zoheleth stone, and proclaimed himself king. He invited other king's sons, military commanders, and the priest, Abiathar, to the ceremony. They are now eating and drinking with him, crying out at the same time, 'Long live King Adonijah!' But he did not invite me or the priest Zadok or Benaiah or Solomon. Has all this happened according to your will? Did you really not want to reveal to us, his servants, who is to sit on the throne of Israel after you[7]? You let Adonijah put on the crown?"

"Nathan, who knows the will of Yahweh better than you. I am his faithful servant." David found new strength with every spoken word. "What Adonijah did, happened without my knowledge! After me, Solomon is to be the king of Israel. Not Adonijah, nor anyone else, but So-lo-mon!" he spelled each syllable. "It's decided."

Bathsheba watched her husband with increasing joy. She deluded herself, thinking that what was happening would make him get his strength back for good and recover. *"Maybe he needed just such a challenge,"* she thought.

"Here's what you'll do," the king decided. "Immediately, as soon as I'm done talking, you will go with Solomon to Gihon. There, priest Zadok and you, Nathan, will anoint him with holy oil. Let them blow the horns and shout as loud as they can, 'Long live King Solomon!' Benaiah will be with you and so will all my bodyguard. Sing, praise, dance and rejoice - let the world know that we have a new king. Then come to the palace, let Solomon sit on the throne. I'll be waiting for him, and I will put a crown on his head.

"Let my lord, David, live forever!" exclaimed the happy queen.

It happened just as he ordered. They went to Gihon. There, the prophet Nathan and the priest Zadok took the horn filled with oil and anointed Solomon. When the trumpets sounded, the people shouted: "Long live King Solomon!" Then they all

---

[7] These words are almost exact quotation from the Old Testament, First Book of Kings.

followed him to the palace. They played flutes and rejoiced so much that the earth trembled.

Meanwhile, the sounds of trumpets in the city reached Adonijah and those who feasted with him at the Zoheleth stone . It was a sign to them that something special happened there. Adonijah worried. A moment later, Jonathan, the son of the priest Abiathar, came running.

"Lord," the boy bowed his head before Adonijah.

"Priest," he also bowed to Abiathar, who was his father, but had taught him from childhood to call him a priest in official situations.

Adonijah sensed that in a moment he would hear something that he surely would not like. The son of the priest, who had just anointed him to be the ruler, should have called him a king, but he did not address him this way. Why? *"What happened in the city?"* he thought and was very worried, but he tried not to show the great fear that suddenly appeared in his heart.

"Speak up!' he ordered the boy.

"Our lord and king, David, made Solomon the ruler. The priest Zadok and the prophet Nathan have anointed him in Gihon. They left from there rejoicing, so that the whole city trembled from singing, music, and cheers. Hence, these noises, reaching all the way to you. Solomon is already in the palace and sits on the royal throne. I was there when King David spoke. He said, 'Blessed be Yahweh, the God of Israel, for having established a successor on my throne today, so I could see it with my own eyes."

Jonathan's words were heard by almost all those present around Adonijah's table. To those who feasted farther away, they also arrived almost right away, because they were immediately passed from mouth to mouth.

After a moment, the square was almost empty. As soon as the people realized that they were the victims of Adonijah's fraud, they went in silence, but in a great hurry to the city, to honor the rightful king. Only Adonijah with Joab, Abiathar, and several soldiers, stayed in the valley.

"What do you advise?" Adonijah knew what punishment he himself would give to someone who behaved as he did. He was upset and did not try to hide it.

"We have to run away!" Joab also had no doubt what fate awaits the one who voluntarily declared himself king and his associates. "Run away. As soon as possible! Soon, the soldiers of Solomon will be here. Then we will be finished! They will not forgive us!"

"Do not panic," the priest tried to calm him. "We did not do anything that would require the imposition of the severest punishment."

"It's not panic, but common sense. You know as well as we do that we are guilty of treason." Joab had no doubt.

"Adonijah will be immediately executed for what he did, and we together with him. The king would be a fool if he did otherwise. Let's flee, while there is still time!"

When none of them moved a step away from the place. Joab bowed his head in front of them, turned away, and walked briskly to the horse, taking the bridle from his servant.

"Do what you want. Maybe we'll meet in better times," he kicked the sides of the animal.

They watched in silence as the rider quickly receded.

"Lord, the temple will guarantee your safety," priest Abiathar advised Adonijah when Joab disappeared behind the first rock. "Hold the horns of the altar. The eternal law says that those who have not acted properly, but were not guided by evil intentions, are protected. No one will dare to defile the sacred right of asylum."

"Are you sure?" Adonijah was looking for hope in his words. "What if Solomon does not respect this law?"

"He will respect it; he is wise," assured Abiathar.

"I wish!" He held on to his words like to salvation. "Promise me, in the name of our friendship, that you will now go to Solomon and ask him to promise that he will not order to kill me. I am only afraid of death," he added quietly. "Will you do this?" He approached the priest at a breath distance and grabbed him by the skirts of his long coat. "Promise!"

Abiathar shivered. He had never seen such terror in the eyes of the one who just a moment earlier proclaimed himself king. Adonijah's fear infected him.

The Kingdom of Sheba, Mariba

At the same time

"He for whom I am destined, will soon sit on the throne," Makeda stretched just after waking.

She was pleased and happy. She was lying in the big bed, which the king recently ordered to make from the best Lebanese cedar wood. Nikal pampered his daughter without restrain. I thought he was trying to compensate for the absence of her mother in this way, but I did not see anything inappropriate in this.

"He will sit on the throne? You had a dream?" I asked, sitting down beside her.

She embraced me with her little hands, and she said, in accordance with our agreement that she would always whisper about her visions into my ear so that no one else could hear.

"He was walking toward the great throne. I looked at his back. He was already on the steps, but something stopped him from entering higher. He stopped. As if he were wondering. I was hoping for him to turn around so I could see his face, but he disappeared."

"Something else?" I asked.

"Where he was, the sun was shining."

"Were there any people with him?"

"I have not seen anyone besides him..."

The Kingdom of Israel

At the same time

"May the God of Israel be blessed for having appointed a successor on my throne today,"[8] surprisingly for everyone, King David's voice was very strong. The coronation of his son gave him strength. His eyes sparkled, he was proud and convinced that Solomon would be a perfect ruler.

"Be brave as befits a man," he added, addressing him directly. "Remember, serve God by walking his paths, obeying his laws, commandments and ordinances, as it is written in the law of Moses, so that you succeed in everything you do and wherever you go. In this way, the words spoken to me by Yahweh will be fulfilled: 'If your sons are faithful to me with all their heart and with all their soul, you will never run out of a descendants who sit on the throne of Israel.'"

Solomon knelt.

"So, it will happen. I will fulfill God's will, father."

He did not have time to get up when a messenger came running into the throne room. He bowed low, out of breath, and then panted, turning his gaze from David to Solomon and back, and gasping for air, "Lord, there is no one left with Adonijah. Everyone left him. People are now running into the city to bow to the rightful king. The priest Abiathar will be here soon. Adonijah asked him to beg you for your grace for him."

---

[8] *Millennium Bible - Holy Scriptures of the Old and New Testaments*, Old Testament, 1 Kings, Poznań 2000 (the remaining words of the king, which he says here, are also a quote from this part of the Bible - author).

The eyes of the gathered people focused on Solomon, for it was him whom the messenger addressed with his last words. David was also looking at his son expectantly. But Solomon was silent.

"What should I do?" he wondered. *"If I have him killed, it will be my first decision as a king. I do not want to start my rule from sentencing. If I let him go free, the people will see it as weakness or fear. I know that Adonijah will always think that he would be a hundred times better king than me. He will want to remove me at the first opportunity."*

His thoughts were interrupted by the entrance of priest Abiathar.

"King, I want to pay tribute to you," he began, bowing.

David smiled at his thoughts. He was sure Abiathar would behave exactly like this: he would bow down low and pretend that he had nothing to do with Adonijah's coronation.

"You are the rightful king, given to us by Yahweh," he said, obsequiously.

"What brings you here, priest?" Solomon's expression was impenetrable. "Speak honestly. I want to hear the truth from your lips."

"I come from Adonijah, who made a terrible mistake. However, he realized it and begs for forgiveness. Shaking with fear, he clings to the horns of the altar and says: 'May King Solomon give me a promise today that he will not kill his servant!' Adonijah believes in the right of asylum in the temple for those who have committed a crime unintentionally."

Solomon considered the answer. Finally, he said, "In the law of Moses, it is written: 'If it turns out that he had fair intentions, the hair will not fall from his head, but if they prove him guilty, he will have to die!'"

"King, you speak in a riddle." Abiathar understood the king's words perfectly, but he hoped that Solomon would nevertheless show mercy to the traitor.

"Let Adonijah stand before me immediately."

Solomon signaled that the time allowed for the hearing was over, then he beckoned Benaiah, the commander of the soldiers, "Bring Adonijah here. Right now!"

Benaiah left to obey the order, and a discussion started in the room. The gathered did not heed the presence of the old and the new king. They wondered, quietly at first, and after a while more and more loudly, what the punishment for the self-proclaimed king should be.

Benaiah returned faster than anyone expected. He was not alone. The eyes of the audience focused on Adonijah. The soldiers surrounded him from four sides. He did not resemble the man who had spontaneously proclaimed himself king in the morning. Hunched, he looked contrite. He did not take his eyes off the floor.

"Adonijah?" Solomon greeted him when the man stood before the throne.

Only then did the culprit dare to look up. Apparently, he read something in Solomon's eyes that gave him hope, because he straightened up.

"If what we've learned is true, and if you understand how great a sin against God you carry on your shoulders, you should humble yourself immediately."

There was silence. Even the air did not tremble. Time flowed, and Adonijah stood unmoved. The tension was growing. Finally, the meaning of what he had heard apparently reached him, for he fell to his knees and bowed his head. One could hear a sigh of relief among those present.

However, Adonijah's gesture was not enough for Solomon. He kept looking at him expectantly. The kneeling man raised his eyes slightly to meet the king's eyes fixed on him. He understood that he should humble himself more. The gathered men, seeing what was happening, froze again in anticipation.

Adonijah closed his eyes and bowed his head so that his forehead touched the stone floor.

The gathered people looked at Solomon. The usurper received a chance and he used it.

"What will the king do now in this situation?" they wondered.

The king waited long enough for Adonijah to realize what his situation really was. He also wanted the present people to recognize that the ceremonial was done and that they had a king in front of them who was strict albeit understanding in his wisdom.

"Adonijah," said Solomon. "There are six things the Lord hates; seven things are an insult for him: haughty eyes, false tongue, hands stained with innocent blood, a heart hiding evil plans, legs chasing the evil, false testimony containing only the lie, and causing quarrels between brothers[9]. Remember this, I am warning you. From now on, live in righteousness, and not a hair on your head will perish. For the Lord fulfills the desires of the righteous, and always rejects the lusts of the ungodly. Trust the Lord and his decisions. It was Yahweh who has put me on the throne. And he is the one who directs me. The divine judgments come from the mouth of the king; his lips are not mistaken when he makes them. Respect my decisions and you will live.

When David learned the decision of the new king, he smiled proudly. He was certain that also this time, Yahweh knew what he was doing, placing Solomon on the throne of Israel.

"Now go back to your home and do not dare do anything that would anger my heart!" the new ruler finished.

Solomon gave his first sentence as a king. It was symbolic: he left his greatest enemy alive, but he did so publicly and under the loudly announced condition that Adonijah would never come against him, and that's how the gathered people understood the

---

[9] *The Millennial Bible - Holy Scriptures of the Old and New Testaments*, Old Testament, Pr 5: 16; Prov 10,3; before 16.10, Poznań 2000.

verdict. They admired the wisdom of David's son and nodded with approval at the ingeniousness of the punishment. They were glad that Solomon had just become David's successor.

A few days passed. The forces that God gave David to finish his earthly work, began to fade. The old king felt that the time was coming to go to Sheol, the eternal home of all living.

In order to leave royally, in harmony with the world, and without leaving unfinished business, he called for his son and gave him his last will without any witnesses.

"As you know, every ruler has countless friends. However, he also has many enemies. A reasonable king should remove those most ardent and unyielding from his path. For they will always plot and do everything to deprive him of the throne."

"I know, father. The ruler has many different duties. He must perform each of them in deep faith and for the common good."

The face of David was illuminated by the wise smile of a departing man.

"You will be a good king..."

"I would like to be good and wise, father."

"The children are the pride of their fathers. I am glad that I lived to the moment when you sat on the throne," he sighed at the memory of the last days' events. "It's good that you have dealt with Adonijah, but do not expect that this is a finished matter. You can still have a lot of problems with him. It will be difficult for him to be obedient; he is disappointed and embittered. When I leave, he may try again to take over the crown."

"I will keep an eye on him."

"Watch out also for priest Abiathar. He is the one behind Adonijah's ideas."

"Father, I have been watching your ruling for years, I know the mechanisms of power."

"God will give you strength and everything you need." The king straightened on his bed. "I leave some unfinished business here on earth. Please take it over and finish the work, necessarily within a year since my death. During this time, cleanse your field, that's what wise rulers do. Then the time will come to build."

"I will finish anything for which you run out of time; I promise."

"Do you know what Joab, the son of Serua, did to me? What did he do to the two commanders of Israeli military troops, how he killed them, shedding blood during peace, as if it were during the war? You will be guided in your actions by your own prudence and you will not let me leave to the afterlife not avenged. Get rid of them."

David was tough, and Solomon turned out to be his father's true son. He did not hesitate for a moment with the answer.

"I will avenge you, father."

"On the other hand, you will show much kindness to the sons of Barzillai of Gilead and you will count them among those who will sit with you by the same table. They showed me kindness when I fled from the war. They supported me. We will repay with the same."

"So, it will happen," he made his father happy with another answer.

"Shimei from Bahurim is close to you. He threw hideous insults at me when I was on my way to Mchanaim. But because he came to meet me all the way to Jordan, I swore to Yahweh that he would not die from my sword. But you do not have to save him. You are wise and you will know how to deal with him. Let his white head be red with blood on the day of his death[10]."

"Father, it will be according to your will." Solomon was an obedient son.

Soon David left to his fathers and was buried in Jerusalem. He had ruled Israel for forty years. Horns were blown in the city. A

---

[10] All David's commands come from 1 Kings; The last command and description of his death is the fragment: 1 Kings 2.1-12.

prayer resounded over the grave of the king. "Listen, Israel! The Eternal is our God, the Eternal is the only one! You will love God with all your heart, and with all your soul, and with all your strength."[11]

According to Moses law, burials were carried out as soon as possible. Most often on the day of death. From that moment, the period of mourning began. The strict mourning, or shiva[12], lasted seven days. At that time, life was on hold. One was not allowed to work or read the scriptures, nor have intercourse, but not even wash or wear sandals. After this period, the month-long shloshim time began. At that time, the mourning continued; one could not participate in the festivities. At this time, for example, you could not cut hair or nails. Then came a twelve-month avelut, when the entertainment was withheld, and the son and the immediate family of the king prayed at least twice a day.

The Kingdom of Sheba

At the same time

I have been sleeping together with Makeda in her bed for some time. Falling asleep, she held my hand. I sang old songs to her, hugged and caressed her. We laughed, comparing our hands and feet. We put them one next to the other.

"When will mine be like yours?" she asked.

"The time will come for this."

"And when I grow up, will my skin be as black as yours?"

---

[11] Shema Israel - a fragment of one of the two most important prayers in Judaism; the form currently in use was adopted in II/III century A.D. (author's note).

[12] Shiva means seven in Hebrew; shloshim - thirty; avelut - twelve (author's note).

"No. But you know that. We talked about it many times. Mine is black as ebony, and yours is only a little darker than cedar wood."

"You once said that wood darkens with time."

"It does not apply to skin. Your mother was the same as you."

"My father is darker than me," she teased.

"But only a little," I tickled her with the hope that it would make her change the subject.

Makeda often stressed that she would like to look like me and was disappointed that nothing could be done about it.

"People are different," I told her. "Those who live north of us have skin even more fair than you. And most people on the other side of the Red Sea look like me. But people like you are there too. They say that a long time ago, an expedition sent by a great Egyptian queen came to Punt, where the parents of Prince Den, whom you adore so much, rule today."

"Hatshepsut," she guessed at once. "I know about her."

"How come?"

"I'm talking to her in my dreams."

I did not comment on what she said, so she added, "You are not surprised? Different people come to me in my dreams. I talk with them."

"What did Hatshepsut tell you?"

"That I will be a queen too, and that it is my destiny."

"Right. Did she tell you about the trip to Punt?"

"Ha, ha," Makeda chuckled happily. "I was joking! And you believed it! You really believed, admit it!"

"I admit," I confessed surprised, disarmed, but also a little saddened by her joke.

She attacked me with kisses.

"Father told me about Hatshepsut. I'm sorry. I did not want to sadden you," she added, seeing my face.

When I smiled at the sign that there was no reason to feel offended, she added, "I wanted to see if I can talk about what is not true so that you would believe me. If you believe me, and you know me best of all people in the world, then everyone else will believe me too."

"What do you need such a skill for? Queens do not lie," I scolded her gently in rematch for her joke.

"They do not lie. And I do not want to lie. I will always tell the truth, but you never know what skills can be useful in your life, right? You keep repeating it to me."

"You're right. I encourage you to learn and always find out something new, because I am convinced that what we learn will stay in our heads forever. Nobody will take it away from us."

"All right," she concluded in a conciliatory tone, "tell me about Queen Hatshepsut and her trip to Punt. I know only as much about her as my father told me."

She put her head on my shoulder and closed her eyes.

"Hatshepsut was the most powerful women who ruled Egypt. She lived a long time ago. It was said that her father was Amon, the greatest god in this country. Her mother was Queen Ahmes, the wisest and most beautiful of women. Hatshepsut knew since childhood that she would become a pharaoh. Not the queen, the king's wife, but the king. Like a man. She could do everything: she knew languages, math, geography, she dealt with architecture. To this day, the temple that she raised is the joy for the eyes and hearts of not only the Egyptians. She built a lot of roads, sacred buildings, and palaces. It was on her order that the great trip to Punt was organized. The queen's ships came there mainly for incense. Soldiers and priests of various specialties spent several months there. They left not only gifts and a new temple for the king, but also something more. Few months after their departure, children with light skin color started to be born. That is why to this day, some inhabitants of those lands have a fair complexion."

"Not because these lands belong to Sheba?"

"Of course, also for this reason. For a long time, these areas belonged to our kingdom, so the diversity of people there is big."

"I'd rather be as beautiful and black as you..." Makeda looked admiringly into Seshep's eyes.

"I told you that skin color is not important. What counts is the heart and what we have in our heads."

"Was Hatshepsut very wise?"

"Extremely. She ruled over priests and soldiers. She could also fight. As a pharaoh, she put on a male outfit and attached a beard."

"A beard? Really? Why?"

"She wanted people to see a man in her. Masculinity is often identified with strength in our world."

"You are strong, and you are not a man."

"Because I'm hemet. We can do everything. Anyway, just like every woman."

"Is every one of us strong?"

"Everyone. Sometimes we do not even know it, but we are. And even if we are not, we can be."

Makeda fell silent. After a moment she rose and sat down in front of me.

"If I become a queen, I will not wear men's clothing or put on a beard," she assured me.

I remember this conversation not only because of the words that were said then, but also because the same night Makeda had another vision.

She slept calmly, but at some point, her breathing became short and interrupted. Her body covered with sweat, and the hair and shirt became wet in an instant. I knew I could not wake her up. She was in a sleep trance. At some point, she opened her eyes.

"I saw him again..."

"Who, honey?"

"The one that is intended for me."

I wiped her wet forehead with my hand.

"I saw him with the crown. He became the king. It is in front of him that I will bow my head one day. And he will bow to me."

I reached for the cloth. I did not want to interrupt her, so I just wiped her wet hair and neck. She did not seem to notice what I was doing.

"I also saw a lot of blood. Sharp swords pierced the hearts of his enemies... And you know what else? I experienced something very strange: I felt the presence there of an unknown, powerful and all-encompassing light to which I am supposed to go. It was a power I do not know, nor can I name it.

"Not everything has to be name," I assured her.

"I also saw camels, a big caravan," she continued, as if she had not heard my words. "I was grown up already. I saw myself in colorful airy scarves, traveling on a covered light palanquin placed on a white camel. You were there too. You were riding alongside me. The journey took many long months. We were battered by storms of rain and sand. It happened that oases lacked water for our animals, not everyone survived the journey, but I know that we succeeded to arrive at the destination in good shape. And that later, also in good condition, we returned to Sheba, which was safe in our absence. In this vision, I could feel the sand of the desert in my mouth and the blowing wind on my cheeks. I was there, I saw everything exactly. I looked at us from above, I felt like I was a bird. Do you know what else I saw? We were carrying rich gifts for the king."

The Kingdom of Israel

At the same time

When the time of shloshim was over and the avelut was still in place, Adonijah came to see Bathsheba.

"What does this unfortunate man want?" wondered the queen.

She felt sorry for him. She knew that her son deprived him of all the privileges and most of his rights. Although she remembered perfectly well the events from several months ago, and how uppish and arrogant Adonijah was then, seeing now his remorseful attitude and expression, she invited him to sit down.

"Lady, mother of the king, queen, I am asking you for your grace and support," he began, rightly sensing that Bathsheba was sympathetic to him. That was what he counted on. He thought that if he had her on his side, he would manage to implement the clever plan that the priest Abiathar had shown him, and Joab supported.

"Until recently, the eyes of the whole Israel were focused on me in the hope that I would be the king. But, well... Yahweh predestined my brother for the power. I accepted it; one does not argue with God's will. However, Queen, I will not hide it from you, a woman who has such a big heart, how much I suffer."

"It's been a long time. You should get used to what happened," the queen took his words at face value.

"I know I will not be a king. I have accepted this, and I am grateful to Yahweh for inspiring Solomon to forgive me for what I did."

"A mistake that teaches humility is better than success that makes one arrogant. Thank God, Adonijah, that he has not made you a king, because I feel that you would be arrogant as a ruler. I remember your expenses, chariots and horses rushing through Jerusalem without paying attention to people or animals. Do you remember how, on your orders, wherever you went, fifty people would always run ahead of you, to let others know that they were looking at the future king? You were overbearing and conceited. God did not like it."

"Who knows how the fate of the world would have gone if I became the king? However, it does not matter, because it did not happen. Today, there is only humility in me," he replied, remembering why he came here. "Humility and begging for help." He looked at her with such eyes that she began to suspect that he might be plotting something, but his emotion seemed sincere. So, despite her previous bad experiences, she wanted to believe in his good intentions and decided to listen to him.

"Queen, I love a woman," he confessed in a low voice. "Who else will understand me better than you?" He touched her tender point. He knew that according to her, love was the most important thing in the world. He was right. At the sound of the word "love,' Bathsheba leaned in his direction."

"Speak!"

"In you, there is my only hope and rescue, queen! Promise me that you will not refuse to help me, please!"

"I'll hear you. Speak."

"This is my greatest desire, which, if fulfilled, will help calm my heart," he sighed. "I am asking you, lady, to please tell the king to give me Abishtag for a wife; he will hear you for sure. Ever since I saw her, I have no peace. Earlier, I did not even try to approach her from respect for my father, whom she looked after both day and night. After the death of the king, we were all mourning, so there were no proper circumstances; but now, I think the time has come for me to reveal my feelings and plans for her."

"Does she know?"

"I don't think so. But the King's brother's proposal will certainly be the greatest honor for her."

The queen liked Abishtag. During the last months of the King's life, she cared for him with the utmost care. Bathsheba thought that maybe Solomon would be interested in taking over the girl after his father, but he did not express the slightest intent for that. Therefore, according to her, there was nothing in the way for Adonijah to receive her. *"He has not become a king, let him at least have the one he loves,"* she thought.

"All right, I'll tell the king about it," she finished the meeting.

***

On the same day, she presented the Adonijah's request to Solomon.

"Mother, he still counts on getting the throne. Can't you see it?"

"I admit that I can't."

"If Abishtag, who warmed my father's bed, would become his wife, people would recognize that he inherited a woman from David, so he has also the right to the crown."

"What are you talking about!"

"That's the old way. The eldest son inherits the last woman of his father, and everything else with her. So, he deserves also the crown! Traditions are difficult to change. The people believe that Abishtag wasn't just warming up the king who had suffered from a disease. How could they know what it was really like? The power of tradition is powerful. Besides, Adonijah still has Abiathar and priest Joab on his side, and they are strong. Asking me for Abishtag for him, you may as well ask me to give him the crown."

"Son, I did not suspect him of such evil intentions. He played me with a love story. I believed him, despite the fact that I do not like him, let alone respect him."

Solomon got up from his chair.

"May God send all the worst upon me, if he did not cause his own peril with this request! He has gone too far! I will deal with him, and tonight. For God, who gave me strength and seated me on the throne of my father, I swear that Adonijah will give up his spirit tonight! And very soon, the punishment will also reach his supporters!"

That's what happened. Later that same day, Benaiah, called the militant arm of Solomon by the inhabitants of the city, carried out the order. Adonijah, the greatest adversary of Solomon, was killed from his hand, pierced by the sword.

At the time when this was happening, the king called priest Abiathar.

"I condemn you to exile. You can be happy, because I allow you to go to your estate in the country, even though you deserved to die. However, I will not put you to death today because you carried the Ark of the Covenant in front of my father. Because of my respect to him, you will live. But get out of my sight immediately."

This, however, was not the end of the cleaning of the field, which Solomon's father recommended before his death.

As soon as Joab, the third of the conspirators, heard the news of what was going on, that Adonijah was slain, and Abiathar exiled, he ran to the temple. He thought that since grasping the horns of the altar protected Adonijah one day, so the right of asylum would also save him.

"Commander of troops, the king orders you to leave the temple," called Benaiah, sent there by Solomon.

"I will not leave. I prefer to die here!"

Benaiah feared to desecrate the temple, besides Joab was his commander after all. He immediately passed Joab's words to the king.

"Let it be as Joab wants, execute the sentence in the temple," replied the king. "During the time of peace, he slew the best commanders of my father, men who were just and better than him. Their blood will fall on Joab's head and on the heads of all his descendants forever. On the other hand, always let the peace of Yahweh come down on the descendants of David. Benaiah, do my will without hesitation, because the law of asylum is only valid for those who have committed crimes unintentionally. And Joab not only murdered the innocent, but he sought refuge in the temple, knowing that he had no right to do so."

Benaiah returned to the temple and carried out the order. On the same day, Solomon appointed him the commander of the royal troops, and to replace the priest Abiathar, he appointed Zadok, who was faithful to him.

Of the three greatest enemies of Solomon, two were dead; and from among those his father indicated for extermination, only Shimei remained in this world.

The king called him to himself and ordered him to build a house in Jerusalem and never leave the city walls.

"If you leave the capital, know that the death penalty will find you," he added. "You take responsibility for your life."

"Thank you, king, I will follow your orders," Shimei appreciated the goodness of the king.

That's how the first months of Solomon's rule passed.

The kingdom of Sheba, Mariba

A month later

A man with a scar on his face left the royal palace through a side exit, shielding his head with a shawl. Nobody noticed him.

Moments later, the voices of servants resounded, filled with fear and terror.

"Prince Sirah, the heir to the throne, is dead!"

The Kingdom of Israel

Three years later

The last person whom King David ordered Solomon to kill, was Shimei. Three years had passed from the moment the king forbade him to leave Jerusalem under the death penalty. Throughout that time, Shimei did not move even a single step away from the city. One day, however, his two servants fled to the city of Gath. Without thinking, he decided to bring them back in person. When he was in Jerusalem again, Solomon called for him.

"Have I not beseeched you in Yahweh's name? Did I not warn you that you would have to die if you would one day leave the city and go any direction? Did you not answer me at the time that what you heard seemed right to you? Why, then, have you not kept the oath of Yahweh? Why have you not obeyed my order[13]?"

The king fell silent not only because he finished speaking. Those present saw clearly the effort with which he tried to restrain his anger. After a moment, he spoke again, "You know well the harm you did to my father, David, and you carry it in your heart. Yahweh made you bring all your perversity upon your own head. You will die because you have broken the arrangements we have made, and you agreed on."

Then he gave the order to Benaiah, who killed Shimei with a single blow. This is how the last of the three men, of whom David spoke before his death to his son, died.

The royal power in Solomon's hands was growing stronger.

---

[13] Millennium Bible - Holy Scriptures of the Old and New Testaments, Old Testament, 1 Kings 2.36, Poznań 2000 (literal quote, End of the opponents of Solomon - author's note).

CHAPTER II

TIME OF FIGHTING AND PEACE
PRINCESS MAKEDA IS NINE YEARS OLD

The Kingdom of Israel

Jerusalem

Tamrin, the richest merchant of the kingdom of Sheba, was a portly, strong, almost forty-year-old man. He just came to Jerusalem. He did not want any merchant or mighty he might meet, to recognize the envoy of King Sheba in a humble traveler. Thus, he moved around in the company of only two servants. He was in this city for the first time. He arrived at Nikal's command to see the remarkable Jerusalem, as it was said to be, and to see what was the genius of King Solomon, whose fame spread throughout the world as fast as the north wind.

His face, windswept and sunburnt on numerous expeditions, was lined with wrinkles. However, they were arranged in such a way that he did not look older than he was, but rather they gave the impression of a man knowing all about life.

From an early age, he accompanied his father in trade expeditions. When he was sixteen, he managed a small but important caravan for the first time. He led camels carrying priceless incense then. The route was not long. He sailed first on one of his father's ships from east Sheba to west, from where he moved to southern Egypt. Nor was it dangerous, because there was peace in the lands of the pharaohs at that time, but the responsibility for delivering the goods more valuable than gold was enormous. People and animals had survived the expedition without any harm. So, if anyone had even the slightest doubts before whether the young Tamrin would be worthy to represent his father, they were allayed after that expedition. Even the oldest and least trustful drivers were confident that Tamrin could lead the caravan efficiently.

Since then, he traveled so often that he did not had time to start a family. He did not get married even when his father died, and he inherited the main part of his estate as the eldest son. Many people tried to convince him to do that, and there were many beautiful and wise women willing to accompany him, but he entrusted the management of the estate to his younger brother, while devoting himself to expeditions and trade.

At this time, he was already the owner of two hundred camels and thirty ships. He was widely regarded as the wealthiest inhabitant of Sheba, of course, right after the members of the royal family. Wherever he went, as his father did before, so also him now. He often represented not only himself. He was sometimes an envoy of the king. As a trusted man, he delivered letters, gifts, and information. At the most important courts of the world, he collected news that he gave to Nikal. He also used them himself. Thanks to this, he was able to double and then triple the property left by his father within a short time.

"Information is power," he used to say. "Nothing is as valuable as it. Neither gold nor incense."

Tamrin had heard stories about distant Israel many times. He had been promising himself for a long time that he would go there, and here was the opportunity. King Nikal asked him for it personally. He wanted him to bring information about King Solomon, about the country he ruled, and about his god who seemed to have more power than any other.

So, when he successfully completed another trip to Egypt, he sent his people back to Sheba and went to Israel himself.

Here he was in Jerusalem, the capital of the country, about which he had heard so much from his earliest childhood; whose king, for reasons not entirely known to Tamrin, intrigued Nikal so much.

***

Two days later, he stood among the crowds listening to Solomon's decisions. It was a day of judgment.

Those, whose disputes the overseers of the twelve lands that are part of Israel were not able to judge, came to Jerusalem to submit to the judgment of the ruler. His decisions were final, because it was common knowledge that the king's wisdom came directly from Yahweh. Tamrin heard about it even before he went on the journey commissioned to him by Nikal. In the oases where he was staying, at the evening bonfires, in the guest houses where he spent the nights on the road, everyone knew who Solomon was. It was said that his wisdom was superior to all the sons of the East and the Egyptian sages because his God gave him wisdom, mental acumen, and extensive knowledge. He knew the nature of people, understood the language of animals, knew everything about plants. The world had no secrets from him. It was even said that he could control the demons who performed whatever he ordered them to do at his command.

Before Tamrin reached Jerusalem, he heard so much of Solomon's splendor that when he finally saw him, he felt disappointed.

When he entered the assembly hall, he saw a tall, handsome and at first glance confident, but still an ordinary man. He smiled at his thoughts.

"I have many springs behind me and lots of experience, but after what I learned about this man, I expected to see not a mortal but a god," he scolded himself. *"I'm naive."*

Then two harlots were brought in front of the king. Both were young and pretty, and both extremely desperate. Behind them stood a guard, holding a bundle with the source of dispute in it.

"Speak. I want to hear what each of you has to say in this matter," Tamrin heard Solomon, and he had a revelation. It was the voice of good and wisdom. It seemed to him that he did not hear the words of a man, but someone who is above everything mundane, who is in direct contact with another world. It sounded loud and bright. It was clear and melodic, yet powerful enough to get the impression that it was reaching the farthest corners of the city, maybe even all of Israel. Tamrin shuddered. Finally, he felt that the stories he had heard were not exaggerated - he was indeed dealing with someone extraordinary. He also knew that whoever saw and heard Solomon once, did not forget him until the end of his days.

"Mercy, my lord," the first woman said. "She and I live under one roof. I gave birth to a child. She gave birth to hers three days after me. There were only the two of us, nobody except us was home." She looked at her opponent with contempt. "That woman's child died at night because she crushed it in her sleep. Then she got up, took mine, and put it on her lap, while leaving hers, dead, with me. When I woke up to feed the baby, I saw it was dead. But then, watching him more closely, I noticed that it was not the child I had born."

"No, my child is alive, and yours is dead!" the other woman shouted.

"Never! It's yours that is dead, mine is alive!"

"You're lying!"

The women came on each other with fists. The guards quickly separated them. The struggle lasted only a moment, but even when it ceased, both were still spouting insults at each other. The agitated audience expressed their support once for the one and once for the other.

When the emotions seemed to rise all the way to the ceiling, Solomon raised his hand. Discussions and shouts ceased immediately. It was evident he enjoyed a great authority.

"Here's what I heard," he said confidently. "One of you says, 'The child who lives is mine, while the one who is dead is hers.' The other says, 'No way! The one who is dead is yours, my child is alive.'" He paused. "Here is what the king orders: Bring me a sword here. Cut the child and give one half to one woman and the other half to the other."

The guard took the child out of the bundle and approached the throne. The second guard raised his sword to execute the king's order. The gathered people held their breath.

Then one of the women cried out, throwing herself at Solomon's feet, "Oh, my lord! Let her take the boy; just do not kill him! I beg you!"

"Let neither me have him nor her!" cried the second. "Cut!"

There were shouts of terror among the gathered. A turmoil ensued.

The king waited a moment, then raised his hand again.

"Guard, hold the sword! Give the living child to this first woman. She preferred to give it away so that it could live, rather than to see it dead. She is his mother."

That day Tamrin understood the greatness of Solomon.

The Kingdom of Sheba, Aksum

At the same time

"The last time it went smoothly for you," Seth looked at the assassin bowing in front of him. "Now, do it equally discreetly. It's been four years since your last visit to Mariba, Nikal has lost his vigilance. He is no longer watching the son that has remained to him as closely as before." He pulled a purse from behind a wide belt. "As before, this time it must look like the will of the gods too, you understand?"

The assassin made a grimace that was supposed to mean a nodding.

"It's part of your pay," Seth tossed the purse at his feet.

"Always at your services, sir."

The Kingdom of Israel

A few days later

Solomon had power over all Israel. He ruled wisely and justly. His mother, Queen Bathsheba, sat on the right side of the throne, giving him advice. He trusted those who did not disappoint him in the tough time of taking over the power, their sons, as well as the young and talented who had previously been far from the palace and royal power.

Benaiah, called the king's militant arm more and more widely, commanded the army, Sadok was the most important priest, his son Azariah also became a priest. The sons of the prophet Nathan received important functions: one became the supervisor of the overseers and the other a trusted adviser. Josephat was the king's plenipotentiary, Ahishar managed the palace, and Elichoref was a writer. Adoniram controlled those working at heavy works.

Throughout the country, Solomon was represented by twelve land overseers. They had the duty to provide food to the king, his household, guests and service. Each of them did it for one month a year.

Such news and much more, Tamrin gathered in Jerusalem. In street pubs, he heard stories about the righteous king, about his wisdom, management, and also about his beautiful wife, the daughter of the king of Egypt, and the princesses, of whom more and more came to the palace to become his next wives. For the king, as it was said, wanted to have as many children as possible on the order of Yahweh himself.

Tamrin, who had known many lands in his life, could not stop being amazed at the extraordinariness of the customs which he discovered every day in the world of Yahweh's followers. The Jews intrigued him, they had a right, a rule, an order or a law for everything, which they had to follow to avoid arousing the wrath of Yahweh.

One day, as he paced around the market, a dignified looking young man approached him. He was accompanied by two servants.

"Lord, I am Josephat, the king's representative," the newcomer bowed his head slightly. "Solomon invites you for a short chat. It would please him greatly if you would accept the invitation."

The witnesses of the event watched carefully the man to whom the king himself sent one of his most trusted men. They were sure that he could not be just anybody, since Josephat personally went to meet him.

"The king's plenipotentiary, it is an honor and an unexpected distinction for me." Tamrin bowed his head as low as Josephat had done. "Why have I deserved such a great honor?"

"Will you come with me, lord?" Josephat answered the question with a question. "The king is waiting."

"Let's go, then," said Tamrin, following Josephat.

They passed between the stalls and walked one of the narrow streets leading towards the old palace, but they did not reach it. They stopped by a group of workers. Solomon was talking with the overseer. As soon as he saw Josephat and Tamrin following him, he finished the conversation and turned to the guest with a smile.

"Lord, here is the merchant Tamrin," Josephat introduced the newcomer.

"King, I'm honored," Tamrin bowed low and added in Hebrew. "Shalom aleichem!"

This welcome made Solomon happy.

"Shalom aleichem," he answered in a similarly courteous manner, looking the visitor in the eyes. "I hear you have been in Jerusalem for a few days..."

The merchant understood at once that one can only give the words of truth to this man. His eyes were so piercing that there was no way to try to smuggle an understatement or a half-truth. Tamrin met people with similar eyes maybe twice in his life. Nothing eluded them; they understood every word and they could recognize who they were dealing with in an instant. One was a priest in Egypt and the other a hermit in the desert. Now, he met the third one.

"I come from the kingdom of Sheba, king."

"You are one of the richest merchants the earth bears. What brings you here?"

"Your wisdom, sir."

"Has your king sent you?"

"I was guided by my own curiosity and willingness to get to know this place, but I am here with the king's approval."

"Nikal is old already. Was he in good health when you left him?"

"He is a strong ruler."

"And he trusts you?"

"I appreciate it very much."

"What answers are you looking for in Jerusalem?"

"What god has given you so much wisdom, king? I would like to know who you are and what you are like that such an abundance of gifts comes to you? The news of your power is shared by not only people. Our priests say the gods are talking about you too."

" Gods, you say? Interesting…"

While they were talking, busy workers were passing by them. At one point, the king stopped one of them. He carried a large stone on his head, a water bottle hung on his neck, and he wore sandals and a bundle of food attached to his belt.

"Look at this man," he said. "How am I better than him? And how should I show him my glory? Just like him, I was made of ashes, which tomorrow will be eaten and decomposed by worms, and yet I look like I should never die. Aren't we both the same beings and people? He lives and I do. He will die and so will I.[14] Get back to work." he turned to the worker, ending the lecture.

"Wise words, king."

"Yahweh, my God and the God of all Israel, tells us all to remember this every day. 'Do not be vane,' he teaches. Each of us is convinced that he lives in the right way, but only He can judge the inside of man. Entrust God with everything you do, and your intentions will come true[15]." He paused and looked up at the sky. "Tamrin, and who are you praying to? Who are you asking for blessing and strength every day?"

"We have many gods in Sheba. The largest of them is Illumkuh. The Silver Mother, called the Lady of the Moon, also has a great power. Women like to pray to her. Makeda, the only daughter of King Nikal, is surrounded by the priestesses of the goddess. She is her follower and of course, like her father, of Illumkuh as well."

"Makeda is still a child, isn't she?"

"She's nine years old. And I will admit to you, lord, that while I spent all my life in my travels and met a lot of girls, none of them matched her beauty or wisdom. She will grow up to be a wonderful woman."

---

[14] Kebra Nagast, XXVII Worker (author's note).
[15] Millennial Bible, Old Testament, Book of Proverbs 16.3.

The king did not respond to this information, but he remembered it.

"You did not answer my question," he rebuked the guest gently. "Which of the gods is the closest to you?"

Tamrin thought about it.

"I got to know many of them during my travels."

"And?"

"I think they were invented by people," he said boldly, and understanding that he might be exposing himself to the king's anger, he got silent, preparing for the worst.

But this opinion apparently did not make an impression on Solomon, because he just said, "Really?"

"If they cannot deal with the world that surrounds them, people create gods and make them responsible for their failures and successes, the storms in the sea and in the desert, diseases of relatives and animals," he said more boldly, seeing that the king had an open mind.

"They ask them for help in various matters, hoping to be heard. It is good that they have someone to pray to, that makes life easier.

"So, you claim, Tamrin, that the gods are a figment of people?"

"In Egypt, they pray to cats, crocodiles, they have a goddess-lioness and hundreds of others, and yet, for example, Amon, which they claim is omnipotent, does not have power in Syria or here in Israel. Why? People are inventing the gods they need at the moment and for whom they are ready."

"Then who created it all, Tamrin?" the king made a wide gesture, showing the buildings, trees, the sky and the hills surrounding Jerusalem. "Where did the world in which we live come from? What force caused us to exist?"

"Probably everyone who considers himself a thinking being and spent even one night looking at the starry sky or the endless sands of the desert or the vastness of the sea, asked himself this question. And it was not different with me either," he gave himself time to sort out what he wanted to say. "I think there is one huge, endless primordial force that moves everything. It is the eternal energy that was, is and will be. The power that makes the children come into the world, the rivers flow, the earth yield, and the sun always rise at dawn. It is an indestructible and all-encompassing force. And the gods we know are only a small emanation and a human image of what shape this force can take."

"Your words are wise," Solomon put a hand on Tamrin's shoulder in a friendly gesture. "You know that the power you are talking about is the God of Israel?"

"Oh!" Tamrin blurted out.

"Other gods are a human invention; I agree with you. In fact, there is only one God."

"What does he look like?"

"He does not look. He just is. He is the beginning and the end, alpha and omega. He embraces and encompasses everything. He is the light and the source. He was and will always be, as you say. He is the energy you talked about."

Tamrin looked at the sky, just like Solomon did a moment ago. He saw clouds that lazily moved across the sky. He inhaled the air into his lungs, listened to the sound of the wind. He kicked lightly a small pebble lying on the road with the tip of his sandal. Solomon's simple words reached his heart and touched it. They roared in his head.

"King, I will pass your words on to Nikal," he said quietly. "Thank you for them."

"Before you leave, look carefully at everything here. I would like you to convey to your king what you saw and what you found here as faithfully as possible. Tell him about the power of Yahweh. Know also that all my wisdom and everything that surrounds us comes from him. Alleluia, Tamrin!"

The kingdom of Sheba, Mariba

At the same time

I was standing by the window bay in Makeda's room, when I saw a human skittering along the wall. He wanted to be unnoticeable. His robes were in the colors of earth, his head covered by a hood, he moved smoothly, as if he wanted to blend in with the background. He was not looking at anyone. I knew the assassins' behavior. I had no doubt, he was one of them. Suddenly, as if called by my gaze, he raised his head slightly. It was a mistake. I saw his face. The face of a man with a large scar. I stiffened in terror. It was the terrible face from Makeda's dream.

Four years earlier, when the older son of the king died suddenly, Makeda had a vision. At first, she could not sleep for a long time, disturbed by the prince's death like everyone else in the palace, and when she finally closed her eyes, she quickly woke up with a loud scream.

"I saw him," she said, terrified. "A man with a terrible face killed Sirah."

I hugged her, tried to rock her and calm her down, but she did not let me do it.

"Watch out for him, he will come back here again," she said a little more calmly, but still shaky and wet with sweat. "Watch out for a scarred man. Death follows him."

"Do you see anything else?" I inquired.

"He will come into your hands one day," she assured, and exhausted, fell into my arms and fell back to sleep. I remembered that day perfectly. The servant found the dead prince when he came to wake him up at dawn. He was cold. He looked as if he had fallen into an eternal sleep. Illumkuh's priests examined his body and found him poisoned. The investigation did not show that anyone in the palace was involved in the case. The perpetrator remained unknown.

Now I saw the man Makeda had seen in a nightmare. I was sure he was the one guilty of Sirah's death.

The blood hit my head and I rushed into a chase. However, I stopped almost immediately. Goddess of the Moon made me realize that I should first run to the chamber of Prince Tomaj, the only male heir to the throne. That maybe, if he is still alive, I will manage to save him.

"Run to the city with the guard. Look for a scarred man. He did not run far," I shouted to Ashenafi, the security commander. "Get him, he is an assassin! Announce an alarm!"

Ashenafi knew what to do. He was efficient. Running, I heard him give the proper orders.

"Prince!" I shouted, rushing into Tomaj's room without warning.

He was not inside. I was terrified.

"Where is Prince Tomaj?" I shouted as loud as I could because I wanted as many people as possible to hear me.

The servants looked at me, frightened.

"He is in the temple with the king," stammered one of them.

"Do not touch anything in the room," I ordered and continued to run. "And let no one enter it," I added loudly already on the stairs.

I got to the temple as fast as I could. Fortunately for me, some time, a long time ago, it was erected a short distance from the palace. I took three steep steps in a single jump and ran inside.

The king and the prince were burning incense before Illumkuh's statue.

I breathed with relief. They were both safe.

Disregarding the sanctity of the place, I quickly approached them.

"I saw a man with a scar," I said, catching my breath.

"Is Makeda safe?" King bowed to Illumkuh calmly, as if not hearing my words.

"Yes, king. I am afraid that a scarred man is all about Prince Tomaj. Fortunately, I see that he is with you."

Tomaj straightened up. He looked like his father, but even though he was only sixteen, he was taller and more strapping.

"What's happening? Who is a man with a scar?" he wanted to know.

"I'll explain everything to you," Nikal promised him. Meanwhile, let's go to the palace. We should all be together now. Makeda is probably very worried."

She was calm, however. She was sitting in her room and drawing something with a reed brush on a piece of papyrus.

"It's him, you have to look for him," she said, demonstrating her work. A terrible face with small eyes and a huge scar on the right cheek, from the temple all the way to the chin, looked at us from the papyrus.

"And search Tomaj's room," she added. "Something hisses in the chest."

The prince's chamber was closed before I left the palace, as I ordered. By Ashenafi's order, guards stood in front of its door.

"We've been waiting for you, hemet," Ashenafi said. "The search for the assassin continues, but he seems to have fallen off the face of the earth. Nobody has seen him, he's gone. If it was not for your eyes, we would not even know he was here," he said, as if he had some doubts that someone could have entered the palace, escaping the attention of his guards.

"Let's go inside," I suggested.

The guards began searching. I ordered to check everything minutely – each place, cubit after cubit, every corner, fabric, clothing, weapon, trunk and dish, and to watch out for snakes, after all Makeda warned us that something was hissing in her brother's room. At one point, one of the guards raised the lid of a stone box. Usually, it contained favorite amulets and cufflinks that Prince Tomaj put back in every evening. There were also Illumkuh's protective bracelets, which during the day usually decorated the prince's right wrist. Tomaj always put on his jewelry himself. The guard lifted the lid, and then, before he knew what was happening, his hand was bitten by a viper which suddenly jumped out of the casket.

The guard shouted in terror and grasped his hand, putting it instinctively in his mouth and trying to suck out the venom.

Ashenafi cut the viper into two parts near its head with one movement of a long knife, and covered the casket with the lid, in case there were other dangerous creatures in it.

Meanwhile, I rushed to help the bitten guard. Blood was flowing from the wound, the hand got almost immediately swollen and dark. The guard could not stand, he staggered and fell. I knew there was no help for him. The viper who had bitten him was one of the most dangerous that the earth bears. A moment later, he was dead. It was not the end of the day's emotions. When I returned to Makeda's chamber, to my horror, I did not find her there.

"Where's the princess?" I called to the maidservants huddled against the walls in fear of my anger.

"She ran out. Nobody dared stop her," one of them finally stammered.

"When?" I boiled with rage that they let something like that happen.

"Well..." the same one who had previously dared to answer my question, was speechless from fear.

"Where is she?" In anger I caught her by the hair with such force that I put her on her feet. "Where is she?" I yelled, forgetting for a moment that I should control my emotions.

The maid pointed at the window bay. I looked in the direction she indicated. A black mare, fast like the wind, rushed along the road lined with sycamore trees. I was relieved to see Makeda cuddled in her mane.

Since then, whenever there were problems which she needed to face herself, she jumped on the mare and galloped till the loss of her breath. It helped her.

The Kingdom of Israel, Jerusalem

At the same time

"Shalom, Tamrin."

"Shalom, prophet Nathan."

The men exchanged greeting courtesies and sat down. They were in the palace, in a small but comfortably furnished room where the highest dignitaries received important guests.

"I know that King Solomon has given you his attention and time."

"I had this honor. I'm still impressed by his wisdom. I admire him, especially since I also looked at his sentencing."

"I wanted to talk to you before you go back to Sheba."

"Thank you for the invitation. Here I am."

"I know that you are interested about how and from where Solomon got his wisdom.

"I can't deny it."

"Well, listen then, I'll tell you before you hear about it in one of the street bars. I do not know if you know it, but in our country, and especially in Jerusalem, everyone has their own story and likes to talk about everything. We Israelis are experts on everything and know everything," he joked. "I'm saying this in case you have not noticed it yet."

"I realized that, prophet. Furthermore, I managed to get to like not only your wisdom, but also your sense of humor. It is quite perverse."

"My story will be real. And very serious," Nathan lowered his voice and made a long pause, thereby giving a sign for Tamrin to listen carefully to the words that were about to come.

"Remember what I tell you and pass it to your king as best you can. And to princess Makeda. I predict that it may be of interest to her."

"I will do so, prophet."

"Here is the story," Nathan lowered himself into a wide leather armchair. "One day, in the first days of his reign, the king went to Gibeon to make a thousand burnt offerings. After a long ceremony, when he was asleep, God came to him, 'Tell me what you want me to give you,' he asked. Solomon replied, 'You have deigned to show great kindness to your servant, my father David, for being faithful and just in the simplicity of his heart. It is you, my God, who passed the power after my father to me, your servant. And I am still young, and I do not know how to act. I live among people that you love. This is a great nation: it cannot be counted or evaluated. Therefore, give your servant a heart full of wisdom, so that he could judge the affairs of your people, carefully distinguishing good from evil.' The Lord liked what he heard. 'Because you have presented to me such a request, and you have not desired a long life for yourself, or any riches, you did not demand the destruction of your enemies, and only asked for the wisdom needed for a just governance, here I fulfill your request: I give you a wise and penetrating heart, as nobody has had before you, and no one will have in the future. What's more, I will give you what you did not ask me for: wealth and fame, unmatched among all those in power during the whole time of your rule.'"

The prophet Nathan finished speaking, and Tamrin was still listening intently. He was pondering what he had heard. But he also thought about Solomon's wise judgments and the king's words that he gave him when they talked face to face for a moment. He counted in his mind how old Solomon was when he sat on the throne. He figured he was twenty-five. So, only four years passed since he took power, and he managed to do so much and so strongly affect the imagination of people in even the distant corners of the world. "Is there anyone left on this earth who has not heard of the great Solomon," he wondered.

"Tamrin, when you came to Jerusalem, we knew who you were, even though you intended to remain unrecognized," Nathan interrupted the silence. "News of you reached us long before your feet crossed the borders of Israel."

"I have always thought that information is more valuable than gold," the buyer liked what he heard.

"It is difficult to disagree with you in this matter," the prophet nodded approvingly. "You will soon return to Sheba, won't you?" He wanted to be sure, and when Tamrin nodded, he added, "I have a royal proposal for you."

"I am listening with the utmost attention," he was happy to think about what he expected to hear.

"You are a wealthy, experienced merchant. You have ships and camels. You are expert at what you are doing. God has given you many talents. As you know, Solomon begins building the temple for the glory of God. Everything that it will be built with, and what will be found in it, should be the best. You know the quality of goods like nobody else."

"Those words are music to my ears, prophet," he wanted it to sound like a joke, but Nathan took it seriously.

"You're an expert," he repeated his praise. "And Sheba is famous for its ability to obtain the best things that come from the Black Continent. We want you to provide us with everything that will be necessary for the construction and can be found in the areas where your king's power reaches. Tell your ruler that Solomon wants a cooperation. That he would willingly support him in what he cares about most, and so, as we think, in the commercial mediation between the worlds and the peoples who live north and east of us, in exchange for goods that you have access to. But they must be the best of the best. And it will be on your head to give us just that."

"Prophet, I will pass on your words to King Nikal. But already today, being authorized by him, I can express interest in the cooperation. We are sure that it will be mutually beneficial."

"Before you leave, we will prepare for you a list of what we will need. Solomon's payment will be generous."

The Kingdom of Sheba

Makeda is 15 years old

I know who, when and how clipped Makeda's wings. Who caused that for many years, maybe even all her life, with one exception, she found it difficult to trust a man?

Here is how it happened: For centuries, the kingdom of Sheba had quite mobile borders. Depending on how strong the king in power was, we controlled the territories on either side of the Red Sea, or not. If the alliances were lasting and there was peace, the trade between the Black Continent and the east coast belonged to us. If we had enemies on the west side, there were problems with the flow of goods, so Sheba had less gold and other goods coming from those areas.

For centuries, we have ruled over vast lands on both sides of the sea. Our army and the whole country was once even stronger than Egypt. Some called our lands on the west coast Punt; others called them Kush. The largest city and duchy on the west side was and is Aksum.

The capital from which King Nikal rules the two parts of the country is Mariba. It is located on the east side of the sea, in the area where one can reach Babylon, Israel, and other distant countries, known for their wealth and great culture, on dry foot, without using ships. On the Western land we have important allies, formally subject to Nikal. They are so fragmented that without Sheba's support they would not be able to resist Egypt, so they are keeping an alliance with us. Nikal must care for good relations with the rulers from those areas, because our wealth and the ability to trade with the world depends on it. Because it is out of those lands that the goods from all the Black Land, desired by the rich kings, originate – exotic animal skins, gold, electrum and myrrh of the best quality, more valuable than gold. Ships transport them to our side of the sea, and from there the merchants transport them further. This is the source of our wealth and power. That's why we care for those territories, and the princes from the western areas have influence in the palace. Why am I talking about it? This is important for my story, because it was the son of the richest Prince of Aksum, Den, who broke Makeda's heart, and it had serious political consequences. Den's behavior, the princess's hurt feelings, and the damage of her own self-love, which may seem unlikely or even impossible to many, led to a war. Yes, I say it with full responsibility: what happened between two young people really led to a war. That's what I want to tell you about.

***

Den was only three years older than Makeda. It is not much, but at such a young age, such a difference can be significant.

I met him almost immediately after I started to live in the palace. His father was a frequent guest of the king, and Den accompanied him. Sometimes, although not often, Den's mother was also with them, a quiet, meek woman, fully subordinate to her husband.

Den was a bright, lively, and cheerful boy; very excited that as the only son, he would once take the rule over from his father. He tried to meet the expectations of his parents and his childhood image of being a young prince. I tried to like him, but from the first moment, something in him disturbed me. I did not know what it was. Maybe his too confident eyes? Perhaps the superiority with which he looked at my ward? Or maybe something else that I could not define at that time? As it turned out, my premonition was not wrong.

Makeda and Den spent almost every spare moment together. Something, some invisible threads, attracted them to each other from their earliest childhood. They gave the impression of being created for each other. The older they were, the more their mutual sympathy grew. It seemed that his parents and King Nikal looked kindly at this. I heard Prince Seth remarking many times that in a few years, the children would make a beautiful couple, and if it would so happen, it would be beneficial for both sides. Nikal would be assured of peace and friendliness in the western part of the kingdom, and young Den, as the husband of the king's daughter, would become the most powerful ruler on the western side of the Red Sea.

The children's relationship, and later the youthful friendship, had thus both permission and all means to flourish.

Time passed quickly. Before I knew it, Makeda turned from a charming girl into a young woman aware of her talents, skills, and charms.

I do not deny that I had a significant effect on what she was like. Of course, she owed a lot to the royal blood of her parents. It was said that she got the appearance and intelligence from her mother, and she got courage and relentless character from her father. I did not know her mother, but I was told that besides her beauty, Makeda also inherited from her the independence and feminine wisdom. To me, she owed knowledge of books, languages, astronomy and martial arts. I also taught her how to value her own worth, know what she wants, and be able to communicate it to the world. I showed her how to keep the balance between the needs of the body and the spirit. It seemed to me that when she became a woman and Lady of the Moon gave her the monthly blood, she was fully independent, wise, reserved and responsible, that is, prepared for life. However, it was not exactly like that.

When Makeda was fifteen, she caught the eyes of everyone who was in her company. She was slim and delicate, yet there was strength showing in her every movement. Her figure revealed the skills of fighting and horse riding and high fitness of her body. She had hard muscles, and at the same time she moved with such grace as if she were floating in the air. Long hair, softly falling over her shoulders, formed an unusual veil around her head, heaving with every movement. She had big black eyes, beautifully cut lips and a small, slightly upturned nose. She looked like a princess from a story that mothers or nannies tell their children in the evening, and at the same time she was the toughest, strongest and the most intelligent girl I've ever met. She knew what she wanted, she was disciplined, and she was able to submit to even the most rigorous order of the day I suggested to her, if she clearly saw the goal and identified with it. When she knew what was at the end of the road, she could follow it without regard to the effort and costs she had to bear. She was consistent and persistent, and at the same time, extremely sensitive and attentive to the spiritual side of life.

While teaching and educating her, advising the king, which teachers to choose for her, I always had a vision in front of me, in which Makeda sits on the throne. I remembered that I am looking after the future queen and it is my duty to properly prepare her to rule. I divided Makeda's life so far into two parts. At first, she was a girl who had dream visions. She was smart and brave, but at the same time delicate and absolutely trusting.

The first stage ended when the Lady of the Moon made her a woman. From the moment her monthly blood began to appear, the night visions ceased completely, and she entered the time of keeping both feet on the ground. She absorbed knowledge even more than before, learned and developed every day. She accompanied her father in the expeditions, she went hunting with her brothers, and participated in the royal councils, although she could not speak at them, but even just listening to them was valuable to her. She visited temples, mines, visited a great dam, thanks to which the peasants could cultivate the land and obtain substantial yields. She was constantly in motion. It was a time when she still trusted most people, but she realized more and more often that life has many colors, and the truth usually lies in the middle. She noticed that someone is rarely only good or only bad, and the river current is not just what we see on the surface. In a word: she matured.

This stage of her development ended quite abruptly and was not pleasant. For it meant for her the clipping of the wings of power that she had since birth. Because, as the Lady of the Moon says: "Each of us has wings. Some smaller, others bigger, in different shapes and colors. Sometimes we do not even notice that we have them, but we are born with them. Every one of us. We get them from our mothers, grandmothers, and women who give us support." Makeda's wings were clipped by prince Den.

Den and his parents had been staying in the Mariba palace for several days. The relations of King Nikal and Prince Seth did not work well for some time. It was about issues related to myrrh trade. The dispute was growing. At one point, the marital future of Makeda was also at stake. Den's father wanted to see her as a daughter-in-law in his palace, and Nikal dismissed this topic on the excuse of Makeda being too young.

I was sure that the king was deeply concerned about the development of events when I received his instructions to be on the watch out even more than ever before, and to not leave the princess alone while Den and his parents were in the palace. I sensed that this was related to the sudden death of the young prince Sirah many years earlier, which still could not be solved. Could the king suspect that it was Seth's job? My intuition also told me that he should be the first suspect in this case, but I did not have any evidence for it, so I kept silent. I was sure that sooner or later, we would find out who was behind the murder.

Den was eighteen at the time. He was no longer a boy but a young, strong, fit man.

One evening, after a sumptuous supper, Den invited Makeda for a stroll around the city. I walked a few steps behind them. Along with me, unofficially and in disguise, were the warriors from the king's team. I did not know what to expect and what Nikal was afraid of. All the more my vigilance was increased. The young people walked, talked, laughed, looked as if they felt as good in each other's company as usual. Nothing disturbing happened during the whole evening. I was sure, however, that I should not lower my guard. Nikal certainly had good reasons when he told me to not step away from the princess.

Late in the evening, when I was almost asleep, I heard knocking. Someone was standing outside the door of Makeda's chamber. My room was adjacent to her bedroom. I could come to her room at any moment if she called me. All she needed to do was to hit any of the gongs set up in such way that they were always within her reach. Some time ago, we agreed that I would accompany her only when she called me, and that's what I did. Makeda was already at the age when she sometimes needed to be alone. Someone always accompanied her in the chamber where she worked, but the bedroom was her private space, isolated from the world, where even I tried to enter only when she expressed such a wish.

The knocking became urgent.

"It's me, Makeda..." I heard Den's muffled voice, and then her steps.

"What are you doing here?" she asked, surprised, when she opened the door.

"This is the only place where we can talk without witnesses."

"But this is my bedroom! Nobody from outside comes here," she protested, but it was so weak that it seemed to be an invitation.

"That's why I came. No one will disturb us here," he explained, and from the sound of footsteps I guessed that he had passed by Makeda, who was still standing at the door in a surprise. "Shut the door, we have to talk."

"What is so urgent that we must talk about it in the middle of the night, and so unusual that we cannot have witnesses?"

I was ready to step into action at any moment. Makeda had to be aware of it, because she stated in a loud and very clear voice, as if addressing these words especially to me, "You know that whenever I want it, my guard will come in here immediately? It can happen anytime."

"But you do not want it, right?" he asked almost innocently.

"You are my friend. You have different rights than everyone else."

"Thank you. Can we talk then?"

It seemed from the sounds that they sat on the chairs by the window bay. Makeda knew that when she was in that place, I could watch her freely from my room through the narrow gap between the door frame and the wall. We once called this crack, laughing, a security window. Each of us hoped then that we would never have to use it. But it was not the case. It came in handy. Standing at the door, I was sure that my lady felt safe, aware that I was so close.

"What are you coming with?"

"We've been together forever," he announced, his voice even more confident than before. "Your father and my parents looked at our relationship with approval from the beginning. We played together when we were children, and when we started to mature, our sympathy turned into a serious feeling. I believe that we are created for each other. You are old enough already for us to think about the upcoming wedding. My parents think that we should not postpone the official announcement. This will strengthen both King Nikal and the power of my family, and it will favorably affect the trade with Egypt, Syria and even with far-off Israel. Let the world know that you will be my wife, that the kingdom of Sheba will grow even stronger, and that thanks to the joining of families, our alliance will be so strong that no one will dare to undertake any trade with the Black Continent without our consent and brokerage."

Makeda listened in silence and sometimes glanced my way, as if to make sure that I was there, and I was paying attention.

"As my wife, you will live on the western side of the Red Sea and you will become the lady of the duchy, of which I am the heir. You are the daughter of Nikal, so it will be a clear sign for all that his wealth, and most importantly - the army, are and will be a support for us. We are already powerful, but with you at our side; we will become the strongest dynasty in those areas. You will give birth to many children. Who knows what other good things the gods are preparing for us?"

I saw her eyes widen with his words. She was astonished. When he finished, she straightened up and spoke royally, just like her father during an audience, "Den, I've had an affection for you from an early age," she began. "You know that I had two brothers, my father's sons with his first wife. I admired them and I have always respected them, but both of them were much older than me and that's probably why I did not have too close contact with them. As you also know, Sirah died in unexplained circumstances," Makeda made the triple sign of the Lady of the Moon, honoring her late brother. "I grew up in the shadow of both of them. When they were already riding horses very well, I was just beginning to learn to walk. At that time, you were always next to me: strong, brave, wise. You showed and explained the world to me. Since I remember, you did everything perfectly. I wanted to be like you. I dreamed to match you. You were a model for me. And I always loved you very much," she said and fell silent.

She lowered her head, as if wondering if she should add something. After a moment, she straightened up again and looked him straight in the eye, "I have always loved you. And I always will."

He smiled radiantly and let the air out of his lungs. He felt relieved.

But she had not yet finished what she had to say.

"I will always love you like a brother!"

He jumped from his chair.

"Like a brother?" he cried out, agitated. "What are you talking about? I want you to be my wife," he knelt in front of her. "Not a sister! Together, we will create a great dynasty. This is our mission! I have known that since I saw you for the first time."

"Impossible," she remarked realistically. "We were small children then."

"I want you to be my woman. You are destined to me," he announced and rose from his knees.

"Destined? By whom?" She crossed her arms on her chest.

"Gods decide about our lives. They want you to be mine."

"Yours? They want that? How do you know that?"

"From the priests. They told my father about it a long time ago already."

"Long time ago?"

"The moment you were born. Our union is written in the stars. You cannot oppose it. You will be my wife, whether you like it or not. That is the gods' will."

"Sit down," she said calmly. "I'll tell you something."

He sighed deeply and exhaled again, pouting his mouth to show that he knew better, anyway.

"All right, tell me," he said conciliatory, still not believing that what he had heard might be true.

"I will tell you my great secret. I will tell you something that almost nobody knows."

I shivered because I knew what words were about to come. In the first reflex, I wanted to open the door and stop it. However, something stopped me. Some force made me pause. I thought that the Lady of the Moon had her part in it, so I submitted to her will.

"Give me your word that you'll never ever tell anyone about it," Makeda demanded.

"You know that I can keep a secret. Do you think I ever revealed our secrets to anybody?"

"Our childhood secrets were just a play. Now, I want to tell you something that absolutely no one can find out. There are situations when silence is a hundred times more valuable than gold. In this case, it is infinitely more valuable."

"You amaze me, Makeda," seeing her seriousness, he calmed down and listened attentively.

"It's a matter of national importance. The fate of the dynasty depends on it. So, you must swear to all your gods!"

"I worship various gods, but as you know, Almakah[16] is the most important for me and my family."

"So, swear to him!"

"What's this secret that makes me swear to Almakah?"

"It's a secret that I cannot reveal to anyone," she lowered her voice. "I promised it to my father. He fears that if someone found out about it, it could even lead to a war."

Den leaned toward her. He was certain that in a moment he would learn something very important. Something that may be significant for the future of his family.

"I will not tell anyone," he promised.

"Swear by Almakah," she whispered.

---

[16] S.H. Selassie, *The Deity of Sheba ALMAKAH*, The Establishment of the Ethiopian Church, in: The Church of Ethiopia, Addis Ababba 1997

The situation got tense; time stood still. It was not only Makeda and Seshep behind the door that were listening to Den, but also the gods, especially Almakah, whose name was summoned.

"I swear to Almakah that I will not tell anyone what I will hear now," he said quietly, but slowly and clearly. "I swear to my god. And if I break this oath, let me get a well-deserved punishment."

Makeda nodded gravely. She knew that if Den would break the oath, he would not escape a punishment.

"I had visions in my childhood," she began, putting her hands on her thighs.

Den let her talk. He was educated and prepared by his parents and teachers to exercise power in the future. He knew well that there were situations that required absolute silence. He decided that this was one of them.

"I had visions. It always happened in a dream. Until some age, I could not distinguish sleep from waking. It seemed to me that everybody was the same. That everyone can look at reality just like me. That when they sleep, they find out what will happen in the future. I thought that I wasn't the only one that can see images and look at events that have not yet occurred. I once told my father about this. At first, he did not understand what I meant, but he always listened to me carefully, asked me about everything. The priestess of the Lady of the Moon told him that I had an extraordinary gift. And that I need to be particularly protected. Together, they decided that no one should know about it. And so, it has been. My father, the Great Priestess and I, know my secret. And now, also you."

Den was moved by what he heard, but he was equally surprised that there was something that his parents' spies did not know, and thus neither did he.

"Well," he said conciliatory and as gently as he could, "I understand that you had visions in your childhood. I regret that you never told me as your friend about it. I'm going to get over it somehow, at least I'll try. But tell me, why do you think you cannot be my wife because of this?"

Makeda straightened up.

"Well, because you're not meant for me!"

"The Almakah priests say I am."

"You are not! I am sure."

"How do you know who your chosen one will be?" he got impatient.

"I saw him."

"Who is it?"

"I saw him in my dreams."

Den fell silent wisely, though one could see how much he did not like what he had heard.

"I saw him. Not just once. I know that when I am a queen, I will go to him. The caravan will be in a tiring journey for a long time, but I will get there successfully, and I will come back with a great treasure. This man is meant for me. I have to wait for him," she fell silent, and after a moment, she added, "You will not sit with me on the throne."

He was silent. He was trying to order his thoughts. It was obvious that he was wondering if he understood what he had heard and how he should react. He was especially intrigued by the last sentence she had uttered. He took her hand.

"Have you had a vision that you will be a queen?"

"Yes. And I cannot talk to anyone about it."

"None of your brothers will sit on the throne?"

"I saw myself on the throne of Sheba."

"You will be the queen?"

"I will. But nobody can talk about it. Even you. You took the oath to Almakah, remember!"

"The man you are going to go to will be your husband?"

"He will give me a great treasure."

"Are you saying that you will not be my wife because of a child's dream?" He stood up abruptly, clenching his fists.

"It was a vision, not an ordinary dream!" she protested angrily and also rose.

They stood opposite each other. He was a head taller than her, well-built, strong. Their upset breaths were so loud that I could clearly hear them where I was standing. I was sure that Makeda was already sorry that she had revealed her secret to him a moment ago. But it was too late to change it.

"You will be mine, whether you want it or not," he called.

He grabbed her night gown and ripped in two parts with great force.

"What are you doing!?" she managed to shout.

She stood before him naked and more surprised than terrified by his behavior. And he, panting, caught her by the head, completely immobilizing her, and clung to her lips with some bizarre fierceness and rage. She threw her fists at him and kicked him, trying to scream at the same time.

"I will not be yours! Or anybody else's! I belong to myself! Only to myself! Get out!" she struggled.

I wanted to rush to help, but we agreed once that in case of danger, if she could not hit the gong, she would call me by raising her hand with her index finger up or by stomping her foot three times, or just by calling me. She did not give any of these signs, even though she knew I was next door. So, I waited, promising myself that if the situation becomes even more dangerous, I would step in.

"Get out!" she yelled again through clenched teeth, finally breaking free from his grip. "Out!" she pointed the door to him.

She was still standing in front of him, in a torn dress, with bitten lips and traces of abrasions on her wrists. She looked at him with disgust from under half-closed eyelids. She was shaking, but she was in control of herself. I was proud of her.

"Get out," she said more calmly now, still pointing at the door.

Then, instead of doing what she told him, he pounced on her like a tiger on a prey, knocking her down to the floor. Everything happened so fast!

"Hemet!" I heard her call. "Seshep!"

I was with her immediately. I caught him and kicked with all my strength. He did not expect the attack. He was surprised. He rolled over and curled in pain. I knew that I could not give him even the shortest moment for gathering strength. Everything happened very quickly. I pressed him with my knee and put my knife to his throat. He lay motionless. I watched his hands. I could not let him attack again, because a misfortune could happen, and I did not want that. The heir of Nikal's greatest ally could not die or even be wounded at the palace in Mariba, no matter what the reason would be.

When I decided that Den had cooled down, I let him get up.

"Try telling anyone about what happened here, and I'll kill you, black witch," he hissed through his teeth.

"Try telling anyone about what Makeda told you, and I will personally tear your heart out," I grinned, looking him in the eye.

At the same time, I cut the skin on the outside of my wrist and slowly licked the blood that flowed from there. He watched what I was doing.

"I swear to the Lady of the Moon and my own blood that I will tear your heart out!" I growled. "And, believe me, I never break my oaths."

***

"That was the whole incident, mukarrib," hemet Seshep ended the account of the night events in Makeda's chamber.

"In the light of the fact that Prince Seth with his wife and son hurriedly left the palace before the sunrise, I suppose we should prepare for the imminent trouble," Nikal sighed.

"They left?"

"The prince left an apology and the news that urgent matters were calling him home."

"Hmm... King, how are you going to react to what happened to Makeda?"

"We will see what Seth is plotting, but it seems to me, as far as I know as his aspirations, that we will soon have a war."

"A war? Do things look so bad?"

"Seth has long been looking for an excuse for the princes to leave me, because he dreams about the crown. Information on what he was trying to do to gather supporters, how he instigated people and tried to bribe them, have been reaching me for years. He is too crafty to go against me directly, in any case, he has not been able to do so yet, but I suppose that the situation will now be favorable for him."

Drops of sweat appeared on Nikal's forehead. It happened when he was not sure how to act, which was seldom.

"From your story, it appears that Den learned that he has no chance for Makeda's hand. I suppose he immediately shared this information with his father. I can imagine his rage, because it looks like even their best spies, who have their men in the palace, did not know about Makeda's visions.

"Only we knew about this, you, lord, and me..." Seshep made sure that the king did not reveal this secret to anyone else.

"And Makeda," he laughed bitterly. "At least it was so until yesterday. From today, our secret is common knowledge."

"We need to think about how to behave in this situation."

"Their leaving was not an escape from my anger. Seth wants to reach the princes as soon as possible."

"Right," Seshep knew what the king meant.

"He will tell them that they have been fooled by me, because my daughter will not marry Den, nor any of their sons! He will give them the information about Makeda's visions, and he will say that she has had them since childhood; so, I have known for a long-time what path the gods have designed for her. It is unfortunately likely that they will feel offended by my lack of trust in them and will stand by him."

"What are you going to do, king?"

"That's the last straw," he patted his thigh. "I will immediately summon the princes' council and it will become clear who is on Seth's side and who is on mine. And depending on the situation, we will either defend ourselves or I will be forced to make an armed incursion into the rebellious principalities."

"Is it so bad?"

"Unfortunately. I wonder now, shouldn't I treat his departure as an escape? It is true that, as you say, Makeda is fortunately all right, but maybe I should immediately go against Seth, without waiting for the opinion of the princes? He has been long undermining my authority, and what his son did certainly requires vengeance."

"Your every decision will be right, mukarrib," Seshep knew that soon, without anyone's advice, the king would as usual, decide on his own what to do next.

"Thank you, you helped me a lot," he laughed a little ironically, but cheerfully.

"I wouldn't dare advise someone so experienced. I know only one thing," she added, "it is not a time for debates. You have the chance to attack Seth and win, even by surprise. This situation will not repeat itself anytime soon."

To her surprise, he spread his hands helplessly.

"I think I'm getting old, but I feel like I need advice. I don't know what decision I should make " he sighed and shook his head in disbelief. "Hemet Seshep, you have a strange influence on me, you make me say what I think. And I shouldn't do that.

"Maybe Den was right saying I was a witch," she laughed.

"No matter what Seth's son called you, you are a wise woman," he looked at her with admiration, then waved his hand, surprised that he allows himself such unusual behavior, and ordered in his everyday tone, "Go to Hendake as soon as possible and tell him to come here with the advisers. I want you to be at this meeting too."

***

The persons that appeared in Nikal's chamber were: the eunuch Hendake - the king's trusted man and the manager of his palace, General Tesfa - the commander of the army, Sethon - the highest priest of Illumkuh, High Priestess of the Lady of the Moon, and Seshep. At the king's request, the twenty-two-year-old heir to the throne - Prince Tomaj, and Princess Makeda were also to attend.

The king's chamber was one of the larger rooms in the palace. The only one bigger than it was the throne room, in which Nikal received guests, gave parties, and organized large councils with princes subordinate to him, who in such cases were invited early enough for each of them to arrive on time. They ruled the principalities located on both sides of the Red Sea, and the furthest of them required a travel sometimes even ten or fifteen days long.

The palace was vast and high. The great-great grandfather of the king built it from evenly hewn stone blocks and wood, mainly acacia, because the worms avoided it. Time did not damage the thick walls. Every arriving prince found hospitality in the palace. Some advisers and trusted people of the king also lived there. Some of them had their own houses in Mariba but located not far from the palace. This way, they could appear for the ruler's call at any time; so, it was also this time.

"Things require urgent decisions, which is why I called you," the king began as they took their places.

He told of what had happened at night, not hiding his upset, ending with information about Seth's sudden departure.

There was silence after his words.

"Anyone's going to say something?" He looked at them in surprise. They were moved by what they heard.

"King, Princess Makeda has visions?" Priest Sethon dared to begin.

"I had them until the time of my first monthly blood," unasked, Makeda shifted in her chair. "The king thought there was no need to tell anyone about the little girl's dreams," she added, because she felt she should justify her father in their eyes.

She knew that they could not only be offended for not being informed about something so unusual, but that they might regard it as a lack of trust on the part of the king.

"I thought it was better not to burden anyone with this information. Even you."

The king was not in the habit of explaining himself to anyone, but in the new situation he decided that he should clarify the matter thoroughly. Hard times were coming, and he knew he would need their support.

"The king did the right thing by not informing us of the princess' visions," the High Priestess supported him. "It's not about lack of trust, but about the fact that, as each of us knows, the less people know a secret, the greater the chance that it will not see the light of day."

The king did not know that hemet informed the High Priestess about everything that concerned the princess, and therefore also about her visions. Makeda and the priestess were bound by a vow of secrecy and were certain that what they were saying remained only between them.

Since the time it turned out that she had visions, Makeda was under the care of the Lady of the Moon, so the High Priestess knew everything that concerned her and had an impact on the girl's upbringing and development, because Seshep not only informed her about everything, but also consulted most decisions with her.

"I'm sorry, but it was only because of my recklessness that things took such a turn," Makeda admitted remorsefully. "I really thought I could trust Den; he has always been my closest friend."

"Princess," General Tesfa, whose daughter was of a similar age as Makeda, decided it was time to speak, "sooner or later there would be a conflict. Prince Seth has sought it for a long time. Forgive me, but you are young, and you don't understand a lot of matters, especially those military and political. They are quite complicated."

"What do I not understand?" Makeda was outraged by the general's good-naturedness.

"That Seth would rather be a king than a prince? That he incites others to go against my father? Or maybe I do not understand that Den wanted to use me, and I was to be only his tool on the way to power? I understand it, as well as the fact that we were being spied and overheard. Furthermore, I even understand that my brother's death, a long time ago, was not accidental. Isn't it enough? Just because I'm only fifteen years old and I'm a girl doesn't mean I don't think!"

"Princess, I did not mean to offend you," moved by her outbreak, the general jumped up from his chair.

"Sit down, Tesfa," the king calmed him down. "Makeda has a royal temperament."

His words didn't sound like an excuse, but they were the praise of his daughter and that's how they were received by those present. At this point, Makeda realized that she had used the wrong tone to present her arguments and added more calmly, "There's a lot of my fault in what happened, I'm sorry. I know I should still learn a lot. Thank you all for your understanding."

Then Seshep spoke, "Makeda is not guilty of anything, the general is right. Prince Seth was just waiting for the right excuse. And here it came. Let's be wise and anticipate his moves."

"Hemet is right," said Prince Tomaj. Until now, he had only listened, but it was obvious that he could hardly stay sat in place, and would prefer to go to fight immediately, instead of doing politics.

"I think we should rush after Seth and strike him before he can talk to the princes. I promise that as Makeda's brother, for the insult she suffered, I will personally get Den!"

"I threatened him that if he would reveal the secret of the princess, I would snatch his heart out with my own hands," said Seshep calmly and seemingly to herself. "Thus, prince, forgive me, but I'm first in line!"

Tomaj grabbed the handle of the knife he wore under his belt.

"I'm ready to fight!" he called, rising from his chair.

"Let's go, there is nothing to wait for," the general picked up and stood up as well. "The troops, as always, are ready. We can leave even today."

"Let's also hear the voice of reason," the king stopped them. "Priestess?"

The general and the prince sat down again and, like everyone else, turned their heads toward her. She nodded to the king in thanks. She was a woman whose beauty went hand in hand with wisdom, and who knew perfectly well what impression she made on people, including the king. With her right hand, she held a tall cane crowned with a silver scepter symbolizing the Lady of the Moon. She always had it with her in official situations, as if drawing power from it. She clenched her fingers lightly, uniting with the goddess in her thoughts.

"We're talking about a possible war," she began calmly. "But do we really want it? Have we considered its effects? Our troops will cross the sea, attack Seth, many will die. Let us remember that our subjects will also fight on the other side. Do we want it?

Maybe it would be better to find out first if Seth has a chance to realize his evil intentions? Who will stand by him, who will support him, what is his strength? After all, all we are talking about is just presumptions."

"Priestess, with the utmost respect for your wisdom, knowledge of the world and experience," said Hendake, who had been silent until now. "Our scouts have been reporting Seth's activities for years. We can be almost sure that he will do everything to lead to war. The first thing he did when Den passed the words of Princess Makeda to him, was sending messengers to the princes to give them the message. Of course, thanks to our efforts, most of them did not reach anywhere, but to my regret, some of them succeeded. We are under a threat of if not war, then surely a rebellion. Perhaps the termination of the obedience or an attempt to separate from Sheba by the principalities on the west side of the sea."

The face of the Great Priestess most often did not reveal any emotions. But this time sadness appeared on it.

"The Lady of the Moon warns us that this war can bring us heavy losses," she said, clenching her fingers on the silver cane.

"Do you know anything more?" worried Nikal, who always took her opinion into account.

"No," she answered truthfully. "I only know that many will die, and tears will flow."

The king stood up.

"I listened to your voices. Thank you. I know what you think. Seth has long been a pain in Sheba's body. It's time to get rid of it. We've only trouble with him."

The gathered nodded their heads.

"King, please think again." The High Priestess wasn't going to give in so easily. "We are stronger, we have definitely bigger and better army, gods are on our side. However, let's win in a different way. This war will bring us losses. We may lose land overseas, but worst of all, there will be blood."

"We can finally gain peace and free the country from Seth's plotting," the general was ready to fight. "This trip can give us peace for very long years."

"Priestess, there is loss in every war, that's the way the world is," it was obvious that the king had already made his decision. "In the worst case, we will lose the western part of the Sheba, but as you say, we are better than them in every respect, so the risk is small. By getting rid of Seth and his followers, we'll make Sheba enter a new stage in history."

"May it happen," the priestess looked up towards the sky, and furrows appeared on her forehead without her will.

"The general is right," concluded the king, patting his thigh. "Let's not discuss it any longer. Tesfa, order the march of troops and make sure that the soldiers reach the coast as soon as possible and that the ships are fully ready to sail. We're going to war! In my absence, I hand over the rule over Sheba to Sethon," the king looked at the priest. "Hendake will be your right hand."

"When are we leaving?" Makeda was almost as excited as the men.

"Princess, you stay," Nikal cooled her excitement in a decided tone. "You will be looked after by the Great Priestess and hemet Seshep."

"No way. I have to be there!" She jumped to her feet. "Is Tomaj coming with you?"

"Of course," her brother had no doubt. "I am the heir to the throne and a man."

"I have to be there," Makeda repeated, knowing that her father accepted only strong arguments in a firm but calm tone. "I want to be there when Den is deservedly punished."

The king hesitated, but only for a moment.

"Fine," he decided. "But you will be accompanied not only by Seshep, but also by the High Priestess. Priestess, would you like to do us the honor?"

"When do we leave?" she replied when asked.

Kingdom of Sheba

Fourteen days later

After the council, at which he decided to go to war with Seth, King Nikal sent messengers to his subordinate principalities, asking how many soldiers each of them could send.

Almost everyone brought back promises to send troops at every king's request. Only the ruler of Punt did not answer unequivocally. He reported that his troops were fighting wars in the south, so he could not support the king. However, he sent Nikal generous gifts in order not to provoke his anger.

Punt was more loosely connected with Sheba than other principalities, and it needed less royal protection. That was because between Punt and Egypt, before which all the principalities in the Nile Valley trembled, lay the land of Aksum and Nubia, which constituted a kind of security buffer for that principality. Although the powerful ally in the person of the king of Sheba was needed by the prince of Punt, not feeling any direct threat from Egypt or apparently from prince Seth, the same prince wanted to convince the king of his loyalty by gifts alone.

Nikal counted his strength. He had an army of 20,000, and additionally, the princes on the west side promised to send a total of several thousand people. And Seth, together with the mercenaries, could have a maximum of fifteen thousand soldiers. So, he felt that if the princes would not betray him, and the prince of Punt would not stand on either side, the advantage was definitely on his side. He had also a better equipment. He knew that his bows with new strings were able to pierce the leather shields of Kush's warriors, and that his swords and axes made of iron would not break in battle like the bronze swords of their enemy's warriors.

"We will win this war," the king thought. *"Let's start, in the name of the gods!"*

There was a tense but joyful atmosphere in the palace. Not even a week had passed since the king's decision to war was announced, and the army was ready to leave.

On the day indicated by priest Sethon, at the king's order, twenty thousand warriors, led by General Tesfa, set out for the bay. The army had three hundred horses and a similar number of camels. It was planned that it would take ten days to reach the coast.

The king and the retinue, Tomaj and Makeda with the High Priestess and Seshep, were going to leave five days later, to reach the bay at the same time as the soldiers.

Ships floated on the water. A forest of individual masts with rolled up sails could be seen from afar. Skilled sailors were bustling on the decks of the wide, bulky hulls, and there was a swarm of warriors prepared for embarkation on the land. With calm sea, light wind and unfurled sails, they should reach the small harbor of Adulis on the other side of the Red Sea, where they were heading, within two days.

The flotilla consisted of a hundred transport ships that were used commercially in Sheba every day, and four warships. The one on which Nikal was supposed to sail was not only the newest, but also the most impressive. Like the others, it was a single-masted sailing ship with one row of oars, but the sails were gold in color, the bow cabins were lined with carpets, and the furniture was worthy of a king.

At the given sign, the ships left the shore, heading west. The initial turmoil and noise caused by the sailing out and crackling of the oars subsided. One by one the ships were unfurling sails and the sea began to look like a meadow with white flowers. Light gusts of wind filled the sails.

Makeda, standing on the deck, looked around. She was proud of the army, the ships and her father. She realized how much she loved Sheba, which she thought was the greatest country in the world.

The trip was indeed short. Favorable winds blowing from east to west allowed the ships to sail quickly, almost without using oars.

Adulis was a large fishing village, which thanks to its safe location in the bay, was readily used for unloading and loading goods.

The army quickly left the ships. Some of the soldiers not used to sea travel did not feel well and were happy to feel the ground under their feet. Horses and camels going down the makeshift gangways also gave the impression that they were happy to do so.

It was evening, the sun was setting. Departure to Aksum was scheduled for the next morning.

The soldiers lit fires on the beach and went to sleep. Even the officers did not pitch tents but lied down near the fire. Nights around this area were cold at this time of year. The warm sun was shining during the day, and already in the evening, the exhaled air turned into visible steam. That night, soldiers were not only kept warm by the bonfires, but also by the emotions before the fight awaiting them.

For many hours, the king consulted with General Tesfa, Ashenafi and four senior officers. Prince Tomaj also sat at the table. Makeda knew her father would not agree for her to be with them during the discussion of the final preparations and strategies of the attack, fearing that she could talk uninvited. So, she crouched in a corner of the tent, trying not to let anybody notice her. Everyone saw her, but since the king pretended that he did not know anything about the presence of his daughter at the meeting place, others did the same. Makeda listened, watched, and learned.

The meeting lasted several hours. Thanks to the intelligence agents, it was known that Prince Seth had set up his army in a wide ravine leading through the last mountain range before the capital. His army had twelve thousand soldiers, no horses or camels. The neighboring princes, to whom Nikal had sent messengers beforehand, did not respect Seth. They feared him, so with the choice of either Seth's support or loyalty to much stronger Nikal, they chose the ruler of Sheba.

***

Nikal's army moved from Adulis in a long column. At the head rode a group of scouts on a hundred horses and a hundred camels. A column made of infantrymen, archers, and slingers followed them. The long procession was closed by riders on horses and camels, armed with spears and swords.

Nikal's soldiers had swords, spear points and arrows made of iron. They carried leather shields made of oryx skins. The sons of richer families had iron shields, much heavier and more resistant to blows. Few, mainly officers, had iron flap armor on their tunics, but most of the soldiers made do with leather tunics and vests.

The column was approaching Aksum in a fast march. The king, who was riding in the middle of it in the company of General Tesfa, commander Ashenafi, Tomaj, and Makeda, knew about Seth's army waiting in the gorge. The gorge was a convenient place for defenders, and difficult for attackers. However, he had no choice: Aksum was surrounded by high mountains, and the few roads leading to it led through the gorges.

On the third day of the march, in the afternoon, the long serpent of king's army entered the gorge. The front guard noticed the soldiers defending the entrance from afar. The column stopped.

It was clear to everyone that troops would meet soon.

"What's your advice on the best way to attack?" Nikal began the evening council. "We know that there are twelve thousand of them and that they are poorly armed. There are twice as many of us, but in a gorge, we cannot attack with full power. What is the easiest way to defeat them? How to open the way to Aksum?"

"King, I think archers and slingers must climb the surrounding mountains at night so that they can reach the bottom of the ravine and shoot at the enemy," General Tesfa knew where they would fight and had repeatedly discussed the attack with the officers. "Infantry, with spears, axes and swords, will go to the battle straight ahead. Let the horses and camels stay behind, in this gorge we will not be able to use their strength. The officers and I will go in the front row, you king, with Prince Tomaj and Princess Makeda, watch from a proper distance, as befits a king. If we need help, we'll send a messenger."

The king considered all the pros and cons in his mind.

"The plan is good. That's what we will do. We will start the battle early in the morning. Now let the soldiers rest, give them tella, tej[17] and a lot of meat, let them eat well before the battle."

"King," Tomaj waited until only Nikal, Tesfa and Ashenafi remained in the tent, "let me accompany the general. I am already twenty-two years old and I want to fight.

All eyes turned to the king. His older son was killed, Tomaj was the only successor. Should he agree for Tomaj to go fight? Especially that the visions of Makeda and Seshep gave much food for thought. He was afraid for his life, but on the other hand, he was proud that this brave, courageous boy was his son. Saying "no" in front of the generals listening to their dialogue would weaken him in their eyes. After all, young men who just turned sixteen, fought as part of the army. Tomorrow they could die. Does he, therefore, have the right to prohibit the prince from fighting together with them?

---

[17] Tella - beer with low-percentage of alcohol, tej - honey wine (note by author).

"General, I entrust to you the heir to the throne, Prince Tomaj," the king decided finally. "Let him fight by your side tomorrow."

Tomaj hit his chest with his fist, as soldiers did, and it was obvious that he would jump with joy if he could.

No one noticed how sad Makeda became, sitting quietly in the corner.

The morning greeted everyone with the sun. The armies faced each other. Seth was in a better position because the narrowing ravine prevented Sheba's forces from spreading. Both sides knew this well.

Seth's army, armed with bronze swords and axes, spears, bows, and slingshots, was dressed in dark tunics made of thick fabric, and the soldiers' chests and backs were protected by large pieces of hard, untreated skin of antelopes and zebras. Shields were also made of these skins. It was not an army that could win in open battle, but it could defend access to the road in the gorge for a long time. The soldiers were commanded personally by Seth, with his son Den at his side.

At the behest of General Tesfa, the walkers set off in a wide line. Spearmen in front, followed by archers and slingers, then soldiers armed with swords and axes. It soon turned out that the general's plan was not fully successful: the archers and slingers, who had climbed the mountainsides at night and hid themselves, were too far away to successfully attack the enemy with arrows and stones. Their missiles did not reach the defenders of the gorge outlet.

The general then attacked directly. Better and more modern weapons gave the Nikal's army an advantage. This time the arrows of the archers easily pierced the leather shields and caftans of the Aksum soldiers, and the strokes of the iron swords broke the bronze swords. Soldiers were killed. They were quickly replaced by others from further ranks.

At first, General Tesfa only watched the fight and gave orders, but seeing strong resistance, he threw himself into the fight, hacking his opponents with his sword. Tomaj followed his example. He killed with a single cut a spearman, intending to hit the general, and knocked over another one. Defense was weakening, but soldiers on both sides were still dying, screaming or silently.

At one point, the victory tilted significantly to the side of Sheba, and the ranks of Seth's soldiers dwindled. However, the gorge of the ravine was still not conquered and the road to the capital was closed.

Finally, Prince Seth and his son appeared. It was obvious that they wanted to strengthen the fighting spirit among their own.

Seeing Den, Prince Tomaj rushed towards him. There were still several ranks of soldiers separating them, but Tomaj did not care. Dressed in a silver armor made of iron scales, with a sword in his hand, and energized up by the fight and his victories so far, he wanted to catch the one who was planning to dishonor his sister and take away the crown from his family. Cutting with the sword in all directions, he approached Den. Recognizing him, Den shouted at the soldiers standing between them, and when they parted, he accepted the fight.

The swords of both warriors crossed. Despite the difference in years, Den was eighteen and Tomaj twenty-two, the strength was similar. The only thing differing among them was rage and revenge. Tomaj, trained by fencing masters, found a worthy opponent. Den fought off attacks and pushed himself. They did not care about the ongoing battle around them, they were focused only on themselves and their swords. Besides, the soldiers, knowing who the fighters were, did not intend to disturb them. The princes' struggles continued. Their strengths were slowly leaving them. Feeling this, Tomaj attacked with fury and hit with all his strength. Den's sword swung back, leaving his whole body unprotected. Tomaj's second cut reached the target, his sword cut to the bone in Den's shoulder and deeply wounded his side in between the halves of his armor. Den fell on his back. For Tomaj it was a moment of triumph. Here, his enemy lay defeated at his feet. With him wounded and in captivity, it will be easy to force his father to surrender. He was proud of himself.

He did not manage to turn around and find with his eyes the general, before whom he wanted to boast about his victory, when an arrow whistled and hit his neck. The arrowhead pierced the larynx. Darkness enveloped him.

The general, fighting a few dozen meters away, saw Tomaj's glory. He was already happy, knowing that this could end the fight and cause Seth's surrender. Then, he was scared by the sight of the arrow in the prince's larynx. He looked in the direction it came from. He saw a man with a scar, who watched out of the bushes behind a small rock to make sure his shot was fatal.

Disregarding the enemies, the general rushed towards the wounded prince. Despair gave him strength. He moved forward, ignoring the retreating Aksum soldiers who carried with them Den, not showing any sign of life.

Only dying Tomaj remained on the battlefield. When the general reached him and knelt down beside him, he smiled proudly.

"I killed Den. It's the end of the war," he whispered and gave out his last breath.

Tesfa stopped the battle. They were victorious, more than four thousand Aksum soldiers were killed, while they lost a thousand of their own at most, but he felt that he lost. For the one who was the future of Sheba, whom the king entrusted to his protection, was not alive, and nothing could change that anymore.

The king, watching the incident from above, clutched his heart. His face tightened. One of his sons had previously been killed in a treacherous act, now he was losing another one. He stared at the distant figure of Tesfa. When the general rose from his knees, the king was certain of what had happened. His world collapsed.

Although the war was won, he ordered a retreat.

The soldiers who tasted a victory and hoped that their next stop would be in Aksum, accepted the king's order with bitterness but also with understanding. The more so because a news that the son of Seth probably survived the blow inflicted on him by Prince Tomaj traveled around the army with the speed of a lightning. The column came back the way it came. However, while it was a joyous march before, the return looked like a funeral procession. The despair of the king who did not speak to anyone was understandable to everybody. Makeda, whose sadness and sorrow was similarly immense, did not even try to comfort her father, understanding that nothing would alleviate his suffering.

She was riding right after her father. Seshep was on her left side, and the High Priestess on the right. All three rode horses.

"If Den is really alive, I'll get him!" Seshep drawled through her teeth. "I should have killed him a long time ago."

"I'll return here someday and take back Aksum," Makeda said firmly, without looking back.

The High Priestess was sure that this would happen. But she didn't say a word.

Kingdom of Israel

At the same time

"Tamrin, we have received information from the Sheba kingdom today."

"Is that what you wanted to tell me, prophet?"

"Prince Seth, you probably know who I am talking about, came against Nikal. The only heir to the throne was killed in the war and the king is seriously ill and it is not certain whether he will survive."

Tamrin was so impressed by the words just spoken that he covered his mouth with his hand so as not to shout.

"Do you have news of Princess Makeda?"

"She's safe."

"Do you know anything else, prophet?"

"The deadly arrow that struck the successor was shot by an assassin hired by Seth."

Tamrin shook his head in disbelief.

"I should go back as soon as possible," he said. "When did this happen?"

"Three days ago."

"Three days?! And you know it already, so soon? How is this possible?"

"God is with us. And he works miracles," the prophet adjusted the edge of his robe. "You once said that for you the information is more valuable than gold. So, it is for me, too."

Preparations for the road did not last long. Before leaving Jerusalem, Tamrin went to see Solomon.

The king received him in the chamber in which he used to work. Scrolls filled mainly with architectural plans and calculations rested on long tables. Evenly arranged long wooden rulers, compasses, calipers, inks, scribers and brushes, used in his work, lied next to them.

"Look, Tamrin, here is my pride," the king pointed to one of the largest drawings. "This is what our temple will look like. Come here," seeing the delight of the guest, he went to the corner of the room, where a model of the temple was placed on the second table. "Look! What do you think?"

"King, this is more beautiful than anything I had the joy of seeing in my life," Tamrin was so delighted with what he saw that for a moment he forgot about the matters because of which he had to return to Sheba earlier than he intended.

Solomon folded his arms over his proudly outstretched chest.

"I think so too. We do everything according to God's instructions. Look, feed your eyes. Next time you come here, a lot of what you see will take real shape. Also, thanks to the materials you send me."

Tamrin took in the view. The model was made with the greatest care. Every detail was perfect: from gold and copper offering bowls, through walls, columns, altars to stairs, walls, and the roof.

"It's breathtaking, king," he assured Solomon.

"Remember this view and tell Nikal about it."

"I will, sir."

"And may God lead you straight to Sheba. May he bring peace to your country and solve its problems, because I have heard that things have not been going well there lately."

"May it be so, king."

"Amen."

Kingdom of Sheba

Fifteen days later

"The worst is over." The High Priestess straightened up from over the king's bed.

She spent by Nikal all days and nights that came after the moment when the king boarded the ship, stopped by the body of his dead son, then clutched his chest, staggered and fell.

"Protect the king!" a command sounded.

Almost immediately, Nikal, lying on the ship's boards, was surrounded by soldiers.

"King in danger!" one could hear on the ship.

Who knows what would happen if it wasn't for the presence of the Priestess who knew what to do? If it wasn't for her, the king would inevitably join his dead son. As soon as she understood what had happened, she knelt down next to him and began to pass her breath to him and hit his chest.

"Stay here, don't leave," she kept yelling.

Finally, summoned by her magic voice and enchanted by her breath, he opened his eyes.

"Goddess, Lady of the Moon, thank you!" whispered the Priestess, first raising her arms to the sky, and then bowing so low that her forehead touched the deck.

Terrified Makeda, standing motionless right next to them all the time, knelt beside her father and cried. The fear for his life left. It cracked like ice, which froze her heart the moment her father slumped aboard. The soldiers, seeing that the High Priestess had just performed one of the miracles, looked at her with admiration mixed with fear, but at the same time they breathed a sigh of relief, like Makeda, seeing that their king was alive. The priestess knew that in order to save the king, she needed the support of the Lady of the Moon, but also the knowledge that the priestesses before her had accumulated for centuries. She also used magical resources known to her for the next few days when they sailed, and later, when the weakened king was laid on special stretchers placed on a cart pulled by mules. During the journey, she gave him herb infusion to increase blood circulation. When sweat poured over him, she covered him with cooling leaves and stones, and when he was freezing from exhaustion, she warmed him with her own body.

Finally, they arrived at the palace in Mariba.

Everyone felt safer here, but just as during the journey, Makeda, Seshep, and the High Priestess did not leave the king. So, all three were present when he opened his eyes on the second day after arriving at the palace.

"Have   the   gods   left   Sheba?"   he   asked.

CHAPTER III

WEIGHT OF THE CROWN
MAKEDA IS 17 YEARS OLD

Kingdom of Sheba, Mariba

Makeda was standing by the bay window in her chamber, staring at the green, flourishing city in front of her. It belonged to her. Just like the whole country.

She had just become the queen, the Great Kandake of Sheba. Her father passed away after long months of illness. From the time when his heart almost broke with despair after Tomaj's death, he had not recovered. He reigned, but he was getting weaker day by day, and when one day he lost consciousness during a long ceremony in honor of Illumkuh, he never got up from his bed again. It was then that he finally decided to pass the crown to her. After the death of his two sons, she was the only heir.

Now she was looking into the future, which carried many challenges. She had the landscape, so close to her heart, before her eyes. The whole area was visible from the palace built on the hill, from her chamber on the top floor.

In Mariba, the palace, temples, houses of the mighty, and all other major buildings were built centuries ago from stones and baked clay. The city looked as if it emerged from the earth and it was an integral part of the landscape. The buildings were surrounded on all sides by lush greenery. Avenues of trees stretched from the palace to the eight monolithic pillars of the Illumkuh temple. It was there that the great ceremonies were most often held, where the god who supervised the royal family and the whole country was worshiped.

"Illumkuh, I'm left on my own," she complained quietly. "There is no one else left in the family who can support me. Is that what you wanted? What are your plans for our family? Why did you let all the men leave?"

But Illumkuh, as it usually is with the gods, was silent. Makeda moved her eyes to the temple of her patron, Lady of the Moon.

"Maybe she would answer my questions," she thought.

But the Lady of the Moon remained unmoved. Yet she was so close, almost at her fingertips. Her temple, whose base resembled an egg, was perfectly visible from the window of the chamber. A tall, ornate portal led to it, which had delighted Makeda since she had seen it for the first time a long time ago. The temple was surrounded by walls that were nearly twenty cubits high. Its main part, in which the ceremonies in honor of the Lady of the Moon were held, was not roofed. Lush vegetation covered the area around it. Colorful, fragrant flowers and herbs grew between palms, sycamore, and tamarind trees. The priestesses tended to the temple gardens. It was Makeda's favorite place beside the palace.

When she looked left, she saw another temple, the oldest one in the city. Its five high pillars called residents to worship not only gods, but also ancestors. Once a year, great ceremonies were held there in honor of those who had passed away.

On the right the gardens stretched, fed with water flowing through channels from a great dam, built at the same time when the greatest pyramids were built in Egypt. The most magnificent plants the earth knew grew there. Among them, were trees giving the resin from which valuable incense was obtained, fragrant myrrh trees - the source of myrrh, and also the perfect substance for relieving pain, healing wounds, strengthening wine and embalming corpses. Myrrh and incense were Sheba's most valuable trading goods. They were sold not only to Egypt, Babylon or other countries that were within the reach of ordinary caravans, but even to distant India.

"If it wasn't for the wisdom of my ancestors, we would live in a desert," Makeda thought. *"God, who inspired them to build a dam, was wise and foreseeable. If it wasn't for it, there would be no water, and we would be a poor desert country that no one would care about."*

The dam collected water from the river that was flowing abundantly only in the rainy season. For the rest of the year, the river either dried up completely or turned into a weak stream. The construction, for centuries the pride of Sheba, was more than one thousand three hundred cubits long[18]. It was built centuries ago in the form of an earth embankment reinforced with stones and mortar. Sluices were erected at its ends, through which water fed the city, gardens, and two huge oases. Each of the oases was so huge that yields from just one were enough to feed not only the city and the royal army, but also the inhabitants of the less water-rich areas of the kingdom. The yield of them was the most valuable commercial commodity of Sheba, next to myrrh and incense.

"No one in the whole world has such a dam and such gardens," Makeda admired the reason, skill and foresight of her ancestors. "The kings who ruled here before me were really wise. They knew how to turn the land of desert and poverty into the most beautiful and prosperous garden. What can I do to match

---

[18] Ancient Egyptian and Sumerian cubit is about 52 cm; today's English ell measures 114.3 cm; the dam at Mariba was about 680 meters long; The northern oasis in Mariba occupied 4300 ha, and the southern oasis 5300 ha (author's note). [*ell* and *cubit* are the same word in Polish]

them? So as not to just maintain what I inherited, but to make my successors proud of what I did?"

She was thinking about the future. She realized three things. First of all, that she was left completely alone, because no one from her family was alive. Secondly, she doesn't need a husband because she wants to be an independent queen. Thirdly, that Sheba is not only the lands on the east side of the sea, but also the fertile and beautiful territories on its west side. When Nikal died, Aksum remained in Seth's hands. Makeda ruled only over the eastern part of the country. Since that war, the state had fallen asleep. Mourning for the king and his son made everything stand still.

Now, with the spring and the awakening life, she felt it was time to do something about it.

"I had visions in my childhood," she sighed. "Thanks to them I knew I would be a queen. In my dreams, I also saw that the one who is destined for me, is waiting in a distant land, and here I am the queen. I rule Sheba, I sit alone on the throne of a wonderful state. It happened as it was meant to be. So, probably one day, there will be time to meet the one whom the gods intended for me. However, for now, I need to sort out the issue of Aksum. Time to end this split of the country. The people, gods, and our ancestors deserve it! Oh, if only I could get such visions as in my childhood, maybe I would know what I should do?"

Kingdom of Israel

At the same time

The temple Solomon was building was sixty cubits long, twenty cubits wide and thirty cubits high. The length of the vestibule was twenty cubits, the same as the front wall of the temple to which it adjoined, and it was ten cubits wide. A multi-story building was erected along the walls, as well as around the

Holy Place and the Saint of Saints. Side rooms around the entire temple were also built[19].

When construction began, the walls were built of blocks prepared in quarries. That is why there was no noise of hammering, axes, or other iron tool heard in the city.

When the walls were completed, the whole structure was covered with a ceiling made of cedar beams and boards. Similar boards were used for lining the internal walls from the ground to the ceiling beams. There were flowers and garlands carved on them. The floor was covered with cypress boards.

The interior was lined with pure gold. Although the construction was still underway, the whole building shone, delighting everyone who had the privilege of entering this place. Solomon wanted as few people as possible to see the inside before finishing the work, but still the news of the wealth that was accumulated there, reached the most distant corners of the world with the flight of the northern wind. Yet the temple contractors still had a lot of work to do. The outer part was still in the early stages of construction.

Solomon knew that he would have years of effort ahead of him and that he would have to bear great costs before completing his extraordinary work. He was building a temple that was supposed to show the greatness of the God of Israel, so he should not hurry. He knew that everything that was good and that would last for centuries required time and effort.

Kingdom of Sheba

One day later

---

[19] All information about the Temple of Solomon comes from the Old Testament; this part is from: First King's Book. Construction of the temple 6.1-37.

Waiting for the council, which was called by the queen, Tamrin shared stories of Solomon and Israel. He stood in the council hall with the commander of the royal guard Ashenafi, Hendake, managing the palace, and general Tesfa. He told them how wise Solomon's judgments were and he cited the incident of women claiming rights to the same child as an example.

"Let him finish," Makeda said to Seshep accompanying her, stopping her with a gesture at the chamber door. "Let's listen."

They stood in such a place that they were not seen by anybody.

When Tamrin finished, the men nodded approvingly.

"Well, well..." Tesfa was impressed by Solomon's decision.

"Moreover, I will tell you that he is not only appreciated but also liked," assured the merchant. "There are many anecdotes about him."

The queen ordered Seshep to remain still.

"At a tavern in Jerusalem, I heard the story: Two women came to the king, dragging a young man with them. 'He agreed to marry my daughter,' said one. 'No! He promised to marry mine,' shouted the other one. They started arguing until Solomon commanded silence. 'Bring me the greatest sword,' he ordered the guard. 'We will cut the young man in half. Each of you will get an equal share!' 'Sounds good,' said the first woman. 'Lord, don't shed innocent blood,' the other one sobbed. 'This woman's daughter can marry him, just let him live.' The king didn't hesitate. 'The young man is to marry the daughter of the first woman,' he announced. 'But she wanted to cut him in two!' people exclaimed. 'Well, now you can see already that this is the man's true mother-in-law!' said the wise King Solomon."

The men laughed out loud, perfectly understanding the joke and the reference to the earlier story of a child and two mothers.

"Do you want to say, Tamrin, that the Israeli mother-in-laws are the same as ours?" the anecdote amused Tesfa the most.

"They are the same all over the world," confirmed the merchant. "That's why, among other things, I don't want to have a wife."

"I don't have anyone for the same reason, too," Hendake, who everyone knew was a eunuch, remarked humorously.

"Sure," Ashenafi concluded, and abruptly straightened, seeing the queen entering the hall.

With her came the Great Priestess, priest Sethon and hemet Seshep.

"I hear you are in good spirits," said the glad queen, letting them sit down.

"Let the gods lead you!" as the highest rank among those present, General Tesfa uttered the formula used to welcome the king, and bowed duly, like the others.

She nodded in response.

As soon as she took power, she ordered all guest seats in the royal council hall to be the same. She sat on the one that was higher and more ornate. The others were arranged in a semi-circle and there were always as many of them as the people invited.

"I am just telling stories about King Solomon, lady," Tamrin, like everyone else, took the place indicated to him.

"You have been fascinated with him for a long time," Makeda remembered how much the merchant was impressed with the ruler of Israel when he returned from Israel for the first time just over two years ago.

In addition to gifts, news and orders for goods from Solomon, he brought something, or rather someone else. With him came a young talented boy, the son of one of the merchants from Jerusalem. His father asked Tamrin to take him with himself to the land of the queen of Sheba, to learn the customs of her court, and also to see the world, and as Tamrin was connected to him by not just the business, but also sympathy, because for years they met on trade routes in many different places around the world, he complied with his request. This way the boy arrived in Mariba. His name was Ben.

For two years, Ben, at the queen's request, had taught her the language and customs of Israel. And as the memory of childhood visions was still vivid in her mind, and more and more often she connected the man who appeared in them with Solomon, so she too began to share Tamrin's fascination.

"I heard your story," she said, sitting down. "I like his way of judgment. From what you say, Solomon has something far more valuable than all the gold of this world, because he possesses wisdom."

"Our ancestors used to say that whoever gains knowledge loves himself, who cares about reason, finds happiness," priest Sethon recited.

"The king is famous for his wisdom, and because he is also effective in what he does, legends circulate about him all around the world, and people in oases and taverns tell anecdotes and sing songs about him," Tamrin did not hide his appreciation for the king's achievements.

"I want to talk to you also about him today," the queen began the main part of the meeting. "We have three things to discuss. I expect advice from you because I don't know what to do yet."

The faces of those present expressed interest. As a matter of fact, none of them knew what to expect from the young queen and how she would do as a ruler. So far, she had not yet made any decisions that could significantly affect the shape of the country. Since the death of the king, Sheba had been lethargic. Nothing was happening. However, they sensed that the time for action was coming.

They were right.

"The first issue concerns our western lands. I decided it was time to settle accounts with Seth. We need to discuss how to do it most effectively," she began firmly. "The second issue, related to the first one, concerns the trade with the world. At the moment we have no influence over the principality of Aksum, where, as we know, Seth has proclaimed himself king. We are currently not acquiring goods from there. This is not good for our treasury and for Sheba's reputation that our ancestors have developed over the centuries. At the same time, we have a problem with the kingdom of Hijaz. This is the third thing, and because it concerns trade, it is necessarily linked to the previous ones."

She looked at the advisers and, assured that they understood what she was talking about, she continued, "Taking advantage of our temporary weakness and sleepiness, caused by the departure of my beloved father to the gods, Hijaz is trying to take away our exclusive brokerage between distant India and Egypt, and the rest of the world. In short: we are threatened from two sides. Our problems are Seth and the kingdom of Hijaz. Fortunately, Sheba's army is strong, and everyone is afraid of it, so no one tries to attack us, but if we don't do something with the problems we have, things can go differently. Seth is growing stronger; he will soon want to attack us."

She saw the advisers nod their heads.

"The time of passivity is over," she hit the table with her hand. "We've waited too long!" Her eyes burned with fire and she fell silent, holding back her emotions. "But as you all know, we couldn't have done otherwise," she added to her excuse.

She looked into everyone's face again. She slowly and carefully looked from one person to the next. As she found support in their eyes, she straightened up even more, took a deep breath and announced solemnly, "Today I am opening a new part of Sheba's story. I want those who will come after us to have reasons to be proud of us."

Despite being tough, Seshep was touched by her mistress's speech. After all, she remembered her as a little girl who trustingly cuddled next to her shoulder each evening while falling asleep. Now, when she looked and listened to her, she was proud of her. And she saw that she was not the only one impressed by Makeda's speech.

"Queen, you are very young," General Tesfa looked at her with admiration. We have always known that the gods have equipped you with great deal of wisdom, but I must admit that I just felt like I was listening to an old strategist, someone with a mind capable of deciphering, naming, and ordering everything that is most important. Experienced leaders have this skill. I bow my old knees to you," he stood up and, as he had said, knelt down with a deep bow.

"The general has expressed also my thoughts," Ashenafi joined the praises. He was about to kneel before her, but Makeda wouldn't let him.

"General, commander, thank you for your appreciation. I am grateful for it. If others think alike, thank you too. However, I want you to know that we will not be meeting to praise the queen's wisdom. Everyone," she pointed her finger at each of them in turn, "you have incomparably more experience, knowledge, and wisdom than I do. I expect advice and support from you. Let's make Sheba powerful and strong as in the days of my greatest ancestors."

She said it with such strength and certainty that they shuddered. She knew what she wanted. A powerful internal fire burned within her, warming them.

"So, queen," General Tesfa was the first to speak again, "I believe that we should immediately set out with the army and take Aksum from Seth's hands. I guarantee that the victory will be complete!"

"I second the general," Ashenafi was also a supporter of the war. "Let's strike quickly. We have many supporters there. When the princes learn that we have set out, they will immediately abandon Seth. They are tired of his rule. Since he proclaimed himself king, he imposed huge exaction on them and greatly restricted their power in the principalities. I know that they will gladly come back under our wings."

"Why do we need war again?" asked the High Priestess, who had been silent until then.

"We'll win it quickly," said the general.

"Probably yes, but why go to the other shore with the army, why should people die? We recently had a war in which the heir to the throne was killed, and then the king joined him. We have suffered only losses. It is better to transfer soldiers to the eastern and northern borders, let Hijaz feel our strength. Seth must be dealt with differently.

"I agree with the Priestess of the Silver Mother. The wisdom of the goddess speaks through her," Priest Sethon supported her. "We must use the army where it is needed and deal with Seth quietly."

"Maybe it's not a bad idea," Tesfa admitted after thinking. "I'll send few specially trained soldiers for him. They'll capture him when he won't expect it and bring him here. They will also grab the man with a scar."

"With a scar?" Seshep was interested.

"Today we are already certain that this man is to blame for the death of Prince Tomaj. He shot a poisoned arrow. He wanted to make sure that the prince would die," Tesfa explained. "We have long suspected that he was on Seth's service. He's the one you tried to capture in Mariba some time ago. As you said it yourself, Hemet Seshep, he was here on the day when a deadly venomous viper was found in Prince Tomaj's chamber."

"I also noticed him in the palace on the day of the death of Prince Sirah."

"And I saw his terrible face in my dreams at that time," Makeda added.

"Now we are sure that Seth is behind all the tragedies at our court," the general was glad that finally, after long days of mourning, he could speak openly, because things were at last starting to happen. "We must remove him from this land as soon as possible! Both Seth, and the assassin, and preferably also the poisoned fruit, that is Prince Den. Otherwise, we will always be at risk. Vermin should be crushed!"

The general stamped his foot and crushed the nonexistent worm with the thick sole of his sandal, demonstrating how to do it. A discussion broke out, to which Makeda listened in silence.

"Thank you for your suggestions for resolving this matter," she interrupted them when the emotions seemed to reach the vault of the chamber. "Common sense wins the battle, and having many advisors gives the advantage[20]. Thank you for your wisdom. I will make a decision by tomorrow " she assured, thus quelling the fever of the arguing debaters." "We'll discuss the second point now," she ordered, because all voices stopped immediately after her words.

Those gathered felt again that day that Makeda had royal strength and was able to make use of it. She was able to control her emotions, even in matters that were difficult for her, and such was certainly the death of both her brothers. They appreciated it. Earlier, men gathered in the room saw her as a beautiful girl, smart and intelligent, but still just a girl. Now, they were pleasantly surprised, because they realized that they were dealing with someone who was born to be a queen. This role was written to her.

"Trade is what has been creating Sheba for centuries. It builds our power and provides wealth. Gold, silver, myrrh, incense, precious fabrics, animal skins, wood... As we all know, we send them all over the world. Caravans going from Egypt to India pass through Sheba, we collect goods from the Black Continent by sea and send them on. Products from our gardens have been going to royal tables and temples of distant gods for centuries," she listed. "How can we manage our affairs so as not

---

[20] Old Testament. Book of Proverbs. Life rules 24.6.

to lose control over trade between the worlds?" she suspended her voice in anticipation, but no one spoke. "We have always been the best at it, and I will do everything possible to keep it that way. I expect from you that you will advise me, using your knowledge and experience. How can we make Sheba remain a powerhouse. Or even to make it more powerful than ever before!"

Of all those present, Tamrin was the most competent in trade matters. After the queen's words, the eyes of those gathered focused on him.

"As we know, Solomon builds the temple of Yahweh. I was there, I saw it: believe me, this is the greatest place under the sun. There is nothing else in the world built with such momentum and more filled with wealth. In admiration for what he does, the monarchs of neighboring countries send ambassadors, who congratulate the king and pass valuable gifts."

"Maybe we too should send an ambassador there, queen?" Handake suggested.

"One needs to know that Israel has great power right now," Tamrin went on, without addressing Handake's question, for it was obvious that Sheba should send a representative with generous gifts to Jerusalem. "King David, Solomon's father, once captured the strategic harbor and the surrounding land, where the desert stops on a narrow road leading to Arabia. This harbor is Ezion-Geber and provides access to Ofir, where there is the most gold in the world. We should do something to make this harbor belong to us, at least to a small extent. It's an entrance into the world. Israel is now a powerful state, believe me, we should form an alliance with it at all costs. Solomon is a wise king. Everyone respects him. He made many strategic moves. For example, he married the daughter of Pharaoh, so he has no enemy in Egypt. He is friends with King Hiram, thanks to which his fleet now sails not only the Middle-Earth Sea and the great ocean leading to India, but also, as you know, our Red Sea. I predict that in a moment the trade between India and Egypt will bypass Sheba and will only move by sea. Do you know what this means for us?"

"I think we know," Hendake said again. "We have been profiting from brokering trade between continents since the dawn of time. Almost all caravans going from India to the rest of the world pass through Sheba. In our oases, buyers buy camels, pay for water, food ,and accommodation. If they chose the sea way, it would be an unimaginable loss to the royal treasury. I prefer not to think that this could happen."

"I was hoping that the main threat to the trade is that our neighbors are trying to discourage caravans from using our oases in order to attract them to theirs?"

"Unfortunately, queen, the threat from the north in the form of Solomon's harbors and sea fleet, even though it is imperceptible to us now, can be really serious at any moment," by addressing the queen with these words, Tamrin wanted to make everyone aware of the impending threat. "If we cannot reach agreement with Solomon in this matter as soon as possible, our trading power will soon be just a distant memory. And believe me, what I am talking about is not a distant future that will concern our grandchildren or great-grandchildren. Solomon acts quickly. If we are not among his friends within two or three years at the most, we will be pushed to the margins of the world."

Mariba and Aksum

the day after the royal council and the following days

The queen's conversation with the High Priestess regarding Seth did not last long. I listened to it.

"The ruler should also take actions that are morally difficult for him, but serve a greater good," said the Priestess at the end, as if to assure Makeda in the rightness of the decisions made a moment earlier.

I had the impression that sometimes she still wanted to see her as a little girl, as if not fully realizing how much Makeda had changed in the last two years; and from the moment when the war broke out because of her carelessness and faith in the Den's ability to keep secret, until the death of her brother, and finally the departure of her father, my beloved protégée underwent a metamorphosis.

I watched her wings, undercut by Den, slowly grow back, and her powerful, dormant female strength wake up in her. She was always mature, but recent events made her think like an adult strong ruler, despite her still young age. There was power in her! For those who met her, she was a reflection of the face of the Lady of the Moon. I felt that she had entered this stage of her life in which she could consciously hold her strength and share her light with others. I knew her since childhood, I replaced her mother; I was her companion and guardian. I protected her and at the same time I admired her. Perhaps also because I knew her pure heart and innocence, I watched with admiration how she approached Seth's case with dispassionate reasoning. When I noticed that she could distance herself so much, I realized that she stopped being a little girl and became a queen: wise, prudent, foreseeing, and one who was able to put the matters of the state above personal ones, but without losing feminine sensitivity at all.

"We will finish it quickly, efficiently, and effectively," the High Priestess concluded coldly. "Seshep, I want Seth to know for sure who sends you when he is dying. Den should die too."

"No. We will spare Den," Makeda said firmly. "I've known him since my childhood. And I don't believe that he wanted to lead to the evil that happened. He revealed my secret to his father, not knowing that he would use it in such a shameful way."

"You want to believe it," said the Priestess without emotion.

"I do," she replied almost provocatively, and understanding that the Priestess did not approve of her decision, she added:

"Seshep, if you can, bring Den to me. I want to talk to him before we make the final decision about him."

"It will be done according to your will, queen," I bowed my head.

She wasn't my little girl anymore. She was mukarrib. She gave me orders, and I wanted to follow them with the greatest devotion. I was proud of it. When Seth proclaimed himself king, we placed one of our priestesses in his palace in Aksum. She served the ruler in his chambers together with other servants, taking care of his comfort. Thanks to her, we knew what was happening in his immediate surroundings and the habits of this terrible, self-proclaimed king, whom I hated.

We, hemet, always act quietly and discreetly. So, I crossed the sea unnoticed by anyone. I knew the places where I was going to quite well, so I managed to get to my destination - Aksum - without any obstacles. Nobody noticed the single black woman, wrapped in dark, low key robes.

I got to the city at night. The guards didn't notice me. As a priestess of the Silver Mother, and furthermore, a hemet, I can be invisible; I have known that for years. I entered the king's chamber, sneaking by the walls. It was a full moon. I consciously chose that night to fulfill my mission because I knew that thanks to its bright face, I would be able to see the surroundings, and to move when the favorable goddess covers its face with thick clouds.

The palace was sleeping. The guards kept the watch in designated places, closing their eyes every now and then and falling asleep while standing. There were not many of them. Clearly, Seth was feeling confident. He did not expect any danger so soon after Nikal's death.

Sneaking quietly, I silently got into his chamber. According to the words of our priestess serving there, there was nobody inside apart from the king. Also, as she said, a cup of wine stood on the low table by his bed. Sometimes he would wake up at night because he felt thirsty. He ate hearty dinners that did not let him sleep soundly. *"Perhaps he was also troubled by remorse,"* I thought, looking at the sleeping man.

Everything was going unusually smoothly. I admit it worried me a little. I was supposed to get to Aksum and I did, to enter the palace imperceptibly - and I did it too, then to get to the king's chamber and still remain unnoticed - I was sure that I was - after which I was supposed to pour the poison into his cup and wait until he drinks it.

When I was beginning to worry about the lack of even the smallest obstacles, there was a small glitch in the implementation of my plan. Fortunately!

I felt the blood that had been running quickly through my veins that night start to flow even faster, but at the same time I calmed down a bit, because my experience told me that when adversity arose, it meant that everything was fine. What happened? I heard someone trying to get into the room through the window bay. Seth was sleeping soundly, but his ears seemed to catch something in his sleep too, because he opened his eyes for a moment. I froze. The movement outside the window stopped immediately. I thought that whoever was there, knew his job well. After making sure everything was all right, Seth turned to the other side and fell asleep again.

A few moments passed, the clouds began to reveal the shining moon, it was getting brighter, so the unexpected guest decided it was time to go inside. First, a short rope appeared, then bare feet, and soon a man dressed in black. He looked around the chamber with a trained eye. He could not see me in the place I stood. I did everything to calm the energy radiating from me, so he did not sense my presence. I watched him approach Seth's bed with the movements of a predatory cat and retrieve a short knife from behind his belt.

I left my hiding place, gesturing to show that I was on his side. He froze. He stared at me for a moment, trying to get into my energy field. I opened up to him as much as it was needed so that we could communicate without words. We understood that although we did not know each other, we were on the same side. We both breathed a sigh of relief. I showed him the bottle with poison. He nodded.

From that moment on, everything happened quickly. I poured the liquid into the wine cup and we both moved a safe distance from the bed, waiting for what would happen. I made a sound that would make Seth wake up again. Indeed, after a while, he sat on the bed and reached for the cup. He was thirsty. The dinner he had, had to be abundant. He drank almost everything, while the lethal dose was two or three sips. The body's reaction came immediately.

He clutched his throat, trying to breathe. He could not. His eyes opened wide – I don't know if it was more in pain, surprise, or helplessness. The poison acted quickly. The victim was almost immediately paralyzed, unable to utter a voice. Death followed a moment later.

"This is how the gods of Sheba punish the murderers of kings," I said into his ear. "Great Kandake Makeda sends her greetings," I added.

A witness to what had just happened stood next to him, ready to finish my work if necessary.

When Seth got still, the man in black bowed and blessed me with the sign of Almakah, the god whose zealous follower Seth was too. It became clear to me that not only the Lady of the Moon and Illumkuh, but also the god watching over Aksum ceased to favor Seth. I bowed to him, making the sign of the Silver Mother.

Mariba

The next day

When the dry season slowly began to change into the rainy one, the air in Sheba was sometimes crisp. One could breathing easily, and thanks to the moderate temperature, the clothes did not stick to the body, even when the sun was at its zenith.

A light breeze blew, the scents of fragrant balm, incense, refreshing sage, lovage, and mint hung in the air. It was morning. The general walked briskly along an avenue lined with sycamore trees. He was pleased. He had good news to tell.

The queen was sitting on a stone bench under a tree in the palace garden. She saw Tesfa walking down the alley her great-grandfather planted. The trees had spreading crowns and were just in bloom. Male flowers looked completely different than female ones. They had more petals and stamens; they were smaller and seemed to come from a completely different plant. Sycamore had always been considered a sacred tree in Sheba; it had a hard, mighty trunk and it did not give in to winds, storms, sun, or water. When it was broken, buried or flooded, the trunk and branches sprouted roots and the tree continued to grow, thus lasting forever. Therefore, it was considered indestructible, just like the kingdom of Sheba, which had always existed, and despite numerous falls and temporary weakness, it was able to recover again and again, just like a sycamore.

Makeda was not alone. She was accompanied by the High Priestess, who received news from Seshep at night. The queen already knew that the task was done.

"May the gods lead you, lady," Tesfa greeted the queen. "Great Priestess," he bowed to the other woman.

"General, I see joy on your face," Makeda guessed what Tesfa was going to communicate to her, but she didn't want to deprive him of this pleasure.

She wasn't wrong.

"Seth is dead," he announced. "They say he died in his bed at night, without anyone's help. It seems that the gods favor us. It happened as you wanted, lady," he said to the High Priestess. "Without war or bloodshed."

"You are right, General, it looks like the gods are on our side," said the Priestess, smiling kindly.

At this point, maybe the soldier's instinct, often called experience, or maybe some gesture or expression of the Priestess, caused the general to think about what happened in Aksum.

"I see, queen, that Seshep is not with you?" he noted. "She has always been like your shadow."

"She is in Aksum, making sure that the gods favor us in the way we think is the best," she laughed, thus hinting that his assumptions about Seshep were accurate.

"She settled the matter very quickly and efficiently," he admitted, because he realized that Seth's death had not been accidental.

"Where you do not want to send troops, send a hemet."

Tesfa had long known that the Priestess of the Silver Mother has wisdom, and her hemet possesses many amazing skills, but he sometimes thought that it would be best if she and her charges focused on healing people and looking at the past and future, and not on matters of war.

"My admiration," he admitted. "It seems that thanks to Seshep we got rid of our biggest problem."

"Our information shows that Prince Den was in the south of Aksum when it happened," said the Priestess in a firm voice. "He already knows that his father is dead and is on his way to the palace.

"We can't let him get there," the general straightened, and exclaimed with such zeal as if he were a young boy.

"I think so too," said the Priestess. "That is why Seshep will stay in Aksum for some time."

The general nodded, finally acknowledging that the Priestess was in full control of the Aksum case.

"What about taking over the palace?"

"Caleb will be announced the new prince of Aksum today. We know him. He has always been faithful to Nikal to such an extent that when Seth proclaimed himself king, he refused to cooperate with him and did not support him, despite threats."

"General, I would like you to support Caleb in Aksum with the presence of your soldiers," Makeda knew that Tesfa should not feel unnecessary, for he was the type of man who always had to act. "Go to Aksum as soon as possible, and send your best people there tonight and bring balance to the principality."

Seeing the smile returning to his face, which disappeared when he realized whose merit Seth's death was, she added, "Soon the queen will want to visit the western lands of Sheba. You need to restore the old order there by then. Nobody will do it better than you."

"Queen, I will do everything according to your will," once again in his life the general appreciated the clarity of thinking of the young ruler.

At the same time, however, as an experienced soldier, in court service from an early age, he was able to predict how the fate of the queen could unfold if she did not choose the right spouse soon. He decided that the time had come, and the place was right to tell her that.

"Do you have any concerns, general?" Makeda asked, noticing that Tesfa was thinking about something.

She liked him. He reminded her of her father. She felt safe with him.

"Forgive my boldness, queen," he looked at her with concern. "I'll go right away to fulfill your orders, but I'd like to say something before."

He took a breath.

"As you know, I've served your father all my life, I've known you since you were a child. As you also know, I have a daughter who is almost your age."

Makeda nodded. She saw Warda, usually at big ceremonies, but she did not know her well. All she knew was that she was beautiful, smart, and she still had no husband.

"I certainly don't give you the love that Nikal gave you, may the gods favor him on the other side, but you are very close to me. And it is because of the respect for your father and the feelings I have for you that I must tell you – I would add that these are not only my thoughts – Ashenafi, who also knows politics well, shares my view. I'm sure most of the people in the palace think so, but no one has ever dared to tell you that."

"Then tell me, general," she encouraged him gently and added, "When a true friend says what he thinks of you, even if it hurts, we should know it is needed and constructive, and thank him for his care and honesty. So, thank you now for what you are about to say. You are the bravest of the brave. Speak!"

Seeing her serious face, he bowed his head respectfully. He was still standing in front of the bench where she was sitting, but he took a step forward to be closer to her. Her words encouraged him.

"Well, Great Kandake can't be alone," he lowered his voice almost to a whisper. "You should have a husband. It won't be easy to find the right one, but we're thinking about it. A kingdom cannot be ruled by a woman alone."

"It can," the High Priestess said. "If this woman is a virgin. This is what Sheba's eternal law says. And Makeda is one."

The general swallowed hard. He dared not question her words. Anyway, he had no reason to do so. He had heard that a woman could sit on the throne and exercise power on her own as long as she was intact, and everyone in Sheba knew that Makeda didn't have a partner.

The queen got up and standing closer to Tesfa, put her hand on his shoulder.

"Actually, why can't a woman be a ruler, general?" she asked, looking into his eyes.

He was speechless. Her question surprised him.

"It's an eternal law," he replied with genuine surprise after a moment. "Every king has a wife, and the queen should have a husband. It is obvious."

"Ah yes?"

Tesfa didn't hear the slightly mocking tone in her voice.

"Everyone has a role to play in this world. And everyone needs the support of others. You are a woman, very wise one, but still young and inexperienced. If you are alone, it's a matter of time before Sheba becomes a tasty morsel for your neighbors."

"It is your responsibility to prevent this from happening, General," she was still facing him, but her arms were now folded on her chest. "As the commander-in-chief of the army, you will soon receive authority that no general had before you. Our safety will be mainly in your hands and on your shoulders.

His chest seemed to expand. He was pleased.

"You know how much I trust you, don't you? You also know that I love you almost like a father. But don't suggest any of the regional princes for me. We don't need to strengthen Sheba in this way. We are strong and rich enough for me not to have to tie up myself with one of the princes of our countries, at least for the time being. Do you agree? Anyway, you know very well that someone else has been written for me..."

"Lady, you've been stubborn since childhood and always did what you wanted. So, it's hard to expect that something would change when you became the queen," he laughed amicably, flattered by the promise of new powers he was to receive. The Grand Priestess watched and listened to the conversation. She was proud of Makeda and sure that the girl would achieve all that had been written for her.

Makeda had a storm in her head. She remembered her youthful visions, but they were increasingly becoming a thing of the past and were fading away against the sheer volume of matters and events. The man on the throne she had dreamed about might indeed exist somewhere, and perhaps it was even this mysterious Solomon she knew more and more about, and to whom something was strangely attracting her, but she was less and less sure about it. There were even days when visions seemed to her as only the colorful dreams of a little child and she stopped believing in it.

She was busy with responsibilities, looking to the dam, visiting managers, controlling the day-to-day functioning of the state, and at the same time the Aksum case, which was still not fully taken care of, kept her awake at night.

All this caused her forgetting her old visions and her trip to somewhere in the world where she was supposed to meet someone who would give her the greatest treasure.

She was a queen, and enemies began to threaten her divided country from different sides. However, despite this, Sheba was still a powerful, rich state, which all local rulers took into account.

No one from her close family was alive, she was alone. She was aware of it more than ever before. She was sure that in order to maintain the throne and the dynasty, she had to carry on the line. But she also knew –   and it was the most important thing at the moment –   that she had to be smart and strong. She was the queen, the Great Kandake of Sheba. It was obliging.

***

When the news of Seth's death spread over Aksum with a speed of the northern wind, Prince Caleb, Makeda's supporter, came to power almost immediately. These developments did not surprise anyone. Furthermore, people have been waiting for a long time for the old order to finally return, and for the prince appointed by the king, or in this case, the queen of Sheba, to take over the rule in the capital and principality. When almost immediately after Seth's death, the High Priest of Almakah blessed Caleb, no one even tried to object. Everyone was fed up with Seth's two-year rule, his cruelty, disregard for people, and above all, huge taxes. Also, since the greatest god of Aksum, Almakah, was in favor of the new prince, it ultimately spoke in his favor.

After Seth's death, Makeda's soldiers appeared in the palace, and general Tesfa subdued the entire principality quickly and without any fights. It became clear to Den that not only he should not try to return to the capital, but he had to run as far away from it as possible to save his life. It turned out that he had no supporters in Aksum, and the soldiers he thought were faithful to his father and him, immediately passed to Sheba's side when the situation changed. So, he decided to go to Egypt, hoping that the pharaoh would give him shelter.

Seshep followed the escaping Den. However, before she could reach him, Makeda told her to return to Mariba. The queen's order did not please the hemet. She thought that while Den was alive, it was more than certain that he would cause trouble for Makeda and the whole kingdom. However, she could not and did not want to oppose the ruler.

***

Den had no doubt that what had happened in Aksum was no accident. His father's death and taking power immediately by Caleb must have been the result of a conspiracy. While escaping, he wondered if General Tesfa was behind it, or was Makeda personally directing everything?

"Could she participate in something like that?" he wondered. "She is very young and has no experience at all."

On the other hand, however, he knew that it was the same Makeda who had rejected him, who had fought him, who most likely blamed his father for the death of her brothers, and even indirectly also for Nikal's passing.

"What to do?" he thought frantically, considering various options. *"Caleb took power and will do anything to capture me and get me back to Sheba. My supporters, if there are still any somewhere, will wait for the development of the situation. My return to Aksum without troops to support me would be a suicide. I have to wait it out. Preferably in Egypt. Father always said that Pharaoh did not like strong Sheba and would do a lot to weaken it. If I succeed, I will return to Aksum at a convenient moment with his troops."*

When Den was still small, Seth explained to him the intricate interests of the neighboring kingdoms. So, he knew how much each ruler makes sure that another one does not grow in strength. Pharaoh Siamun gave his daughter to King Solomon as wife to ensure peace from Israel. He maintained a powerful army that guarded Egypt's borders and cared for its interests. This also applied to the southern borders, and Aksum was right behind it. Hence, Den was almost certain that helping him, the rightful heir to the throne of Aksum, could be a good move for Egypt.

Once there, however, he was disappointed. After two weeks of waiting, he received the message that the pharaoh would not receive him in audience. The ruler of Egypt, in his wisdom, taking care of good relations with neighboring kingdoms, and in this case with the Queen of Sheba, did not intend to openly support her enemy. He did it in a secret way. He sent Den, along with his companions, up the Nile to the fourth cataract. The city of Napata in which Den was to be hosted by Pharaoh, was a fortress, the last point defending Egypt against the southern principalities and tribes. According to the Egyptians, it was the place where the civilization ended.

Kingdom of Israel

Two months later

Elichoref was Solomon's writer. He wrote down thoughts, took down ordinances and king's sentences. He also wrote letters on his behalf, and because he often met other writers and visited taverns, he was for the king a source of anecdotes and stories that circulated among the people.

"Lord, I heard something interesting yesterday," he said one morning.

Everyone in Jerusalem knew what Solomon looked like, so wherever he appeared, he was worshiped. People bowed low, and as he was considered almost a saint, no one thought to tell him the latest jokes or gossip. Therefore, he eagerly listened to the stories Elichoref brought him.

"If at least half of the anecdotes circulating about me were based on the truth, especially those that speak of my extraordinary skills, I would have to be not a human being, but one of the gods to whom the unenlightened pray," he laughed, thinking that his favorite writer would tell another story about him.

"People believe that there are djinns at your service, that you understand animal speech and can talk to them."

"And I can't?" Solomon was in good mood, as he always was in the morning.

"People's stories indicate that you can do everything."

"And let it stay this way,"   Solomon, who used to browse the construction plans or documents written the previous day while talking to Elichoref, stopped what he was doing and sat down. "Tell me please, what amazing feat of mine did you find out about yesterday?"

"I heard, for the first time in such a place, about the Queen of Sheba."

"Oh, so we have a new character in the series of stories about King Solomon?"

"Yes, she has never appeared before."

"Interesting…"

Solomon sat back, stretched his legs in front of him, and folded his arms. Then Elichoref began, "Every morning, after waking up, King Solomon talked to the birds sitting on the tree growing by the window of his chamber. In this way, he learned what was going on in the country and abroad. Birds told him everything, because nothing escaped their attention. One day, the king noticed that there was no hoopoe among his bird friends. The next day it happened again. And on the third day too. 'Where is he, where did he go?' the king wondered. On the fourth day, the hoopoe finally appeared. It turned out that he had fun in the land of Sheba. A beautiful, wise and very rich queen, Makeda, ruled there. He flew there because he heard about her attributes and wanted to check how things were going with his own eyes. He told Solomon about her beauty and extraordinary intelligence. He also said that he saw in Sheba the most beautiful gardens in the world and the greatest pure gold throne set with precious stones. 'King, my eyes did not see anything that precious in any kingdom,' the hoopoe was delighted. The king was intrigued by the tale. He summoned one of the djinns on his service and ordered him to transfer the queen's throne to his palace in Jerusalem. He believed that in this way he would make Makeda come to Israel in effort to get her property back. Then he would be able to meet this most beautiful woman who walks the earth, for whom wisdom is more valuable than all the gold and silver of this world. And as everyone knew, this queen had more gold and silver than there is sand in the desert," concluded Elichoref.

"And what was next?" Solomon wanted to know.

"This is the end of the story," Elichoref spread his hands. "For now," he added, as if he were sure the story would go on.

"How come it's the end? There must be some conclusion from the story."

"King Solomon is waiting for the arrival of the beautiful and wise queen from the south, because he hopes that she will want to regain her precious throne. To be continued. Undoubtedly."

"You really intrigued me. But, I think, that's exactly what this story was about. Someone wants the inhabitants of Jerusalem to learn about Queen Makeda. The merchant Tamrin told me about her. He praised her beauty and wisdom. But in Jerusalem, except me, few have heard of her."

"So far," said Elichoref. "I think it will change soon. You can see that it is really important for someone."

"Great. So, let's wait for the developments."

Mariba

Tamrin's house

Tamrin had a big house. It was not a palace, although he could afford to buy more than one. His father erected it, and Tamrin never expanded it, he only took care that it was equipped with everything necessary to let him live comfortably when he was in Mariba. He employed quite a lot of servants who cared for the house in his absence.

His younger brother lived in a palace he built nearby. He took care of family interests in Mariba whenever Tamrin set off on another journey. Unlike Tamrin, he already had a wife and four children. The fact that the older brother devoted himself to traveling, and the younger settled in Mariba, was convenient for both of them.

All rooms in the house were laid out on one level. There was a large room here, which served as a party hall, but it also served as a banquet hall. When their father was alive, family celebrations took place there, too. Next to it was a room in which meals were eaten. A fire, surrounded by a carefully finished stone circle, burned in the middle of it once. Meals were often eaten around it. However, since Tamrin as a young man first saw in the countries he visited with his father that it was possible to feast while lying on beds or sitting on chairs, set by wide benches, similar solutions were also introduced in their home.

On the other side of the room, there was a chamber in which his father once received individual clients. Tamrin continued this tradition now, with just small changes to the place. He only added some valuable travel souvenirs.

It was in this chamber that he was hosting the queen.

"What are these beautiful scrolls?" Makeda picked up a partially unfolded roll, placed on two richly decorated rollers.

"It's sacred Sefer Torah," Tamrin explained. "I unfolded the scroll because I tried to study it, but I don't know the language well enough."

She studied the letters on the white, carefully crafted lamb leather, and the cedar wood rollers with almond flowers carved at their ends.

"Why is this scroll sacred?"

"Because it is in the Torah that the words of Yahweh are written," Tamrin knew that Makeda knew who Yahweh was, because he told her about him when he returned from his first trip to Jerusalem. " There is everything that is most important for Jews there: the history of the creation of the world, the history of the Israelites, the covenant that their God made first with Abraham and later with Moses, the plagues that fell by God's will on Egypt, when Pharaoh refused to let them leave his lands...There are plenty of amazing stories here. And most importantly: the Ten Commandments[21]. These are the rules dictated to Moses personally by Yahweh at Mount Sinai. All other rules are subordinated to these laws. Jews must strictly follow

---

[21] The Ten Commandments (The Ten Statements in the Jewish tradition) - a collection of the most important orders for the Judaism followers, and later the Christians, dictated by God to Moses on Mount Sinai (author's note).

them. And the stone tablets on which they were engraved are kept as the most valuable relic in the Ark of the Covenant."

"Ben told me about it. Apparently, it has magical power. Do you believe this?"

"They say that it can move people in space, that the divine power that is hidden in it can destroy the most powerful army. There are unusual stories about the Ark."

"Like what?"

"They say that whoever sees its contents will be immediately killed; that its energy can tear down the highest walls; and that even a high priest who can come near it once a year should look at it only through the veil of holy incense smoke, because he would be struck by its power."

"Ben told me that Solomon had seventy-two demons at his service. That he trapped them in a brass vessel and made them serve him. He knows secret spells, makes magic charms, can become invisible, knows where hidden treasures are, knows how to heal people, knows the language of animals and can magically move from one place to another, and even be in two places at the same time."

"Well, maybe, according to Ben, Solomon is not a king, but a magician?" he laughed, pleased that the stories of his mentee affected her imagination. "In the scroll you are looking at, you will not find anything about it. The Torah is a holy book," seeing that Makeda was still stroking the soft skin of parchment without even realizing it, he returned to the previous topic. "The priest who rewrites it cannot make a single mistake, because he would have to start writing again. It cost me a fortune."

Makeda's fingers felt not only the smoothness of the wonderfully cured leather, but much more. As if she touched something she knew perfectly well and had been waiting for a long time, dreaming that it would finally appear. As if she knew these scrolls and their contents. It seemed to her for a moment that she was dreaming. That she was a little girl again and saw images. The feeling of unusual excitement that she knew from her childhood, came back to her. She trembled, touching the scrolls.

"I wish I could know their language well enough to read it myself," she said quietly, her thoughts circling other worlds. "Ben has already taught me to speak a little but writing and reading is not going well yet."

"I have a present for you, queen," seeing how impressed she was when she touched the parchment, he said equally softly.

"Tamrin, you keep giving me gifts," she shook off the bliss that overwhelmed her and scolded him, trying not to offend him at the same time.

He gave her jewels, gold and expensive fabrics. He brought her jewelry from distant countries, gold and silver mirrors, valuable furniture, often even plants and unusual animals. This time he drew a small leather pouch from a casket.

"Please accept this gift," he said, holding the pouch on his open hand. "It is extremely valuable to me because King Solomon gave it to me."

She looked with interest.

"What is this?" She took out a small golden plaque with letters engraved on it from the pouch.

"That's the Ten Commandments I told you about, lady."

"I am the Lord your God," she began to read. She shook her head, dissatisfied with herself. "I don't think I can do it," she said helplessly and handed the tablet to Tamrin.

"I am the Lord your God who brought you out of the land of Egypt, out of the house of slavery," he read. "You will not have other gods before me."

She shivered. She felt again as if she knew those words, as if they had been in her head for a long time, as if they belonged to her. And again, the atmosphere of childhood dreams returned to her, only with even greater force.

He noticed the change in her.

"Queen?" He worried.

"It's all right," she reassured him and herself, chasing away the traces of old dreams in her thoughts. "You will not have other gods before me?" She returned to reality. "I wonder what the Lady of the Moon or Illumkuh would say to that?"

"Solomon has no such doubts. His God is possessive. And he punishes severely for worshiping a golden calf."

"I am very curious about Solomon who believes in only one god."

"He also believes in wisdom."

"Oh? So, do I!"

"You have a lot in common, lady."

"Really? What, for example?"

"Belief in wisdom. When I first met him, he said that wisdom is more valuable than silver, and possessing it means more than possessing gold[22]."

"I think exactly the same."

Tamrin told her how Solomon asked God for the gift of wisdom. She listened carefully to him, and when he finished, she said, "I have always known that the beginning of wisdom is to acquire wisdom, so you should strive to obtain it with all your might[23]. I feel that I should go to meet Solomon as soon as possible."

"Lady, this is a long and exhausting trip," he objected weakly. "And if Queen of Sheba is to participate, it will require a lot of preparation."

"So, start organizing it today already, Tamrin!"

Mariba

[22] Old Testament, Proverbs 14.

[23] Old Testament, Proverbs 7.

One year later

"I desire wisdom and my mind is seeking knowledge," she announced. "Wisdom is better than all treasures of gold and silver. It is the greatest creation on earth[24]." The assembly hall was filled with dignitaries.

Everyone was staring at the queen and listening carefully to her words.

"What can wisdom be compared to? It is sweeter than honey, it gives more joy than wine, shines stronger than the sun and attracts attention more than precious stones. It is fatter than oil, satisfies more than exquisite delicacies, and gives man a greater reputation than thousands of pieces of gold and silver. It is a source of heart's joy, light and brightness for the eyes, a donor of speed for the feet, a shield for the breast, a helmet for the head, a chain for the neck, and a belt for the loin. It makes ears hear and hearts understand. It is a teacher of students, a comforter of the calm and thoughtful, and a donor for those seeking fame. No kingdom exists without wisdom; without it you cannot get treasures and reach the desired place on foot. When a tongue casts words that lack wisdom, they cannot be accepted. Wisdom is the greatest of all treasures. Those who accumulated gold and silver did not benefit from it until they had wisdom. However, from those who accumulated wisdom, it will not be stolen by anyone. What fools accumulate, wise people get rid of. Because of the wickedness of those who do evil, the righteous are glorified, and because of the wicked acts of fools, the wise are beloved."

Everyone listened to the words that flowed like a calm river. The queen's voice caressed the hearts and ears and soothed the souls of those who heard her. She spoke in such a way that

---

[24] Kebra Nagast. Glory to the Kings, translated from English by P. Żyła, Sandomierz 2011 (Kebra Nagast is a book originally written in the Etiosemite language Geez - author's note).

nobody doubted the truth of what he heard. Every sentence coming out of her mouth sounded like a Divine message.

"Wisdom is a sublime and rich quality. I love it like a mother, and it embraces me like its child. I will follow the footsteps of wisdom and it will always protect me. I will seek wisdom and it will always be with me. I will follow wisdom and it will never abandon me. I will lean on wisdom and it will be like a firm wall. I will seek asylum in wisdom, and it will give me power and strength. I will rejoice in wisdom and it will give me abundant grace."

She hung her voice and looked around the room. Everyone looked at her as if she were a goddess and seemed to be drinking words from her lips. She smiled at them and to herself and continued.

"It is just as right to follow the trail of wisdom as it is right for our feet to stand at the doorway of the gates of wisdom. Let's look for it and find it. Let it love us and it will never leave us again. Let's follow it and we will catch up with it. Let's ask and we'll get an answer. Let us turn our hearts to it so that we do not forget about it. If we remember, it will also keep us in its memories. By sticking to fools, one can't remember wisdom because they don't worship it and it doesn't love them in return."

Many of the listeners nodded as a sign that they completely agreed with what they heard.

"The honor given to wisdom is the honor given to a wise man, and love of wisdom, love of a wise man. Let's love a wise man and he will never leave us. At the very sight of him, wisdom penetrates our bodies. We observe the places where he set his feet to see the remnant of wisdom. I love a wise man even though I can't see him at all. I love with my thoughts of the one I don't know, who reigns far away. His story and what I know about him is as much desire for my heart as water is for the thirsty," she finished.

The silence that lasted during her speech, although it was difficult to imagine, because even the hearts of listeners seemed to be beating more quietly, deepened even more. The dignitaries understood that, apart from declaring love for wisdom as a divine gift, the queen's words also meant the expedition that had been talked about everywhere in Sheba for a year already. Since Tamrin started preparing it, there had been no place where people would not talk about it. The road to the kingdom of Israel was long and full of dangers. Tamrin's caravans had done it several times and the participants felt that the route was extremely tiring. They also knew how experienced the merchant was and how fit, and at the same time hardy and used to inconvenience, his people were. They wondered how a gentle woman could travel such a distance, let alone the queen, accustomed to luxuries.

What really pulled her to Jerusalem? Many thought that the real reason why their mistress wanted to reach such a distant place was a secret that perhaps they would never be able to know.

The high priest Sethon was against the expedition. He talked to the queen about this many times. He hoped she would accept his arguments. He submitted them patiently. He did not want her to go on such a long journey, leaving the state without a ruler. He did not like that she would go to a king who worships a god that does not allow the worship of other deities. He was also afraid that in the absence of Makeda, Den would raise his head and plead for the throne of Aksum, and maybe even attack Mariba.

Sethon noticed the queen's fascination with the Israelite god, and as he took seriously her childhood visions and what hemet Seshep saw behind the veil of time, he was very worried about the future of the state. In his temple, he performed rituals to ensure a safe return trip for Makeda and tried to find out what the future would look like. But it appeared to him hidden behind a fog. Illumkuh either didn't want to show it, or there was no place for him in Sheba in the future; and that was what the priest feared most. After all, the faith of the ancestors could not simply disappear because of the queen's departure to some distant kingdom. Sethon wanted to believe that Makeda was a faithful daughter of Sheba.

However, despite the spells and sacrifices made to Illumkuh and other lesser gods, the high priest felt that the expedition would take place and that it could bring Sheba such powerful changes that they would shake the world as he and other Shebians had known it so far.

His thoughts kept him awake. He talked about the expedition and what it could bring to Sheba to everyone who could influence Makeda's decision.

"High priest, you can stop worrying," General Tesfa assured him. "The state will be in good hands during the queen's absence. We have a powerful, well-equipped army; no one will dare to assault us. Den is too weak to try to do anything. He sought support at the Pharaoh's court, but he got turned down. Messing with us is not in Pharaoh's interests or, I assure you, in anyone else's. We are rich. We have a powerful, well-trained army. We are safe. I think the queen can and should go.

"This journey will give us tangible benefits," the eunuch Hendake also tried to calm Sethon down. "If the queen achieves what she wants, for many years no one will dare to try to undermine or deprive us of exclusive trade and brokering between India and the countries with whom we have been cooperating since the dawn of time. If we gain the sympathy of Solomon, whom the whole world respects, then even the grandchildren of our grandchildren will have guaranteed a peaceful, rich future. So, if you are not happy with this trip yourself, then enjoy it on behalf of your grandchildren's future grandchildren."

"The Lady of the Moon has long been giving us signals that changes will come to our world," the High Priestess also wanted to ease his worries. "But after all, the only thing that is permanent in the world is change. We can be afraid of it, of course. But we can also just prepare for it as best we can. As you know, Sethon, the priestesses of the Lady of the Moon have long been expecting the queen to embark on this journey. It is written in the stars. The changes it will bring, cannot be avoided."

Seeing the fear in the eyes of the high priest, she added, "As I said a moment ago, and as we both know well, this is a higher plan, written in the space of the eternal cosmos. You can oppose it, but it won't change much. And yet, it is like this – if we cannot change something, we give in to the current. It is a proven strategy." She noticed that Sethon nodded, so she assumed he'd agreed. "High priest, flow with the river. There is only one energy in the world. Its nature is the eternal pursuit of harmony. Join it."

" ...or leave with dignity," the high priest whispered quietly, when after finishing the conversation with the Priestess, he was certain that the leaving woman could not hear him anymore. Of all the most influential people in Sheba, the high priest did not speak only to the commander of the royal guard, Ashenafi. He looked forward to the expedition more than others, because he would accompany the queen and protect her all the time.

The old priest decided to make the last attempt to convince the queen immediately after her appearance in the throne room, during which she clearly announced her departure. Her words were followed by a long silence. Then a loud uproar erupted. People commented on her words one over another, and she let them. Finally, she raised her hand, commanding silence, and gave the old man the right to speak. All eyes turned to him.

" Oh, my lady," Sethon hit the floor with a long cane with a snake's head on its end. "Hear me because I am the voice of your people."

The gathered did not know what to expect. They understood, however, that Illumkuh, and thus also the high priest, did not support the expedition. Sethon looked at the queen with care and devotion, leaned even more on the tall cane and used the last argument he hoped could get through to her heart.

"You love wisdom, queen, and you want to follow it. It's glorious. As for us, when you leave, we will follow you, when you sit down, we will sit down too. Your death will cause our death because your life is our life[25]. We love you very much. You are our sun and moon, a beautiful gift from the gods. You have a big heart and embrace all the inhabitants of your lands." Saying that, he bowed his head low, and when he raised it, his words sounded like begging. "Don't go to Israel. Do not orphan your people. Don't leave your children unattended. You are our mother!"

There was silence, and a moment later the turmoil rose again, this time much bigger than after the queen's speech. Everyone wanted to share with the ones next to him what they think about the high priest's speech, all at the same time. Many began to shout calling the queen to not leave Sheba.

The Priestess of the Moon looked at the ruler, and when the latter nodded almost imperceptibly, she stood next to the throne and raised both hands, silencing the gathered.

"Queen, priest of Illumkuh, this trip will bring only benefits to Sheba," she adopted such a posture that no one had doubts that her words should be binding for all who listen to her, and that they are fully in accordance with the will of the gods taking care of Sheba.

"The arrangement of stars is favorable for the travel. Gods are with us. This trip will be a great triumph! Those who will participate in it, will remember it for the rest of their life. It will also be a blessing for those who will stay in Sheba, waiting for the queen's return. The gods direct the thoughts and actions of Great Kandake. And they know what is best for us!"

---

[25] "Kebra Nagast" as above XXIV p. 30 The queen's preparation for the travel.

CHAPTER IV

THE CARAVAN OF THE QUEEN OF
THE SOUTH

Fifteen months later

On the Mariba - Jerusalem route

After over a year of intensive work, Tamrin finished the preparations for the expedition.

He organized it according to the queen's wishes. Everything he prepared was of the best quality, the greatest, the most magnificent, and durable.

The royal team commanded by Ashenafi received new rich outfits, the maids got dresses, scarves, sandals and jewelry, and servants tunics and coats. Even the camel drivers were equipped with identical vests that they were supposed to put on right before entering Israel. Camels were given new seats and rugs, donkeys received new leather harnesses.

Tents for the queen, which were to be put up during stops, were especially carefully prepared. One of them, especially fancy and exquisite, was planned to be set up just outside Jerusalem, so that Makeda could prepare in it for entry into the city, and if anyone saw it, he was to be sure that it belonged to someone extremely rich.

Tamrin was, of course, the manager of the caravan, and it was protected by the commander Ashenafi, who took a hundred soldiers with him for the expedition. The queen was accompanied by hemet Seshep, the High Priestess with her retinue, and numerous servants managed by Varda. While Queen was absent, Mariba was looked after by Hendake, and Aksum by General Tesfa.

Splendor and majesty - these words most faithfully reflected what the Shebeans were proudly thinking, looking at the caravan leaving the city. Seven hundred and ninety-seven camels carrying heavy load walked in it, as well as countless mules and donkeys. The soldiers were on horseback.

They walked through the desert sands, along the Red Sea, pass towns, villages and settlements. Most often, however, they moved through areas unfriendly to people, therefore almost uninhabited.

Their tall, strong camels could withstand up to twenty days without water and food, covering 20 miles each day, carrying riders and huge luggage. People had to stop more often though. With this in mind, Tamrin planned his trip so that every few days of the walk, he would stop in the oases or set up a camp in the desert, so that both people and animals could rest.

One evening after a meal, when the caravan had been staying in the oasis for two days, the queen invited the Grand Priestess to her tent.

"I want to talk about men," she began as they both settled on the nearby sofas. The frames were made of bamboo to make them light for the transport. After unfolding them, the servants put comfortable mattresses on top, over which they spread soft, colorful fabrics.

Makeda's tent was furnished with a luxury worth the queen. There was everything she needed for the trip. Jugs with wine and beer, fruit platters and her favorite fig and date cookies were placed on the low tables. Part of the tent was intended for a bathhouse, not very large, but comfortable, in which the central place was occupied by a copper bathtub designed for morning and evening baths. There was also a large mirror made of gold plate, and travel cases with oils and perfumes.

The servants reported to noble-born Varda - general Tesfa's daughter. From childhood, Varda dreamed of exploring the world. She wanted to meet people in countries that lay behind mountains and rivers, to see the statues of their gods, houses and palaces. And she only knew Mariba and Aksum. So, when the news of the expedition spread over Sheba, she begged her father to recommend her to the queen. Tesfa gave in to his daughter's request, although reluctantly, because Varda's mother was not thrilled with the idea.

Till then, Makeda had only known her from big ceremonies; she was not sure if the girl would bear the burden of managing the servants during such a large and long-lasting expedition, but she agreed because of her sympathy for Tesfa. In addition, Hendake's word did weight in for her. He had known Varda almost since she was born and he was sure that she could deal with any challenge, and even if not with all of them, she would have the opportunity to quickly learn whatever she could not do yet.

The daughter of General Tesfa joined Makeda's closest circle as her trusted assistant. She was wise, well-organized, joyful, and because she could write and read, and was not much older than the queen, she quickly became her favorite. It did not escape Makeda's attention that Varda had showed interest toward Tamrin's since the beginning of the journey. She liked the random looks she gave him whenever he appeared in the area and the way she listened to what he was saying. She also understood her sadness when the merchant, instead of responding with even the tiniest smile, seemed to pay no attention to her.

"Tamrin doesn't notice her or wants her to think that way, but she is in a much better position than I am anyway," Makeda watched Varda with understanding. "At least she knows the one to whom her heart goes out."

She thanked for what the servants had prepared for her meeting with the Priestess.

"I'll let you know if I need anything," she told Varda, asking her this way to let everyone leave the tent.

She didn't want anyone to listen to what she was going to ask her mentor about. She did not feel uncomfortable about the topic, because she thought that it was one like any other, but her ignorance intimidated her. What could connect a man and a woman was one of the few spheres that Seshep, who was involved in the education of the princess, did not take care of.

"As you know, priestess, I have never met a man," she began. "And I think that it will never be given to me as a queen who wants to sit on the throne herself. As we know, the ruler of Sheba must be a virgin."

"That's what the tradition says," the priestess smiled, understanding her embarrassment. "But remember that the gods gave us bodies to use them in various ways. Our eternal souls are placed in them, so we should take care of them, nourish them well, give them sleep. We need the body to taste different colors of life. Thanks to it, we know what suffering is and what pleasure is. Not all souls, as you know, receive bodies. Many of them have been waiting for their turn from the beginning of the world, and sometimes it never comes. So those who are lucky, should do everything to spend their time on earth in the best possible way. Isn't it so?"

"Of course!"

"Since we were given this joy to be able to taste life, we are obliged to take care of our own balance and harmony with everything that is around us," the priestess reached for the goblet of wine that the maid had placed on the low table before leaving the tent. "Do you feel that you live in harmony now?"

Makeda wondered. She felt good. There were many difficult moments in the life she had led so far, but after all, it was beautiful. Its beauty was not only in the wonderful moments, but also in difficult moments, defeats, despair after the death of loved ones, loneliness, distressing lack of her mother, disappointment with Den's behavior, whom she had considered a friend, the wars in which she took part, and the fights she fought every day.

Her life was also the awaiting for her vision of first, the throne to be realized, and then for her to meet the king of her dreams. She knew that her father, while he was still alive, suspected that the one she dreamed of was the king of Israel, and had sent Tamrin to have a look at him and establish contacts with him.

"And if it turns out that the man from my visions is the king of Israel? What should I do then? What should my pursuit of harmony be like?"

"The Lady of the Moon will lead you. Trust her like you have done so far."

"How do I know it's him? I never saw his face in my visions."

The priestess closed her eyes.

"The Silver Mother will tell it to your heart," she assured her. "She has gathered the energy of women who were before us. She knows everything; she contains the wisdom of which you can speak so beautifully. The Lady of the Moon is the eternal wisdom we seek. It has existed and will always exist because it is everything and everywhere. The goddess is guiding you; she is watching you all the time. She is always with you. You can find strength in her. You are like each of us, a feminine emanation of divinity. What you do is always right. Listen to yourself; to your inner rhythm. The goddess who is within us will be your guide, trust her voice in you."

"She's been leading me since I can remember. Her guidance is the most important thing in my life," Makeda also raised her cup of wine. "Who I am now, has been decided by you and Seshep, or the Moon Lady, because she speaks to me through your lips. If that is the case, and it is, then you will admit that she has not told me much about men."

They laughed at the same time.

"As you know, the priestesses of the Moon don't start a family, because all their lives they serve only the goddess."

"But you can meet men, isn't it so?"

"Not all of us, but of course we can. You know that there are hemet who have sworn that they will not be touched by a man all their lives. They serve at the altar. Others are free in their choices, they can decide about their bodies, but their main duty is always to serve the goddess."

"Can they leave the temple, for example?" Makeda, who had not heard a similar case happen in her lifetime, kept asking.

So far, similar topics have not concerned her much. Sheba's custom dictated that the ruling queen would remain a virgin. And this knowledge was enough for her. She didn't need to know more. However, the closer the caravan approached Jerusalem, the more intrigued she was about the relationship with men.

"They can if they turn out to be pregnant. Then they should marry the man whose child they are expecting."

"I don't remember anything like that happen in my lifetime."

"The Lady of the Moon has revealed to us the ways to experience the body pleasure without creating a new life."

"Will you tell them to me?"

"Of course, immediately, if the need arises. But you don't have to worry about that now, because you're a virgin." The priestess put down the chalice. "If it turned out that you received the gift of a new life from the gods, it would be a great joy for all of us and a cause for celebration for Sheba. Because it would mean an act of special grace that your guardian, Lady of the Moon, would give you."

"Have you ever experienced such a grace?"

"What do you mean?"

"Is your child walking around the world somewhere?"

"Just like in the case of Great Kandake, so also the High Priestess has offspring only when the Lady of the Moon wants it."

"In your case, she didn't want to?"

"No."

"But you could have them with the king."

"I could," it was obvious to her that Makeda knew the nature of her relationship with Nikal. "I've always visited your father on a full moon. This is one of the high priestesses' ancient duties and privileges."

"You don't have to excuse yourself. I was glad you were with him. He was so lonely."

"When your mother died, he wasn't looking for a woman. He sent away those that came to his bed. Over time, the eunuch Hendake and priest Sethon stopped trying to introduce to him women to marry, or even concubines. However, once, almost three years after the queen's death, during the full moon, he invited me to his chamber. He confessed that your mother was the love of his life. I have visited him every month since then, and it was so until his death."

"Thank you for that."

"I suffered a lot when he passed. He was the only man I loved."

"I knew you were visiting him, and you had a great affection for him, but I didn't think it was love."

The priestess touched her ring that she never took off.

"It's from him," she said, turning it on her finger. "I wish you could ever love someone as much as I loved him."

They fell silent, each remembering Nikal in their own way. Makeda spoke after a moment.

"How can I be sure that this is the one I've been waiting for all my life, whom I miss, even though I don't know him? Once, in my childhood, I thought I loved Den, remember? I liked to cuddle with him when we looked at the stars together. We felt good together. It wasn't until later, when he confessed to me what plans he and his family had for me, that I understood that it certainly wasn't love between us, but rather a friendship of children and then teenagers, and it seems it was mostly on my part. I felt lonely. I didn't know my peers. I have been raised to be a queen since I was a child. And as my father used to say, queens don't have friends."

"They do sometimes. But Den wasn't one."

"Don't say that! I believe that he had good intentions, he just surrendered to his father. And he wasn't a good man."

"The time will come when it will turn out what the truth was."

"Exactly!" Makeda laced her hands into a basket, as she often did when she wanted to focus. "What's the truth about my visions? Perhaps the one I dreamed about is just a figment of my imagination? Does he even exist? King on the golden throne," resigned, she lowered her head. "Sometimes I feel like I'm chasing a phantom from a dream. Perhaps the high priest Sethon was right in saying that I should not go to an unknown land, sent by dreams remembered from my childhood? 'Know that your dreams, even those that seemed like a real vision to you, could only be an illusion,' he told me that before leaving. 'If you leave the country, you may lose the grace of Illumkuh. God will leave you and Sheba.' Priestess, what if it really happens?"

"Do not be afraid, and always believe the voice of your heart. All the truths of this world are contained in it. You know the old principles of priestesses. Live now and here. Do not think too much about the past and the future. Do not focus on what is not here. You know them."

Makeda nodded.

"The high priest is afraid of losing power. Illumkuh is an old god, not as strong as he once was. Sethon knows that, after all his priests can also look into the future. He is worried about what may come; he wants to prevent what is inevitable."

The last words of the priestess were drowned out by the sounds of commotion in front of the tent. After a while, Varda came in.

"Queen, please forgive me, but the commander Ashenafi and merchant Tamrin ask for an urgent hearing."

"What happened?"

"The guards caught someone."

"Let them come in," Makeda ordered. "We will not be able to finish this conversation today, priestess."

"All the most important things have been said."

They sat down, assuming poses suitable to receive guests.

"May the gods lead you, queen," began the commander.

"Tell me what happened that was important enough to disturb the queen's evening rest?" Makeda asked gently, confident that no one would dare to worry her for a trivial reason.

"We captured a suspicious man. He does not belong to the caravan, but he follows us."

"Who is he?"

"He claims to be Solomon's man."

At the sound of the royal name, Makeda stood up. So did the Great Priestess too.

"Bring him," she commanded, hiding her excitement.

After a while, a tall, swarthy young man stood before her, who looked not much older than her.

Makeda's beauty must have made a great impression on him because, despite the fact that he knew who he was dealing with, he stared at her as if enchanted, instead of humbly dropping his eyes.

"Bow to the ruler of Sheba," Tamrin admonished him in Hebrew, and only then did he make a clumsy bow.

"Ask him who sent him and why," Makeda told Tamrin, not wanting to reveal to the stranger that she knew his language.

"I am acting on the order of the greatest of kings, Solomon," he said, with his head bowed. "He ordered us to watch your caravan, and in case something bad happens, to support you, lady, and let him know immediately."

"Did he say: us? Have I understood well?" Makeda asked Tamrin.

"That's what he said."

"Then ask who he means by that?"

Tamrin repeated the queen's question in Hebrew.

"Even though you still have a long way to go, you are already in the lands of Israel. The territory of our kingdom is vast. The king sent a group of six scouts. Solomon wants the queen to reach her destination safely and without any unexpected adventures."

"Give your king thanks and greetings from Queen Makeda," she said, and Tamrin translated. "And to thank him for the care that he has shown us, I have a gift for him," she nodded at Varda and said something quietly to her.

After a while, the girl came back with a beautiful cage made of gold wires, shaped intricately into floral patterns. There was a small bird inside.

"It's a hoopoe," the queen explained. "My present to Solomon. There is a long way to Israel. Promise me you'll bring it alive."

Tamrin smiled. In this company, only he and Makeda knew why the queen had given Solomon a hoopoe.

Jerusalem

Seven days later

"Lord, the Queen of Sheba is sending you a gift," said the palace manager Ahijah, entering the chamber in which Solomon worked every morning.

The king, in the company of Yoshenaf, Nathan, Sadok, and Elichoref, looked at the designs of golden equipment that was to be placed in the temple of Yahweh.

Everyone's eyes turned to Ahijah.

"A gift from Queen of Sheba?" The king did not hide his surprise.

"One of the scouts you sent to watch the caravan brought it."

"What is it?"

Ahijah gesticulated at the servant who, after a moment, brought a golden cage.

"It's a hoopoe," Elichoref noticed, laughing, remembering when not long ago he had told Solomon about the role that this inconspicuous bird played, according to folk tales, in the life of the King of Israel.

"I like the Queen of Sheba's sense of humor," Solomon appreciated the gift, then shared the story of the hoopoe with the men in the room.

"Apparently, this story also reached her," he concluded, amused, because he was almost certain that the story reached the people of Israel on her order, most likely through Tamrin and his men.

"She can build tension skillfully," he thought with appreciation, more and more intrigued.

The caravan

last stop before Jerusalem

"How to welcome the king who knows everything, has everything, and has seen everything?" the priestess wondered aloud. "How can a young girl intrigue him, when there are still seven hundred women married to him, all of whom are ready to do anything for him?"

Makeda, the High Priestess, Seshep, and Varda as well as everyone else trusted by the queen, wondered for a long time how their ruler could not only be noticed at Solomon's court, but also make an unforgettable impression. They wanted the requests for Israel's future trade agreements to take the utmost account of the interests of the Sheba kingdom. This was the main purpose of their ruler's visit to this country, for many of them the real one.

Actions initiated by Tamrin the year before were successful. At a time when it was already known when the queen would go to Jerusalem, the merchant paid the people who saw to it that the news of the beautiful, wise, and unimaginably rich queen reached Jerusalem. Through the wandering storytellers, they spread wider and wider. The story of the hoopoe, already known to the king, was also created in this way. So, when Makeda, sometimes also called Bilkis or the Queen of the South, came to the lands of Moses, she was already a known and expected figure there.

"Men are not my passion, I don't know much about them," Seshep said what each of them already knew. "But if I were Solomon, forgive me my honesty, lady, I don't think the thousandth woman coming to me, even as beautiful as you, could really interest me. She would have to be... I don't know, I don't know..." she wondered loudly and ended up perversely, "richer than the Pharaoh's daughter?"

Makeda laughed out loud, and so did Varda as well. Even the High Priestess smiled a little. They all knew that Pharaoh's daughter occupies the most prominent place among all Solomon's wives and that she was considered the richest of them.

"I am Solomon," Seshep assumed a haughty pose and looked at the women as she had imagined the king might look. "My god gave me everything I wanted. The surrounding kings send me gifts, the country is developing well, I have powerful friends, and women cling to me like bees to honey."

"What do you need, sir?" Makeda asked, joining the party joyfully. "Is there something you don't have that could touch your heart?"

"I don't know. I don't know," Seshep repeated the words she had used before and crossed her arms over her chest. "My heart is devoted to God. It's in him I find fulfillment."

"Oh," the High Priestess sighed, "maybe Seshep is right? After all, it may turn out that Solomon is a ruler so inspired that our most original ideas and efforts will be of no avail."

"Not at all!" Varda exclaimed excitedly. "Tamrin said, and you must have heard it, that Solomon knows the joys of life. Although he is reserved, he can enjoy what the world offers him!"

The priestess looked at her gently.

"We know about your weakness for Tamrin. None of his words will escape you, so we believe in what you say unreservedly. You said, 'Solomon loves life.' Have you heard it, Solomon?" she asked Seshep, who was still standing in a man's way and with her head raised high.

"I am Solomon, a wise king who knows everything and has everything, and at the same time loves life and can appreciate its charms," the hemet announced in a loud voice. "How will you surprise me, Queen of the South?" she asked Makeda directly. "What will your pretty head come up with for me?"

"My head, King Solomon, is not only pretty, but also wise," she replied, and the tone of her voice indicated that the situation was no longer amusing to her.

Seshep noticed this and immediately sat down.

"Forgive me, queen."

Makeda was young and did not have much self-confidence yet, even though she was trying to make people think so. So sometimes, especially when she was overtired, she was annoyed when someone doubted her reason or her mind, even jokingly.

There was tension in the air. The Great Priestess fell meaningfully silent. She knew that there were situations in life when people needed time to breathe and get some perspective on other people's statements and thoughts. This was one of those moments. The fatigue from the long journey and the tension that each of them felt, had to vent. Makeda was the most burdened. The difficult duties, arising from the role she played, were on her shoulders. She was the queen and no matter how hard the people around her would get involved and try, the whole odium of victory or defeat of the expedition would fall on her.

Makeda was in a double difficult situation. On the one hand, she wanted to do everything to achieve the purpose of the expedition regarding trade agreements. On the other hand, she had a great, troubling hope of fulfilling her visions in which she meets a man who gives her the most precious treasure in the world. She carried these burdens, fears and responsibilities alone, despite the fact that she had so many kind and devoted people around her.

"I know I can do it," she said when the tension over the prolonged silence passed, and each of them had already calmed down her thoughts. "Everything that is going to happen is written up there," she raised her head and smiled at the stars.

"Of course, you can, Makeda," said the High Priestess. "You are strong! The Moon Lady watches over you."

At these words Seshep, who didn't say a word from the moment she apologized to Makeda for her jokes, stood up again, and assumed the pose of Solomon once more.

"I know, my queen, what my desire is," she said loudly, holding her head high, as befits a king. "Women make themselves available to me, each of them comes with a snap of my fingers. I am the ruler they are waiting for, whom they desire and before whom they open like flowers in the morning. I would finally like to meet the one who will be a mystery and a puzzle for me. Whom I will have to try my best and strive for, one that will not give in to me, who I will want to fight for. One that would be beautiful and wise, good and kind, but at the same time unavailable. That's what I want! I, King Solomon!"

Kingdom of Israel

At the same time

The inhabitants of Judah and Israel were as numerous as sand on the seashore. Everyone had something to eat and drink and all were happy*. Solomon had power from the Euphrates River to the land of the Philistines and all the way to the borders with Egypt. All countries paid tribute to him and were subjected to him during his days of life. Solomon's empire was so huge that he considered it necessary to divide it into twelve provinces.

The royal overseers, who each managed in a different province, took care, each for one month, of the food for the king and those who were invited to his table*. They made sure they didn't lack anything. The daily food supply for Solomon was: thirty kor of the purest flour and sixty kor of plain flour**, ten fat oxen and ten oxen taken straight from the pasture, a hundred sheep, and deer, gazelles, fallow deer and specially fattened birds.

The overseers also imported barley and straw for both draft horses and the mounts. They delivered it to the stables, of which the king had four thousand for the horses to his chariots and twelve thousand for the mounts.

Solomon stood on the terrace. In the same place where his mother once told him how she met and got to love his father. He was looking at his city. It got more beautiful and strengthened every year. He was proud. The work in the temple was still going on and there was a lot to be done, but it was slowly coming to an end.

There was peace in the country and its borders.

"Blissful harmony," he said to himself. "Nothing disturbs the peace of the state. Thanks be to God."

He raised his head, looked at the sky, smiled and spread his arms wide as if to fly.

On the way

Somewhere in Israel

One night, while we were still walking but already quite close to Jerusalem, and we stopped for the night, the priestess came for me. There was a full moon. At such times the Silvery Mother was always more eager than at other lunar phases to give us her support and open the gates to the unknown. I did not sleep, as usually on full moon nights. The priestess wanted me to look into the future.

We left the camp watched by the guards. None of the four that we passed on the way dared to ask where and why the hemet, with a white dagger strapped to his belt, and the High Priestess, leading one of her two favorite leopardesses on the gold chain, were moving away from the camp. They knew that as it was full moon, we could have important things to do. Besides, who would have the courage and audacity to stop or even ask a question to the High Priestess?

We left far enough away from the camp to not see the lights of its bonfires. There was a bloody full moon that night, which is extremely rare. Lady of the Moon reveals her secrets for those who can properly ask for it.

We knelt to worship our patron. We said a long thanksgiving prayer and asked to give me the grace of learning the future.

"Lady of the Moon, reveal the secret of the world to us, show us what awaits our queen Makeda. How can we support her so that she achieves what you have destined for her? Please show us what is important to us. Show us the future," cried the High Priestess, still kneeling, but with her hands raised. "Let us look into the power of the cosmos and in return take what I offer you from the bottom of my heart. Let the energies of giving and taking remain in harmony. Accept the gift and send what I humbly ask for."

Saying this, she reached out, asking me to pass her the dagger. We used it only to make sacrifices. It was the property of every successive High Priestess. It was said that it has been in our temple since its inception. Apparently, it was given to the first

High Priestess by the Lady of the Moon herself, who personally made it from moon dust. It never rusted or blunted. In addition to the dagger, we had a small silver bowl with us. It was used to collect the blood needed to perform the ritual. Both the dagger and the vessel were protected by the power of the Lady of the Moon.

In ancient times, the priestesses of the Silver Mother made human sacrifices. They were usually girls with clean, uncontaminated bodies or boys before initiation. I saw drawings showing such rituals on the walls in the oldest part of our temple. Centuries ago, the Moon Lady banned such sacrifices. Perhaps, had I lived many centuries earlier, I would have been one of those whose lives were sacrificed to her? In the meantime, however, I was here and now, and I made the sacrifice, or at least participated in it. The High Priestess's leopardess was to be laid on the improvised altar. It was a huge gift on her part because she had the female cat for at least ten years, and she loved her very much. Just like her sister from the same litter, who had stayed in the priestess's tent that night. The blood sacrifice meant that, just like centuries ago, the goddess had to receive something valuable that someone gave her with all their heart, knowing it would cause them a great loss and regret. However, this was done for a higher purpose. Therefore, the choice of the priestess fell on one of the leopardesses. I appreciated her decision because I knew how attached she was to her cats, but I also understood that the goddess's favor required giving her something special. Otherwise we wouldn't get an answer to our questions.

"Come here, my little one," the priestess patted the place on the small blanket she laid out in front of her. Beside her stood a silver bowl prepared to receive blood. The leopardess, who had been lying quietly a few steps away from us till now, raised her head and, seeing that her lady was calling her, obediently lay down in front of her.

The priestess patted her head tenderly.

"Goodbye my love," she said softly. "Go to the Silver Mother now. Serve her as best you can and love her as you love me..." With her left hand still on the animal's head, she raised her dagger with her right hand and dug it straight into the heart of the cat.

The leopardess jerked her head in the last defensive reflex and dug her teeth into the priestess's hand. The blood that spurted almost at the same time from a punctured heart and a torn hand, merged into one sacrificial stream.

"Lady of the Moon," cried the Priestess, as if she felt no pain. "Take this sacrifice as the proof of our love, faith and trust in your power. Protect us and give us strength to fulfill your will. Let us look into the future and let what we see inspire us to act properly. Let it be so!"

"Let it be so," I repeated her words and we both bowed low.

The moon's disc was bright above us. It was blood red in color. The goddess favored us.

Still kneeling, I leaned over the bowl that the priestess put in front of me. It was filled with blood. I leaned even lower so that I almost touched the surface of the red liquid with my nose and inhaled its smell. I felt dizzy. Then the priestess took out a tiny vial, opened it, and poured its contents into the vessel I was bending over.

"Drink it," she said.

I knew that in this way I would quickly connect with the Lady of the Moon. I had done it before more than once. I picked up the bowl and drank enough to leave some blood on the bottom, because it was in it that I should see what the Silver Mother wanted to show us.

My head spun. The priestess again helped me lean over the bowl. I stared at it motionless and felt my senses sharpen.

After a while, I first saw great brightness, and then the images.

"Speak!" I heard the priestess's voice coming as if from other words. "What do you see?"

"I see the queen on the throne. A boy is sitting next to her. He is beautiful."

"Anyone else there?"

"This boy is her son. She loves him very much."

"Isn't Solomon there?"

"He is not there. The queen is alone; great, strong, and lonely."

"Just like each of us ," I heard the priestess's voice. " Every woman is great, strong, and lonely. Even if she is a queen. Or maybe even more so? This is our path in this world," she said very quietly, thinking that I could not hear her.

"Look around," she ordered. "Is this our palace?"

"It's the throne room."

"Where?"

"In Mariba. The throne is huge. Steps guarded by two golden lions lead to it. Makeda puts her arm around the boy."

"Look at the people."

"I see you. You are dignified and beautiful. There is General Tesfa, Tamrin. A woman is standing next to him. She is his wife. She is pregnant."

"Who is this?"

"It's Varda."

"Why is everyone in this room? What are they doing there?"

"I do not know. I am looking at them, but I don't understand. They are moved but satisfied."

"Look closely. See what happened. Why are they there?"

I tried to understand what I was witnessing for a long time. I looked at people, but I didn't hear what they were saying. I saw their gestures and how they moved their lips, commenting vividly. I finally got it.

"I think we've won the war," I said with relief.

The priestess tried to learn more from me, but the picture was getting foggy. Before it disappeared completely, she managed to ask me one more thing.

"Look at the boy again. Who is he like?"

"He has dark hair, dark eyes, and fair skin."

"How old is he?"

"Two? Three? Four at most. I don't know much about children."

I saw and told the priestess that much. Fortunately, it was enough for her to stop worrying about Sheba's future.

Then my head rumbled, I felt as if something burst inside me and I fell asleep.

When I woke up, the sun was rising. The priestess, with traces of tears on her face, lay near me with her hand on the dead body of the leopardess.

Jerusalem

At the same time

Shalom means peace in Hebrew. Solomon was the one who, according to God's will, was to bring shalom to the lands of Israel, and make the kingdom powerful, rich, and stable like never before. The completion of the construction of the temple for Yahweh was to be the culmination of the first stage of the implementation of the divine plan. This moment was coming but work in the temple was still going on.

Ever since he sat on the throne, he used his wisdom to reach agreement with all the neighbors. The wars fought by his father came to an end. He preferred other methods of acting and finding allies. He married the daughter of Pharaoh, which not only ensured him peace with Egypt, but also new territories. Together with the princess, he received the city of Gezer. He loved Pharaoh's daughter with sincere love, and Gezer, like several other border towns, served him as a city-warehouse in which he kept horses and chariots*.

He won over King Hiram, the ruler of Tyre, with whom his father was in almost constant conflict, by ordering from him huge amounts of cedars needed to build the temple. In this way, Hiram became not only his largest trading partner, but also a political friend**. The cooperation worked so well that the kings reached an agreement that was to result in the expansion of the port and the creation of the largest merchant fleet in the Red Sea. Hiram knew shipbuilding and sailing like hardly any ruler, and Solomon had a small but perfectly situated port. They made a deal. They planned to create a new trade route, competitive for the one that had existed for centuries and was controlled by Egypt. The port belonging to Solomon was on the road from India to Tarshish, the largest port in the south-east part of the Iberian Peninsula. So, it was perfect to be the most important point of the new way.

Solomon's wisdom and justice were known in the world. The fame of his verdicts was far-reaching, as was the information that scales weigh fairly in Israel, and that efa and hin weights do not cheat***.

Solomon thought proudly of the recent years of his rule. God favored him. Thanks to him, Israel became a new market center for buyers from around the world. Taxes collected from them enriched the royal treasury and allowed for incurring huge costs of building the temple.

The king thanked Yahweh every day for the protection of his nation.

Shebeans' camp

Two days later

"Lord, I'd like to talk to you," Varda came up to the tent of the caravan manager.

It was late evening. Tamrin was getting ready to rest after a hard day. The servant standing in front of the entrance put his finger to his lips when he heard her voice.

"He's sleeping," he said in a whisper. "If everyone is alive, nothing is so urgent that it can't wait until morning."

However, seeing her desperate eyes and understanding who he was dealing with, he added, "Unless it is something very urgent indeed..."

Varda pushed him aside and without entering the tent, stood close enough to touch the cloth covering the entrance. She spoke so loudly that she was sure Tamrin would hear her even in his sleep.

"Administrator, I need to talk to you urgently. It can't wait until morning!" she added a little quieter, because she realized that she did not behave quite as befits a queen's confidant, "Would you like to give me a moment?"

There was movement in the tent, and before she could repeat her plea even louder, Tamrin pulled the curtain back and stepped outside.

If she wasn't the queen's confidant, the daughter of general Tesfa, and in addition a virgin, he would let her inside. Their conversation could take place in the tent. However, out of respect for her, he had to go outside and talk in the open.

"What happened, lady?"

"Excuse me, administrator," she realized that when he would find out what she was coming with, he might be angry, but she couldn't wait any longer with her confession. " This doesn't concern the queen or the caravan, or anything related to our service.

"What is it then?" he asked.

"It's a completely private matter," she confessed already very quietly.

"Let's take a walk then," he suggested, pointing with his hand.

He signaled the servant to stay. He understood that the situation was special, and seeing Varda's unusual behavior and her restraint, which replaced the previous desperation, he thought that he would hear something truly unusual.

He had been watching her for a long time. She always listened carefully to his words, observed him, watched his management activities. He felt that she liked and admired him. He liked her too, and he had moments when looking at her he was thinking that if he decided to start a family in the right time, sometime long ago, his daughter could be just her age. Before leaving Mariba, General Tesfa entrusted her to his particular care.

"Tamrin, treat her like your own child," he beseeched. "She is leaving home intact; I want her to return like that too. You are responsible for her."

"General, I will treat her like my own daughter," he was sure he would keep his promise.

When they went to the edge of the camp, he spread a cloak on the sand, which the servant handed him at the last moment.

"Let's sit down," he suggested. "Nobody will disturb us here."

She took a seat on the edge, he settled in a proper distance to her.

"So?" he encouraged her when he thought the silence was getting too long.

She cleared her throat. She was abashed. She left her tent with a decision that she would tell him everything, even if she had to do it in front of all his service, because she could no longer bear the tension. She could not cope with it, so she decided to take care of the matter, maybe not in very typical way, but - in her understanding - efficiently and unequivocally. She was still ready for it while in front of the Tamrin's tent, but the walk silenced her excitement. The emotions subsided. She realized that the situation was not only unusual, but also funny.

"What if he rejects me," she thought. "He will make fun of me, will say I'm too young for him and he treats me like a daughter? What if my words offend him? After all, he is the richest man in Sheba; he can have every woman he chooses. He doesn't have to wait for someone like me to give him affection. Hundreds of women must admire him. If only he wanted, he could have any of them."

"Actually, I think I can deal with this problem myself," she said quietly, looking at her feet.

"What?" he pretended to be upset. "You pull me out of my bed in the middle of the night and drag me into the desert to say you can handle your problem?!"

"I didn't bring you here," she protested.

"You better come up quickly with a sensible reason why we're here, otherwise we'll stop being friends tomorrow!"

"We have been friends?" her intimidation was over. "Really?"

"Yes. Haven't you noticed?"

"No. You always treat me as if I were a burden to you," she complained. "You hardly talk to me; you don't let us ever be alone."

"I treat you like a daughter," he assured her.

"Exactly!"

"What's wrong with that?"

"I don't want you to treat me like that."

"How would you like to be treated?"

"I'm a woman!

"It's hard not to notice."

"Somehow you manage not to!"

"Are you making a scene? Am I hearing right?"

Until then, they were at a distance which they had determined for themselves by sitting on the two ends of the coat spread on the sand. Now, however, Varda turned to him sharply, knelt down and looked into his eyes.

"Don't you really understand anything?" she raised her voice, emphasizing her words with spreading her hands. "I will go crazy because of you! Can't you see that I love you? Is it so hard to see?"

He looked into her eyes and said nothing. His face didn't express any emotion, even though his heart almost jumped to his throat.

"I got to love you when you visited my father's house a long time ago. I remember it as if it was today. You came back from one of your trips, bringing an air of extraordinary far lands to our chambers. You brought presents and stories. I could listen to you for hours. When you treated my parents and their guests with them, I sat quietly, always somewhere near you, so as not to miss a word. I dreamed of being able to go on a trip with you, to get to know the places you talked about, see people and animals with my own eyes. And every year I became more and more attached to you. As I grew up, I realized that I would do anything to be with you. I begged my father to ask the queen to be her confidant because I really wanted to be with you. I could not imagine that you would once again go away for long months, and I would wait for your return hoping that maybe someday you would notice me and give me at least a part of the feelings that I have for you. I rejected everyone who wanted me as a wife, waiting for you. My father announced that I must choose a husband after returning from Israel, because a woman my age, if she is not a priestess, should have children. I gave him my word that it would happen according to his will. I was hoping that this journey would bring us closer, that you would notice how I feel about you."

She finished. She closed her eyes and gently placed her hands on her knees, feeling that her long held emotions had finally found a vent. Now she was waiting for his reaction.

"Varda," he began calmly. "I really like you. And thank you for what you told me. I imagine how hard it was for you to hide the feelings you are talking about. You have decided to tell me about them. It is good."

She looked at him hopefully.

"But I want you to know it: I'm not a man for you."

Her heart froze. She expected what he would say next.

"Don't tell me we'll be friends. I can't take this!"

"That's what I want to offer you."

"So, don't offer it!" She got angry.

"Varda, you are a beautiful and smart girl. Pure and honest. The whole world opens the gates for you. Come through them. You will see how it will delight you. You deserve it. But be sure that I am not the one with whom you should go through life. After all, I could be your father."

"It doesn't matter," she protested weakly, painfully realizing that he had a completely different opinion about their being together.

"I promised the general that you would be safe and that you would return home intact. And that's what will happen."

"So, it's because of my father?" she called, rising from her seat.

He also stood up and seeing that Varda was about to flee, grabbed her hands.

"I am a mature man, I got to know the sides of life you are better off not knowing about. I know its darkest and most hideous corners, I'm a man worn out by life. I am not suitable for you. You need someone like you: fresh, good and undefiled. You will marry one of the princes or a noble son of your age, who has not come to know the dark sides of life as I did."

"Maybe I don't want it?" she shouted desperately.

"Do you want to live with a man who has met dozens of women before you? Corrupted by what he saw and survived, spoiled by abundance?"

"Do you think you'll discourage me by talking about the women you had?"

"That's exactly what I think."

"You're wrong! No matter what you tell me about yourself, I will love you anyway," she said.

He felt that even though she was trying to break free, he should hold her for a moment longer and stop her from crying. He did not want her to run tearful around the camp because he knew that it would draw the attention of everyone who would see her. Rumors would start, which would be humiliating for her. He wanted to avoid it at all costs.

"If you calm down, I'll let you go," he promised, looking into her eyes. "And don't cry. You are a strong girl, I know you; you can do it."

"I hate you " she hissed, trying to free her hands."

"All right, I understand," he nodded, trying to smile. "But I won't let you go anyway. The queen's confidant should not run in tears among the servants."

"I am not crying," she said firmly, taking control of her emotions.

"And that's good. Why would you cry? You have no reason. You are just furious." He laughed, knowing that he would help by calling her emotions.

He was right.

"Have I told you I hate you?" she said almost conciliatorily.

"Yes, you more or less mentioned it."

"I'm calm now, as you can see," she said. "You can let me go."

"We'll have a tough day tomorrow," he reminded.

"I know. We enter the lands adjacent to Jerusalem."

"Exactly."

"And what about that?"

"We should be well rested."

"Of course, administrator Tamrin," she folded her arms. "Thank you for your time and I am sorry for the excessive emotions that I could not control."

"You have nothing to apologize for, Varda," he was almost tender. "Maybe we will return to this conversation in more favorable circumstances?"

"May the gods give you a quiet night," she said between clenched teeth. She turned on her heel and walked away.

He followed her with his eyes.

"What   a   woman!"   he   murmured   in   awe.

CHAPTER V

JERUSALEM

Kingdom of Israel

Six months after leaving Sheba

The Great Kandake, the Queen Makeda, was approaching Jerusalem.

People said that when the beginning of her caravan reached the city gates, its end was still in the kingdom of Sheba, it was that long. No one could count the camels, and there were so many pack mules and donkeys that even when many years earlier the Pharaoh's daughter, considered the richest of Solomon's women, arrived in Israel, no one saw such an amount of animals, wealth and splendor that accompanied the Queen of the South.

Her fame traveled ahead of her. Although Jerusalem had only recently begun to talk about her beauty, kindness, wisdom and power, the stories were so colorful that she became the heroine of the imagination of the inhabitants of not only Jerusalem, but all of Israel, and even the neighboring countries.

The caravan stopped outside the city in the place indicated to Tamrin by Josephat, the king's representative. The camp was set up there. Solomon invited the queen and the most important people from her surroundings to the palace, where he allocated numerous chambers for them.

Makeda crossed the city gates preceded by Ashenafi soldiers, led by their proudly upright commander. They rode horses.

People's costumes and animal's accessories shone with gold and silver. Merchant Tamrin was riding behind them, on a white horse. He was known in Jerusalem as the one whom Solomon trusted, and because he was also generous and liked fun, he had many friends in the city. This time he came to Jerusalem not only as a merchant and the ambassador for Sheba, but as a trusted guide for his queen, of whom Jerusalem inhabitants heard mostly of due to him.

The Queen of the South looked at the city from the height of a fancy golden palanquin mounted on a camel. It looked as if she was sitting on a giant four-poster bed, with transparent curtains made of delicate fabric shielding her from the sun. The camel was not only huge and white, which made him look haughty and proud, but it was also generously decorated with gold and precious stones.

She watched the surroundings. Unlike in Mariba, where there were two city gates, there were many more of them here. Most of the streets were paved, almost all the buildings were built of stone. She was amazed at how little wood was used to build them. The people she passed looked with admiration and wonder at her palanquin, the mighty camel, and the adorned retinue.

The High Priestess, Seshep, and Varda followed the queen on slightly smaller, but impressively decorated animals, hidden behind the curtains of smaller palanquins.

The queen's court went directly to the part of the palace designated for them. The two most important people of the king waited there - the plenipotentiary Josephat and the palace manager - Achishar. The writer Elichoref accompanied them.

They hoped that they would be able to see the ruler, whose beauty and wisdom were the subject of legends circulating in Israel. They hoped to see her, just like it was given to a scout who was in her tent a few weeks back, and later told everyone that the Queen of Sheba was the most beautiful woman he had ever seen. Their hopes were only half-fulfilled. They saw her getting out of the palanquin, they bowed, welcoming her on behalf of the king, so they saw her figure, but they neither heard her voice nor saw her face. The queen nodded in a greeting without saying a word, and as she was veiled from head to toe, she only showed them her long-fingered hands, decorated with rings, and narrow feet in soft gold-colored sandals.

After two days of rest, came the meeting for which all Jerusalem had been waiting with bated breath.

Makeda brought with her countless precious presents as a gift for Solomon. She wanted to impress not only the city's inhabitants, but above all the king, with their quantity and quality.

That day, Solomon sat on a throne that was placed in front of the palace especially for her. Queen Bathsheba sat at his right, and the most important of his wives, the daughter of Pharaoh of Egypt, on his left. The priest Sadok, prophet Nathan, Josephat, Achishar, Benaiah and others stood next to them on both sides. Everyone was waiting for the queen to appear.

However, it was the merchant Tamrin, preceded by drummers, who came first as her envoy. He bowed low.

"Solomon, please accept these gifts for your royal majesty as an expression of the Queen of Sheba's admiration for your wisdom and your works, the news of which has reached her," he said in Hebrew. "The queen has come to pay tribute to you."

He bowed again, waiting for the king's permission to present the gifts. When Solomon nodded in agreement, the drums rang again, the pipes, flutes, horns and lutes echoed, and an unusual performance began. The procession with gifts was preceded by servant girls in identical costumes, all of them equally beautiful and all carrying censers on their heads, supporting them with one hand. A smoke of the world's best incense, sweet and at the same time sharp and disturbing, spread throughout the city.

Camels, mules, and donkeys, bearing gifts and led by festively dressed drivers, followed the servants. People and animals had garments made of the same precious fabric adorned with gold fringes. The queen's insignia were visible on the clothes and all the vessels.

Behind the loaded animals came young, strong men. Each of them was carrying something. The heavy pitchers contained white, yellow and cream resin from incense trees, and a red one from myrrh trees. Myrrh leaves were carried in numerous canvas sacks. Enormous amounts of ivory were laid on huge copper trays, reinforced with cedar wood. Nard, ambergris, and black resin obtained from flowers, called laudanum in many lands, coriander, myrtle, fragrant roots, and many valuable spices unknown in Israel till then. They were transported in sacks, bottles, jugs, trays, bowls, small and large glass bottles, and vials.

The servants also placed before the royal palace the furniture from the most valuable types of wood, they brought honey and wine of the best quality, and spread valuable fabrics. Finally, pink and white pearls and precious stones were brought on gold platters and in bowls and placed on the highest part of the stairs leading straight to the palace.

However, what made the biggest impression on those watching the extraordinary spectacle, was one hundred and twenty talents of gold*. The precious metal was brought by servants with naked, wide torsos, whose bodies were covered only by a loincloth. The gold, placed in carefully woven baskets lined with soft materials from India, was carried on litters built so that they could bear the heavy weight of the ore. Each litter was carried by four men. Each was placed near the throne, almost at the royal feet.

The impressive gifts were laid with a wide path created between them, so that the impatiently awaited perpetrator of the admiration of her generosity, The Queen of the South Makeda and her entourage, could pass.

As soon as the bringing of the gifts was completed, a litter appeared, carried by two strong servants, whose ebony skin was thoroughly oiled, which emphasized the beauty of their bodies. A beautiful, mature woman with long dark hair was sitting on a highchair resembling a throne. She had a silver dress, and her head was decorated with a wreath of silver stars, crowned with the image of the full moon.

"The High Priestess of the Moon," Tamrin announced loudly, standing halfway between the throne and the stairs, so that both sides could see and hear him well.

The priestess got off her chair, bowed to the king and stood near Tamrin. She stared at the golden litter, which had just stopped in front of the lowest step of the stairs.

"The Great Kandake, the ruler and mukarrib of the kingdom of Sheba, Lady of Mariba and Axum, Bilkis, Michalide, the Queen of the South, Makeda," Tamrin announced in a loud voice.

At these words, the servants who came shortly after the Great Priestess and were standing in front of the queen's litter, unveiled the silk curtains. A female figure appeared before the eyes of those gathered.

She had a long, light, tight-fitting gown made of a thin fabric, but her body shape could only be guessed because a semi-translucent shawl covered her from head to foot. However, as she walked up the stairs, the lightness of her steps and posture showed how shapely she was. It was also not difficult to notice that she had a narrow waist, because it was emphasized by a wide golden belt decorated with precious stones. Small, but still strong arms and wrists, and hands with long delicate fingers were visible. They were decorated with numerous gold bracelets and rings shining so that their glow could be seen even from under the shawl. Her face aroused the most interest. However, no one had a chance to see it, because the veil covering it was thick.

As she approached the throne, Solomon rose to greet her. He came close to her, hoping that as a king he would be the first to have the pleasure of seeing her face.

For her, it was a replay of her childhood dream. Here the man, for whom she had been waiting for years, was standing before her. The one who had visited her visions so many times that she knew his silhouette, movements and voice almost by heart. The one destined for her by gods was here at her fingertips.

She couldn't get words out, she felt her throat choked by emotions, as always in difficult times, and she thanked the Great Priestess in her thoughts. It was thanks to her that she covered her face with a veil, so no one could see her surprise and stress. Nor the relief that what she had been waiting for, finally happened.

She was trembling. Her body was covered with goose bumps. A moment later, she felt hot.

"Queen of Sheba, on behalf of my people and my own, I welcome you to Israel. It is an honor for us that you wanted to travel such a long way and give us gifts personally. We are grateful to you. I hope that you and everyone who came with you will want to be our guests as long as possible."

Solomon stood in front of her and tried to see at least the outline of her face under the veil. He spoke freely, with warm and soft voice. It made her feel more confident.

"My presence didn't impress him as much as I wanted," she thought. "Seshep was right, joking that he probably didn't dream of me as a child. You can see it in his gestures and words. It's good that he doesn't see my tremors and doesn't know about my fears."

"Mighty Solomon, on behalf of the Kingdom of Sheba and my own, thank you for welcoming us, accepting our gifts and hosting us," she said, causing quite a stir with the melodiousness of her voice, but above all, because she spoke Hebrew fluently.

"You speak the language of Israel " he noted with pleasure.

"Getting to know the language of the king famous for his extraordinary wisdom was and is a great joy for me. I came from afar. I stand here, look at you and see immeasurable wisdom and inexhaustible reason, which are like a lamp in the dark, a pearl in the sea and moonlight in the fog. I come to you not only as to a great king, but also to a master, hoping that the splendor of your wisdom will illuminate also my spirit*."

Solomon thought he could see her eyes shine through the veil. He wanted to reach out and reveal what was covered. He wanted to see the face of the one whom he had been seeing in his imagination for some time. He was already intrigued when he heard for the first time about the unique beauty and wisdom of King Nikal's daughter from Tamrin. It was then that he began to look more closely at Sheba and what was happening there. He found out about the conspiracies, Seth and Den, the priests, but above all, he looked at the princess from a distance, and he knew what was happening to her much better than she might think. When she became a queen, he was almost certain that their fate would merge one day.

Now that she was finally standing in front of him, he felt unsatisfied. Here was the one who recently sent him a hoopoe, thus signaling that she knew the stories circulating about their mutual relations, the one of whose wisdom, beauty and wealth the men of Israel told in the evenings in taverns, and women at the wells, in the fields and in the kitchens. The one who made him wait for this meeting, even though he did not know her, promising him an extraordinary experience. Now that she was finally standing in front of him, he couldn't see her face?

"Wisdom is better than all the treasures of gold and silver; it is the greatest creation on earth," she continued, not abashed by the fact that he was staring at her.   I am looking for asylum in wisdom. I follow it. That's why I'm here, king. I have come, hoping that you will let me draw on the countless resources of your knowledge.

He was delighted with the mystery surrounding her and the sound of her voice, which was to his heart like honey to the tongue. He was dazzled by her outfit, jewelry, but above all, the subtlety and humility flowing from her words. He wanted to see her face so much! As a king, he could ask any other woman to take the veil off, but custom did not allow him to do so to the ruler. Makeda was a queen. Not a princess or a noble daughter, but an individual, independent ruler of a powerful, wealthy state. Therefore, although she was a woman, she had the same rights as any other king visiting Solomon.

"Be my guest for as long as you wish, and for the duration of your stay, let my home be yours. I hope that the rooms I have at your disposal, are at least in part worthy of you and meet your expectations."

It was so. The chambers in the palace that Solomon offered to Makeda were extraordinarily furnished. In addition, the king ordered to supply her every day with fresh fruit, the most beautiful roses from his gardens, and specially sewn dresses from the best fabrics. Furthermore, the queen's court received every day from Solomon's pantry forty-five sacks of flour, ten oxen, five bulls, fifty sheep, as well as goats, deer, cows, gazelles and chickens, wine, honey, fried locusts, and sweets. In addition, twenty-five men and the same number of women sang daily in Makeda's chambers to make her stay more pleasant.**

During the first meeting, the most important people from their circles were introduced, and from the first day, threads of sympathy and agreement, or antipathy, were established. There were people at Solomon's court who felt threatened by Makeda's presence. This was the case of the royal wife, the daughter of Pharaoh, who occupied a unique place in Solomon's life and heart. She immediately sensed a serious rival in the Queen of Sheba. As the most important spouse, she had lived at the court for almost ten years. She felt that the feeling the king had given her many years ago had weakened, but she was certain that he needed an alliance with her father. She thus felt that her position should not change, although she could not be sure about it.

Bathsheba, seeing her son's delighted eyes on the mysterious beauty, was able to perfectly imagine the future development of events.

Joshaphat and Achishar were delighted by her, but as the treasury managers, they admired primarily the size and value of the gifts she brought with her. They wondered what she would want in return, and they were sure that her requests would not be small. They expected that they could relate to trade and perhaps some assurances regarding Sheba's participation in the operations of the maritime fleet, of which the world was talking more and more.

Elichoref noted with pleasure and satisfaction that there was no exaggeration in the stories of the queen he had heard in the taverns and fairs, and because he saw the king being excited about the visit, he rightly thought that there was also a bit of his merit in it.

Benaiah, looking at Ashenafi, his soldiers and their horses, wondered what the armament of the Shebean army looked like compared to Israel, and promised himself to discuss these issues in detail with Ashenafi. Meanwhile, the priest Sadok and the prophet Nathan, appreciating the extraordinary value of the gifts, including gold and the best quality incense, looked at the queen of Sheba as a threat to the peace of their king's mind. They were both worried, because, just like with the queen Bathsheba, the life experience allowed them to predict what would happen next.

Since the moment the prophet Nathan saw the Great Priestess getting out of her litter, despite the fact that she was beautiful and wise in appearance, or maybe because of that, he felt a strange fear, that was in his opinion unjustified. Fear of something perhaps familiar to him, but pushed into such an abyss of his heart, into which he was afraid to look. He felt that these fears, even though he had only experienced their first signals, were going out of control.

"Who is this woman to disturb my peace of mind?" he thought, asking God for support and trusting that nothing that was not Yahweh's intention would happen.

***

Every day, Makeda and Solomon, filled with joy, visited each other. The queen saw his righteous judgments, splendor, and glory. She heard in his words the traces of wisdom, which she knew from the oldest papyri and parchments. How admirable the king was delighted her heart, her mind, eyes and ears. She wondered about what she saw: his perfect figure, reason, wisdom, and mercy. She was touched by the gentleness of his voice, the slight movements of his lips as he gave orders and announced his answers, mindful of the God's presence. She saw all this with her own eyes and was amazed at the enormity of his wisdom. His perfect words lacked nothing*.

He couldn't wait for the moment when she would finally want to show him her face. Despite his great wisdom, he did not know how he could affect her, so that she would like to do it sooner. He couldn't order her to do it, all he could do was to wait and hope that she would do it before she decides to return to Sheba.

Every day he sent her gifts. In addition to dresses and flowers, his servants put in front of her unusual fruit or precious stones of unusual shape, fancy jewelry, or insects that she had never seen before, enclosed in glass boxes, dishes prepared especially for her, and even old papyri and parchments of great value.

The queen always thanked politely, but it seemed that the gifts did not have the slightest impact on the place her voile still occupied. There was no day that Solomon would not wonder what was behind it. The more he thought about it, the stronger the desire to win was awakening in him because he began to treat the matter in terms of a game, or maybe even a fight that he wanted to win. He did not consider any other outcome. The Queen of Sheba was the first woman in his life he had to fight for. He felt the blood in his veins circulate faster, and he liked it a lot.

***

The prophet Nathan, in agreement with the Moses laws, worshiped one God. He believed that Yahweh contained all the male and female elements of this world. He was sure that only him could be prayed to. He condemned faith in idols and regarded it as a manifestation of not only barbarism but of the civilization's immaturity and backwardness. So, when he saw the High Priestess of the Moon, he felt a strange anxiety on one hand, and a mission on the other. He assumed, and was getting more and more convinced with each passing day, that the Supreme himself had sent this woman to him, so that he, the prophet Nathan, would help her get on the right path.

"I understand that people need an image of the gods they pray to, and it is difficult for them to live without it," he said once, when the priestess kissed in his presence her ring with the symbol of the Silver Mother and raised her folded hands to the height of her forehead in a gesture of thanksgiving directed at the goddess. "But you, the High Priestess, who has read more papyri in your life than all the Sheba kingdom's inhabitants put together, do you really believe in the existence of the Lady of the Moon?" he asked, half doubtful, half incredulous.

She knew his intentions before he even spoke those words. She saw through him when she saw him for the first time. A woman can know everything about a man if she wants. All she has to do is just listen to his heart. She already knew that she would have to face him when she saw him for the first time on the stairs in front of the palace, when he was standing next to the

Solomon's throne. It was then already that she looked into his heart and sensed what it contained. She understood his anxiety and knew that it stemmed from a concern for Israel and his king. She also knew that they would come into dispute more than once, which was strange to her because she was convinced that they were both on the same side. At the same time, however, she noted that the prophet Nathan did not think so.

"Gods, in one form or another, are necessary for people to help them every day," she replied calmly. " You believe in Yahweh who has no face and you can't even try to imagine him. This is a rule like any other. It does not bother me, just as the fact that we carry with us the image of the goddess, or some part of it that can be called its symbol. Why not if it makes us feel better? Who is bothered by that, which god?"

"I spoke to Yahweh," he answered with conviction, "he enlightened me."

"And I talked to the goddess," she said with equal solemnity. "She revealed the truth of this world to me."

"The goddess doesn't exist!"

"She exists exactly like your God does."

"Wise people know perfectly well that there is only Yahweh, the only God who is everything."

"Do you think Israeli people are smarter than others?"

"The God chose us. He gave our king the extraordinary wisdom, and makes other kings give us gifts. He has the power to cause other nations to bend their knees before us. Finally, we have the Ark - a symbol of God's covenant with people, and as long as it is with us, we will be the most powerful nation in the world, because we are under the protection of the Most High!" he raised his voice, convinced to the rightness of his truth.

"The Moon Lady is eternal. She had been before the world heard about your God, and she will be long after people forget him."

"Be careful, priestess, Yahweh might punish you for these words," warned the prophet. "He is harsh on those who blaspheme."

"Thank you for your care and the warning, but I believe that I am in a good care," and to emphasize that she was sure of what she was saying, she made a gesture of thanksgiving again, directed at the Lady of the Moon.

***

The time at Solomon's court passed quickly for Makeda. The king gladly met with her, despite the fact that he was busy supervising the construction of the new palace and thousands of other matters related to the management of the state. Everything pointed to the fact that they both took great liking to each other, and it was talked about not only at the court, but throughout the city as well.

Feasts, shows of dance and other arts and skills, expeditions to construction sites and outside the city, long talks about joint commercial ventures, meant that each day they got closer. Still, even though many days had passed since the queen had crossed the gates of Jerusalem, Solomon never saw her face without the veil. Sometimes he could see her lips as she lifted the cloth slightly to taste the dishes served at the feasts, but he couldn't see anything more.

This situation, instead of discouraging him, as his Egyptian spouse hoped, ignited his curiosity even more. He knew hundreds of women, but none of them dared cover their faces from him longer than until the wedding, that is at most for a few days from the moment she arrived at the palace as a gift from one of the kings or princes, grateful to him or willing to earn his favors.

No one could count the women living in Solomon's household. It was said that there were hundreds of them in the palace and other estates throughout Israel. Solomon himself claimed that it was God who commanded him to be with so many of them, so that in the future his descendants could spread throughout the world, live in its various parts and rule over the lands from which their mothers had come. So, even though every man who was subject to the Moses law could have only one wife, Solomon - apart from the daughter of Pharaoh - had many. Among them were Moabites, Ammonites, Edomites, Sidonites, Hethites, and many others. They all came from the nations of which God told Israel's sons: 'Have nothing to do with them, nor let them have anything to do with you, or else they will pull your hearts over to their gods' side.'"*

These words did not apply to Solomon. In any case, he was convinced that it was so. He had many women, yes, but he never prayed to their gods. He allowed them to worship their gods, but none of them lived in his palace so as not to offend the God of Israel. Even the daughter of Pharaoh, whom he loved the most before he met the Queen of Sheba, lived in a separate palace built especially for her.

Managing the court, Achishar, was one of the few who knew how many women the king had, because he knew the living cost for them. He tried not to make this information public, because the financing of the royal court already required great expenditure, and people complained more and more often about the high taxes.

Thus, according to Achishar, Solomon had seven hundred wives and three hundred** concubines, who not only cost the people of Israel a lot, but also worshipped foreign gods.

The Queen of Sheba was different from all the women he had known before. First of all, she was not a princess like most of them, but she ruled a big, rich kingdom. And she not only did it alone, but also with the utmost success.

He admired her. She was twenty years younger than him, and had so much consequence, restraint and wisdom! Unlike the women he knew, who willingly demonstrated the beauty and charms of their bodies to him, her face was still covered by a veil and the body by a shawl. In addition, she seemed not to be interested in the king's physical aspect at all, but only in his mind. He still liked it, but he believed that soon the moment would come when Makeda would want to show him his face.

When they were together, they often played riddles and word games, as was customary at the courts at the time. One of his favorite pastimes was creating proverbs and searching for situations and words that, he said, raised individual human cases to the generalized rules.

The king's writer, Elichoref, accompanied him almost constantly, always having a tablet, piece of papyrus or parchment on hand, on which he recorded Solomon's best thoughts, and almost every one of them was valuable, because God gave his favorite an uncommon mind. According to Solomon's plan, they were the bases for a book to be created that could support and guide people in making choices and living in accordance with God's laws.

Makeda flourished in his company. Her heart was happy. She felt fulfilled. She quickly discovered that getting to know him was a way for her to know herself.

Every day, she entered new paths and discovered new areas of life. She admired Solomon's lightness of mind, wit and openness, accompanied by an unforced, calm peace of mind. He was never in a hurry. He spoke in a calm, confident voice, was polite and treated everyone around him with great respect. She wanted to be like him. Their time together gave her not only spiritual pleasure. With each passing day, with each subsequent smile and look, she felt the joy of being with him more and more physically. Every morning, right after waking up, she dreamed of seeing him. In the evenings and at night, she thought about the questions she would like to ask him. When they met, she gave him the ones that seemed most interesting to her.

"What do you think the evil is?" she asked him one day.

"The eyes of the Lord, who misses nothing, see both good and evil. These words themselves contain their definition, which means that it is given to us at the moment we are born. We always know what is good and what is bad, isn't it so*?"

"I know that the opportunity of being with you is good for me. I knew that already when I was born," she laughed.

He did not comment on these words but remembered them.

"If you had to choose which is more important for a man: eyes or ears, what would you point to?"

"The Lord has given us both eyes that see and ears that hear. But the level of deafness and blindness depends primarily on a man. That is why we have eyes to look at the world and ears to listen to its sounds. The Lord has given us senses to use them."

After these words, Makeda wondered if she could fully draw on what her body had. Does she see the world and hear its music fully?

"And what is, in your opinion, king, the most powerful organ of a human body?"

He didn't answer right away.

She didn't show that she noticed his frivolous look.

Elichoref, who wrote down the previous answers meticulously, smiled to himself, waiting for what the king would say.

"A tongue has power over both death and life," he answered after a moment with a serious expression. "Yes, definitely a tongue has the greatest power."

Makeda shuddered. She thought that if you could fall in love with wisdom, then she undoubtedly loved Solomon. His words flowed upon her heart like a balm and caressed her mind that soared into the lands where all-knowing gods live. She felt bliss and happiness. Never before had anyone, not even the Illumkuh's priest, or even the High Priestess, whom she considered the wisest people she knew, made her feel so fulfilled and happy. In the presence of Solomon, she had the impression that her spirit slips out of her body and rises above her with joy of the sensations she experiences.

"Tell me, king, who knows everything, how are body and spirit connected? What does Yahweh say about this?"

Solomon didn't hesitate for a moment.

"The condition of the spirit is rooted in the body, and the nobility of the body results from the spirit," he said.

"So, a body and a spirit are connected?"

"Of course."

"Seshep, who raised me, told me every morning that a healthy spirit lives in a healthy body."

"Every morning?"

"Before I became a queen, I was woken up almost every day at sunrise. Each day began with an intense exercise to ensure that the body was ready to meet the challenges that the spirit could be faced with."

"I like Seshep."

"She likes you too, king."

He smiled at that confession. And he thought he would take the opportunity to speed up, at least a bit, the moment when Makeda would show him his face.

"I wonder what the hemet would have advised to an unknown queen if a king had asked her for an extremely generous payment for what he offered her," he laughed mysteriously.

"It is difficult for me to answer for her, but I think that first of all she would be surprised by such a demand, and secondly, she would wonder what perverse trick hides behind the king's question." Makeda was sure that what he said was a witty provocation to her intellect.

"Seshep is smart, isn't she?"

"Mhmmm... and experienced."

"Then please, be so kind to me and ask her what she would think of an unknown king who would like the queen to come up with three difficult riddles and three tests and present them to him for solving."

"What happens if all the answers are correct? What reward does this unknown king expect from the unknown queen?"

"If all the answers and solutions turn out to be good, and it can't be taken for granted, because the questions will certainly be difficult, this unknown king would ask the queen to remove the veil and show him her face."

Makeda smiled under the veil.

"So, the queen you are talking about does not show her face to the king?"

"To the king's great regret."

"Maybe she has an important reason? Maybe her face is not beautiful? Maybe she was disfigured by illness, or has scars from wounds inflicted in a battle? Maybe the look in her eyes does not reflect the depth of her soul? Maybe she is afraid of disappointing the king, and she really would not want it to happen? Or maybe she dreams that this king would love her not for the beauty of her face, but for the beauty of her spirit? Maybe it is not like what you just said that a beautiful spirit is always clothed with a beautiful body?"

"Your words are wise; I will take them to my heart. Thank you for them. I vouch for you that the king wonders what the reasons are that the queen does not reveal her face for so long. The more that he knows from the accounts of one of the scouts who has seen her, that she is flawless and unusually beautiful."

Solomon fell silent and looked at Achishar, entering the chamber. His appearance meant that the king should go back to daily duties.

"Queen, I must leave you. I would be grateful if you would ask hemet Seshep what she would think about the offer of the unknown king we were talking about?"

Seshep was amused by his words.

"You were right to tell him I liked him," she concluded.

She did indeed like him. Not only because he was the way she always imagined him. It seemed that thanks to the Lady of the Moon, the feeling overwhelmed him, unexpectedly even for himself. What's more, it looked serious. In his look and gesture, in every gift he sent every morning, in the actions he took to be close to her, there were signs that something that rarely happens to men like him, had happened.

Here, to the one who was considered the smartest of all people, who knew the ancient scriptures, understood history, astrology, geometry, mathematics and other sciences, played instruments, wrote songs, had the knowledge of craftsmen, met and talked to the kings of other countries in their languages, who understood the speech and behavior of animals, and got all these talents and skills straight from God, came the greatest gift that a man can receive: love.

It came to Solomon like a light from heaven, stunned him, overwhelmed his body and mind, and decided to stay.

From the beginning, Seshep closely watched what was happening to the king. When she found that the events recorded in the stars were coming true, she breathed a sigh of relief. She wanted Makeda's childhood visions to come true, for her to love wholeheartedly and, most importantly, have her feelings reciprocated.

She saw that God's plan was being carried out, and as she thought about it, she became more and more convinced that not only the Moon Lady, but also the God of Israel favors it.

***

After a few days, Makeda had her riddles ready.

"What is this: a casing with ten doors. When one door is open, nine doors are closed, and when nine doors are open, one is closed?" she asked him when they met.

Solomon answered that question the next day.

"The casing is the womb, and the ten doors are ten holes in the human body: eyes, ears, nose, mouth, excretory and urine holes, and navel. When the baby is in the womb, the navel is open, but the other holes are closed. However, when the baby is born, the navel is closed, and the other openings are open."

This was obviously a good answer.

"First point on my side, right?" asked Solomon happily.

She confirmed.

"And will you tell me what is the surest thing in the world and what is the least certain?"

"Is this the second question? Or are we just talking to each other without scoring?" he asked mischievously.

"If you answer correctly, the second point will be on your side. So?"

"The death is the surest thing, and participation in the next world is uncertain," he answered without hesitation.

"Although I have also heard the voices of ridiculers," here he looked towards Elichoref, "who say that death is the most certain thing in the world, as I said, but they add that high taxes are also equally certain!"

"I believe it," she laughed, and knowing that taxes in Israel were considered to be the highest in the world, after the Egyptian ones, she added to comfort him, "Until now I was convinced that the inhabitants of Sheba complained about them the most."

The next day, Makeda asked the king to meet in the garden. Six strong servants came with her. They carried a large barked tree trunk.

"It's a cedar tree trunk," she said as they laid it at the king's feet. "As you can see, there are no leaves or roots. It is naked.

How will you know, Solomon, on which side was the root once and on which side were the branches?"

He knew wood. He used it a lot to build the temple. He knew from the carpentry and joinery masters that one should always remember to arrange all wood being used in such way that the part where the roots were would be at the bottom, because the structure and cohesion of the wood at its base is different than in at the crown. This is of great importance when constructing buildings. So, he didn't have a problem with the answer. He ordered the servants to take the trunk to the water and led Makeda there.

"The part that sinks into the water is heavier because it was closer to the ground. It means that a root was there. The part that floats above the water is the side of the leaves. It is lighter because it was closer to the sky."

The queen admired his knowledge and wisdom. From the speed with which he answered that question, she concluded that it was simple for him. She decided that the next tasks would be more difficult.

"Maybe you'll lift your veil soon, Makeda," he said as they parted. "I gave the correct answers to three questions."

"Yes. There are three more tests awaiting you. We'll see how things will go," she laughed. "Come to my chambers tomorrow, please."

"Sounds encouraging," he joked, knowing perfectly well that her words were not a promise of fulfillment, but meant another task for him.

He was looking forward to it. He liked the game they played. He felt a bit like in his childhood, when his masters gave him riddles and praised him for the right solutions. Now he enjoyed the challenges he was facing and felt a pleasant excitement at the thought of the reward ahead.

"Girls are different from boys, yes or no?" she asked him the next morning.

"Yes," he answered without hesitation. "Was that your question for today?"

"I wouldn't dare offend your intelligence like this, King," she appreciated his joke. "As the smartest man in the world you deserve something a little more sublime."

"Thank you," he bowed his head.

"If the children have identical dresses and hair, how will you recognize which of them are girls and which are boys?" she asked and led him to a room in which ten children were standing politely.

They all looked the same, they had identical linen knee-long dresses, with long loose sleeves, tied at the waist with a rope. Their dark hair was cut by the same hairdresser. The servants made sure that all of them had clean nails and that there were no scratches or bruises on their skin, suggesting, for example, that the child was a boy, because he took part in a fight which left its marks. They were all at an age in which their gender was difficult to guess.

"King, which of them are girls?"

"Let's get them to lift their dresses!" he laughed. "The simplest solutions are the best. Why make life difficult? "

She appreciated his next joke that day, knowing that he wouldn't do what he was talking about because he knew the rules of the game, he had proposed himself. She liked the lightness with which he talked with her, the warmth of his words, the gentleness and his cheerful sense of humor.

"Let the servants bring here ten bowls of water, ten washing oils, and ten cloth for wiping hands," he said. "Before I start the experiment, I want every child to wash hands."

After a while, a bowl of water was placed in front of each of the children, according to his wishes.

"Wash your hands!" he encouraged them.

The children knelt down or squatted down and did as he asked.

"I won't need the experiment anymore. Here are the girls " Solomon pointed to five children.

"How did you guess?" she didn't believe what she saw.

"It's simple," he said. "I watched them carefully. Before washing their hands, the girls rolled up their sleeves. All of them. None of the boys did this!"

"Indeed..."

"We are all born people. Bodies are given to us. Most often we come into the world as women or men, although as we know God also allows other solutions. What gender is given to us at birth largely determines our lives. Both girls and boys fit into this tradition quite quickly. Because after all, the fact that the girls rolled up their sleeves is not given to them by God. They didn't come to this world with this. They learned it from their mothers and care takers. Each of us is taught to function properly in the world we come to. Rules and laws are good and needed. They make life easier for us. People like an orderly world because when they follow the rules, they know that their lives are in harmony with God and his laws. It's easier that way."

"Weren't the boys taught how to roll up their sleeves?"

"Maybe they were. But probably their mothers did not push this skill as much as they did for the girls. In our culture, it is accepted that a woman cares more about this type of trifle. A man doesn't have to."

"It's not fair!"

"Life is not always fair. Let's take it as it is; it will be easier for us."

Makeda wondered if the riddles she was giving Solomon were a greater challenge for him or for herself. Because after each answer he gave, she thought about it for a long time and each time she realized more and more how valuable the lessons he gave her were. Her admiration and love for him grew with each passing day.

She was beginning to lose herself in the feeling. It enveloped her more and more, absorbed her gently, and step by step caused her soul to spin. The moment came when she no longer knew if she loved him, or her image of him. If the reality she was experiencing was a dream come true or just a fantasy.

"Give this emerald to him," the High Priestess handed Makeda a large stone. "Look, there's a hole in it, see?" she made sure that the queen could see it and added, "But it is so twisted and irregular that no needle can pass through it. It is impossible to thread a thread through it. Give him that stone and ask him to pull a thread through this complicated hole. We'll see how he does with this task."

"Is that even possible?"

"Of course. There is no problem on earth that cannot be solved."

It turned out that the Priestess was right. Solomon dealt with this task too. He sent for a silkworm,* which crawled through the hole, pulling the silk thread behind it.

"One can find a way for everything," he concluded. "It is good if we can use what exists in nature for finding solutions. If we look closely at the animal world, we can find a lot of solutions that will be useful to us in everyday life."

As he spoke, he watched Makeda's reaction. Even through the veil and the shawls covering her, he could see that she was admiring him more and more every day.

A few days passed since he let the silkworm crawl through the hole, and he had not received a signal from the queen that she was ready with the last task. When she finally invited him over, he was very happy.

She put two beautiful flowers in front of him. There was nothing different between them. They were a mirror image of each other. But only one of them was real. The other one, masterfully made of the finest silk imported from overseas, was identically beautiful, but artificial.

"You can look and smell at will, but don't touch them," Makeda said. "I'd like you to guess which one is real."

Solomon leaned over the flowers to see them closely and found them both equally beautiful.

"One of them is God's work and the other is human made. Both are an expression of extraordinary artistry. Art, the greatest one, is always an attempt to imitate the divine idea, to depict something that exists in divine space. That's how it is with this flower. Which one is the work of man? Queen, give me a moment..."

He nodded at the servant and whispered something in his ear.

"Soon, with God's help, I will try to answer your question, and meanwhile let's drink our best wine," he encouraged.

The servant brought two goblets filled with sun-colored liquid on a golden tray.

They were standing on the terrace of the chamber, which the king gave to Makeda on the day of her arrival in Jerusalem. The city stretched out before them. It was long past noon, but the sun's rays were still strong, flooding the room with a bright glow.

"Let's drink to God's works that make the world beautiful," he raised the vessel.

"Let's drink to human works, which are created because of a divine inspiration," Makeda said.

"To women, whom God gave to the world."

"And for men, whom the Moon's Lady brushed with its wing that gives sensitivity to beauty..."

Solomon liked Makeda's mischief. He even liked her faith in the moon goddess. He felt that Yahweh would be understanding about this, or at least he hoped so.

"When the time comes, we'll talk about your goddess."

"She knows you, king," Makeda assured him with conviction. "She's been watching you for a long time."

"I wonder what Yahweh thinks about this?" he asked quietly enough that nobody heard him besides her, neither Elichoref or

Seshep, who were engaged in the conversation, nor any of the servants accompanying them.

"I know he favors us, but I can only suspect what he thinks of your goddess. As far as I know him, he is not impressed by her presence."

"Everyone loves the Moon Lady," she assured him. "She is a cosmic element of the eternal world, a female part of divinity."

"Are you saying she's part of God? That she is contained in him?"

"That's how you could put it."

Their quiet conversation was interrupted by a servant's entrance. Behind him was a gardener with a small pitcher, closed tightly with a lid. He held his hand on it to make sure that nothing would get out from under it without his permission.

"Come closer to these beautiful flowers, gardener," Solomon said, pointing to a table deep in the room where the flowers were. "My friends will help me solve the puzzle that the Queen of Sheba gave me."

The gardener bowed and standing next to the flowers, raised the lid. There was a buzzing sound.

"Help me, God's messengers," Solomon said loudly.

The confused bees circled the chamber for a moment, then, guided by the smell, headed for the flowers. They sat on one of them, buzzing.

"Do you think, Makeda, that they have made the right choice? Did they do well? Did they help the king solve the puzzle?"

"They say you know animal speech."

"When you use the right words, you can count on your request to be fulfilled," he answered mischievously. "They flew to a real flower, because the artificial fragrance, even the most beautiful, will never match the natural one."

Makeda took him by his hand and led him near the bees. They stopped at a safe distance.

"I've heard a lot about your wisdom. Now that I met you, I see that it exceeds your fame*."

Elichoref, who listened to her words, recorded diligently what she had said.

"Blessed are you, my Lord, and blessed is your wisdom. I would like to be at least one of your servants so that I could wash your feet, absorb your wisdom, comprehend your reason, serve your majesty and enjoy your closeness."

He also accurately wrote Solomon's words:

"You too exude wisdom and forbearance. I have them because God gave them to me after my prayers and pleas. Although you don't know my God, you have the wisdom in your heart that had brought you to me. I preach all wisdom according to his will. Even what I say now flows from my mouth thanks to him. Whatever he orders me to do, I will do. Wherever he orders me to go, I will go. Whatever he makes me learn, I will learn. Because he gave me wisdom, I understood how I became a body from ashes and water, how he shaped me and all of us in his own image. It is also his merit that you are here. He brought you to me. For which I am extremely grateful to him."

Makeda no longer held the king's hand. His words reached the deepest recesses of her soul and touched the most sensitive areas.

"Queen, are tears flowing from your eyes?" he noticed that the movements of her arms and chest betrayed strong emotions. "Can I wipe them off?"

She took a step back and sighed.

"You guessed my riddles and solved the puzzles, so following the agreement, even though the virgin queen should not show her face to the followers of foreign gods, it is time for you to see me."

Saying this, she took the edges of the veil and slowly lifted it over her hair, making it a veil.

Solomon held his breath. He had waited for this moment for a long time.

He heard a lot about the beauty of the Queen of Sheba. First from Tamrin, who was delighted with her, then from Elichoref, who brought him stories about her from the city, later, from his scout. Her voice, posture, gestures, and above all the brilliance of her mind, worked his imagination with such power that there was no night that he would not imagine her face. What he saw exceeded his expectations.

"If the Lady of the Moon existed, she would look like you," he was captivated. "In your eyes one can see the wisdom of the ancestors, your features reflect goodness and nobility, and your lips betray the passion of the heart. Welcome to my life, Makeda, Great Kandake, Queen of Sheba, the greatest woman in the world!"

***

"Queen, we've managed to achieve everything we wanted. The prudence of your mind made it happen," the High Priestess respectfully bowed her head to the queen. "Solomon promised you everything you asked for. Our trade routes are safe, we will have shares in the fleet in the Red Sea, and even in trips to the most distant lands beyond the seas. Our mission has been a success. We can return home."

Apart from the High Priestess and Seshep, there were also Tamrin and Ashenafi in Makeda's chamber. They were celebrating the victory. The day before, Solomon agreed to fulfill almost all the queen's requests. The details of the agreements were discussed for many days by Josephat and Tamrin. The doubts and disputes related mainly to the percentage share in the expenditure for the construction and operation of the fleet, and the subsequent distribution of profits. Everyone wanted the expenses to be as low as possible and the profits as high as possible. They managed to meet halfway. Everyone was happy with the agreements they had made.

"Not only will we have access to new trade routes through the seas, but the old ones leading through Sheba are no longer threatened." Tamrin was also pleased with the agreements reached. "We can feel safe. If Solomon keeps his promises, we can go home and, as the ancients said, live happily ever after."

Indeed, the Israeli king allowed the Queen of Sheba to participate in the merchant fleet being formed in the Red Sea. The contract said that because of the obvious loss to Sheba that would have arisen if the trade had been taken over by Hiram and Solomon's fleet, the queen received the opportunity of financing one-third of the costs of building and operating it, but also of similar profits. She, in turn, agreed to deduct one-fifth of the profits she had each year from the caravans going through her land to and from India. In addition, the trade route leading from the southern part of the Red Sea to the Black Sea coast, rarely used until then, was to be developed. New oases were to be created there, the profits of which would go to Sheba and Israel proportionally to the number of new oases built in the area controlled by each of them.

"We've got everything we've come for," Ashenafi agreed. "We've worked hard for it. The gifts we brought did their best, but I think we all will admit that the contracts would not have been so favorable without what Queen Makeda has done. I talked to General Benaiah; you know that we meet often. We're both soldiers, we've found a common language. Benaiah says, and his words are like iron, not like Elichoref's writing stories, that Solomon gave his heart and lost his mind to our queen, and that is why our contracts are so favorable."

"Solomon has not lost his mind, I can assure you, general," laughed Makeda, whose vanity was flattered by Ashenafi's words, even though not quite proper. "He has exactly as much of it as he had before we came here. No offence to anyone, but he could generously share it with us all, and he would still have enough left to rule the state."

"I did not mean to offend anyone," Ashenafi excused himself. "What I want to say is that if it wasn't for your feminine charm, queen, we would probably go back to Sheba with nothing. Without you, lady, I am going to repeat it because I know what I am saying, our victory would be much smaller."

Makeda nodded. However, it was not possible to deduce from this gesture whether she agreed with the general's words or simply considered this part of the meeting coming to an end. For at the same time, as her father used to do when summing things up, she patted her thigh.

"If we are all happy, and it looks like that, then we can set out on our way back in the coming days," she said.

Tamrin and Ashenafi were clearly happy, while the High Priestess and Seshep kept a straight face. As if they both knew that it was not the time to return, because the will of the gods was not completely fulfilled yet.

Makeda was pleased. She received even more than she had expected. However, she felt sad at the thought of returning home. As if something was holding her back and calling, "Stay!" As if she should do something else that was written for her and inevitable.

"Maybe I haven't had enough of this city's atmosphere yet?" she asked herself, trying to find a source of her anxiety. "Maybe it's not time to go back as yet? Maybe I need to stay longer in the aura of Solomon's wisdom? Take a look at the way he governs? See more closely how the state works? Listen to the words of his god? But maybe since we got what we came for, there is nothing to wait for! He dazzled me with himself and his wisdom, I wish I could still be near him, but I am the queen after all, I have duties, Sheba is waiting!"

"Notify our host that the queen has decided to return," she decided.

On the same day, Tamrin conveyed her words to Josephat, and in the evening a messenger bowed before Makeda with a letter written by Solomon himself*.

Queen,

Now that you have come to me, why are you leaving without a thorough look at my kingdom? You haven't tasted enough of what I can offer you. Leaving so fast, you will not acquire the wisdom that your mind is gravitating toward and intended for. Come with me. Or at least give me one whole evening. Please, be my Guest. Come to my terrace tomorrow. You will have a wonderful feast waiting for you. I promise that I will follow your every order and answer your every question, no matter what it will concern. You love wisdom after all. Know that it will live in you until the end of your days, forever.

***

I saw that the Great Priestess and prophet Nathan did not like each other from the beginning. From day one, they watched everything that was happening between Makeda and Solomon with worry. The priestess was alert, but as usual, also this time she approached calmly what she saw and sensed. She had information about something that the prophet probably could not know. Although, perhaps, he was well aware of what the future would be, just like us. If this was the case, then what was he afraid of? Was it what had to come, and what he wanted to prevent with all his might?

I saw what the Lady of the Moon was planning for Makeda. At the same time, however, I realized that my goddess was only showing me what I was asking her. And nothing more. Because I'm primarily interested in the fate of my lady, I see Makeda when

I open the veil of time, it's obvious. On the other hand, the prophet Nathan, who was said to have talked to God many times in person, could have known and probably knew the future from a different angle. Was that why he had a reason for concern?

***

The musicians could not be seen from the tent, but they could be heard well. They were seated in one of the corners of the terrace, while a place to prepare dishes was created in the other.

At the king's request, the royal chef, Enri Her, was going to prepare special dishes for the evening. Solomon left him a free hand as to the choice and method of preparation, for he knew that he could fully trust his skills. He made only one condition.

"Prepare whatever you choose, delight my guest," he said. "Let everything be delicious and wonderful in every respect. However, I would like you to season dishes so that their taste and quality was intact, but later, after dinner, the queen would feel such a great thirst that she could in no way stop it. I want her to have a need to satisfy it at any cost."

Enri Hera was surprised by these words. He knew full well that no woman could resist Solomon. Why, then, did he need to give aphrodisiacs to any of them to make her want to give in to him?

"Lord, it will happen according to your wishes. I will prepare dishes that affect women so much that after eating them even the least submissive one will be yours."

"No, that's not what I mean," Solomon understood that his words about thirst and satisfaction had been misinterpreted by the chef. "She needs to want to drink! Drink! Understand? The dishes need to be so salty, or so spicy, or I do not know what yet, so that she would be thirsty sometime after eating them, not immediately, but a little later!"

Enri Her looked at his sandals, smiling at the tips of his toes, amused by the situation. He was restrained in expressing his feelings and opinions. Hardly anyone knew that he was venting his emotions by moving his toes. Solomon noticed it.

"I see your toes are amused," he smiled. "You're right about aphrodisiacs. I don't think they are necessary because Queen Makeda is tough in character, so she certainly won't do anything she won't feel like doing."

***

The chef had one day to prepare the feast. He knew that the work had to start immediately. Dishes had to be prepared as soon as possible to only need finishing touch before serving on the next day.

Near the tent, in which the king and his guest were supposed to feast, a hearth of stones was erected, which was needed for one night. When the place was selected, the chef left the construction to be done by the best royal craftsman, and himself focused on his work.

Making a properly seasoned dish seemed quite simple. On the other hand, the cook remembered that he was to give it to a woman, and additionally, a queen. He had to prepare dishes with a delicate taste. He knew that people in Makeda's homeland eat spicy food, but not salty, and he was to lead the queen to thirst!

The more he thought about it, the more convinced he was he had to use garum. He got to know it thanks to his contacts with the Greeks. He knew that this liquid spice was not accepted by the people of Israel. Like most blood-based and uncooked dishes, they were not accepted by Yahweh's followers, especially priests. He understood that. He knew that God's principles should be followed, but curiosity pushed him to experiment.

Of course, if he prepared the garum himself, the matter would be out very quickly. Fermentation of fish entrails in the sun caused such a stench that it would arouse curiosity in the court and throughout the city, and thus uncomfortable questions. However, thanks to his contacts with the Greeks, he occasionally bought small clay pots with garum. For this evening he chose the one made with tuna blood and guts from among its various types. He decided it will be best for the occasion. Earlier he used it for decoctions, in which he cooked meat for special meals for Solomon, when he entertained guests that were most important to him, and knew that these dishes did not cause a sensation, except for the questions, "How was it prepared? What are these spices?"

At such times, Enri Her just smiled and said that he had picked the herbs himself, but he would not say where, because then everyone would imitate him, so he would inevitably lose his job after some time.

He worked alone that evening. He sent the cooks away, even the boy guarding the fire. He didn't want to have witnesses while using garum. Besides, when he was alone, it was easier for him to focus, and preparing dishes for the king required the highest form of concentration. He planned a quail breast and lobes of a thigh of a young ox for the main course. He cut the raw bird's breast into small pieces, mixed with finely chopped onion, garlic and pepper, and marinated in olive oil, pomegranate juice and a few drops of garum. Then he took two lobes, cross-cut across the fibers, of the leg of a young ox, fed only with his mother's milk until his death. He broke the meat structure with a stirrer from tamarind wood, turning it over from time to time. When the meat was almost transparent, he sprinkled it with oil and garum and set it aside.

He put more wood to the hearth. He moistened the dry grass and herbs that hung on all walls in his kitchen. He placed a copper plate with holes on the hot hearth. He put herbs and grass on it, and when they started smoking, he placed a tray of marinated meat over them and covered it with a clay pot. After a few minutes, he removed the dish, then transferred the slightly smoked pieces of quail to another one. He cleaned up the mess that had arisen, and then put a large portion of quail stuffing on the ox meat sheets, sprinkled it with garum once more, added some pepper and skillfully wrapped it all in a roll. He stuck a wooden pin into the roll, preventing it from unfolding. He did the same with the second lobe. He heated up the copper plate on the hearth, sprinkled it with goose fat and waited until the first light smoke began to rise. After a while, he turned the rolls over once, and then twice more, frying on each side. Then he placed them in a clay pot. He poured some fig wine on the copper plate, evaporated it, mixing and scratching the remains with the tamarind stirrer. Then he poured it into a dish with ox rolls, added the right amount of vegetable stock to cover both rolls, and added the garum and pepper again. He hung the dish over the hearth and slowly stewed the food.

In the meantime, he took the dish in which the yam was cooking from the hearth. He decanted the water and crushed the cooked vegetable with a blunt tip of the stirrer, threw in a goose egg yolk, a few drops of garum, a pinch of turmeric and a handful of spelt flour into it. He kneaded everything with his hands to a smooth mass. Then he formed balls the size of a date and put them into water that was boiling in a dish above the hearth. When they surfaced, he waited a while longer and took them out with a spoon woven from tree branches. He moistened thus prepared balls with olive oil and wrapped them in the leaves.

That was how he spent the night before dinner.

CHAPTER VI

SONG OF SONGS
THE QUEEN'S PROPHECY

That evening a tall, spacious tent supported on five columns of red sandalwood, stood on Solomon's terrace. The vault was formed by heavily draped light fabrics with golden threads. The roof remained wide open so that the sky could be seen clearly. Finely draped purple curtains, finished with golden fringes, hung from the beams connecting the columns. Between them, on gold chains, lamps made of colored glass were hung, whose star-shaped rims were made of gold plates. Each lamp had a container with oil, the amount of which was calculated so that the fire could burn all night.

The floors were decorated with thick carpets. Low tables with gold and silver sheet tops stood on them. Their legs were made of ivory and cedar wood and were additionally decorated with precious stones. Wide mattresses covered with soft fabrics and pillows were arranged around them.

"Follow me, queen," Solomon greeted her at the door of his chamber.

The way leading to the terrace was lit by dozens of star-shaped lamps. There was a subtle scent in the air that Makeda was happy to recognize as a blend of amber, musk, lavender, lemon, and vanilla. Soft music could be heard in the background.

When they arrived on the terrace, she stopped. Before her stood a lit, royally decorated tent. It delighted with its lightness and splendor, but something else took her breath away. Here she saw a city stretching to the horizon. Yellowish lights flickered in the windows of the houses standing on the hills side by side, so densely that they seemed to be fused at this distance. There were thousands of them. They all resembled to her the starry sky, which she sometimes saw on cloudless nights in the desert. The lights trembled just like her and seemed to be waiting for what was about to happen. And a lot was happening. The evening, and then the night came that Makeda and Solomon remembered for the rest of their lives.

***

"You are among women like a lily among thorns, queen*," he bowed his head low before her and gestured with his hand to invite her in.

"You are among men like a proud apple tree in the forest," she took a few steps forward. "I would like to plunge into the embrace of your shadow. It is an honor to be a guest in your chamber, king."

She walked slowly, looking around discreetly, occasionally brushing the soft fabrics with her hands or putting them on the hardness of perfectly smoothed furniture wood. Near the centrally placed tent, the view of which impressed her so much, the cook set up the hearth. Next to it was a large table, on which he gathered vegetables, fruits, flowers, and other products needed to prepare dinner. He had also dishes for serving meals.

That evening, Enri Her did not work alone. An assistant, whose task was to ensure the adequate strength of the fire, was bustling around the hearth. The chef communicated with him without words, they were such a close-knit team that they did not exchange a single sentence during the dinner.

The hearth was built so that the smells and smoke went in opposite direction from the tent.

Solomon's servants were to receive the trays with ready dishes, and the most important of them let the chef know when to serve the next ones.

Enri Her prepared the first course from fresh vegetables from the royal gardens and decorated it with edible flowers. He mixed the evenly chopped ingredients with shallots, a little pepper, and olive oil. He deliberately did not use salt, so that in the next course the eaters would fall into the trap he had prepared for them, as requested by Solomon. He put small portions on the platter to increase hunger. He decorated them with flowers, sprinkled with pomegranate juice and oil before serving, so that the dish pleased the eyes.

He looked furtively at the eaters.

The queen first looked at the vegetable structure for a long time, and then, when Solomon took one of the colorful chopped vegetable cubes with his fingers and put it in his mouth, she did the same.

"The composition is so elaborate that it's a shame to touch it," she was delighted.

"My chef prepared works of art in your honor," he liked the praise, as if he was the author of the delicacies that the guest liked. "He assured me that everything is edible."

"Let's eat then," she looked at the piece of a carrot she was holding.

"And let's drink wine!" he beckoned to the servant, who immediately filled the goblets. Good God created it for our pleasure. It would be a sin not to taste it."

"Drinks from King Solomon's vineyards enjoy great fame in the world," she tilted her head, as she always did when she said something mischievous. "But they are also considered extremely strong. Should I be careful? I'm not used to them. The drinks in Sheba are not strong."

"You'll always be safe with me."

"I can't imagine it could be different, king."

"In Israel we say: Guest in our house is God in our house."

"I am honored."

At the sign of the servant, Enri Her began the final preparation for the main course. A clay pot with the rolls of meat in a sauce had been already hanging over the hearth for some time, and slightly lower, above the fire, there was another one filled with water, and still smaller one with oil next to it. The chef took from the table the yam dumplings prepared on the previous day, wrapped in leaves on the platter. He gently unfolded them and threw them into boiling water. Meanwhile, the helper took off the first dish and carried it to the table. The chef tasted the sauce again. He smiled to himself because he knew that what he had prepared would definitely have effect on the queen exactly as his master wished.

After a while, the assistant brought a second dish with boiling water and two pomegranate flowers sprinkled with spelt flour. The cook arranged meat rolls in the center and the dumplings, removed from boiling water, on one side. He sprinkled them with oil. When the helper came with crunchy pomegranate flowers, previously dipped in boiling olive oil, he poured a large portion of the sauce on the other side of the roll and covered it with a flower.

The dish prepared in this way was placed in front of the talking couple.

The cook was pleased. He hid the dark brown stain of the sauce under a six-pointed, dark-orange pomegranate flower, the shiny yellow dumplings and brown meat completing the whole with their color. The composition was beautiful and the dish very tasty.

He watched with pleasure as the meat melted in the mouths of the eaters; it was so delicate. He imagined each bite revealing a range of flavors, tender beef and savory filling, previously slightly smoked with herbs, mixed perfectly together. The spice of meat was lost in the delicacy of the structure. This was just the beginning, because in contact with meat, the sauce flowing from under the flower was to provide the palate with another sensation.

Makeda had never eaten yam in this form, and at first, she did not know that its true taste is only revealed in contact with the sauce. She saw Solomon cut soft, springy pieces and mix them with the sauce. She did the same. When she tasted it, she felt that she could eat this dish endlessly.

However, she controlled her appetite. Being a queen obliged her to be restrained also in eating. As customs dictated, she never spoke with her mouth full.

"Delicious! What is your chef's secret?" she asked when she swallowed. "I've never eaten yam prepared this way."

"The tubers, from which he can conjure up something so unusual, were brought from one of the hunting expeditions for the wild honey. I don't know how he does it. I asked him, but he claims that it is a secret that he cannot reveal even to me. Ask him if you want. Maybe he'll open his cook heart to you."

"It's a special species, lady," Enri Her confessed. "These tubers are intended only for the most important occasions and for the exceptional guests of the king."

"I'm glad you are with me, Makeda. This way I can also enjoy eating this amazing dish," Solomon joked.

The salt and spicy sauce in complement to the pleasant structure of the yam made Makeda feel like asking for more after eating a portion of it for the first time in her life. She didn't do it though. She knew that a feeling that is not quite satisfied is better and provides the body with much more pleasure than satiation.

They ate and talked until late. The moon was already high in the sky, and the last lights went out in the windows of the houses in the city.

Time disappeared, they forgot about the place where they were and the people who surrounded them. They no longer paid attention to the decorated tent, music, and shadows of Jerusalem.

Only they existed. Staring at each other. Blind to the world beyond them.

He took her hands. She didn't move, didn't protest, didn't move away. She was sitting staring at him, waiting for what had long been written in the stars.

He stroked her hands. She raised his hand and kissed it. He dipped his fingers in her hair. She arched her neck and closed her eyes. He put his index finger on her lips. She opened them slightly.

"How beautiful you are, the lady of my dreams*."

"You dreamt about me?" There was hope in her voice. She wanted to be the fulfillment of his dreams. She imagined that he, just like her, had been waiting just for her from the earliest childhood, knowing that their lives had been joined by the gods.

"I have dreamt about you since I saw you."

She straightened up.

"How come?" she thought. "So, it's not him who the Moon Lady has chosen for me?" She was disappointed. "It's not him who is supposed to give me the greatest treasure in the world? It's not him to whom I have been coming all my life? He dreamed of me only from the moment he saw me? Not before?!"

Her heart was beating so strongly that she felt that even a chef could hear its beat. She felt her throat tighten.

"I have to go now, king," she stood up.

"What happened? Makeda?" He also jumped to his feet.

"It's late. At this time, the queen of Sheba should have been in bed for a long time."

"The Queen of Sheba can decide for herself what she does at different times of the day and night, can't she?" He tried desperately but gently to return to the previous atmosphere.

He didn't understand what happened. He considered his every word and gesture.

"Did I offend you?"

"Not at all," she wanted to look honest. "I just realized how different we are."

She was already breathing more normally, and her heart stopped beating madly.

"Well, yes," he laughed. "We are from different worlds: you are a woman and I am a man."

"You're right. We are very different. Your God has given you an extraordinary mind. My Lady of the Moon, beyond my reason, gave me a sensitive heart and a great imagination."

"And an unearthly beauty," he added quietly, but loud enough for her to hear it clearly.

She did hear it, and although she wanted to be adamant and tenacious in her resolution, what he said and how he behaved, flattered her pleasantly. She was sure he was very interested in her. At that moment she was really close to tell him something else. That besides beauty, the Silver Mother also gave her the gift of seeing. But his words that he had dreamed of her since the moment he saw her, not since childhood, made her fall silent.

"Each of us received different gifts, coming into the world. We differ not only in gender," he said, as if he were reading her mind. "There is a different path written for each person. Sometimes our paths cross. Most of us don't know why this is happening. I believe that what happens to us, you and me, is God's will. I feel it. I am not sure what your heart is hiding, but mine tells me that our souls want to be close to each other and are made for each other."

She sighed and sat down. He did the same and took her hand again.

"He is right. After all, not everyone has visions, I know that very well," she explained in her mind the fact that he had not dreamed of her since childhood.

"Let us allow it..." he whispered softly, feeling that she had given up completely. "I don't know stars. The Moon Lady doesn't speak to me in my dreams. But I feel that God likes that we are here together and that you let me hold your hand. Everything we experience is done at his will."

He felt that the momentary crisis, the reason of which he did not understand, was over; that the time they had been waiting for was coming; and that they both wanted the same thing.

"It's late, I'll better go..." She was still teasing, still not quite sure of her decision, but weakly enough for him to know that she probably wanted to stay.

"I won't let you go this late," he adjusted to her tone. "They say Jerusalem is a safe city. But you never know. It is better not to let such a beautiful woman walk around the grand palace alone at this time."

"Do you think I can get lost?" Her good mood had almost returned.

"Or maybe someone will kidnap you?"

"And instead of reigning in Sheba, I will end up in a harem of some magnate?"

"Let's not rule out such eventuality!"

Both of them were already very amused. Wine, the warmth of the evening, the charm of the surroundings, music, the taste of dishes all worked together, and above all their dancing souls clung to each other.

"Don't you think my chamber and the greatest terrace in Jerusalem, queen, are comfortable enough to spend the night here?"

"As you probably heard, Solomon, in Sheba a woman can be an independent queen only if she is a virgin. I sit on the throne alone and I want it to stay that way."

"An interesting answer to the question about the room and the terrace," he laughed. "Be sure that no one in Jerusalem would dare to do anything against your will. And certainly, I would never do anything that offends you in the least."

"I trust you," she said.

"I will take the oath!" he called and knelt before her on both knees. "Do you want it?"

"Are you serious?" Like a little girl, she clapped her hands in joy. "Yes, I want you to do it!"

"I swear, Makeda, the most beautiful queen of the world, that nothing will happen against your will. I won't take anything from you by force. But beware," he raised his finger to emphasize the importance of what he was going to say. "It will happen under one condition!"

"What condition?" She was surprised.

"That you too will not take anything valuable that belongs to me either."

"Oh, Solomon!"

"Nothing valuable that belongs to me and is in this chamber," he added.

She laughed, convinced that she could do it without any problem."

"Is that your condition?"

"Yes, it is!"

"Let it happen then.

" In this situation, please, take your oath, too.

She knelt down in front of him. They were at their fingertips. They heard their breaths.

"I swear I will not touch anything valuable in this chamber that belongs to King Solomon " she said slowly and solemnly.

"What will happen if you don't keep your promise?" he wanted to know.

"It is impossible."

"But in case it happens anyway?"

"It's impossible, I can assure you. I have everything I could ever want."

"Well, but if, however, it happens? For some reason unknown to us now?"

"Oh, and if it happens, and I emphasize that it is impossible, then, dear king, you can do whatever you like with me," she spread her arms as if she was getting ready to fly.

"Let it be so," he was happy.

"It won't," she assured him.

"Everything is in God's hands," he looked at the sky with hope.

Then they talked for a long time, laughed and joked. They drank wine, chewing on treats prepared by Enri Her.

In the middle of the night they moved from the tent to the chamber, where they settled on wide, comfortable sofas and talked while drinking wine. Finally, exhausted, they both fell asleep, not even knowing when.

***

Makeda woke up in the middle of the night, very thirsty. Her mouth and throat were dry. She wanted nothing more than to drink water. She looked around.

Solomon ordered to leave only one pitcher of water in the chamber. It was placed near his sofa.

Believing that the king was asleep, Makeda crossed to his side tip-toeing so as not to wake him up. She reached for the pitcher, filled the goblet, and drank it all in one chug. It seemed it was just what Solomon had been waiting for. As she took a last sip, he opened his eyes and caught her hand.

"Why did you break the oath?"

"I didn't," she got scared. "I just came for water. Let me drink it. It's just water."

He stood beside her, holding her hands.

"Are you saying water is not valuable? There is no life without it! Without the great dam and the water accumulated in it, what would your kingdom be?"

"You're right," she lowered her head in remorse, understanding her mistake. "Water is valuable. Very valuable."

"You broke the deal."

"Yes."

"And now what?"

"Exactly. Now what?"

***

"You are the man I have dreamed of, you know?" she murmured quietly, lying next to him with her eyes staring at the morning sky. "I always knew you existed. I knew you were somewhere and that the time would come when we would meet. I waited for this day for so long that sometimes, in moments of weakness, I stopped believing that it would ever come. Now I know that my life has been a path leading to you."

He rolled over to his side and rested his head on his bent arm. She knew he was looking at her, but she didn't want to get distracted with his sight. She was looking at the sky.

"You are here, next to me," she spoke to him, to herself, to the Lady of the Moon and even to Yahweh, whom she did not know, but she had long felt his existence because he was the God of the man who was destined for her.

"Not only was the Silver Mother watching over our meeting, but also Yahweh must have agreed for it," she thought.

She put her hand in his hair and tugged. He hissed.

"You exist," she stretched, pleased. "I see your face, one that I have known since the beginning of the world, the eyes with wisdom in them, the straight nose, the lips that kissed me, dark hair with silvery threads in which I dipped my fingers tonight, as I do now. I touch your skin. When I do it, you tremble, so I do it again and again because I know we both want it. Your scent floods my body in waves. I give in to it because

I've missed it all my life. You smell like my dream man," she snuggled into the hollow behind his ear.

Immediately afterwards she jumped up and knelt down. She bent her legs under her and sat on her heels.

"This is really happening!" she called out. "You exist. Real and tangible! I was so scared that you only exist in a little girl's dreams."

"You dreamed about me?" Curious, he put his hands under his head to see her even better.

He knew that dreams were the gate through which God speaks to people.

"I had visions in my childhood," she explained. She knew that now she could tell him everything. "Not dreams but vision. Serious, full, sent by the gods. It was thanks to them that I knew you were meant for me. And because the priestesses of the Moon said the same, a husband was not sought for me. In Sheba, the will of the gods is holiness. We implement it and comply with it. We do not break the oaths we make to them. We live working, praying, caring for the gardens and our life-giving dam that provides us with water without which Sheba would die. As you know well, we have been involved in trade for centuries. It is this, that by the will of the gods, determines our wealth. Everything we do is always according to their will. That's why my father took my visions so seriously, that's why I have so much support from the priestesses of the Moon, and that's why I came here. I'm your guest because the gods decided so. Being born, I brought information that we would meet. And that was the main and recurring duty of my life."

He was moved. He sat down opposite her.

"What did you see exactly?"

She told him about the visions that appeared like light flares, exploded in her head with images, and were so strong and unambiguous that they did not let her forget about themselves. She told him that as a child she believed that everyone was dreaming similarly, and that this is how the gods announced to people what could happen in the future, what their purpose might be, and what they should strive for. The visions show something that can potentially happen.

"I saw you ascend the throne. I watched the fight you fought with enemies. I saw how much blood was spilled before you began building the temple. The priestesses explained to me that I could see a future that could happen and that the Moon Lady shows me the one that is meant for me."

He listened to her carefully.

"I don't know if you know it, but Seshep has the ability to see through the veil of time. Before she became my hemet, she saw that it had been written to me to be an independent queen. She knew the future long before it happened. She, just like me, saw us together. You and me."

"So, you know what awaits us tomorrow?"

"Unfortunately, not. My visions ceased when I became a woman."

"But you are sure that I am the one who was destined for you?"

He wanted it to sound a bit as if he was joking, but she answered with the utmost seriousness.

"I already knew it when I saw you for the first time. When you got up from the throne to greet me, I shuddered. Everything was happening exactly as it had been previously revealed to me."

"Do you know what will happen to us next?"

She denied. "Seshep doesn't know either?"

Something stopped her from telling him the whole truth. Maybe it was the memory of Den, who once spilled the secret she entrusted to him? She did not want to say that her dreams stopped when she learned about something very important: that the one she was destined for would give her something that is most valuable in the world. That she would receive an incredibly valuable gift from him. Something that will not only delight her but will change her whole life. She did not know why, but she felt that she should not share this information with him. Not yet, and maybe never.

"The gods don't reveal all their intentions to us," she changed her tone. "You not only do smell like the man in my visions, but you taste so as well," she bent and touched his skin with her mouth. "Yum..." She showed him the tip of her tongue. "That's exactly the taste from my dreams."

He laughed.

"You dreamed with all your senses, you know? You have already told me about the sensations that you experienced thanks to the gifts of sight, touch, taste, and smell. I skipped the hearing, but my ears knew you too. Just as I can hear your voice and breath now, so each of your words sounded like the most beautiful music to me when I was a child. You are right, I met you with all my senses long ago. And yet, now that I am so close to you, I still don't know if I should allow myself to believe that my dream has come true? Because you know what?"

"Yes?"

"What if, after waking up, it turns out that it was just a beautiful vision? That what happened to me has been blown away, leaving my heart so hugely dissatisfied that it will be impossible to live with it? What if I see you are gone, and I'm left alone with a great desire to catch up with my dreams?"

"I do exist. Really," he pulled her to himself. "Your senses are not wrong. You can believe them, I assure you. And furthermore, you are saying that the gods brought you to me and that you have dreamed of me since childhood. I don't know why yet, but I am sure that God has brought you to me in His infinite wisdom. And he always knows what he is doing."

***

In the evening, when Makeda rested in her chambers, recollecting the night, she heard agitated voices of the servants, and after a while Seshep stood before her.

"Lady, King Solomon is coming," she managed to communicate.

She was lying on the bed with her eyes closed. She had not opened them yet, when she heard a man's voice already.

"He's not coming, he's already here," he laughed, entering the chamber.

"What are you doing here?" she jumped off the bed.

"Come," he took her hand, unabashed. "I will show you a place in Jerusalem that is the most important for me."

"In this outfit?"

"You look as dignified and beautiful as ever," he assured, not releasing her hand.

They walked along the corridors leading along the shortest path to the eastern exit from the palace. They turned north behind the gate.

She was excited.

She guessed where they were going. They had been more than once in the square where they were walking now. It was surrounded by very important buildings, and was crowned by a famous temple, of which it was said that in the mind of Solomon it was designed by Yahweh himself. It was separated from the city by a wall of evenly hewn stones. After a while, they were in front of the entrance leading to it.

"I have been building it for seven years," he boasted, leading her into the courtyard. "The hill we're on is called Moriah."

"Does it mean holy rock?"

"Exactly. Abraham sacrificed his son Isaac here."

"Tamrin told me about it. He said that Yahweh wanted to test Abraham's faith in this way. When he saw that Abraham did not hesitate to comply with his request, he allowed to sacrifice a lamb instead of the boy. He also made an alliance with him, that's very important. Apparently, Isaac lived a hundred and eighty years, is that correct?"

"It would give me hope that maybe I will be able to accomplish everything that God has planned for me."

"You will live long. He is extremely good to you."

"Because he is love. What is the use of us, human children, if we do not experience goodness and love on earth? Aren't we nothingness, barely grass in a field that withers and is consumed by fire*? God always loved those who could humbly follow his path and let them rejoice in his kingdom. Blessed is the man endowed with wisdom and compassion and fearing God. This temple, and everything I do, is for his glory," he said, walking.

"Why didn't you let me come here earlier?"

"This place is intended only for those who preach the glory of the Lord. Worshipers of other gods are not allowed here."

"So, why am I here today?"

"Yahweh brought you to me," he said with conviction. "He gave us each other. And I feel that today he allowed you to come in here."

They stopped in the main courtyard. A giant basin stood near the stairs leading to the main entrance. It was round and ten cubits in diameter*. It was five cubits high, and the cord that measured its circumference was thirty cubits long. Two rows of flared flowers were placed beneath it, ten for each cubit. The vessel was supported by twelve oxen, three of which faced north, three west, three south and three east. The thickness of the walls was equal to the width of a hand, and the brim resembled an open lily flower.

"People call it the sea," he explained. "It's made of bronze."

"Delightful," she raised her head and slowly circled the massive vessel. "Everything I see is beautiful and made with such precision, as if God Himself was leading the craftsmen's hands."

Ten other vessels, also made of bronze, stood nearby. All of them were used during the ceremony.

"As a follower of other gods, you can't go any further. But I will show you one of the vestibules. Come."

They headed toward the entrance leading to the side vestibules. They walked along a narrow, long corridor.

"Our greatest treasure, the Ark of the Covenant, used to wander with our ancestors. For many years it stood on a hill under a special tent, and now it is here. It is sacred, only priests can see it. But if you stand here," he pointed next to himself, "you'll see a large chamber."

They were on such level of corridors that she could see the golden hall she had heard so much about.

"What do you think?" he wanted to know.

She couldn't find her voice. Her throat tightened and tears came to her eyes. She had never seen anything so beautiful. Chills ran through her. After a while, she couldn't control her tears anymore. This place was undoubtedly God worthy.

The walls, ceiling, floor, doors, columns, carvings, garlands, flowers - everything was covered in gold. The altar, a table used to lay breads** on it, candlesticks, flowers, lamps, pliers, bowls, scissors, cups, and censers, were all made of gold***... Everything that her eye could see. Two massive golden cherubs stood against the long wall. Each of them was ten cubits high, with wings stretched both ways and ten cubits long. The wings met in the middle of the temple.

Solomon stood beside her in silence. He spoke only after a long moment.

"The place behind the curtains, there at the end, is the vestibule of the Saint of Saints. The Ark is there," he said quietly, because he did not want to disrespect God. "There are tablets there with the commandments that Yahweh has given us."

She looked in the direction he was pointing to her. She thought that she recognized a shape of a chest behind the curtains.

"Yes, it's right there, but you can't see it from here," he explained.

"I've heard a lot about it. And about the Ark and about the temple." She confessed. "When the tabernacle was ready, and when the Ark was moved here, the news of what sacrifice you made to God spread all over the world. It was said that you ordered twenty-two thousand oxen and one hundred and twenty thousand sheep to be killed, and the ceremony lasted fourteen days.

"Yes, that's how it was."

"I have also heard of the words that God addressed to you."

"Which of them?"

"I sanctified this temple that you built so that my name would always be there. If you obey my laws and ordinances, I will strengthen you on the throne forever, and you will never lack a descendant who will sit on the throne of Israel."*

"Yes, it's true."

"But I've also heard of his other words that sound like a threat and a warning."

"Really?" he guessed what he was be about to hear.

"'If you turn away from me and stop maintaining my orders and laws that I gave you, if you go to serve and bow to other gods, I will remove Israel from the land I gave to it, the temple will disappear from before my face, Israel will be the object of contempt and a laughing stock for other nations.'"

"That's right, that's what he said."

She hoped that perhaps he would declare that he would never break the laws and that he would make the temple and Israel last for centuries. But he did not speak. She waited a moment, then, when he was still silent, looked again at the golden hall. She felt chills again. It was hard to believe that what she saw was a product of human hands.

He noticed what was happening to her.

"This is how the Shekhinah works," he was sure that she was not cold, but the extraordinariness of the place made her feel the Divine presence.

"Shekhinah?" She didn't know what he was talking about.

"It's the perceptible presence of God," he explained. "But you, the Queen, feel it every day, don't you? Because you have him here," he put his hand on her heart.

She covered it with her hands, then lifted it to her lips and kissed.

"This is also your God, even if you don't know it yet. Everyone should worship the one who created the universe, sky, sea, land, sun, moon, trees, stones, domestic and wild animals, feathered birds, crocodiles, fish, whales, hippos, lizards, storms, lightning, clouds, and good and evil. It is fitting for us to worship him, trembling and rejoicing. He is the master of the universe, the creator of angels and people. He is the one who gives and takes life, punishes and shows mercy, raises the poor, lying on the ground, who can grieve and rejoice."

Seshep and Elichoref did not accompany them to the temple. They were standing in the square. When they noticed Makeda and Solomon coming, they stopped talking. They waited for instructions.

"God speaks to us in various ways," they heard Solomon's words. "You are an unexpected gift for me and inspiration that God has sent me. Thanks to you, my soul rises to the heavenly meadows of knowledge. I rediscover what awaiting means. The purity of your heart, combined with the visions you have experienced, is like being allowed to the altar of God's secrets. You and the world that I am getting to know through you, is intriguing to me. When you left in the morning, you left me with my delight. I want the words I wrote then to be a chronicle of our feelings. I want to offer them to you right here in a place that is sacred for me."

He nodded at Elichoref, who, together with Seshep, kept a distance that allowed the rulers to talk freely. The writer handed him a small scroll wrapped around a wooden post, with its ends shaped like almond flowers.

"Makeda, Queen of Sheba, I know God has brought you to me. In the temple, this thought has been confirmed. You feel him with all your heart, you open it to him," he said solemnly. "Thanks to what happened tonight, you have become my wife. I would like you to become one also in the light of our law. Please accept my words written on this parchment as the evidence of my love."

How delightful is your love, my sister, my bride!
How much more pleasing is your love than wine,
and the fragrance of your perfume more than any spice!
Your lips drop sweetness as the honeycomb, my bride;
milk and honey are under your tongue.
The fragrance of your garments is like the fragrance of Lebanon.
You are a garden locked up, my sister, my bride;
you are a spring enclosed, a sealed fountain.

***

At night, I heard Makeda's scream. I immediately appeared at her bed. I saw her and I felt like in the times of her childhood again, when I hugged her, sweaty and shaky.

She was sitting on the bed and rocking back and forth. She was hugging herself, as if she wanted to cuddle. She was crying.

"I had a vision," she confessed. "Similar to the one from the old days. I have already forgotten how I felt in such moments," she sobbed. "I thought it would never come back..."

I let her calm down. I wiped her wet forehead and brushed her hair, wet from sweat, away from her face.

"My head is cracking," she complained. "It didn't hurt me before. What's happening? Why did it come back?"

Having learned from experience, I knew I shouldn't talk too much. I was right: after a moment she calmed down enough to start the story.

"I dreamed that I forgot my name, that I didn't know where I came from, that I didn't remember whose daughter I was, in what city or country I was. I even forgot the name of the man I spent the night with. I didn't remember anything; I was like a blank white parchment. It terrified me. I tried to scream but I couldn't. Besides, I didn't remember whom I should call. Seshep, do you understand, I even forgot that I got you."

She took a sip of the water I gave her.

"In addition, I couldn't use my voice. So not only did I lose my memory, but something also tightened my throat. I knew that until it let go, I wouldn't be able to get out the quietest sound. I was afraid. I knelt and wanted to pray, but I didn't know how. I forgot all the texts I have ever known. I had a terrifying emptiness and a terrifying, terrible nothingness in my head. Then a strong voice appeared and a golden brightness that accompanied it. I heard that if I don't do my duty, it will deprive me of my memory, and I will forever forget the words I know. Everything that I know and what I have learned so far will disappear. I will have a void in my head, and at the same time the cruel awareness that I had a memory once. He said there is no other way."

She fell silent, ordering her thoughts.

"It sounded like a gentle threat. A kind of a contract, but not negotiable."

She took another sip.

"I promised I wouldn't forget, and I would fulfill my duty. I said that even though I didn't remember what it was, that is, I agreed to something that I didn't even know it existed. Maybe I did it out of fear of a force that I couldn't understand? Or did I trust this extraordinary voice? When I made the promise, the pain that had been holding my head in an iron grip, disappeared, and the memory came back. I felt relief and peace. My thoughts became clear. I felt as if the one who was talking to me, smiled. And I think it really was so, because after a while I heard him again. He said that he was speaking to me in a human voice, because I wouldn't understand him if he used his own. I asked, what is my duty? "I'll show you the future. Tell Solomon about it. Let what you will see be a warning. Whether it will come true or not will depend on people and their choices. And remember there is one God, Only one. He is the beginning and the end. He is everything and everywhere. Those you consider to be the gods, you pray to, are the sons and daughters sent by me, my emanations. I give you the gods you need, you can understand, and you are ready for."

Makeda said the last sentence in a very weak voice, then she fell asleep, lulled in my arms, exhausted and still shivering.

When she woke up, we told the High Priestess about everything.

"Who was talking to you?" she asked quietly, even though she knew perfectly well whose voice Makeda had heard.

"'I am, who I am,' that's how he introduced himself. He was the one talking to me."

"It was the voice of the God of Israel." The priestess had no doubt that a new, long foretold chapter in their lives had just begun.

***

I watched the most important members of our expedition and saw how quickly they made contact with the inhabitants of Israel.

The soldiers fared best. For example, the commander Ashenafi entered such a close relationship with Israeli general Benaiah that it could even be said that they had become friends. Since the time it became obvious to everyone that Solomon favors

Makeda, the connections between the king's people and ours have become even more stronger.

Both commanders met frequently to drink honey, beer, and wine under the pretext of discussing defense strategies. It's not new that men like to do business over drinks. The drinks always facilitate their contact and loosen the tongues that are normally slow to speak.

One time, I witnessed how easily Ashenafi and Benaiah found agreement.

"Shalon, don't make a fool of yourself..." Benaiah was telling Ashenafi a joke. "You go everywhere praising the charms and virtues of your Sarah, as if you didn't know she had four lovers?"

"So what? I prefer to have one-fifth share in attractive goods than all shares in a junk."

The men laughed so hard that even I smiled too, but not because of Sarah's conduct or because her husband was so good at counting, while at the same time practical. I laughed because their joy was so contagious that I couldn't help it.

I stopped by the wall then. They didn't see me. I heard another story. This time Ashenafi spoke.

"A man comes to the priest for advice. 'Something terrible is going on and I need to talk to you about it.' 'What's going on?' 'My wife wants to poison me.' 'How is this possible?' 'Really. I'm sure she wants to poison me. What should I do?' 'I'll tell you soon,' says the rabbi. 'I'll talk to her, find out everything and let you know.' After two days, the priest calls the man to himself and says, 'Well, I talked to your wife for a long time. Do you want my advice?' 'Yes.' ;You will be better off swallowing this poison.'

Commanders clinked the jugs with honey and came to the conclusion that no matter what gods were worshiped; women were the same everywhere – In Sheba and Israel, and probably in every other country.

Then they started talking about something that really picked my interest. The case concerned security, which was what I thought was the most important. I listened to what people were saying because I had to make sure that the queen had the latest news, but above all that nobody and nothing was a threat to her.

"This is an old matter, but these are the worst, because sometimes they unexpectedly resurface years later," Benaiah began.

"Yes, the unsolved past is the hardest," Ashenafi nodded.

"In the time of David, my predecessor General Joab took at the king's order Edom, which did not want to submit to him for a long time. For punishment and because of too long resistance, Joab ordered to kill all men in the city. Only the little son of the prince, Hadad, managed to escape. His father's servants placed him in the care of the king of Egypt, who gave him shelter. When he became a man, he gained the favor of Pharaoh so well that he gave him his wife's sister as a wife. Pharaoh is wise, he thinks far ahead."

"These are the attributes of great rulers," admitted Ashenafi.

"After David's death, and when Joab fell out of favor with Solomon, Hadad returned to Edom, because he finally felt safe."

"And?"

"Joab has been dead for years, and Hadad rules his father's country."

"... and now he wants to take revenge," Ashenafi guessed.

"I have worrying information that he felt strong enough to plan a revenge on the heir of the one who killed his father."

"You mean on Solomon?" Ashenafi wanted to be sure.

"Exactly."

"So, you need to increase vigilance."

"It won't be easy to explain it to Solomon. He believes he has no enemies."

Listening to their conversation, I came to similar conclusions as they did. Vigilance had to be increased, and significantly. I backed out unnoticed by anyone. I went straight to the Great

Priestess with this information. Of course, I also told her the two newly heard jokes. She particularly liked the one about poison.

***

Solomon wondered how to make Makeda want to stay with him as long as possible. He was sure she would leave him one day. He understood her duties better than anyone. He knew that the day would soon come when her caravan would have to leave for Sheba. No country can stay too long without a ruler, even if he is represented by the best proxies. The king thought her departure was only a matter of time, and he tried to postpone this date for as far as possible.

She was also looking for excuses not to leave Jerusalem yet. She wanted to be with him so much! She felt unsatisfied, not only when they parted, but even when they were as close to each other as possible. She asked the Lady of the Moon and God to let them be for each other longer. She felt fullness, breathed with whole herself, had the impression that she had found the part she had missed all her life. She was complete. She had never experienced anything like that before. A flame enveloped her, which, however, did not burn her, but created her, gave her new, unimaginable strength and power she had never felt before.

She was glad when one day he suggested that she should take a short trip with him.

"Since we are so close to each other, and we have also entered into important trade agreements, maybe you should see what Israel outside Jerusalem looks like?" he suggested.

They decided not to hurry. He wanted her to experience the hospitality of his people, to learn their customs, and appreciate the beauty of the lands. He loved her, he wanted to show her everything that delighted him and to share with her what he considered beautiful. He dreamed that she would pick up his love for Israel, at least to a small extent.

They traveled in a single palanquin carried by a huge camel or in two separate ones, moving side by side, when they both needed rest. They often mounted horses and galloped with laughter, trying to keep up with the blowing wind. Their route had been planned so that it was diversified and included not only beautiful views, but also attractions prepared at each stop.

***

Following Moses' law, people In Israel worked for six days, and the seventh one, called the Sabbath, was spent on rest.

"In six days, God created heaven and earth, and on the seventh day he needed rest," Solomon explained to her. "A man is made in his image. He works hard and also needs a moment of breath. Notice how you can live well and wisely by observing the rights given to us. Can you see God's wisdom?"

"God organizes your world. Since I got here, I have the impression that you have the answer for every behavior, event, and question in your scriptures."

"People find it easier to live when they have clearly defined rules. Laws can be cruel, harsh, and even often silly, but compliance must be enforced. This is the basis for the proper functioning of the state."

"In Sheba, we also have a strict law, and whoever does not comply with it, is punished. Now that I see how it looks in your country, I know that when I come back, I will have a lot of work to do. We must organize our laws. I'll do it soon."

He ignored her words about the return.

"During the Sabbath, we not only cannot work, but we do not handle any urgent matters. We do not travel then. We do not light a fire. We pray and make offerings to God," he said with pride, but also with the hope that he would drive the thoughts of return away from her. "We will spend our first Sabbath together in the camp that they are already preparing for us."

When they arrived there, the sun was high. A large, smooth, almost still surface of water gleamed before them. On the left was a range called the Judean Mountains, and on the right was a vast plateau. Makeda jumped off her horse. Her feet, protected only by light sandals with a soft leather sole, met with a rough and hard surface. Everything around them was white. Instead of expected stones or sand, which she usually found on the seashores, here she saw a white solid mass frozen in a variety of different shapes.

She was waiting for explanations.

"It's salt," he bent and picked up a small lump. "And this vastness of water is the Salt Sea. People say that at its bottom lies Sodom and Gomorrah, the cities that God erased from the face of the earth for debauchery that spread in them. Some call this place the Dead Sea."

"Because of the sunken inhabitants of Sodom and Gomorrah?

"Rather because there is no visible life in it. It is so salty that when the water taken from it into a dish dries in the sun, only lumps of salt like this remain on the bottom. Try it," he handed the lump to her.

She licked it.

"Very salty!

"We sell it. It's one of our riches.

"You said it was the sea and I can clearly see the other side.

"It's forty-seven miles long. From here, we have about three miles to the other side. And it is over nine miles wide at its widest point.

He stood behind her and hugged her, embracing her waist.

She was only slightly shorter than him. He bowed his head only slightly and he could bury his face in her wind-blown hair.

"You are my queen," he confessed.

He still couldn't stop wondering how much he liked the fact that his touch caused her body to tremble. He did not have such sensations either with his Egyptian wife, or with any of the beautiful women who were at his disposal on a daily basis. He explained it to himself that maybe it was because he had to wait for her longer than for any other. No one had hidden her face from him for so long and so consistently, none was the queen, and none intended to leave him so quickly. In fact, each of them was associated with him until the end of her days, because they had to, they had no choice. Each one except her!

Makeda could leave at any time, without giving her reasons. She could leave him with his unfinished songs, abandon him, or cease to be interested in him overnight, as he had done with many women.

He loved her, and he didn't know why. He didn't want to look for a reason. What good would it make anyway? The feeling overwhelmed him. He wanted it to last.

He ordered his people to prepare such trade agreements with Sheba that would make her happy. He wanted to show her the most beautiful places he knew in order to keep her with him as long as possible. He invented pretexts for meetings and consultations, just to be close to her. Although he knew it was impossible, he wanted the time to stop and the moments when they were together to last forever.

His eyes moistened. He thought of those who had lived before them. Who were also united by the understanding of each other's souls. He saw thousands of past lives bound by invisible threads of feelings. He hugged her tighter. He took a breath.

"Breathe," he encouraged, "feel the smell of the moment and this place!"

"It's beautiful here..."

They were a unity not only with each other but also with the place.

"God gave us the best air that gives health and tranquility. People come here to cure diseases," Solomon pushed aside the thoughts of those who had similar emotions before them, because he felt that he was beginning to melt. "We have hot springs, of which people say that they treat skin diseases if you bathe in them regularly, and such air that those who suffer from shortness of breath should spend some time here every year."

"I've never seen a similar place," she snuggled into him.

"The sun shines almost always here, and you can see the clear sky," he continued, praising what they both looked at. "And we have something else here."

"Yes?"

"From time to time, the sea spits out black bitumen*."

"Bitumen?"

"I'll show you," he took her hand and led her a bit further, where a block that had been found on the shore a few days earlier was kept by the servants under a low tent.

She leaned in to sniff it.

"Can I touch it?"

"Go ahead. It is warm when it is thrown out of the sea, but now it has frozen, and it needs to be heated to be useful."

"And what might it be needed for?"

"We use it on construction sites, it is soft and rubbery. It is suitable for sealing because it is impermeable to water."

"You have salt, bitumen, stables and horses that you sell all over the world, you are building a fleet. You've created an empire!"

"Come, let's take a bath in the imperial sea! You'll see how it's different from others.

He slipped the straps of her dress, and when she stood in front of him only in a short skirt, he undid the buckle of his canvas robe and remained in a narrow loincloth."

"Let's do it slowly," he said, leading her into the water.

They went deeper and deeper. The water looked thicker than any other water she knew. It took her body in a warm embrace, creating a delicate coating on her skin.

"Lie down," he encouraged, laying on his back. She looked at him incredulous. He was floating on the surface, straightened, with his arms folded under his head.

"You can do that too!"

She didn't wait for another encouragement. After a while she was lying just like him. She spread her hands wide.

"It's wonderful! I'm floating on the water!"

"I love you, Makeda."

"I love you, Solomon."

The sea belonged to them. The servants preparing dinner on the shore occasionally took their eyes off their work and looked curiously at the playful rulers.

***

When she woke up, a scroll tied with a golden rope was lying on her bed. She unrolled it. At night, when she was sleeping, Solomon dressed his emotions in words. He wrote down what they said to each other.

Take me away with you—let us hurry!
Let the king bring me into his chambers.
We rejoice and delight in you ;
we will praise your love more than wine.

How beautiful you are, my darling!
Oh, how beautiful! Your eyes are doves.
How handsome you are, my beloved!
Oh, how charming! And our bed is verdant.

The beams of our house are cedars;
our rafters are firs

Lead me to the banquet hall,
and let your banner over me be love.

Instead of a signature, she found the words at the bottom: I love you. To be continued.

***

"Look that way, up high, see?" he gestured at the hill. "This statue is Lot's wife. It is clearly visible now, during the sunset.

"A stony wife?"

They were eating dinner. They sat on chairs arranged right on the seafront. The saltwater touched their bare feet. The servants brought dishes one after another.

"I told you that what is left of Sodom and Gomorrah is at the bottom of the sea."

"I remember."

"Well, that figure up there is, as I said, Lot's wife. Did Tamrin or Ben tell you about him?"

"I haven't heard about Lot or his wife."

"Do you want to hear about them?" he beckoned to the servant to hand him a bowl of water to wash his hands.

He wiped his hands on the canvas brought to him.

"Our oldest books say that the inhabitants of Sodom and Gomorrah were wealthy, and they lacked nothing, but they were licentious and did not want to live according to God's laws. God did not like their lifestyle, especially that they did not care about his admonitions and warnings. Very angry, he decided to destroy the cities and their inhabitants. Abraham persuaded him to waive such a terrible punishment if he could find at least fifty righteous inhabitants in the city. God agreed. However, Abraham understood that it could be difficult to find so many righteous ones. He asked God to limit this number to forty. And God agreed. But Abraham reconsidered the matter and thought it would be good if he found at least ten righteous in this corrupt city. And God accepted that offer as well."

"He isn't always so patient and forgiving, is he?"

"He's pretty strict."

"So, could ten righteous be found?" Makeda did not intend to continue the subject of strict fathers. Her father was perfect in her memories. Gentle and strict at the same time.

"God sent two angels to Sodom to see how things were going. They headed straight for Lot, who was considered the only decent man in town. He invited them in and offered hospitality. Everything was fine, but unfortunately, in the evening, men surrounded his house. Drunk, they shouted loudly to give them the guests, because they wanted to have fun with them.

"Really? How horrible!" she cried indignantly. "I'm not surprised that the God didn't like it there."

"As you know, we say: 'Guest in house - God in house.' We treat the guest as if he were a divine messenger. So, do not be surprised, but because of the respect for the guests, when Lot saw what was happening, he proposed to the attackers that he would give them his two daughters who were still virgins."

"Quite far-reaching hospitality, forgive me, but it's completely incomprehensible to me."

"That's the way we are," he said proudly, not wanting to notice her outrage. "However, the men refused to accept the virgins, shouting and threatening that if he would not give them the young men, they would immediately burn the house. When the crowd began to break down the door, the angels ordered Lot and his loved ones to close their eyes. They caused a big flash and instantly blinded all the attackers."

"They had power!"

"Immediately after, they ordered Lot to take his family and flee the city, because Sodom would be destroyed at dawn. Lot with his wife and daughters went to the mountains. His future sons-in-law refused to join him, not believing in what he was saying. Leaving, angels warned the family that none of them could under any circumstances turn back while escaping. Whoever would not heed the warning, would die."

"You're right, God is a strict father."

"At dawn, as announced by the angels, the Lord punished the place of offenses and evil, where not even ten righteous men could be found. There was a big explosion. Lot with his family were just fleeing through the mountains you see, and in the place, I showed you..." He indicated again the statue in the rays of the setting sun. "Lot's wife, unable to restrain curiosity, looked back. And she turned into a statue. As you can see, she still stands there today."

"Do you think she can see, hear and feel?" The story affected Makeda's imagination.

"I don't know, but this story has always moved me."

"I feel that we will be gone, and she will continue to look from this hill at the sunken cities and at those who will someday stand in the place where we are now. Will they also wonder if there are really cities on the seabed, and if this rock is really Lot's wife?"

***

The next stop was planned in the household of the region's administrator.

A few days earlier his son was born. The host had thus a double reason to celebrate. Not only his firstborn son was born, his king was also to visit his home. And not alone, but in the company of the famous Queen of Sheba.

That day, Makeda and Solomon traveled on horseback. Each of them rode a beautiful mount from world-famous royal stables. The king personally chose an elegant white mare for Makeda, and himself sat on a black stallion.

"It is an honor for them that the king will take part in brit mila*," he assured her when the buildings they were heading to were already visible in the distance. "And if it wasn't for you, my administrator wouldn't have this honor. So, it's not only me who owes you a lot, but also the man you don't even know yet. Let's see if he appreciates it."

He did. He waited with soldiers, advisers and festively dressed servants outside the city gate of the capital of the region he managed.

"Peace be with you," Solomon raised his hand when they arrived close enough.

At these words, the manager straightened up from a deep bow.

"Shalom aleichem, king who visit your land and honor your servant," he said respectfully and bowed low again. "Peace to the mighty Queen of Sheba and everybody coming with you," he added.

For the time of the visit, the chambers of the lady of the house were put at the disposal of the Queen of Sheba. Solomon lived in the private premises of his manager.

There was an atmosphere of excitement throughout the house caused by the visit and the brit mila ritual that was about to take place the next day.

A circumcision was the sealing of the pact between God and Abraham**. Every boy who was born underwent it before he was eight days old. The child was then given a name.

In the morning, after the breakfast, which Solomon and Makeda ate in the company of the administrator and his wife, the king allowed the ceremony to begin. The guests gathered in the square in front of the house. They felt honored to be there.

Solomon rarely attended such family celebrations outside Jerusalem. Now, he came with the famous Queen of the South, about which colorful stories had long circulated also in this region.

Solomon was given the most magnificent chair, used by the administrator to settle court cases and receive the most distinguished guests. For the king, it was additionally lined with valuable clothes and set on a platform. Next to it was a similar but smaller piece of furniture for the queen.

The ruler personally greeted many of the guests. It was obvious that he knew them and talked to them many times before. He was straightforward and extremely polite towards everyone with whom he exchanged even a single sentence. Earlier, in Jerusalem, Makeda was often impressed by his kind treatment of everyone he met. It was similar now. He was like a father to them, he had a calm but firm voice, he demanded, but also rewarded generously, he was able to severely rebuke, but also to praise.

"You are an excellent leader," she looked at him with tenderness of a woman who was in love for the first time in her life. He was a revelation to her. She admired everything he did. His silhouette, manner of movement, gestures, voice, the way he looked at people, all delighted her. She loved everything about him. Even the smallest gray hair on his temple.

After the official greetings, he returned to his chair and signaled that they could begin. Then the mohel* took out a rolled parchment from a decorative bag. He bowed to the king and the parents of the boy, standing before him, unfolded it and read the old words, familiar to everybody:

"'God said to Abraham: 'You, and after you, your offspring for all generations, keep a covenant with me. As a sign of it, you will circumcise the body of the foreskin. From generation to generation, each of your male children is to be circumcised when he is eight days old, a servant born in your home or purchased for money is to be circumcised. This covenant will be always valid. A man whose body of his foreskin has not been circumcised, shall be removed from the community, for he has broken the covenant with me.'**"

With these words, the mohel took a knife and bent over the baby, placed by his mother on the ritual table. Everybody held their breath. The mohel made a quick cut with a skillful movement, and when the child cried loudly, he filled his mouth with strong wine and leaned over. As it was customary, he rinsed the fresh wound with alcohol, using his own mouth. In this way, the wound scarred quickly, and the ritual wine did not allow the disease to enter the boy's body through the place weakened by the cut.

"In honor and with the consent of the king, who honored us and our household today, I give my son the name Solomon." While the mother took the crying baby to calm him, his father finished the ritual.

"If we had a son, I would like him to be ritually circumcised," Solomon leaned over Makeda.

"We do it in similar way in Sheba," she said. " However, with us it is not a result of a covenant with any of the gods. We know that for a boy who will become a man once, this piece of skin is unnecessary because it accumulates fluids that can cause illness. We remove it and bury it in the ground as a sign of unity with those who had been before us.

"A dried foreskin is like a ring, you know? And in Israel we give a ring as a sign of love."

"I will remember it," she assured him.

***

"Varda is crying at nights." The High Priestess used the moment when she found herself alone with Tamrin.

The queen was traveling with Solomon. She took only Seshep and four maids with her. The rest of the court stayed in Jerusalem. In the absence of Makeda, Varda could focus on her grief so she hardly left her chamber.

"As you know, priestess, women go through all kind of different states," he answered evasively.

"Tamrin, I am not one of your many friends from the pleasure house," she rebuked him. "And we're not talking about any woman out there, but the queen's assistant."

"Yes, High Priestess, forgive me," he straightened up, because he remembered at once how much he respected this woman.

"You are the manager of the caravan, you should take care of its participants, especially if they are responsible for the comfort of the ruler," she continued. "Varda oversees all the maids. Her condition affects how she behaves. As long as the queen is not with us, this is not a matter of paramount importance, but it can become one soon if nothing changes. Do you take this into consideration?"

Tamrin and the High Priestess were of a similar age. They had mutual respect, but before they set out on their way to Jerusalem, their paths rarely crossed. In any case, not enough to have the opportunity for even small confrontation, because there was simply no reason for that.

Each of them was an independent, free spirit that hated restrictions. They both developed a strong position and status on their own. And under no circumstances would any of them allow anyone else to enter the sphere of their own independence. They were mature and responsible, and always treated those whom they found equal to themselves with due respect.

"Varda has a problem," he decided he would make it clear because of his respect for the priestess. "She placed her feelings in the wrong man."

"She's been in love with you for a long time. You know it."

"I hoped for a long time that it only seemed so to me," he almost agreed with her. "I did everything to discourage her."

"The effect was counterproductive."

"I noticed that."

"What are you planning to do about it?"

"Nothing."

"What do you mean?"

"I will wait till it passes?"

She shrugged, "You know it's not a solution."

"I delude myself that maybe it is."

"But you like her, don't you?" Appreciating his honesty with her, she decided to get to the bottom of the topic.

"Yes of course. She is beautiful, smart, and sensitive."

"So, what's the matter then?

"Priestess, you know who I am, you know how old I am, how much world I saw and how much I gained," he said. "She deserves someone as pure and innocent as herself."

"Really? What are you afraid of, Tamrin?"

"I can't do it to her or to her father. I promised him I'd bring her home intact."

She wondered what to say.

"You are afraid of a responsibility for another person," she said.

"Maybe so."

"You like things easy, a life without obligations made you lazy."

"Maybe you are right, High Priestess. You are a wise woman. But I think it's probably not like this. I didn't take a wife all my life because I didn't want to leave her for a long periods at a time. A woman alone at home with children is not a good idea. Do you know how long my trips last? Even the shortest one means months of absence from Mariba. What wife would withstand such a thing? I was a child raised without a father. He was almost never at home. This is not good. That is why we shared things with my brother so that he has a family; he is permanently in the city, takes care of his wife and children, of whom you know he has a whole bunch. And he oversees our affairs in place. And I am in a constant journey. And alone."

"Right…"

"I don't have a wife or children because I'm responsible."

"Haven't you thought about finding a woman who would share your passions?"

"Sooner or later every woman would like to nest."

"Maybe that nest that scares you so much wouldn't be a bad idea? Think about it," she made a gesture, as if to enchant space and show him the future. "You're getting older." How many more years will you travel? How many caravans will you lead? Isn't it time to think about a quiet haven?"

"High Priestess, I have really great respect for you, and I am happy to listen to your wise words, but I do not know why today I have the impression that you treat me like one of your hemet. And I'm not one," he laughed, referring to the words with which she scolded him at the beginning of the conversation.

***

"Israel impresses me, Solomon," Makeda raised her goblet of water, "and you are the best king one could imagine. You have wisdom, reason, knowledge and a clear heart. You are the perfect ruler for the time of peace, the existence of which you have taken care of so beautifully.

"My father and those who were before him listened to God and obeyed his orders. That I am lucky to serve Israel in peacetime was done by Yahweh and my ancestors who obeyed his orders. But as you know, it hasn't always been peaceful in this land."

"I know a little, but still not enough. Please tell me about the very beginning. How did it start? Where did your people come from?"

"Should I start from the very beginning?"

"I will make your task easier if you want."

"Sure."

"In the beginning God created the heavens and the earth," she quoted words from the scrolls that Tamrin had once given her. "He worked constantly for six days, creating in turn everything that is given to us. On the seventh day, he was resting. He also created a man and a woman – Adam and Lilith. They were created from the same clay. God breathed a soul into them at the same time. They were equal. However, it was difficult for them to agree. Each of them had their own opinion on almost every case."

"Lilith was argumentative."

"Or maybe rather independent?"

He remembered the old stories. The first time he heard about her, she worried him strangely. His mother was strong and wise, but she always tried to pretend that she had no influence whatsoever on the state policy. It was only when David was dying, and the fate of the throne's heritage was on the line, that she showed how resolute she was and how well she was doing in the difficult palace reality. Other women around him also did a lot so that they would not be accused of being smarter than they would like to show. They were rather withdrawn, as it was said, "They knew their place."

"Lilith was equal to Adam and considered it natural that she should also have her say in everything that was happening around," Makeda knew the legends of the primeval mother of the mankind. "One day, unable to bear the constant misunderstandings and what I would describe as a power struggle, she left Adam. She opened her wings and flew away to never come back to him."

"They say God turned her into a demon," Solomon saddened. "That all newborn babies are in her hands. Boys up to eighth day of life, and girls up to the twentieth. Then, if they are not properly secured, Lilith can take them to her."

"Are they dying because of her?"

"So, they say. God deprived her of the offspring, so she steals the souls of newborns out of revenge."

"Do you believe this?"

"Women tie a red string on their children hands or hang something red at the cradle, because apparently this way you can reverse the effect of Lilith's evil eye."

"Was she punished for wanting to be independent?"

"You can read it that way."

"Solomon, your view of women is such as if you had never met your mother, High Priestess, Seshep, or other independent women."

"Makeda, ever since I met you, I really look at the world differently. You are the first queen with whom I want to spend nights and whom I want to hold in embrace.

"You are joking now, but I think that by sending Lilith to legends and scaring mothers with her, you harmed many women. This could have serious consequences," she wanted him to understand the importance of what she was saying.

In Israel, a woman did not mean much without a man. In Sheba, she could even rule. The priestesses of the Lady of the Moon were strong and for centuries had great influence. There were no women-led temples in Israel, and only men were priests.

"Think about it," she patted his hand. "A woman is asking you. Rather independent one, sitting on the throne, efficiently ruling a large state. I'm a woman, and look: I can do it. And mostly without any problem. I can assure you."

"I am thinking about it. Undoubtedly, I will come back to the issue of Lilith more than once."

"The fate of those who will come after us will depend on what place a woman takes in your world. Believe me. If you deprive a woman of importance and limit her to the role of mistress, babysitter, or someone whose universe is the kitchen, she will not dare for centuries to think that she has the independence and strength of her great grandmother, Lilith."

"I care about women as best I can. I even allow those who are foreign to us to pray to their gods. Even though I expose myself to the wrath of Yahweh for that."

"Think about it some more, please." She was pleased that she had planted the seed of uneasiness in him that she hoped would sprout. "After Lilith, God gave Eve to Adam?" she returned to the previous course of conversation, which pleased him very much.

"While Adam was sleeping soundly, God took out his rib and created her out of it. This was the woman Adam wanted. They lived happily and without disputes in the Garden of Eden, without pain, without the smallest worries, and in love. It was wonderful. In every respect. They received eternal life, health, they lacked nothing. Not only did they have no worries, but they did not even know about the possibility that worries could exist. They lived in an ideal world and they were perfect."

"And what happened?" She knew the continuation of this story, but she wanted to hear his version.

"One day Eve met a snake."

"Ah, a snake," she gestured, as if she were stroking its rounded body. "It is a symbol of eternal life and rebirth."

"Here, it symbolizes a temptation and evil."

"You know that Egyptian Isis, thanks to cooperation with the serpent, gained such huge power that she became the greatest goddess of this country?"

"I heard it. She took away some of her divine father's power by deceit, right?"

"Not by deceit, but by cleverness."

"I love your way of looking at things."

"Indeed, it's a bit different than yours."

"Maybe that's why you fascinate me so much?"

She gave him a smile in response. That they differed in many aspects could not make her love him less.

"So, you say that Eve met a snake?"

"That's how it was," he was glad to return to the story. "She walked around Paradise, singing cheerfully, until she reached the Tree of Knowledge."

"Our goddess's tree is persea."

"Our tree is called in various ways. Some even say it's an apple tree. But this is not the most important thing in this story."

"What is then?"

"A snake was wound around the tree. He was beautiful and like all animals in Paradise, he spoke in a human voice. Eve stopped in front of him and looked into his eyes. She found something in them that fascinated her. It was a promise to discover the unknown. He tempted and enticed her. He promised insanity of the senses, talked about the pleasure of learning a new and different reality. She listened excitedly. For many weeks, she came under the Tree of Knowledge to talk to him."

"She didn't give in to him right away?"

"Not at all! The seduction took a while. Eve was not just any woman. It wasn't easy for the snake; he had to work hard."

"Acquiring things easily is just taking them. Sometimes chasing a prey is more enjoyable than the moment of catching it."

"A long wait for the prize and the need to make significant efforts to receive it, is a pleasure, but believe me, and I know what I am saying, there are rewards so sweet that nothing in the world can match their taste."

He leaned forward, hoping for a kiss. She appreciated the lightness of his words and his ability to play with them, but she avoided his lips, moving away with laughter.

"You were talking about the tree," she reminded him.

"Right, the tree," he accepted with dignity that she did not allow him to kiss her. "So, the piquancy of the story is added by the fact that the tree under which they met was not ordinary."

"In our legends, the Lady of the Moon writes the history on its leaves. Its roots reach so deep that they are connected to everything that lives and derive power from what was and is."

"In Paradise, God severely and unequivocally announced to Adam and Eve that the only thing they are not allowed to do is to pick and eat fruit from this tree."

"A strong temptation!"

"Exactly," he pointed at her. "The forbidden fruit always tempts the most. You know something about it, don't you?"

She understood that he considered her a forbidden fruit, and she remembered the advice of the High Priestess and Seshep to not show him her face for as long as possible. She also had their words in her head that she should always remain a secret to him. They were right. Then, when they advised her to appear before him in the veil and later, when they urged her not to reveal herself completely to him and to be inscrutable to him, she was glad that she took their advice. It was effective.

"What happened next?"

"Things happened very quickly. Eve persuaded Adam to try the fruit of the forbidden tree with her."

"And...?"

"He tried."

"Oh, poor thing! He gave in so easily?"

"You women have your own ways to make us do exactly what you tell us. We don't even know how it happens that we are so willing to give in to you."

"Really?" she tilted her head mischievously. "Adam seems to me a man who has no opinion of his own. He is weak and easy to control. He barely got rid of independent Lilith, and now it was Eve who controlled him. He preferred her because she did what she wanted in such a way that he did not even realize that she ruled him. Maybe she was smarter than Lilith? Or maybe just different? Each of us can get where she wants to, but we do it in different, unique ways."

"You're confusing me, Makeda. What you say changes my view on many things that I had in order. At least, I thought so until now."

"They ate the forbidden fruit and then what?" She wanted him to return to the main story.

"First, they saw that they were naked."

"Oh!"

"In a world outside the Paradise, nudity is not appropriate. Well, unless in special circumstances..."

They both closed their eyes and smiled at the memory of their caresses.

"Please tell me what happened next?" Makeda was first to return to reality.

"God appeared and banished them from Paradise," he concluded briefly.

"Do you think it's sad?"

"Real life has begun. As we know it."

"That's great!" she applauded. "It's good that Eve reached for this fruit! Were it not for her, the Israelites would live in Paradise to this day and would not know the flavors of the real life? They would not experience its extraordinary beauty. And we couldn't have met!"

"We're not used to making fun of the holy books," he protested.

"I wouldn't dare," she said seriously. "I look at things from a different perspective. In my country, God works on the same level as the goddess. You have only Yahweh. With you, women, together with the goddess, have been removed and excluded. I have already told you about this, but I want to say it again: I have never met a place in the world where only a male god is worshiped and there is no place for goddesses and their priestesses. In Israel, women surrendered to Yahweh's authority and did not even whisper that they would like to worship the female element of divinity!"

"Our God contains both masculinity and femininity. He is everything. An absolute. We cannot make his similarities because he is unimaginable. Do you understand that? Your gods and goddesses are a tiny part of our God, a small element of him. Just like everyone and everything!"

"Solomon, I want to sort it out and think it over quietly," she calmed his emotions. "I need time. I will take as much of it as I need, and maybe one day I will come back to you with this topic," she made a gesture of thanks to the Moon Lady. "Now, please, finish the story of the beginnings of your people."

Solomon, answering her gesture, raised his hands up, greeting his God. He didn't want him to be angry with what Makeda was talking about.

"Adam and Eve lived outside the paradise. They experienced earthly problems. They became people. Next generations were born. It's a long story. So, I will shorten it if you allow?"

She nodded.

"It is important for my nation that at some point God made a covenant with Abraham. I mentioned it to you before."

"I have been looking at your ancient stories for some time. They are so rich and full of names that sometimes it is difficult for me to remember who was whose father, who had the child with whom, who killed whom, or planned to do it and for what reason. Who fought with whom, when and where, and whom Yahweh rewarded or punished. However, I remember who Abraham was, because as a sign of the covenant God has made with him, you do circumcision, of which I think I already know everything."

He was happy with her words, but he did not comment on them, but focused on the story.

"By God's will, a son was born to Abraham, even though he was a hundred years old, and his wife, who was ninety. He was called Isaac. Isaac had a son named Jacob; whose name God changed to Israel. He had twelve sons and twelve tribes come from them."

"These sons were: Reuben, Simeon, Levi, Judah, Dan, Naphtali, Gad, Asher, Issachar, Zabulun, Joseph and Benjamin," she recited fluently, wanting to please him. "As you know, I had Hebrew lessons," she said. "Ben, a son of a merchant from Jerusalem, taught me not only the language. He told me a little about your history. It is complicated, but probably also very colorful because of that. For someone who looks at it from the outside, it may seem terribly confusing at first moment..." she thought out loud and came to the conclusion that she would lie, claiming that she understood it.

"And...?"

"And so, it seems in the second and subsequent moments as well, still confusing," she disarmed him with her sincerity. "I will be grateful if you tell me what happened next..."

"Next? It happened to be the time for Moses..."

" ... who grew up at the court of the ruler of Egypt. Later, when he learned that he was an Israelite, he led his pharaoh-oppressed people to the land of Canaan."

"Exactly. Of course, as you can guess, it happened at the will of God, who appeared to Moses and said to him what to do and supported him all the time. He gave numerous proofs for this. First, when the Pharaoh refused to let the Israelites out of Egypt, he sent plagues upon his country. There were ten of them, each one more terrible than the previous one. For example, frogs, mosquitoes, reptiles, flies, cattle fever, ulcers, hail, locusts, and the changing of Nile waters into blood."

Makeda shuddered.

"Then he helped the fleeing people survive the hard time," he continued. "Thanks to him, the sea parted so that they could cross to the other bank on foot. Pharaoh and his army died in the depths when the sea returned to its former place. There were many miracles that God did for our ancestors. After all, the journey from Egypt to the promised land took forty years."

"And I was complaining that my journey from Sheba to you was long," she said.

"You don't even know how grateful I am to God that he brought you to me."

"I thank him too. I have long believed that not only the Moon Lady, but also Yahweh did it. Maybe they acted in concert, what do you think?"

"Our God has a completely different sense of humor than your goddess. He not only does not like jokes about himself, but he punishes severely for them."

"Because he is still young. As he matures, he will gain distance," she laughed.

"That's a bold statement."

"These are the words of the High Priestess. We sometimes talk about Yahweh. She has nothing against him. Moreover, she thinks it can happen that over time, when Yahweh matures, he will know that every god needs a goddess."

"He has both feminine and masculine traits. He is everything. I told you."

"I will think about it," she promised. "Tell me what happened next, because we are probably approaching more recent times?"

"You're right," he folded his arms. "When my ancestors finally reached the land that God promised us, the time of hard work and building the state began. At first, we didn't have a king. Each tribe chose their representative. The most important decisions for all were made by the council they formed. But around them lived quarrelsome tribes that threatened us. It was clear that if we unite and create a strong state, it would be easier for us to face them. Saul became the first king of the united Israel. The second was my father, David."

"I heard the comforting story of how he defeated Goliath."

"Yes, it's comforting. It says that if God is on our side, we have a chance to win even with the invincible giant."

"It also says that if we believe in ourselves, we can deal with adversities, even those that seem insurmountable."

"Yes," he admitted. "One does not exclude the other."

"Exactly. Just as the existence of Yahweh does not exclude the existence of the Lady of the Moon."

"I can't agree with that."

"Maybe you should still think about it?" she suggested agreeably, and he once again felt how strong a woman he was dealing with.

Would any of his spouses dare to talk to him like that? Would anyone of them dare to suggest that he thinks over something as indisputable, obvious, and inviolable to him as the faith in God? Only a real queen could do that, a person with a powerful, independent spirit. Not only did she say that, but it seemed that she didn't even think of it for a moment as an act of courage. She just said what she thought was appropriate and apparently did not feel the limitations resulting from being a woman!

"Yes, think about it again," she repeated. "But not now, okay? Now tell me about your father, please."

He didn't understand why he was giving in to her, and why the requests or even orders sounded completely natural in her mouth. Furthermore, he was ready to fulfill them immediately.

"David was above all a great, strong warrior. I wish you could meet him; he would delight you."

"I wonder if he would like me?" She showed all her teeth in a smile.

"I have no doubt about it. You are beautiful and smart, and at the same time mysterious. He liked women." He pondered over the memories. "But he loved my mother the most."

"Queen Bathsheba is incomparable," she assured him. "I love her wisdom. When I heard their love story for the first time, I cried all night. I imagined what she felt and dreamed that I too would experience a feeling that would last until the end of the world. I think I received it because I prayed for it. I am with you and I know that you are the love of my life."

"We received a beautiful gift. We should care for and cherish this feeling. Love is like a delicate plant. Without good earth, sun, water and a friendly wind, it can wilt."

She lowered her head and sighed, thinking of the impending separation. But she chased these thoughts away, remembering that the feeling of happiness also depends on commitment to the moments that are given to us.

"So? You were talking about David?"

"He was a warrior. He conquered and subjugated the lands of the Philistines, Moabites, Arameans, in the north and south, making Israel great. And he conquered Jerusalem. It is thanks to him that I can rule in peace. He prepared the groundwork for it for me. He put me on the throne with the task of constructing a temple and strengthening the state. With God's help, thanks to the wisdom that the Lord gave me, I am doing it with pretty good results I believe, right?"

"You are a king whose fame will last for centuries," she was absolutely convinced it would be so.

"I would like to. And that I would be remembered as wise and just, and my rule as the time during which Israel became a powerful state, and whose successors ruled for a long time and in peace. I would also like the faith in the true God to spread all over the world. Because with it there will be prosperity, order, righteousness, and happiness."

"You speak beautifully of Yahweh. Surely you know that long-ago Pharaoh Akhenaten tried to make him the god of Egypt?"

"He managed to introduce the faith in one god, but for a short time only. The god of Akhenaten and his beautiful wife, Nefertiti, was Aton. Some may think that God and Aton are similar to each other. But this is not the case. Aton did not stand the test of time. He was the god of the elite. Egypt was not ready for him. The people were not prepared for him. The old gods were very strong, Aton had no chance against them."

"Do you think God gains power with the strength of the prayers raised to him?"

"You could say so. He gives us strength, and we strengthen him by offering him ourselves, our faith, devotion, obedience, and prayers."

"Does the strength of the state depend on the God who protects it?"

"You can make various political decisions, enter into agreements and alliances, but the most important thing is to have God on your side*," he declared. "I try to rule Israel in this way and that's exactly how my father exercised power."

She fell silent. She wondered how similar her father's view of the world was. Nothing was more important to him than the continuity of the dynasty and the power of Sheba. And he always tried to have Illumkuh and the Lady of the Moon on his side.

"You're right. Caring for the state is our most important duty as rulers. Undoubtedly, we must, and I believe that we both want, to rule in the name of our gods and in accordance with the laws and principles they set for us."

He listened carefully. She saw that he wasn't going to interrupt her.

"I had a dream once that was almost like a vision. It had great power. It was a long time ago, but I remember it as well as if I dreamed it tonight. I heard a voice that almost burst my head open then. I thought it would break in two and I would die. But this did not happen. The voice turned into a bright light and I could not hear it with my ears, but I felt it with my body. It said: There is one God. He is the beginning and the end; he is everything and everywhere. Those whom people consider to be gods, to whom they pray, are the sons and daughters sent by him, emanations of divine power. God gives us exactly the emanations we need. However, someday in the future people will grow up, and then God will send his son to earth, who will be almost ordinary man like everyone else. Before this happens, however, the sons and daughters of the Absolute are gods, not human beings."

"Our books mention the coming of the Messiah," he commented. " So, it's hard for me to argue with what you said. You are right that Aton who we talked about, Hathor, Isis, your Illumkuh or the Lady of the Moon are not human. They are only our image of divinity. The true God cannot be imagined by a human mind. That is why we are strictly forbidden to create any images of him."

She took out a tiny golden plaque, which she always wore in an almost invisible small purse hung from her belt. She placed it on her hand and showed it to Solomon.

"The Ten Commandments," he was surprised. "Where did you get these slabs from?"

"Tamrin gave them to me long ago. I always carry them with me. I like having them close."

"Makeda, God has given you special care, I know that."

"The Lady of the Moon is watching over me as well."

"Maybe…

She loved the time they spent together. She wanted the conversations they had to never end. But with each passing day and each passing moment, she felt more and more that their time together had to end soon. He also knew this very well, so they tried to spend as much time together as possible.

"Solomon, I have to return home," she said one day. "And I know you understand me."

They were holding hands.

"Love is the most important thing in the world, it's worth living for it. But when a man is born for a mission, or when the gods show him a special path, the feelings and his own pleasure must give way to a higher plan. If we have obligations, we cannot give them up just because we come across love. Even if it's the love of our life."

She could feel her pulse throbbing harder and harder. An invisible ring appeared around her head. Her throat was tightening. She knew that in a moment she would not be able to speak, she finished with the last remains of her strength.

"We have to try to cultivate this feeling and take care of it with all our strength, but it cannot be done at the expense of giving up the obligations and commitments we have. We must implement the plans that the gods have set for us. We are rulers, we should live with dignity as befits kings. There is no other way."

She uttered her last words with a completely clenched throat. She paused. Fortunately, after a while the invisible painful ring holding her head broke and the pain eased. She covered her face with her hands and burst into tears. He embraced her. They both cried. They knew their time together was over, and they felt that what they gave each other was the greatest thing that could happen to them in their lives.

"Don't leave, stay with me," he tried to resist the inevitable. "Be my queen. You will sit with me on the throne. We will join Sheba and Israel together. We will create an empire."

"Beloved, you know it's impossible," she justified herself and him, knowing that he was suffering as much as she did. "If I do, all your alliances will be ruined and you will lose most of what you have built so intricately," she stopped sobbing, her voice was strong and calm again. "You know very well that if the Pharaoh's daughter returns to Egypt, because no other solution will be honorable for her, her father will declare war on you. When you have Egypt against you, everyone who has been waiting for your weakness for a long time will come at you. You don't have only friends. Hadad and many others are waiting for your slightest stumble. They would be happy if we did something as unreasonable as joining our kingdoms. Look what a stir our agreements on the fleet and new trade routes caused even though they are secret; nobody was supposed to know about them."

"You know, as well as I do, that there is nothing secret in the world. If something leaves our mouth, it goes to a space from which everyone can pick out our words. You were brought up by priestesses after all, who are experts in these matters, you know it very well."

"Solomon, you understand politics better than anyone. You know very well, just as the High Priestess, Seshep and I do, that I cannot stay."

"You can. I will hide you in my arms and will not give you back, even when the whole world asks for you!" he assured, kneeling at her feet. "I am ready to change myself and everything around, if you just want to stay."

"You would set everything on fire in this way."

"I'm ready to do it for you. Just say the word."

"You are saying that because you know I will never say it."

"I'd like you to do this, really. Because my will is not enough to change our lives."

As he said that, a butterfly sat on her shoulder. It had large wings the color of a clear blue sky.

"It's the envoy of the Lady of the Moon," she guessed. "I wonder what she wants to tell us?"

He closed it in his hands.

"Is it dead or alive now, what do you think?" he asked.

"Let it out," she said.

"Is it dead or alive?" he repeated, and she noticed that he got serious.

"Is this a puzzle?" she guessed.

"Exactly."

She knew that no matter what the answer, she might be wrong. If she says that the butterfly is alive, Solomon will crush it to prove that she is wrong. If she says it is dead, he will open his hands and the insect will fly away.

He knew she understood his thoughts.

"Take it," he offered, moving his hands toward her.

For a moment they created a common space with their joined hands.

"I got it!" She looked inside her joined hands through the hole she had formed with her fingers. "It's wonderful..."

"Yes. And it will live only a moment. But for it, this moment is a lifetime," he said, and it seemed to Makeda that his eyes were watering again. "If you leave me, the thought of the time we spent together will be with me always, all the time and to the end, because since I met you, you are my life."

"What will be the fate of this butterfly?" she struggled to hold back the tears that had accumulated under her eyelids again.

"Everything is in your hands."

***

I watched them and the feeling that united them.

They were like children in their mutual admiration. He was like a dreamed king from a fairy tale, and she was like a princess that almost every girl would like to be in her childhood. They both did everything to create, for the time they knew it would end soon, a world so beautiful and unique that they would never forget it. So that the shared moments would give them strength for the rest of their lives. I wondered if they both were aware of that? Did they create such a world deliberately? A place where there were no worries, no illnesses, no problems, no dangers, and no threats. They both tried to be all the best for each other. However, with each passing day, they felt more and more that the time they were offered was not given to them for eternity.

I was sure that their happiness would end soon. I saw the future after all.

At nights when I was alone, I, the tough hemet, shed salty tears, pitying on the fate of my beloved Makeda.

She was a queen and he was a king. They were born destined to lead their people. For both of them the good of the state had to be more important than anything else.

I knew that Solomon appreciated the gift he had received, because he enjoyed it in such a way that I would never have suspected from a mature man sitting on the richest throne in the world. When they went on a journey, I followed them every step. I trusted Solomon's guards, but I wanted to be close to my lady to make sure she was safe. That was my life calling after all. So, I saw him dancing in the rain, shouting out loud the words of love, throwing off his robes by the moon and bathing naked in the sea with her, I saw the gold ring that he almost made with his own hands for her, I saw him carry her in his arms, anoint her back in a bath...

Makeda? She hadn't known a man before. Love elations was not known to her. Solomon was the man she had awaited and longed for. I watched her closely. In the palace, everyone's eyes were still on her. Although we were protecting her with all our might, I knew that she was constantly watched by the servants of Queen Bathsheba and the Egyptian wife of Solomon. In the palace, Makeda kept her emotions at bay, but when they set off on a journey, she allowed herself to spread her wings.

When I looked at their happiness, I swore that I would do everything in my power so that the moments given to them were exactly like each of them had dreamed. I have never experienced similar love myself, and I was sure that it would not be given to me. So, I wanted Makeda to love for her and for me. So, that what she was going through would be enough for her for the rest of her days, and so that I could draw on it in the process.

I knew that although they were made for each other, they would never be together. Because they have separate lives, a different kind of responsibility, and they were born for different reasons. They were lucky that their fates crossed. I helped them with all my heart and served with all my skills. My life mission was to support Lady of the Moon and protect Makeda. I wanted to do it, I loved it, and I was sure that I was fulfilling myself this way as a human being.

***

"I received the news that Elichoref would want to ask for my permission for Varda to be his wife," the queen knew perfectly well what impression this message would make on Tamrin. She was right.

At the request of Seshep and Varda, she joined the conspiracy. The women concluded that there were many indications that Tamrin was interested in Varda, but he had concerns about the involvement in this relationship. To speed up his decision that they saw would have to be made eventually, they decided to use a trick. However, for the whole action to look credible, the queen had to join this conspiracy. As soon as Makeda returned from the trip with Solomon, joyful, rested, and happy as never before, they decided to introduce her into their plan.

"Fine," she agreed. "If it's for the future happiness of two people whom I like very much, why not?"

Now, sitting next to Tamrin, after she had finished telling the story of her expedition, she decided to fulfill her promise to Varda and Seshep.

"What do you think?" she asked innocently. "General Tesfa has entrusted you with her care, so I decided not to make a decision without talking to you first."

After her first words, Tamrin's breath paused and his heart stopped beating.

Seeing what was happening, Makeda got scared at first, remembering Solomon's words that the human strongest organ is a tongue that can kill. However, the merchant's breathing quickly returned to a steady rhythm, so she decided that Varda and Seshep's idea was good after all.

"So, what do you think?" she urged him. "Elichoref is a wealthy, kind and educated man. True, we would have to lose Varda, because she would have to stay here. After all, the royal writer will not come with us to Sheba, right? Although I would love this solution very much. And you?"

Seeing that Tamrin was still unable to speak, she continued, "We both know that Tesfa has long wanted to have a son-in-law and grandchildren, so this news should please him. Will you finally tell me what you think?" she pretended to be impatient.

"It's great news of course, queen," he swallowed and assumed an official tone. "What does Varda say to this? Does she know about Elichoref's efforts?"

"It's easy to notice that he can't take his eyes off her. Even me, preoccupied with the affairs of the state and many others as you know, even I can see his calf eyes."

"General Tesfa entrusted Varda to my protection." Tamrin was not able to get rid of the official tone, and in addition, a mask of polite indifference appeared on his face. "Solomon's writer is an interesting candidate, but I think Varda deserves someone with a princely title. I would be very happy, but I cannot allow something so important to happen without the knowledge and consent of her father. Besides, Elichoref is a follower of Yahweh. Varda would have to accept his faith.

Makeda listened to him and spread her hands helplessly.

"So what? Are you for or against it? I don't think I understand."

"I am in favor but at the moment, against."

"I see," she was glad she had joined the conspiracy, because she was now absolutely sure that the women were right. "You know how much I value your opinion. What do you suggest in this situation?"

"First of all, I think you should ask Varda. If she is willing to stay in Israel and, as a result, accept the faith in God, you must send a message to General Tesfa as soon as possible. I don't know when we will set out for our way back, because this decision is yours, queen, but we will not stay here forever, will we? So, let us also consider the possibility that we will return to Sheba and Varda will give the joyful news to her father herself. Then they will decide together what to do next. Maybe then Elichoref will come to Sheba? Or Varda will return to Israel? She likes traveling."

"Tamrin, do I understand correctly that you do not favor the idea of consenting to a quick marriage?"

"One shouldn't hurry with such important decisions."

"You may be right." She was glad that the fish had caught the bait. "I'll take your opinion into account. Due to the fact that it is not entirely clear to me, I give you three days to think about the matter. Then you will tell me what you ultimately think about it."

"It will be best this way, queen," he still couldn't get rid of the official tone, so Makeda concluded that the message he received from her was really stirring for him.

She stood up, intending to leave.

"One more thing," she sat down again. "I heard Varda cried almost every night in my absence. She didn't want to say what was bothering her. I have received opinions that it has something to do with you. Do you know what's going on?"

She waited on his response. Knowing her honesty and truthfulness, decided that she was so engaged in the relationship with Solomon that she did not see the life going on around her. He decided that he could only tell her the truth or say nothing.

"Varda is very young and inexperienced," he began. "She has a lifetime ahead of her. She is a good girl. She deserves someone special."

"It's hard to disagree with what you are saying," she encouraged him.

At this point, instead of telling her what was bothering him, as she hoped, he fell silent.

"Feelings are a delicate matter," he said only. "Sometimes you need time for them to mature."

"Or a driver with a whip in her hand," she thought, but decided not to say those words out loud, remembering Solomon's aphorism that sometimes speech is silver, and silence is gold.

***

"Great Kandake, Queen of Sheba, you are pregnant."

Makeda, who was standing when the priestess entered her chamber, sat down. She needed a moment to get the meaning of the words that were spoken.

She closed her eyes. She was silent. Finally, she rose and faced the priestess. She took her hands.

"How do you know?"

"Priestesses always know such things."

"Are you sure?

"Absolutely.

Makeda put her hands on her stomach.

"I will have a baby?

"Everything points to that, lady."

"Everything meaning what?" She still had her hands on her stomach.

"Your blood should have appeared twenty days ago. It's not here. But of course, this is not a proof yet. More importantly, you look different, and above all, your dream visions came back."

"It's true…"

"The goddess gives them to you at special times. You had them before you became a woman. Later, when you needed time to learn and acquire new skills, the Moon Lady stopped them. Now your body has changed again. It has received extraordinary grace. Double one. You have visions again and… you'll be a mother! Thank you for that!"

***

"Tamrin, how much time do you need to prepare the caravan for leaving Jerusalem?"

"Queen, are we coming home?" He was happy.

"It's time," she assured him with such conviction that he was certain that the delayed departure would happen soon.

He did not know what significant thing happened that she finally made up her mind. He was convinced, as almost everyone at both courts, that Solomon and Makeda were doing everything to be able to enjoy each other as long as possible.

He, despite treating Jerusalem like his second home, thought the visit was getting too long. In the palace there were no visible signs of tiredness with the queen's stay yet, but in the city, people talked more and more often about the costs generated by her people and herself, and that she was pulling Solomon away from ruling the state.

Fortunately, the powerful gifts she brought with her were still remembered, so the people's whispers were not dangerous, but they were already beginning to approach the border, which once crossed, never returns to its original shape. Tamrin, who had an experienced ear and was able to sense the moods, knew that it was high time to finish the visit.

"It is better that the host feels unsatisfied than sated," he thought, but obviously found no reason to express this opinion out loud with the queen.

He was thus glad when he heard her question about leaving.

"I've been ready for some time," he said, trying not to show emotion. "As soon as you let us know, lady, we'll be ready within ten days."

"Then I'm letting you know, Tamrin!?"

"Queen, forgive me for daring to ask, but are you sure? The preparations for the journey are, as you know, a long process and a great effort. Our caravan is the largest enterprise of this type the world has seen. I have to gather all the camels available on the spot and bring many new ones, because those in Jerusalem are certainly not enough for us."

"Don't worry. My decision is final."

"I will begin the preparation immediately, my lady," he bowed, ready to leave.

"Not so fast," she stopped him. "I have a question for you because I don't know why, but I get the impression that you are avoiding a certain topic. You know what I mean?"

"I guess," he admitted with remorse.

"You are Varda's guardian because you promised that to her father. I respect you and general Tesfa, so even though as a queen I could make a decision on this matter, I left it to you. But I am not going to wait any longer. Tell me what you finally decided!"

"Forgive me for delaying my answer for so long, lady, but I still consider all the pros and cons. The decision is not easy. I took into account both Varda's happiness and the fact that her father would perhaps be pleased with her marriage. However, the words "perhaps" are essential here. Because we don't know that, do we? Perhaps he would not be delighted that his only daughter would leave the family home, settle in another country, with a different culture and even religion. Besides, maybe he was counting on the husband of his only child to perform a more important function and be wealthier than the royal writer? Just because Varda, who has always had a great desire to explore the world, now thinks that she would like to settle in Jerusalem, does not mean that such a decision will be the right one."

"So, in short?" she urged him, liking what she heard.

"In short, since I have the privilege of being asked again for my opinion by my queen, I believe that if there is a feeling between Varda and Elichoref, it will survive the separation for the time of her return to her father. It is far to Sheba, but not so far that the love that is supposed to last until the end of life will be extinguished. If its flame is large enough, it will last. For Varda and Elichoref, the travel time will be a test of the strength of their feelings, and it will give me the opportunity to present the matter to General Tesfa. I would not like to burden my conscience with this. He is her father and he should make a decision."

"Remember that Varda can make it on her own."

"But she won't do it out of respect for her father, you know that, lady. She is well bred."

"But independent, like all women in Sheba."

"Yes, but sometimes an independent woman also needs time to make a decision that may affect her future life. Let's give her this time. I wouldn't want her to regret it someday. She is a wonderful girl. She deserves the best."

"Fine. Let it be according to your words, Tamrin," she thought for a moment, as if contemplating something, and added, "You're right about the test of time. If the feeling lasts for several months and remains unchanged, it will mean that it is strong and worth fighting for. But it may turn out that it fades away as fast as it appeared, right?"

Makeda thought about the emotions Varda had given to Tamrin, but also about her love for Solomon, about the overwhelming feeling that made her happy like never before.

She understood Varda like none of the women around them. Ever since she learned that her assistant has affection for her favorite advisor, she felt special closeness with her. In a way, they were in a similar situation. Varda loved the man she had met at her father's house since childhood. Someone powerful, unsurpassed, knowing the world and smelling like the wind. Who was almost never there, but she knew that he existed because he appeared from time to time, real, vivid, and tangible. She, Makeda, was in a more difficult situation. All her life she believed in the existence of someone who could turn out to only be a figment of child's fantasy. She wanted to find him, reach him and receive a gift that she knew would be the greatest gift she would receive in her life. But if it were not for her stubbornness, conviction and faith in the rightness of the way from her dreams, if not for the support she received from her father, the High Priestess and Seshep, perhaps she would lose her goal somewhere along the way, forget her childhood dreams and today she would not be where she was just now. So, she understood Varda and was convinced that sooner or later, Tamrin would understand that they were meant for each other. She knew that Varda had the strength and faith that would be enough for both of them. Even if Tamrin was not yet sure that he would spend the rest of his life with Varda, both Makeda and all the women around her were convinced of this. Since Varda decided they would be together, there was no other way. For if a woman decides something about love matters, she gets her way, come hell or high water.

***

Three unusual nights came. One after another. Each of them deprived the queen of strength, but also gave her the feeling that she was admitted to another dimension again' to the otherworldly spheres of knowledge that were always close to her.

As new life grew in her body, the gates of the future parted before her again, as they had once done. She was able to see what ordinary mortals did not have access to. She was not looking for a reason why she was given this honor, but she was sure that her visions were given to her so that she would tell Solomon about them. He should write down and disseminate them, because they were supposed to be a warning sent to people by God.

She realized that the voice she had heard since childhood was coming from the Supreme. Even though she didn't know him then, he was already speaking to her. And it seemed to her that she was beginning to understand more and more: all her life it was not only the Lady of the Moon who cared about her, but He too marked her paths and led her, almost holding her hand. With his power, he made her sit on the throne of Sheba, gave her visions, led her to Solomon, made her pregnant. Now that he reappeared so clearly in her life and she heard his voice again, she felt relief and fulfillment. She was home, safe, sure that she was on the right path.

At the same time, she felt the overwhelming presence of the Lady of the Moon and her acceptance of what was happening. She was with her all the time, covering her with silvery wings, which at times looked like a blue, wide, starred coat. She sent light gusts of wind to her, which brought her relief, blessed her with silver hands and put a kiss on her forehead. She gave strength. At such moments, the round moon over the goddess's head changed its color from silver to gold and made the whole figure, hovering above the earth, shine.

The first prophecy

The queen of Sheba's first vision of the future of the world was so intense that it woke her up. Makeda sat on the bed trembling and sweat-strewn. She was crying. As soon as Seshep heard the movement in her lady's chamber, she was immediately at her side. At night, even the slightest rustle woke her up. Her vigilance did not decrease with age. Seeing what was happening, she wiped the queen's forehead and hugged her.

She was sure that the visions could reoccur when a few days earlier Makeda heard the voice of God in her dream. It was a signal that the vigilance should be increased, especially at night.

She was right.

"Call Solomon, now!" Makeda ordered in a weak but firm voice. "Let him take Elichoref with him. Necessarily. He will write!" she added, lying on the cushions and immediately falling asleep.

Seshep woke Varda and told her to personally go to the king, disregarding any protests from his protection and servants, and make him want to come as soon as possible. She also sent a maid to bring the High Priestess.

While waiting, she prayed to the Moon Lady.

The priestess appeared quickly and seeing what was happening, she knelt beside Seshep.

Varda managed to convince Solomon's guards, who knew who they were dealing with, to let her into the chamber of the king's servant. Fortunately, she didn't have to persuade him for a long time to wake his master. He understood that since the Queen of Sheba called for the king in the morning, something special must have happened. This has never happened before after all. Varda breathed a sigh of relief when after finding out what was going on, Solomon immediately put on a light night coat, which he used only in his chambers, and ordered to send Elichoref to the queen's chambers, and himself went fast in that direction, along with her.

When the king and Elichoref arrived in Makeda's chamber, she sensed their presence and woke up.

However, she did not behave in the usual way. She knelt on the bed, crossed her hands over her arms, and said in an inspired voice, "Your kingdom*, great Solomon, is mighty and abundant in happiness, but know that after your death it will split into two parts, and disobedience to kings will arise among your people, and the last two kings of Israel will be taken prisoners, their eyes will be gouged, and then they will be led together with your people to Babylon, where they will stay until death," she said in one breath.

Elichoref looked at Solomon, and when the king nodded, he immediately took out the utensils and began to note:

"God's terrible wrath will fall on your people because they will not keep his laws and commandments. The holy land will be possessed by foreign people who will bring other gods. However, this people will not even believe in their own gods, and then total ungodliness will prevail. New peoples will come, which will torment them cruelly, until in this tough captivity they will finally convert, turning their prayers and devotions to the true God. Only then, will God have mercy and send to the earth, among His chosen people, the prophets, who will shout in big voice about the imminent woe and punish the bad, but the people will continue to sin, so the punishment will fall on them and God will revenge them terribly."

Solomon, who had been standing next to the bed from the moment he entered the chamber, sat down and sighed heavily, but still with a clear relief. It seemed to him that he finally understood Yahweh's plan, which directed Makeda to him so that he could hear what was just reaching his ears: through the innocent, pure queen, God passed him warnings for Israel.

Words were flowing continuously from Makeda's lips.

"The lineage and the kings will disappear, and the temple built in honor of God, and your cities, will be razed to the ground. Only after many years, when the Israeli people return to God after a severe punishment, will they again take possession of the city, but not as powerful as yours anymore and not for long, because they will soon fall under the rule of the Romans and the pagan will rule completely.

"This land around Jerusalem is holy, for there the Messiah, the son of God, will be born, who will save the people from slavery. He will dedicate his life to the people, teaching and telling them the true knowledge, but the people will not recognize him and will not fear his miracles, and they will crucify him, giving him the most shameful death. Golgotha will become famous as holy, because the Messiah will be tormented on it, his hearty blood and pained sweat will flow down it, he will give out his spirit on it and will give himself into God's hands. After his death, a terrible punishment will fall on Jerusalem, the state will be destroyed, the city will be razed, so that a stone will not remain upon a stone, and the people of Israel will fall apart in all directions because they did not believe in the Messiah and led him to death.

"All your vessels that you have offered to the temple, and all the holy jewels will go to Rome and will always remain there, for Rome will then become a Mose pillar. And the pagan people will gain Jerusalem, but they will value this land more than the people of Israel, because they will recognize the Messiah as a great prophet, and they will keep his grave cared for and will defend it until the last drop of blood."

Makeda finished her speech. She was still kneeling on the bed, arms folded across her chest. Those present were silent. They were stunned. They didn't know what to think about what they had just witnessed.

Solomon was the first to speak.

"You're talking about the Messiah. When will he be born?" he asked, believing that Makeda was still on the side to which none of those present had access.

"One will have to wait for him more than eight hundred years. His death will occur under the rule of the Romans," she replied, as if she expected this question, knowing that when she answers it, the communication with God will be broken and she will be able to rest.

That's what happened. When she answered, her body shuddered, she let out the breath, releasing the air that had accumulated in her tiny body in unusual quantity, and opened her eyes. She looked around, reached her hand out to Solomon, and when he took it, she smiled helplessly, hugged her cheek to his hand and fell asleep.

The second prophecy

She spent almost the entire next day in bed. She was weak, and whenever she tried to get up, she felt so dizzy that she was balancing on the verge of losing consciousness.

Seshep brought a hemet-medic who recommended after some examination that the queen does not leave her chamber. She ordered to cook a light quail soup for her, to which she added a handful of dry strengthening herbs. Makeda slept through the day, awakened only to take a meal or drink water with honey, which was also the recommendation of the medic.

When evening came, and Makeda was still asleep, the High Priestess joined Seshep, who did not leave her mistress. She thought that a vision could happen again. The experience and knowledge accumulated over the years allowed her to believe that the gods appear to people regularly, and that if Makeda heard the divine voice once, it is very likely that she would hear it again. Solomon agreed with her opinion and asked to be sent for him immediately if her suppositions would be confirmed.

She was right.

As the night slowly dawned, Makeda began to breathe louder. Seshep, who had lied downright next to her bed, immediately jumped up. She saw sweat drops on her forehead, and wet hair. She glanced toward the priestess, who was praying earnestly, kneeling by the window. However, as soon as she noticed the movement, she got up and walked to the bed.

"Run to king Solomon," she ordered the maid standing by the door. "Tell him I'm sending you. He'll know what's going on."

She was sure that Makeda would soon hear the voice again.

The queen was kneeling on the bed with her head raised and her eyes closed. She spoke when Solomon stood by her. As if the God, who was communicating with her, had been just waiting for his arrival.

"Faith in the teaching of the Messiah will reach such a power that it will name emperors and kings for thrones, and nothing will happen without the knowledge of priests," she began in an inspired voice just like the previous night. "The Jewish people will wander all over the world, and all rule and power will be taken from them and given to the followers of the faith in the Messiah. But when they come to power, instead of virtues, they will spread only sins. During this time all human sins, like plunder, murders and wars, will propagate, and all in the name of the Messiah's teachings. There will be no shame or virtue, for people will regard shame, evil and sin as a virtue. And harm calling for vengeance to heaven will happen among people: anyone who comes asking for justice, will be pushed away and laughed at. A brother will come against brother, father against son, son against father, laity against clergy, amid the ridicule of the pompous pride, the stronger will rule the weak and treat them worse than a dog. Instead of spreading the knowledge among the wild people and enlightening them, the Messiah followers will fall into the dirt, sin, debauchery, and the habit of making false oaths will flourish.

" Therefore, fourteen centuries after the death of the Messiah, a warning sign will appear in the sky, seen even with the naked eye. This sign will be a star with a peacock tail. God will get angry and will send harsh admonitions, severe punishments and afflictions to pull people away from evil. The people will suffer from previously unknown horrible diseases and pains that will shorten their lives. Four elements, that is water, earth, fire and wind, all this will be against them, it will do great damage through storms, incredible fires, floods and hail. All people will go to arms, wars will arise, the land will burn, it will stand not tilled by anyone, hunger will come, and the first necessities of life will not be met. A farmer will leave his land, a craftsman his workshop, and everyone will take up arms and crave the blood of their fellows. The husbands will leave their wives, children and homes, the wives will incite their husbands over others and for a long-time humanity will sink in unrighteousness.

"Violence and injustice will reign supremely in human souls and scatter to the highest level. Marriage will be disregarded by people, and everyone will taste terrible debauchery, fornication, and lust. In robes, it will be difficult to tell people apart. God will constantly send admonitions to the people to come to their senses and return to the path of virtue " the signs in the sky will be shown constantly, but people will remain hardened in their sins and their hearts will be insensitive to good and virtue. When certain time passes and the people do not show improvement, God will severely punish the third part of humanity."

"When and how will this happen?" Solomon expected Makeda to hear his words, just like the night before. She answered him without changing her tone or moving even a little. As if his question was imbedded in the world she was in. As if hearing his voice and answering questions was a safe thread connecting the place where her loved ones were with the one, she saw in the vision given to her by God.

"When the time of punishment is near, signs will appear. The first one will be that people will get to the deeper part of earth and from there they will get their food, and digging three hundred fathoms deep, they will obtain coal, ore, stones and using these materials they will build various iron equipment and move it with coal.

The second sign will be that trade and industry will flourish like never before, people will bring goods from one land to another and everyone will only think about selling as much bad and cheap goods as possible, as expensive as possible. Therefore, new laws will be created, and one man will remove another from his house and from his land, overwhelmed by limitless greed.

The third sign will be that love and truth between people will disappear, and only falsehood, hypocrisy and deceit will settle in hearts, and no one will tell the truth to others, but will try to deceive them at every step.

The fourth sign will occur when money prevails over the world and becomes as great as God, and man learns to only hold his hand out for it. When God sends the fifth sign to people, a man from royal family will arise in Europe, and strange things will happen in the world during his reign. This man will kill the king in one of the western countries, take his place himself, he will strengthen himself and rule. Terrible oppression will then appear on the earth and blood will be poured abundantly, peoples will rise against peoples, some countries will disappear from the surface of the earth, and this man will rise high with his valor and wisdom. Then, filled with faith in the Messiah, he will create a war with the Roman Empire and gain infinite fame. This man, as a rod sent from God, and announced by the prophets, will fall on the peoples and punish for sins, shedding their blood.

In the end, however, immeasurable conceit will fill this king of many countries, and then he will lose everything he possessed. During his reign, the peoples will be agitated, and boisterousness will appear everywhere like never before. Then languages will arise that no one has heard of now and they will mingle, resounding in both parts of the earth. Many children who leave their home will return under their family roof with many languages, having forgotten their own, and even more will be lost, and their fathers will not see them again. All wars will continue, and one will lead to the next, so that there will be no end to them. Countless troops will move from country to country, but their numbers will be so great that I cannot determine it. These armies will be powerful, relentless iron clad knights will fight against each other, and the human spirit will invent more and more powerful instruments for killing.

And this man will lead to all this, because he will create new laws and will establish many judges. This man will have one rule in his life and deeds. One God in heaven, one emperor on earth. And therefore, he will exalt himself above others, and his lust will be to seize all peoples and all countries into his reign. And behold, listen, great Solomon, for this God will humble his capital, take away what he has won with the Lord's hand, and take away all his dignities. The greatest evil will nest, because the Romans will give a bad example, they will practice usury and oppress the poor. And when simple people see injustice, they will deviate from God's commandments, and they will do wrong, following the example from above. God's vengeance will fall to the people like a punishing thunderbolt.

The patience will run out. God will no longer be able to look calmly at human vileness, so he will send an angel who will blow the trumpet in a powerful voice, announcing God's wrath to the people, and soon afterwards, the plague will come upon the whole world and turn a third of the population into death. Only then will people come to their senses, the wars will cease, and those who stay alive will experience great sadness and despair and regret, they will understand God's wrath, they will recognize his righteousness, they will sprinkle ashes on their heads, and all will do penance together to avoid and prevent further signs of divine vengeance.

However, people will not return completely to the path of virtue, they will not fulfill God's commandments and laws, they will not fill their hearts with their love of neighbor and God. Lots of iniquity will remain until the day of the last judgment, and Sodom and Gomorrah will reign among the people. The Antichrist will have great power over people and will effectively persuade them to sin, so God will send his messengers who will come among the people and will proclaim the righteous faith. And when people convert, when they enter the path of virtue and glory, then the last day will come near. This day will be terrible for all creation. Then beings from earth, fire and water will rise."

Makeda fell silent. She lowered her head and her hands rested limply on both sides of her torso. She was kneeling in silence, parting with the terrible vision.

The third prophecy

On the third night, the revelation did not come until the dawn. The first, still faint rays of sunlight peeked into the chamber, when, just like on the previous nights, Makeda knelt on the bed and crossed her arms.

She said nothing. All held their breath. When the sun fell on her face and lit her in such a way that she looked like a bright goddess, she began to tremble, and tears flowed from her eyes.

"Your face, queen, looks as if it was made of gold," Solomon was delighted with her. "But you are crying. Why?"

"Solomon, he's with me now. Remember when you told me once it was Shekhinah? I feel it now more than tangibly. I am looked after by the Lady of the Moon, and your God has visited me with her consent. Because she and he are one."

Her eyes were closed.

"Now I know and see everything. Ask then and I will answer. I will tell you about people who will be born when we are no longer remembered, about kings, princes and the mighty who will rule many centuries after us. You will gain the knowledge of the future. Because God has given you so much wisdom that there has not been, there is not and there will never be anyone equal to you. Don't waste this gift. You have treasure in your hands. What you do with it depends entirely on you."

Makeda looked different than during her previous visions. She was cheerful, smiling, radiant and bright, as if her body was made of gold, and at the same time slightly floating.

"I would like to know how the world will develop. Which way will it go? Will it end?"

She opened her eyes. Her eyes were bright, clear, unearthly. Keeping her elbows raised, she put her fingertips on her temples. She raised her head. Her eyes fogged, her pupils disappeared, only the whites were visible. Her body began to shine with even more intense glow than before.

"The world will go its own way. What is supposed to be, will be, because people are imperfect. When they feel good, they forget about God and his commandments. They live in sin. Then God must punish them severely. That's how it was, how it is, and it will be. However, before the final punishment comes, God will send minor punishments as rebukes, such as hunger, sickness, fire, floods, storms, and finally great and sudden injuries, frosts in summer, so that the flowers will wither and the seeds in the ground will freeze and die. This will bring tremendous damage, for there will be bad crops, hunger, and terribly high prices. People will have their lives shortened by various diseases, will age early and die early. The sun will become cooler, will stop warming people or give them encouragement to work. As soon as winter ends and there is a short spring, it will already be cold in the world, so that all year-round people will have to wear fur coats and sheepskin coats. These constant colds and frosts will affect crops, because all fruits, plants and grain will freeze before harvest time. Everything will wither and die, and as a result, there will be a constant scarcity of food and hunger will lead people to despair.

"But before God's final vengeance for human signs will fall to earth. There will be twelve signs sent from God to convert people to the right path. The first sign will be that people working hard all week will be forced to work during holidays and Sundays in order not to starve and to prevent crop failures. The second sign will be that people who are fourteen and fifteen will get married young, but there will be no peace in the marriage, hence quarrels, misunderstandings and frequent break ups. The third sign will be that in the world people will devote themselves entirely to earthly affairs, so art will flourish, science and skills will advance, trade and industry will grow to enormous proportions. The fourth sign will be when human skills, having developed, begin to obtain enormous income from a small piece of land, so large that it would have been called magic before. The fifth sign will be the spread of unbelief, lies and godlessness, so that people will love money instead of honesty, they will worship it, respect it and they will consider it their god.

The sixth sign will be the one when the land increases immensely in price, they will sell it very expensive, and thus trade of the land will be created. The seventh sign will be when people do not leave a single piece of uncultivated land, they will graft wine, plant hops, and yet the bread will be expensive. The eighth sign will be when different coins will be minted in each country, various customs duties, tributes, and laws will be imposed so that one country does not bring its goods to another. The ninth sign will be when an extremely short carnival comes, such that people will not be satisfied with it, and they will extend it to the whole fast so that ultimately there will be no fast at all.

The tenth sign will come when people come out to mow hay, already dry from the summer sun, and they will find snow instead that will fall abundant at night like never before at this time of year. The eleventh sign will be that God will send voracious insects as in the time of Pharaoh and the Egyptian plagues. These vermin will sit on all kinds of plants and trees, and will cause enormous damage, stripping them of their leaves. The twelfth sign that God will send will be that, all the trees on the mountain called Blanik will dry, and because of this an extreme hunger will arise in the area.

"God will send these twelve signs to people for their repentance and conversion to true virtue. If there is no improvement, then God will punish people terribly, like he has never punished since the creation of the world. The whole world will be subject to the vengeance for wrongful sins and ungodliness, and as many will not believe my words, it will get worse for them, because God's punishment will meet them unprepared and will be punished more severely, and the truths of these words will be proved by future generations, looking with their own eyes at what is predicted here.

If, however, all people, or some peoples separately, pay no attention to these signs that God will send, and do not think about the imminent punishment. God will send the king against the king and these peoples will have to participate in great wars until lots of blood is shed. Wars will arise one from the other, one after the other, without any break, and thus the emaciated people will have to pay more and more heavy taxes and contributions. That is why the poor will suffer the worst, because money will be hard to come by because of crop failure.

"After terrible battles, by the way of God's grace, there will be fifty fertile and fecund years, with abundant prosperity, because people will lead a godly life and thus deserve God's favor, and with its help the underground will open and all treasures will come to the surface, covered from human eyes since the beginning of the world. Everyone will be rich, there will be no poor, it will be warm in the world, there will be almost no cold weather, therefore the earth will bear fruit abundantly. But it will only last for the duration of the reign of one king. The temporal wealth that gives people the opportunity to use bodily pleasures and delight will draw their thoughts and feelings away from God, from laws and commandments, and fill human souls with pride and conceit, and the people will again forget their duties and will enter the path of godlessness and sin."

"However, they will still have the memory of the last day, the coming of which they will fear. One day, as the signs of God's anger, the moon, stars and sun will shine differently, but people will no longer have the power to get on the right path of duty and virtue. They will get bogged down in their sins until they receive terrible payment: the Last Day. When that day is near, they will repent and regret. Too late."

Tears flowed again from Makeda's eyes.

"When will the Last Judgment happen? Can you see it? Can you tell me?"

"King Solomon, no one can know this but God alone, for God did not even tell his angels that," she replied, without changing her position. "I will only tell you what I know, and I will tell you because you are wise and just. Tell me, what the payment is for good deeds and what is for wrong ones?"

"One repays for good with good and for evil with evil," he said.

"God will do the same to people. If they do good and obey God, he will give them more years, and if they offend him and wade in sins, he will pay them back and shorten the number of years of the world's existence. Therefore, people cannot know when the Last Judgment day will come. I don't know when it will come, but I know the signs that will precede it. Before the end of the world, seven signs will be revealed to people, proclaiming that it is God's will to end the life on earth. Then, to everyone, what is meant to happen, will happen."

"What are the signs? Will you reveal them to me? I will write them down and tell humanity to beware of wrongdoings and prevent God from revealing these signs to them, because his goodness is infinite."

"The first sign will be that all creatures that live will begin to sweat with blood, so that the drops of blood will sit all over their body and flow down, together with great suffering. The second sign will occur when the moon changes and begins to appear from the east, causing fear and dread in human hearts so that they will pray and do penance.

"The third sign will be when the sun, moon and stars shine with blood-red glow, and people will wring their hands in despair and will raise their eyes with regret towards the sky as a show of remorse. As the fourth sign, God will send such a great drought on earth that the trees and all plants will dry up completely, and boundless despair will overwhelm the people who will repent in fear and terror.

"The fifth sign will be when the earth begins to collapse in many places, and fires and smoke will come out in the sunken in places, and people will doubt everything and wait for death. The sixth sign, when the waters rise from the shores and burn with flames, and people will die of fear, unable to really die. The last, seventh sign will be when the surface of the earth moves, when the mountains and hills will sink and collapse, and people will not even know where they are and will start to circle around like lost sheep.

"And truly I will tell you, King Solomon, that before the end of the world, indeed, these seven signs will appear to the people, foretelling the imminent Judgment.

"Before the end of the world, a descendant of Evil will be born on earth. He will walk the earth, teach and spread his teaching, tempt people and distract them from true faith. He will amaze people with numerous extraordinary miracles so that many will think that he has the power of heavenly origin, while it will be Evil One who will give it to him. And those who will not want to join him, will be chased, persecuted and tormented by him.

"This way, having many people persuaded in his favor, he will enjoy great hope together with the whole hell. Then God, to save and help people, will send two preachers to earth, who will teach the people and show them the snares that the demon has set on their souls and possessed them. And these will be called Enoch and Elijah, who, having received their silver-tongued speech from God, will bring people back from erroneous ways. They will point to the origin of the Evil and will bravely fight him. Then the Evil One will become enraged, will order to capture them, kill them and leave the corpse on the street not buried for four days. On the fourth day, a voice from heaven will sound and the two teachers will rise miraculously, and they will rise to the sky in a radiant cloud. And then the skies will break open, lightning will fly, killing seven thousand people, a tenth of Jerusalem will be burnt, and those who will remain will convert to the true God.

"Then the angel Michael of great power will come down from heaven, rise against Evil and throw him and his helpers into the abyss of hell. Peter and another Roman, also Peter, will rule the Messiah's capital. For Peter will be the first to lead the Messiah's flock, and the last one will be also Peter.

"Then the last pagans, seeing the angel Michael and two preachers doing miracles on earth, will convert, enter the path of virtue and begin a God-fearing life. then, the day of judgment, God's wrath day will come upon people.

"First, there will be a terrible lightning made of seven thunders, lasting seven days, which will have such great power that cities, walls, fortresses, and castles will crumble. However, no people will die until it is destined that everything is to end.

"Rocks will crack and pitch-black darkness will envelop the world. After this darkness, a huge sun will rise into the sky, consisting of five giant stars, and whoever looks at them will die a sudden death. Then God will send His angels with trumpets to the earth, and they will sound: 'Let the dead rise from their graves and let every soul appear at the Last Judgment before God.' Messiah will sit on the right side of God. Then those long dead will rise from their graves, and go to the judgment, and everyone will have their good and bad deeds written on their foreheads.

Adam and Eve, Abel and Cain will go first, and everybody will follow him, and God will separate the good ones to the right along with Abel, and the evil ones on the left along with Cain. He will say to those on the left: Go to the depths of hell, to the state of the Evil, whom you listened to in your life, there will be crying and gnashing of teeth there.' And to those on the right hand he will say: 'You who have chosen the thorny and difficult path of good, go to Paradise, that is, to my kingdom.'

"Then the righteous will go before the throne of the Most High and praise him with the hymn."

Makeda fell silent. Nobody dared to move, such was the great impression her words made on everyone.

"Let it be so, for this must happen, so that we too could enter heaven and experience eternal happiness before God," she ended and fainted, exhausted.

***

Makeda's time in Jerusalem was coming to an end. She wanted to come back.

Not only because requests from Sheba for her return were coming more and more often. According to Handake, who managed the country in her absence, things were going very well. However, it appeared from his letters that the priest Sethon, despite the illness that was taking its toll on him, tried to convince people to revolt. It also appeared that Den, who had found shelter with Pharaoh, was planning to recapture Aksum.

Trade agreements on joint ventures were finally and completely signed, which was, apart from learning the wisdom of Solomon, the main purpose of Makeda's visit to Israel.

In addition, God had visited her in her dreams and revealed to her the disturbing prophecies, which Solomon had written down and bound in such a way that they could survive ages and be a warning to people. The Great Priestess and the prophet Nathan agreed that such detailed visions, and at the same time so terrible in their message, had never before been given to anyone who walked the world. They were now absolutely certain that Makeda's visit to Israel must have been the result of God's plan.

Besides, and this was the most important thing for Makeda, her childhood vision came true: she received the greatest treasure imaginable. Apart from herself, the High Priestess and Seshep, no one knew what she was carrying under her heart.

It was the final reason for her to leave Jerusalem. She felt that what had always been written in the stars, was fulfilled. She gave the world a warning - this is first. And secondly, she was pregnant. Happiness filled her. It was all-encompassing. She was certain that the power she had received was enough to last for her life.

She could turn home now.

***

Having confirmed that nothing would change Makeda's decision, and that Tamrin was indeed preparing the caravan for the road, Solomon decided that they would spend the last days in Israel together.

"I will escort you to the port of Ezion-Geber. You will see what the construction of our ships look like and where they will depart from. And most importantly, since your decision is final, we will be able to still spend some time together."

Makeda agreed.

"I would also like you to trust Hiram's sailors and get on a ship that will help you reach Sheba faster."

"Am I supposed to take a boat trip?" She couldn't believe he'd offered her something like that. "It's good for soldiers and merchants! How will I survive for so long at sea with my court?"

"It will be pleasant, and above all, short. You are not afraid of water. You told me yourself that you had been sailing from an early age with your father from the east to the west part of the Sheba and back."

"Our travels were always safe and lasted just two or three days. I have never experienced a storm, and I know how scary it can be on the water. I haven't seen sea monsters and I haven't met pirates. I can't imagine spending many days there. I don't know how I would stand it." She wanted to add "in my condition," but Solomon couldn't find out she was carrying his child. She did not tell him this mainly for one, but extremely important reason: she was afraid that he would not let her go on the onerous journey to Sheba, during which many things could happen. Especially that she was weakened after the visions she had recently. She also thought that he would do anything to make her want to be his wife, although for many reasons it was not possible or good for either of them.

"Think about it, please. Our ships are at your disposal. I have one of them prepared especially for you."

"You surprise me, king."

"Several days will pass before we reach Ezion-Geber. You have time to make a decision."

The port of Ezion-Geber was in a strategic place for the region. It allowed to reach all parts of the world. It lay where the desert stopped at a narrow sea lane. It was the gate to the lands of the black earth and other distant overseas lands, from which roots, spices, fabrics and riches not found elsewhere were supplied. From there, it was also possible to get by sea, the fastest way, to Ofir - the land of gold."

The city was recaptured by King David from the Edomites and it belonged since then to Israel, closely guarded by the army. This was where the Solomon and Hiram's fleet stood, and according to the agreement, the Queen of Sheba also recently received her share in it.

There were many days of travel from Jerusalem to Ezion-Geber. The caravan set off among crowds of locals saying goodbye. Tamrin was leading it. The king and the queen rode almost at its end. Only a small detachment of soldiers followed them. They were still in Israel, so they felt completely safe.

They passed the time on the road admiring the surroundings, making short horse trips, enjoying meals and discussions. They were not in a hurry. They ordered to set up a camp each evening to extend the time spent together. They did not part for a moment. After four days, the caravan split into two parts. The larger, commanded by Tamrin, headed south, and the smaller - royal, headed by Ashenafi, went towards Ezion-Geber. On hundreds of camels, Tamrin carried the numerous gifts that Makeda received from the king, and almost all the traveling equipment of the Shebean court. He also led most of the service and people serving the expedition.

The High Priestess, Seshep, Varda, quite a large group of priestesses and servants, as well as half of the Ashenafi's team, remained with the queen. The general made the other half available for Tamrin.

The plan was that after seeing the ships, the queen would decide if she would like to make some or all of her journey by sea, or she would rather join the slowly moving caravan and, after saying goodbye to Solomon, would reach Tamrin to continue the travel by land.

***

They decided to spend the last evening before their parting together at the seashore.

As they did many times before, they rode on two horses, which were brought from Solomon's stable especially for this evening. Makeda sat on a white mare, while the king mounted a beautiful horse, also white, which surprised her, but she did not comment on this. She thought however that it was of some meaning.

As they reached their destination, he asked her to allow to be blindfolded. She willingly agreed, curious about the surprise he was preparing for her. They rode for a while, then Solomon, holding the bridle of Makeda's horse, stopped both mounts.

"It's your color, Makeda," he removed the blindfold from her eyes. A white tent stood on the white sand, a few steps from where the waves reached. Inside, everything was also white: curtains, mattresses, furniture, carpets, and olive lamp housings, and even flowers decorating an unusual design. As it turned out later, the dishes in which the drinks and the food prepared for the evening were served, were also white.

"Even my horse is white in your honor today," he was pleased to see her delight. "Look," he pointed to the moon. "And it shines especially for you today. It's white, and it's full! What do you think about us spending the evening here tonight?"

They sat on soft, wide armchairs, and the servants immediately gave them a bowl of water to wash their hands and face, and then a white, soft cloth to dry. They also washed and anointed their feet.

As soon as the king signaled, food and drink began to be brought.

They ate and drank. They laughed. They remembered their time together. Time went by quickly. They talked, carefully avoiding the topic of separation. None of them wanted to bring it up first.

It was dark. The sky covered with stars.

"It can't end just like this with your leaving. I won't let it." Solomon looked into her eyes. "You know how much you mean to me. Do not leave me!"

"Come with me, you will be the queen's wife in Sheba," she joked, knowing that such a thought would never occur to him.

"I am the king of Israel; God has chosen me. I can't let him down. Governance is my duty."

"I was also put on the throne of Sheba by Gods. My place is there."

"I'll be left with a broken heart."

"You'll write songs. The ones you've created so far are so beautiful that centuries will pass, and people will still love them."

"Do you know about it from your visions?"

"I saw beautiful books which contained your words."

"My songs?"

"Not only. There were also your thoughts that Elichoref writes down, and many other wisdoms known as your works."

"Do you know the future that awaits us? Do you know everything?"

"No," she reassured him.

She wondered how much of what she had seen in the visions had to happen and there was no other way, and how much it was just a warning of what might occur.

"We will meet again," he assured firmly when he decided she was silent for too long.

"The way to Sheba is over 1800 miles long*. Do you know how much time it takes to make it?"

"We have ships! You will see that one can travel comfortably and safely by them. And soon I will build wings so that I can fly to you. By air it will be faster."

"We say in Sheba that love gives us wings. Let's see if this will be the case for you, too?" She tried to hide her sadness under the veil of humor. "Even before I met you, I heard that you have a flying machine, or at least a host of demons at your disposal, who can move you to any place you wish at any time. In that case, please visit us. Believe me, my country is at least as beautiful as yours. I would like you to see it."

"I'll fly there, don't be surprised," he promised, believing what he was saying.

Then she thought that maybe it indeed would be so. That they will meet one day. Because even if it is not written in the stars, does it mean that it will not happen?

"Man has free will," she thought, wanting to believe the thoughts that came to her. "We create our world ourselves and it is entirely up to us what it will be like. If he really wants us to meet, it will happen, no matter what the will is of the Lady of the Moon, Yahweh, or other gods who speak to me in dreams."

Perhaps he guessed where her thoughts were, because he stood up and gave her his hand to interrupt them.

"We will part tomorrow," they stood face to face. "I would like to give you something special. It is an expression of my love that will be our sign. I made it almost myself; the goldsmith helped me only a little. If you ever need something, if you are in trouble and can't reach me, give it to a messenger. I will listen to everything he tells me as if you were saying it yourself."

He took her left hand and put a large golden ring on her forefinger. It was massive, had the names of Solomon and Makeda engraved, and it was adorned with a convex star.

"Do you know this symbol?"

"Of course. The sign of David and the whole Israel."

"It's our shield and seal at the same time. It is a symbolic combination of masculinity and femininity, a sign of balanced divinity, whose strength lies in the fact that it contains both feminine and masculine elements," he ran his finger along the ring.

"It cannot be different. The world is made up of opposites that are one. A day cannot exist without a night, darkness without brightness, and good without evil."

"I thought of what you said about goddesses and the female element of the universe. I was thinking about Adam and Eve. And about Lilith. Also, about your Moon Lady."

"What conclusions have you reached?"

"In the human world, one element most often prevails over the other. They are sometimes in balance, although rarely, and then there is peace. Yahweh is a God of masculine strength. He requires absolute compliance. Whoever does not listen to him, receives a penalty. But to those who believe in him, he gives great power. The time of one God is coming all over the world. You know it because you told me it was like that in your vision. Others will go into oblivion. The one God will rule the world - and he will be masculine.

"Lady of the Moon will not disappear. Never. She can take on different names and shapes, but she will last forever," she assured him. "You know that I admire your God. He gave Israel incredible strength. I can even say that I love him. Do you know why?"

"Because he is the true God?"

"Because he gave me you."

"Ever since I met you, everything that happens in my life only makes sense if it's connected or at least somehow associated with you. I wish we could go towards God together, all the way to infinity. This ring will be our sign. Wear it, please."

"I'll never take it off. It will for me be like the covenant you told me about when we witnessed the ritual of circumcision. Brit mila unites with God. You said then that the ring is a sign of true love. I remember it well. And I accept this gift from you today as such a sign," she bowed her head, "Thank you."

He took her hand and kissed the ring. A moment later, he hugged her and kissed her forehead. They stood motionless. They breathed in a common rhythm. Time was passing.

"I have something else for you," he said in a voice slightly hoarse with emotion. "Will you let me?"

He took out the bandana he had previously put on his belt and blindfolded her again. She wondered where he would lead her this time.

"Don't move for a moment," he said, stroking her cheek.

She heard signs of movement. A large group of people carried something in, then moved it. Someone was adjusting something, then, at Solomon's sign, something was moved again and again.

Finally, he untied her bandana. A few steps from her was a golden throne. She approached it, fascinated. It was large, with a high back with sculptured garlands, and armrests ending with lion heads. Four solid legs looked like columns topped with palm trees, and open goblets of carved flowers were placed on a leather seat, painted gold. The backrest was decorated with the star of David against the background of the full moon - the symbol of the Silver Mother. On the back was a picture of ships. There were so many of them that they were difficult to count.

"Before I met you, I heard the story that the Queen of Sheba has immeasurable wealth, and among them is the greatest throne in the world. In this story, King Solomon sent one of his demons to Sheba to steal the throne. In the blink of an eye, the demon found himself in Mariba and transferred the throne to Jerusalem. Recently, Elichoref told me that people are saying that you came to Israel to get your property back. And because I serve my people as best I can, I decided to meet their expectations. Here is your throne, queen, do you recognize it?" He smiled with satisfaction, seeing how impressed she was by his present. "I give it back to you, since they say it has always belonged to you."

"King, you must really have demons at your service. It is hard to imagine that a human hand could create something so beautiful!" She was moved. "They say it's the throne that your demons stole from me. Really? And you decided to return it to me? Do I understand right?"

"There is no such thing the king will not do to meet the expectations of his people," he joked again. "It's my gift to you," he added seriously. "Please accept it."

"Is this a gift?"

"I'll be honored if you want to take it with you to Sheba. I would like you to think about me every time you sit on it."

Makeda walked around the throne once again, stroking its backrest and armrests and gazing admiringly at the elaborate details. Each element, even the smallest one, was carefully finished, everything was perfectly smoothed and polished, nowhere was the slightest trace of the tools used, blemishes, scratches or damage. It was masterful work.

"It's unbelievably beautiful," she enthused quietly and sat down, placing her hands on the armrests and resting her head on a comfortable backrest.

He knelt before her. "You are and always will be my queen."

He looked into her face. She looked like a goddess. He raised his head. Just above the throne, as if guarding her, shone the mighty disc of the moon. The Silver Mother watched over her daughter.

"It is full moon," he noted.

"That's a good sign for us."

"I believe that we will always be fully together."

CHAPTER VII

THE WAY HOME

From Jerusalem to Mariba

In Ezion-Geber the queen decided to board a ship prepared and equipped especially for her. She boarded in the company of the High Priestess, Varda, Seshep and servants. She asked Solomon to stay on the waterfront. She did not want to prolong the parting. She was afraid that at the last moment, she might not control her emotion and showing emotions in public did not befit her.

As soon as she got on board, she went to her chambers. She was delighted because everything was drowning in splendor. The furniture was made of precious types of wood, most of them finished with gold sheet, the fabrics used for curtains, blankets, pillows and rugs were made of the best wools, silks and linen from overseas lands. All dishes came from Solomon's palace and were made of gold. Wines, beer and foods were delivered to the ship from royal vineyards, Israel's best gardens and pastures. Makeda's bedroom was connected to a bathhouse and a chamber intended for meetings. A wide door from her bedroom led directly to the terrace at the ship's bow. Next to it was the chamber of the High Priestess, and still further were the cabins, in which Varda placed the servants, priestesses, the queen's closest guard, and all others who were to ensure comfort, safety, and convenience of the trip. To be ready for every call of her lady, Varda chose for herself a small room, which she allocated for Seshep. Neither she nor the hemet had the slightest problem with sharing a small space. Especially that they expected the trip to not take too long.

Ashenafi and his soldiers traveled on the second ship just behind them. Below the deck there were places for horses, who received calming herbs along with their feed during the journey.

Ashenafi kept in touch with Tamrin thanks to the pigeons that they regularly sent to each other. They promised such a connection to each other when it was decided that the caravan would split into two parts. Tamrin was not happy about the prospect of parting with the queen. He preferred to have a direct influence on which way and how she travelled. He thought that only then could he be sure that she would be safe. However, when the king offered Makeda a voyage by sea as definitely more convenient and faster, he could do nothing but agree. The queen did not ask him for his opinion anyway.

On land, drums were struck, trumpets played. It was a sign that ships were setting off from the wharf. Together with the court, Makeda went out on deck and stood at the stern. The High Priestess, her assistants, servants and the entire crew, honored Solomon and his people. The sounds of trumpets and drums sounded on the ship, echoing those coming from the wharf. After a while, when the instruments fell silent and the ship was already sailing, the gentle sounds of lyres, harps, flutes could be heard, and the words sung by the choir of priestesses flowed towards Solomon. It was a farewell song about the beautiful time, the need to part, and the longing that arose in the heart.

Solomon was standing on the waterfront. He recognized the words immediately. After all, he arranged them himself. Makeda added music to them.

He was looking at her. She looked like a beautiful statue of a goddess placed at the stern. The ship sailed out from the shore, and they still kept their eyes on each other. Even when it was already certain that they could only vaguely see their silhouettes, they did not move. They stood as if enchanted. They thought about themselves, about the moments given to them, about the feeling that united them. They were sure that it is stronger than time and will last for centuries.

***

On the first day on the ship, the queen felt nauseous. The next one, she was vomiting so strongly that she didn't even have the strength to get up from bed. It was getting worse every day.

After consulting with an experienced hemet, responsible for the queen's health, the High Priestess ordered to sail to the nearest shore, having obtained the consent of almost unconscious Makeda. However, the maps showed no port or a marina, or even just a place that would allow a large royal ship to land, anywhere in the area. It was therefore decided to speed up and sail a day or two more, and if favorable winds happen, to reach the shores on the west side of the Red Sea and moor in the Principality of Aksum.

The priestess ordered all servants and crew to keep everything regarding the direction of their travel and the queen's health secret.

"Anyone who tries to somehow pass outside the information about what is happening on the ship, will face the death penalty in torture. His loved ones will lose their lives and their heads will be cut," she announced.

Everyone knew that both the queen and the High Priestess always kept their words, so it was certain that no one would dare reveal the secret of the queen's journey and condition.

It was hard to imagine that someone would try to relay messages from the high seas, but the priestess preferred to sensitize people to the need to keep the secret even before they came ashore. Hence, the threat of the most terrible punishment for giving it up. Especially since the secret was twofold: it concerned not only the direction of their journey and the fact that the queen did not tolerate it best, but also something much more important. More perceptive servants were already beginning to guess that the queen was expecting.

However, except for those few who guessed it, the High Priestess, Seshep, and Varda, no one else even suspected that the queen was pregnant. Makeda did not want anyone to talk about it loudly until the child developed in her womb, so that it became certain that it had a chance to be born healthy.

She was afraid of someone's evil eye, worried that a jealous woman or a sorcerer would cast a spell on her, or that one of Solomon's wives would ask her god to not let her baby come into the world. She was also afraid that if Den, who she knew was still watching her from afar, found out about it, nobody knew what action he could take. After his father's death, he fled to Egypt and got Pharaoh's support, as the High Priestess assured, who had eyes and ears of her hemet there. She was convinced that he did not give up his dreams of the crown of Sheba and of her as his wife. So, she preferred the information about her condition to not get outside the closest circle of trusted people, at least for the time being. On the ship, those servants who dared to whisper about it, did so in great secrecy and only among themselves.

Makeda regretted getting on the ship on her first day of the trip already. She realized too late that in her condition, although not the most comfortable, sitting in a palanquin on a camel would be a much better choice compared to a ship swaying on the waves.

With each passing hour, she felt more and more that her spirit was beginning to leave her body. She was scared.

When the ships finally reached the west bank, she was already so weak and exhausted that she wasn't able to not only sit down on her own, but even to speak. She lay limp between waking and sleeping, and the women around her tried to give her strengthening drinks.

They did not call at the port where ships traveling under the Sheba sign always arrived. In accordance with the order of the High Priestess, a secluded place was chosen, away from known routes, but empty, and with a safe shore. No one could find out that there was a queen's ship nearby.

Ashenafi's soldiers came ashore first. They checked that the area was safe. The queen was lifted off the ship on a comfortable, wide stretcher. The servants took her to a tent and laid her on the bed, which was delivered from her chamber on the ship, along with other necessary equipment.

As soon as she felt that she was on the land, she opened her eyes.

"Feels so good," she sighed with relief and looked around.

She saw that Seshep, the High Priestess and Varda were with her, and reassured, fell asleep from exhaustion and weakness. Three women spent the next days with her, simultaneously or alternately, depending on the queen's condition, carefully caring for her. First of all, they took care to provide her with the right amount of fluids. On the ship, she lost a lot of it. During the first days of travel, she returned almost immediately whatever was given to her to drink or eat. In the last two days, she couldn't even hold down water. The irritated stomach rejected everything.

"Solomon, be with me," she cried in fever. "Hug me…"

Later, she was so weak that she couldn't even speak.

If the journey lasted even a day longer, the queen would undoubtedly join her ancestors, as the hemet who knew about the medicine said. Fortunately, they managed to arrive at the firm land, and the rocking that was so bad for her, ceased.

Immediately after reaching the land, the High Priestess sent Seshep to the nearest temple of the Lady of the Moon. According to her calculations, it should be a day, at most two, away from where they were stationed*. Seshep was to ask for help and prepare the temple for the arrival of the sick of special importance, acting in strict secrecy. A few days later, she returned. Four priestesses came with her.

At that time, Makeda felt better. The treatment used by the medic who looked after her, the care of the High Priestess and Varda, and above all being on the mainland, did their job. The queen was starting to regain strength.

"Lady, when you were fighting the sickness, I was wondering what we should do in the near future," began the High Priestess, when Makeda was sitting alone and it was sure that her recovery was a matter of days.

"Tell me," the convalescent was glad that, firstly, she finally understood the words that were addressed to her, and secondly, that the Priestess, as always, cared for her future.

"You are not in the best condition yet, lady. You need time to get your full strength back. You are young, so you recover quickly. However, remember that you are in a special condition."

"Exactly," she realized with worry that the sickness she was suffering from could harm her baby and put her hands on her stomach. "Is everything fine?"

"We think the sea journey was so tough on you because of your condition," the priestess smiled. "Fortunately, despite the fact that you have gone through a lot in recent days, you managed to keep your baby. We gave you herbs that helped in this. And because the Lady of the Moon watches over you all the time, everything goes well."

The priestess's words gave her strength.

"Thank you," she raised herself, trying to get up, but she felt so dizzy that she returned to her previous position. "I'm curious, what are your plans for us in the near future?" she asked when her breathing, which accelerated for a moment, returned to normal.

"Silvery Mother has advice for us."

"I'm very curious, what is the advice?"

***

Three nights later, a small group of women set out from the dormant camp. They were priestesses of the Moon Lady. Seshep led them. They carried a small, narrow litter covered with dense but airy fabric. When they were far outside the camp and were certain that no one could see or hear them, they got on the horses waiting for them. A wide hammock was attached to two of them. It was there that they placed Makeda, who they carried out of the camp in the litter, in the dark of the night.

Nobody noticed them in the camp, so the High Priestess who stayed in Makeda's tent was certain that the implementation of the first part of the plan was successful; and it really was. After two days of a quiet ride, making sure primarily of the patient's safety and comfort, the priestesses delivered Makeda to the temple.

It was a place that was said to be as old as the world itself. It was in the Aksum principality, so it was part of Sheba. However, it was so far away from communication routes and human settlements, that it almost never happened that someone got there by accident. The temple was surrounded by a high stone wall, through which only those who were allowed by the priestesses could enter, and the priestesses had been guarding their headquarters for centuries. They gathered the knowledge that was passed to them by those who had been before them. They wrote it on clay tablets, papyri, carefully curried parchment, but they passed on the largest and the most secret part orally. So, they knew by heart the recipes of medicines created by priestesses since the beginning of the world. They could recite the composition of almost every poison and its antidote; they knew the recipes for excellent wines, beers and other drinks. They knew what herbs to give to relax and see other worlds. They were also able to fight, become invisible, read thoughts and convey them at a distance.

They always guarded the balance and harmony of the world, ensuring that the different colors of energy remain in balance. They fueled the cosmic power of the Lady of the Moon and drew strength from it. They have also been for centuries the guardians and advisers of every subsequent queen.

This was the place Makeda was brought to.

***

Meanwhile, in the camp, the High Priestess announced the will of the queen.

"In a few days, as soon as Great Kandake feels good enough to be able to travel, we will board again and go to the other side of the sea by the fastest possible route. Due to the nuisance of traveling by ship, the queen decided to join Tamrin's caravan, understanding that although the land trip would be longer, it was more convenient and safer for her. She also decided that on her way to Mariba, she would visit places where new oases would be created under the agreement with Solomon and Hiram."

"How's the queen?" Ashenafi wanted to know.

"She's weak, but things are going in the right direction. She should be on her feet soon. What she needs most now is peace."

"When can we expect to depart?" Varda was privy to the priestess's plan, but she asked the question, because she often had questions at such meetings, so in order not to arouse anyone's suspicions; this time, she also tried to behave as usual.

"We will set out within the next few days," the priestess's voice had optimism in it, which she wanted to share with others. "Let us keep praying for the queen's health and her regaining of the full strength. And let's be ready to sail tomorrow."

In the first stage of the plan's implementation, the queen and the High Priestess let Seshep in on the secret, which was obvious, but also did so for Varda. She proved to be trustworthy and the one who can be entrusted with many difficult tasks for simultaneous and urgent implementation, because everybody knew that she would handle them perfectly. They also decided that at the right moment the secret should also be learned by Ashenafi and Tamrin. But no one else.

According to the plan, Makeda was to recover fully and stay in the temple until the child was born. Because only this way, it could be considered a gift from the Silver Mother. The age-old principles of inheritance in Sheba, well known to everyone, said that a woman could sit on the throne provided she was a virgin and would remain one throughout the whole period of her rule. If Makeda returned from her trip to Israel pregnant, it would be synonymous with the fact that she is no longer a virgin.

"You will enter Mariba at the head of the caravan. You will announce to the wealthy and the people the favorable agreements you have made, and what great wealth this means for Sheba. At the same time, you will distribute generous gifts, and everyone will be delighted that the queen has returned," the High Priestess assured Makeda, explaining her plan. "I will show the child. I will say, truthfully, that it is a gift from the Lady of the Moon and Yahweh. It is so after all. There is no doubt about it. And if the High Priestess and the priest of Illumkuh proclaim it, there will be no one who would dare to challenge this truth. The child will become a valid heir. The will of the gods will be fulfilled."

She made a triple gesture of thanks to the Lady of the Moon.

"After all, it was the Lady of the Moon and Yahweh that made you have visions from an early age. They directed your feet toward Israel and made your light merge with the power of Solomon. They have also given you the visions that are a warning to the world. Finally, Sheba will have an heir by God's will."

"How do you know it's a boy?" Makeda was surprised.

"Seshep parted the veil of time." The priestess knew that her words should calm the queen down and encourage her during the difficult time of her illness. "She saw you on Sheba's throne. Next to you was a beautiful little boy."

***

At the same time when Makeda headed for the temple, imprisoned in a hammock, one of the four temple priestesses, whose shape was similar to Makeda's, stayed in the queen's tent to play her role. Varda put her in a bed and ordered to hang opaque curtains around her. From that moment on, only the High Priestess, Varda, a medic initiated into the case, and two trusted servants could enter the tent.

After a few days, as a part of the plan, the tightly covered litter of the "queen" was carried aboard the ship. Varda and the maids followed her. Ashenafi and his soldiers placed themselves on the other ship and both set out off the shore. The High Priestess said goodbyes to them, blessed them, and announced that she would go to the temple of the Lady of the Moon and that she would appear in Mariba when the time came for the caravan to return to the capital. No one dared ask why she was not going to accompany the queen. The High Priestess could only be asked questions by the ruler.

***

More than fifty days passed before the court with the false queen joined the caravan led by Tamrin.

At that time, Ashenafi already knew that Makeda was in the temple of the Moon Lady and understood the need for absolute secrecy in this matter. It was obvious to him that as a security commander, who had long belonged to a narrow circle of the most trusted people, he had to do everything so that no one would learn that the queen was outside the caravan.

In connection with the decision of the High Priestess that she and Seshep would accompany the queen in the temple until the child was born, Ashenafi and Varda, and soon also Tamrin, became the most important persons managing the court and the caravan. It was supposed to be like that until the real queen would return. Varda was supposed to represent the ruler, who was said not to feel well, and that was why she was still in the tent and not showing up in public. Varda was authorized and obliged by the High Priestess to provide Tamrin with all necessary information about the state of Makeda and the reason for her staying in the temple. The priestess knew that the girl would do it diligently and willingly, and it might at the same time lead to Tamrin finally deciding to fully open his heart to her.

The queen's assistant felt the burden of responsibility. She also knew what great opportunity this time was for her and knew that for Tamrin, it would probably be the last moment to decide whether he wanted to be with her.

If he would not confess his feelings to her before they reach Jerusalem [sic], she would have no choice but to fulfill her obligation to Elichoref. She liked and valued him, but she could not imagine becoming his wife. After all, he was only a part of the game, which was supposed to cause jealousy in Tamrin and accelerate his decision about their future together. Neither Varda nor Makeda liked to use people for their own games, especially those unaware of what was happening, but they were both convinced that the one who does something out of love does not sin. This way they felt justified.

Varda prepared carefully to talk to Tamrin. When it was known that their small group, protected by Ashenafi, was approaching the stopping place of the great caravan, she made a special sacrifice to the Lady of the Moon. On the night before the meeting, she went to the top of one of the high brown sand rocks on either side of the gorge they traversed.

She prayed for a long time, asking the goddess for support, then opened the basket with which she climbed the rock, and took a quail out from it. She laid the bird on the stone, stroking it and speaking to it tenderly.

"You will go to the Lady of the Moon," she promised it, believing it understood her. "A small spark of your existence will merge with her eternal brightness. Let your energy enter the cosmic gates, let your blood strengthen Tamrin's spirit, and let the Silver Mother give him the strength to reject his fears and concerns, and the courage to be with me," she bowed her head in front of the moon disc.

Saying this, she cut off the quail's head with one movement of the knife. The bird raised its wings and gave a short scream, the body shuddered. She knew that she had to hold it tight, because although headless, it could stand up and make the last pre-death dance. She had seen such a thing several times and remembering how terrible it was, she wanted to avoid it at all costs. The sacrifice had to be treated with respect, after all its life was devoted to a specific intention.

The equalization of energy meant that there was an exchange: something for something. The Moon's Lady should feel how much the person giving the sacrifice wants to achieve her goal. And the person giving the gift had to drain the blood of the victim with her own hands and at least for a moment fuse with its spirit and join the thread of her life with it.

"Lady, please accept the sacrifice!" she called again, raising her head towards the moon.

When she felt that the quail no longer moved, she raised her fingers, drenched in blood, and made the triple sign of the Lady of the Moon on her forehead, lips and heart.

The next day, they set off at dawn to reach the camp before noon, before the sun would prevent the travel. They managed to do that.

"May the gods guide you, sir," Varda hopped off her horse nimbly and stood in front of Tamrin, inclining her head to such a level as if they had equal positions. "I represent the queen," she said confidently. "I give you her greetings and respect."

Behind her and Ashenafi, who was on his horse, stood the queen's huge white camel. Everyone knew him. He carried a tightly covered palanquin. It seemed that the queen was sleeping, because none of the curtains moved aside even half a cubit.

Tamrin, of course, paid attention to the camel and the palanquin, to Ashenafi bowing his head in salute, but he saw mostly Varda.

She was wearing a long, light dress, covering her body so tightly that her hands were not visible beyond her fingertips. Her head was covered with a wide scarf protecting the face, thanks to which only eyes with long eyelashes were visible. Even her feet were covered. They were protected by sandals lined from the inside with soft fabric wrapping around her calves. From the long sleeves of the dress, protruded the tip of a short little sheaf she was holding. By the wide leather belt around her waist there was a small pouch, a dagger and - what surprised him the most - a short but sharp sword. He had never seen her with it before.

"Is she afraid of someone?" he wondered. "Or is it just a symbol of power that gives her confidence?"

When she stood in front of him and pulled a piece of the veil away from her face so that she could breathe more freely, he swallowed hard. They had not seen each other for over two months. During this time, he tried not to think about her, but he did not succeed in that. She returned to him in his dreams, appeared when he sat on a horse or a camel, and the monotonous road - because such routes also happened - was getting mercilessly long. He remembered how tough, and at the same time helpless and lost she seemed to him that evening, when she had suggested to him nothing less than to marry her. He saw her tearful eyes when he said they couldn't be together. During this time, when she was not next to him, he realized how much he missed her and what an independent and strong girl he was dealing with.

"Lady, as I am always at the queen's service and at her disposal," he bowed and felt that his heart trembled and his legs softened because of her sight, the smell that surrounded her and the memories that flooded his head.

He did not know what made him react so strongly to her presence. He always liked her, but then he had explained to himself a few months earlier that their possible relationship would have no prospects, didn't he?

"Is my heart independent of reason?" he thought. "Isn't my will stronger than a heart's impulse? I am a mature man, experienced, composed, I can direct my own thoughts and act predictably. What's going on? Or is this her imperious attitude working on me? She has gained confidence recently. She has never lacked this quality, but now she is acting as if something has happened that has strengthened her even more. What could it be?" He couldn't find the answer.

He knew one thing: common sense moves out from the areas where love magics comes in, and nobody knows if and when it will come back.

"The queen has decided to go to the country by land," Varda spoke loud and clear so that everyone who stood even a little further could hear her well. At the same time, she pointed to the camel and the palanquin he carried. "Great Kandake personally tested the speed and efficiency of new ships. Now she is sure that the emerging combined commercial fleet of Solomon, Hiram, and Makeda will be the most powerful in the world. She checked the ships capabilities while sailing on one of them. She is satisfied. Now, out of concern for the second part of the agreement with the King of Israel and the financial future of the kingdom, she decided to visit the areas where, according to the agreement, oases are to be built that are going to be part of the extended trade route. Now she is weakened by the travel and tired, so she is resting. You can't bother her."

"Lady, thank you for your words. I am honored to welcome the queen and her trusted ones at our stop," he bowed officially, tilting his head much lower than she had done. "Will you allow me pay my respects to the queen and greet her as soon as possible?"

He concluded with concern that the news of the queen's illness was probably not exaggerated. Since the camel had stopped rocking her in a steady walk, she should wake up, but she did not even move the curtains to greet him by at least showing her hand. It could mean that she was more seriously ill than it was said.

"The queen is weakened by sea travel and a long hike through the mountains. The medic recommended a lot of sleep and rest to her. For a while, no one should visit her, not even her esteemed and trusted man like you, sir. She needs rest."

He watched her carefully, trying to guess what had happened that - he felt it more clearly with every moment - changed her so much? She was official in gestures and words, she tried to be restrained and feigned indifference, but her eyes betrayed that the feeling she had long had for him was still alive.

"She doesn't love Elichoref," he thought. "It is impossible. Maybe she wanted him as a husband to free herself from affection for me? It is hardly surprising given that I rejected her. I hurt her. I was a fool and a coward. What did I get scared of? Her age or loss of freedom?"

"Let us set up the camp, the road was exhausting. We need rest," she interrupted his thoughts. "The queen will receive you as soon as she can, be patient."

"Should I worry about Great Kandake?" he asked, looking again toward the palanquin.

"As I said, the queen is tired," she answered firmly.

He understood that he couldn't ask any more questions.

At that moment, the curtain of the palanquin opened, and the queen's hand appeared. Although no one saw her face, everyone recognized that the hand belonged to her. The large ring that Solomon had given her, was on the index finger. Everyone in her retinue knew that Makeda never took it off.

"Thank god," Tamrin breathed a sigh of relief, bowing before the hand outstretched from the palanquin.

***

Late in the evening, when almost the entire camp was going to sleep, Varda stood in front of Tamrin's tent.

"Tell Tamrin that I want to talk to him," he heard her instruct the servant.

Without waiting for the servant to convey her words to him, Tamrin went outside.

"Lady, I am at your disposal."

"Can you give me a moment of your time, please," she didn't show it, but she was glad to see the joy her visit caused for him.

She guessed rightly that Tamrin might have thought she came late at night to tell him again about her affection, as she had done before. How wrong he was!

"I bring news from the queen," she said coldly.

"Would you like to come in?" he offered, surprised by her tone, which he had not managed to get used to yet.

"Although I represent the queen in conversations with you, I still don't have a husband yet, so as you know, according to the custom, I can't come in, despite the fact that I have to give you the words that should only go to your ears."

"So?"

"Please, take a short walk with me," she pointed the direction to him and walked first, and when he joined her, she added, "Don't be afraid, you are not at risk of any my emotional confessions. I have grown up recently."

"Should I worry?" he tried to joke, but there was a disappointment in his voice.

They walked to the camp's borders in silence, greeting the guards standing at the posts.

"The information I want to give you is strictly confidential," she announced when they reached a place where they were certain that nobody would hear them.

"I noticed something strange happening," he lowered his voice, even though there was empty space around them. "I'd love to find out what is going on."

"Everything I am about to say is a royal secret. You know what it means?"

"The punishment for giving it up is death," he knew the rules.

"Listen then, the queen, together with the High Priestess and Seshep, is in the temple of the Moon Lady in Aksum."

"Is she in danger?" he worried. "Do you know of something I don't know? What's going on?"

"I will tell you everything," she whispered to him.

They stood opposite each other. They were separated by a distance of their arm reach. They both pretended that this closeness was justified by the royal secret.

"The queen is pregnant," she spelled slowly to enhance the effect.

He inhaled, not knowing what to say.

"And nobody knows about it?" he stated more than asked.

"Some have probably guessed," she admitted. "The official information is that she has been ill since the sea journey. Many people saw her in really bad condition. Honestly, believe me, she barely survived this journey. We were very worried for her and for the baby. She kept vomiting on the ship, which weakened her so much that she had no strength not only to get up, but even to speak. In the last stage of the journey, she was almost dying."

"What I hear sounds bad. Is it better now though?"

"When I saw her last time, she was going to the temple, surrounded by priestesses, in a hammock suspended between two horses. She was already strong enough that the medics allowed it, claiming that she and the child who she carries in the womb will survive the journey, if nothing unexpected happens. Later, I got a pigeon with the news that everything was well. These birds that you brought from Israel a few years ago really serve us well."

He ignored her remark about the pigeons, as if he hadn't heard her at all, because something else was more important to him at the moment.

"Who knows about the queen's condition?"

"The High Priestess and Seshep, of course, priestesses from the temple she is in now, although I am sure only some of them, of course, Ashenafi, a few servants and from now on, also you."

"And the queen's tent? Who plays the role of Makeda?"

"At the request of the High Priestess, a girl was sent from the temple who is just as tall and slender as our ruler. She was the one in the palanquin and she is hiding in the queen's tent."

"She had the ring. The queen took it off?"

"She never takes the ring from Solomon off. The one her deputy wears is false. It was made quite hurriedly at the request of the High Priestess. You can't see the difference from afar."

"She is a highly anticipating woman."

"Sometimes I suspect that she knows the future of each of us. She just doesn't tell us about it."

"When is the birth expected?" Tamrin did not comment on her words about the priestess's knowledge, but the thought crossed his mind that it might indeed be so.

"I've been traveling to you taking as much time as I could. The ruler, on the advice of the High Priestess, decided that she would triumphantly enter Mariba at the head of the caravan when the child is already in this world. As you know, only a virgin can be a queen of Sheba. You also know that our lady did not accept Solomon's proposal to become his wife and sit on the throne of Israel. She will return to the country and proclaim that the child is a gift she received from the Silver Mother. This will be true. After all, Lady of the Moon promised it to Makeda a long time ago."

"This child is a gift from the goddess, but also from God," Tamrin raised his head and finger up, pointing to the sky. "I wonder if Solomon knows about it?"

She was silent.

"Not at all," he answered himself. "After all, if he did, he wouldn't let her out of Israel!"

"I'm giving you the queen's orders now," she wanted to end the meeting. "Drive the caravan taking as much time as possible, go slowly between the places where you know that the new oases are to be built. The queen needs time. Move people who saw her up close away from her tent and the space in which she will appear."

He nodded.

"You will receive information from the queen through me. You are to do everything you can to keep what you know about the queen's condition secret. No one can know what's going on, except the people I told you about. Swear you will keep everything to yourself."

"I swear."

"Swear to the god to whom you pray most often."

Instead of saying what she wanted, he fell silent. He spoke only after a long moment.

"Varda, I want you to know that I have been a follower of Yahweh for several years."

"What?" her voice was no longer a whisper.

"It happened during my second visit to Jerusalem. When I was there for the first time and met Solomon, he told me about God. I studied books, learned the history and tradition of Israel and decided that this is the God I believe in."

"What about Illumkuh? And Lady of the Moon?"

"I've always been skeptical. But God has spoken to my heart. I believe in him with all my life."

"What are you talking about?"

He took two steps away from her.

"I was afraid it would happen," he nodded sadly. "I knew you wouldn't accept it. It was one of the reasons why I couldn't respond positively to the beautiful feelings that you wanted to give me. Not only I have my years and habits, I also believe in one God! I thought it was too much of the weight for one girl, so young and wonderful. I didn't want to burden you."

With his every word, her resolve, which she made when she went to the meeting, was getting weaker. She intended to be cold, official, and swore she would turn her emotions off. However, after what he said, she knew that she would not be able to keep her promise.

"What are you talking about?" she abandoned the official tone. "How could you even think that?"

"You're too young to understand."

"If I'm not too young to be the chief trusted person of the ruler and tell you royal secrets, it means I'm not too young for anything."

She was right. Last year changed her a lot. She was neither too young nor too inexperienced anymore. She managed the court, the queen entrusted her with the most important secrets, so maybe also her father would not see anything wrong in the fact that she liked the wealthiest person in Sheba, right after the queen? Tamrin had a lot of time to think recently. He came to the conclusion that the problem was not in her, but in his fears about the inevitability of huge changes, if he decided to live with her.

From the moment they parted, he was certain that if she would only want to repeat the words of love from a few months ago, he wouldn't hesitate.

She waited for what he would say. She dreamed that he would ask her to share her life with him. She felt he was finally ready for it. Her heart was beating with all its might. She was already looking forward to the words she thought he should say any moment. However, something went wrong. Something stopped him. He wanted to confess that he loved her, that he wanted to be with her, that she had captured his thoughts, but he couldn't. He was not able to. He chickened out again. Instead of what he wanted to say and what she would like to hear, his lips, disobedient to his heart, said, "You are the most appropriate person that Makeda could trust so much. I am glad that we will cooperate. I am at your service; you can count on me in everything. And of course, I will keep what I know in absolute secrecy. I swear to my God."

She understood that despite her efforts and premonitions, he was not able to open his heart to her again, so the sacrifice to the Lady of the Moon did not work. Cold sweat covered her. She took a step back and thought that she would immediately turn away from him and start running to get away as far as possible. Almost immediately, however, she remembered how strong she was. She clenched her teeth and fists. She managed to return to her previous official tone and regretted her moment of weakness. At the same time, she was proud of herself that this time she did not tell him much, that she did not confess to him about love again. She exhaled, looked into his eyes, and promised herself that she would never again try to fight for his feelings.

"Apparently, we are not made for each other, or his heart is dead, and I was not able to resurrect it," she thought sadly, and added aloud, "Thank you on behalf of the queen. She was sure that she would always be able to count on you."

***

"It's a boy, lady!" the High Priestess cried happily. "He is born beautiful and healthy," she said excitedly, watching as the medic put the newborn on Makeda's stomach.

His body was covered with mucus, blood, and residual fetal water. Still, it was clear that he had dark luxuriant hair and swarthy blue-tinged skin. He was big and cried loudly.

"Is that you, my love?" she asked, exhausted but happy. "Finally, you are here!" she embraced him with tenderness. The pain that ripped her body a moment ago, was over. She was sore, wet with effort, exhausted, but so delighted that she finally could see her son she has spoken to in recent months, that tears flowed down her cheeks.

"My wonderful, I've waited so long for you," she kissed him.

When he heard her voice, he calmed down.

"It's good that you're already on this side, my baby. I love you most in the world!

Prince Menelik, later also called Bayna-Lehem*, which meant "son of the wise man," was born in the Temple of the Lady of the Moon, on the shores of the Red Sea, many miles away from Jerusalem and many from Mariba, in the lands belonging to the kingdom of Sheba. Many years after his birth, when he was an adult already, it was said that it was no coincidence that God directed the ship on which his mother sailed in this area, so that in future he would rule the lands with which he was associated since birth.

***

The caravan had been camping in the oasis for two days. It was getting dark when Tamrin approached Varda, sitting alone by the water. He sat next to her without a word. She was silent.

It was quiet. People settled in tents and around campfires. Last preparations for the night rest were underway.

When the sounds of the camp falling asleep dwindled completely and the moon shone high, Tamrin opened the traveling purse that he brought with him. He took out a small, beautifully decorated bag made of glittering red fabric.

"Please give me this honor and accept this gift," he handed it to Varda.

"What do I owe this surprise to?" She untied the binding and put her hand inside. "Oh, how beautiful!" She took out a pair of brown leather sandals. They were made of very delicate leather, decorated with golden plates. Their sole was so strong that if it wasn't for the beautiful decorations and the delicate leather, they would look like typical travel sandals.

"An unusual gift..." she met Tamrin's eyes for the first time that evening.

"It's a proposition," he moved toward her.

"Are we going on a journey?" Fearing another disappointment, she refused to think of the obvious.

"I'd love to."

"Is that why you gave me sandals?"

"If you would like to travel with me, I would be the happiest man on earth," he finally said.

She breathed a sigh of relief. What she had been waiting for so long, was finally happening.

"What journey are you offering me, Tamrin?" Even though she knew what he meant, she preferred him to call things by their name; to hear the words she had expected. So that not only her, but above all he, would hear them.

He knelt before her and bowed his head humbly.

"Will you be my wife?"

***

When Menelik was born, a scroll reached the caravan led by Tamrin, and Makeda's tent. It had made long journey before it reached its addressee. It was enclosed in an intricately made gold box, richly decorated with precious stones.

This is our joint work. Although it's not finished yet, I would like these words to be with you. You are and will be the Lady of my heart. This song is an expression of my love and, like the feeling that united us, belongs to both of us.

All night long on my bed
    I looked for the one my heart loves;
    I searched but did not find her .
    I will get up now and go about the city,
    through its streets and squares;
    I will search for the one my heart loves .

***

My beloved spoke and said to me,
"Arise, my darling, my beautiful one, come with me.
See! The winter is past;   the rains are over and gone.
Flowers appear on the earth; the season of singing has come,
the cooing of doves   is heard in our land.
The fig tree forms its early fruit; the blossoming vines spread their fragrance.
Arise, come, my darling;   my beautiful one, come with me .

***

8:6-7

Place me like a seal over your heart,
like a seal on your arm;
for love is as strong as death,
its jealousy unyielding as the grave.
It burns like blazing fire, like a mighty flame.

Many waters cannot quench love;
rivers cannot sweep it away.
If one were to give all the wealth
of one's house for love,   it would be utterly scorned .

[sic - I suppose it is still a part of the song]

***

"Long live the queen!"
"Makeda!"
"May the gods bless the ruler!"
"Great Kandake!"
"Mukarrib!"

People standing on the route of the queen's entrance to Mariba shouted loudly, happy for her return.

News of the tremendous success of the expedition overtook the caravan's entrance to the city. People, sent to the capital earlier by Tamrin and the High Priestess, announced that the queen had entered into agreements with Solomon, which guaranteed prosperity not only for the currently living Shebeans, but also for their children and grandchildren. Everyone said that thanks to the queen, Sheba has a great merchant fleet that will deliver valuable goods around the world, and this means new income to the treasury, and therefore a good life for everyone.

It was also said that the construction of new oases was beginning, and most importantly, that Makeda brought rich gifts from the king of Israel; and that she would divide them among the temples, nobles, and the people will get quite a lot, too.

Inhabitants of the city were invited to a great feast, which was to last three days and begin immediately after the welcome celebrations.

So, when the long-awaited caravan finally crossed the gates, the shouts of joy were endless. As expected, Ashenafi, appointed general by the queen while still in Jerusalem, rode at the head of the returnees on a magnificent steed, followed by half of his soldiers on horseback. The other half closed the procession that stretched many miles outside the city. They were all in shiny, ceremonial outfits.

The priestesses of the Lady of the Moon followed them. They were playing instruments and singing. All in the identical, richly decorated dresses. For this occasion, they, as well as soldiers, servants and others taking part in the triumphal entry into the city, put on the same costumes in which they entered Jerusalem.

When the queen left the country more than a year and a half earlier, the inhabitants of Sheba did not see the costumes prepared to impress King Solomon and his people. They were to be worn for the first time there, in a distant, foreign land. They were used again when the caravan left Jerusalem. Now, extremely rich, decorated with gold, they were presented for the third time. Again, they delighted.

Behind the playing and singing priestesses, on a white camel, in a golden palanquin, with light curtains fluttering in the wind, the queen was sitting. Those who sometimes heard gossips about her illness and weakness, could see for themselves that not only is she all right, but that she looks more beautiful than ever. Maids in golden dresses walked on her both sides and threw flower petals on the road and toward the cheering people.

At the gates of the city, the ruler was awaited by those who managed the country during her absence, namely the eunuch Handake, priest Sethon, and general Tesfa. They bowed low, and when she nodded toward them from the height of her palanquin, they sat down on ornate chairs placed on litters.

Priest Sethon was already old, and while the queen was traveling, he tried to build an opposition. However, he did not have much success. He did not find understanding among the nobles, and because he was very weak and sick almost all the time, he could not get involved properly, so he gave up.

The litters for the three managers were set up primarily because of him. Were it not for his illness, all three would walk before the queen to the temple, thus symbolically bringing her back into the city. The priest's condition did not allow this. The road from the city gates was not long and soon the members of the caravan entered the temple. Everyone who should appear to greet the queen was waiting for them there. The building was filled to the brim.

When the queen entered the temple, followed by the most important people from her retinue, Varda greeted her father. She did it with restraint, because it was not proper to show emotions in front of everyone, promising to herself that as soon as they would be alone, she would immediately throw herself on his neck. She bowed low to him. Tamrin stood behind her.

Tesfa immediately noticed that his daughter and old friend had something more in common than serving the queen. He looked questioningly at her and then at him. She nodded, confirming his supposition.

"Father, we're back," she announced. "And I'm happy."

The general smiled in relief. It seemed that on the long expedition, his daughter had discovered something more than just new lands.

"We'll tell you everything later," she glanced at Tamrin, confirming with the use of plural for her father that he was not mistaken in his assumptions.

Seeing gladness in the general's eyes, the merchant breathed a sigh of relief.

***

All the significant people in the kingdom gathered in the temple of the Moon Lady. There were priests and priestesses of gods worshiped for centuries, princes from subordinate lands, generals, aristocracy, the richest merchants, and officials. Everyone came to greet the queen.

For this day, priestesses from every temple of the Silver Mother from all over the vast Sheba territory, from both sides of the sea, came to Mariba. They sang, danced, and played instruments in front of the statue of their patron. Around them rose the incense smoke and the delicate scent of myrrh, which slowly enveloped those present in a gentle mist.

Priest Sethon entered the temple first, followed by eunuch Handake and general Tesfa. The priestesses dancing in front of and inside the temple knelt along the road, creating a passage. The men stopped only under the statue of the Lady of the Moon.

After them, the High Priestess entered the building. She glided, as if floating in the long black dress. The moon's disc placed on her head shone with an unearthly glow, announcing that the multiplied Divine energy came into the temple with her. In her right hand, she held a cane topped with a silver scepter symbolizing the Lady of the Moon. When she reached the statue of the goddess, the drums were hit, and the trumpets were heard. After a while, the one for which everyone was waiting the most, appeared before the eyes of those gathered.

"Great Kandake, ruler of Sheba, mukarrib of subordinate duchies, queen Makeda!" the priest Sethon announced solemnly.

The queen went along the path formed by the kneeling priestesses and stood in the middle of the platform next to the High Priestess.

Illumkuh's priest bowed his grey head to the queen. The same was done by those who had the honor of standing on the platform.

Those present in the temple knelt down and bowed, touching the floor with their foreheads. When they stood up at a sign of the queen, the drums and the trumpets resounded again, and when the sounds faded, eight huge servants entered the temple. In a litter, they carried the gift from Solomon, which he gave to Makeda when she was leaving. The queen decided that on the day of her return to the country the throne would stand first in the temple, and then would be moved to the palace to be the main piece of furniture in the throne room.

It was similar to the one that Solomon had ordered to be made for himself. It was made of ivory and covered with refined gold. Six steps led to it. On the back was a round canopy. There was only one thing that was different between the throne of Makeda and the throne of Solomon: in Jerusalem, a total of twelve lions depicting the twelve tribes of Israel stood on six steps. In Mariba, there were two lions. They were to symbolize two parts of Sheba separated by the Red Sea.

The servants deftly set up the impressive piece of furniture. Makeda climbed its steps and sat on the throne. She put her hands on the wide armrests and her feet on the footrest.

"Gods bless Sheba and all its inhabitants!" she greeted her subjects.

They knelt again and bowed their heads to her. They had not yet managed to recover from the impression that the throne made on them, when they heard the priestess's voice.

"We bring precious gifts from distant lands. Everyone gathered here today will receive gifts in honor of the happy return of the ruler and the entire expedition to the home country. The beneficial agreements that, thanks to her wisdom, Great Kandake has entered into with the king of Israel, will allow you, your children and their children to live in great welfare and prosperity, and will make Sheba's fame last forever. Let's thank the gods and our queen!"

At this moment, the Moon Lady's priestesses in long ethereal dresses came in amongst those present. Each of them held a small but heavy basket in front of her, filled with thick golden plaques decorated with the image of Makeda.

"Take this gift as a foretaste of the gifts we bring."

"Makeda, Makeda, Makeda!" joyful voices resounded, because after these words, people were already certain that the stories of the great benefits of the expedition that had been circulating around the country for a long time, were not exaggerated. There was a talk of a new fleet, oases, and contracts that gave them a prosperous future. There were legends about the gifts that Solomon gave to Makeda, including the extraordinary throne; and here they have already seen the throne! They also got their first gifts.

While among the stories passed from mouth to mouth, those about treasures and contracts were told aloud and with hope, the next matter was talked about only in a whisper in Sheba. No one wanted to offend the honor of the ruler, and to expose themselves to punishments this way, which the royal guard enforced with the utmost severity against those who tarnished the good name of the Great Kandake.

As people enjoyed the golden plates, the drums and trumpets played again, and four priestesses carrying a golden litter entered the temple. In its center was an elongated basket covered with golden fabric. They came to the High Priestess and set the litter at her feet.

"This is a divine gift from the Lady of the Moon for us all," she announced, raising the basket to chest height. Like other dignitaries, she was standing on a platform, so the gathered could see what was in her hands.

"The Silver Mother gave generously to the kingdom of Sheba. In agreement with the eternal prophecies written in the stars, and announced in the visions of our priestesses, the gods gave us the world's smartest queen, the greatest riches, fame and glory for Sheba, which will last until the end of centuries. We also received the heir to the throne sent to us by the will of the gods. The Lady of the Moon and God Yahweh offer us this boy, sanctified by the power of their cosmic power. By their will, he is the son of the Silver Mother, as well as the virgin-queen Makeda, and when the time comes, by their will he will also sit on the throne, to rule in peace to the glory of the gods, for the good of Sheba and all its inhabitants."

One could feel the significance of the moment. Holding the basket with the baby, the High Priestess climbed the steps leading to the throne, set it at the queen's feet and bowed respectfully.

The subjects did the same. There was almost complete silence. All you could hear was the singing of birds basking outside in the afternoon sun.

The queen got up.

"I accept you as the gift of the gods to me and the people of Sheba, foretold in prophecies," she said in a strong voice. "Be my son and the heir to the kingdom. Let it be done according to the will of the Lady of the Moon and Yahweh!"

She knelt down before the baby boy and bowed to him.

She stood up, raised the basket and showed her son to the assembled.

"Here is Sheba's heir! Menelik, Bayna-Lehem*, the son of the gods," announced the High Priestess. "Let's bow to him!"

Handake was first to kneel before the queen holding the basket with the baby. After him, General Tesfa did the same.

As the third, priest Sethon moved towards the queen, very slowly because of his age and illness, leaning on a tall cane. He was only five steps away from her. When he set his foot on the first step leading to the throne, he ran out of air. He looked at her radiant face. He was about to bow down to her and the heir when he staggered, lost his balance, and although he tried to lean on his cane, he faltered, put his hand on his heart and fell down.

There were numerous shouts of terror.

The dignitaries standing closest to the priest immediately ran to him. Without thinking, the queen passed the basket to the priestess standing by the throne and ran down the stairs. She knelt before the old man.

"Priest?" she managed to ask, looking into his foggy eyes.

"New times are coming," he whispered. "This is the order of the world. The stairs to this throne are not for me, they pushed me away. Illumkuh leaves Sheba together with me," he added.

"Priest," she whispered. "Don't leave..."

"I bless you," he said with the last of his strength.

He realized that the visions his priests had had for a long time, were coming true right now. They said that the queen's trip to a distant country would mean the end of the world. Illumkuh could not be wrong. The visions clearly said that the ruler, who was a follower of the Lady of the Moon, would bring to the country a new god that would knock Illumkuh off the pedestal. The priests seeing future also spoke of a king who would be born by a virgin and would rule the world. So, when Sethon saw Makeda's son and heard the High Priestess, he understood that the visions were coming true.

His heart couldn't take it. It broke. The luminous energy that Sethon received when he came into the world, began its way back to the source.

The priest knew that his death also meant the end of Illumkuh's time. With his departure, a new era began for Sheba.

The High Priestess, watching the kneeling queen and anticipating the reaction of those gathered, stood before the throne. She raised her hands and announced in a powerful voice, "The High Priest Sethon is leaving to Illumkuh, blessing the queen and the heir to the throne!"

She nodded at the priestesses. She was sure that Sethon's death had to be immediately portrayed properly, before anyone would consider it a bad omen. Tamrin, Tesfa, and Handake approached her at the same time as the priestesses surrounded her.

"Let the servants put him on a golden litter," she ordered. "We'll take the body to the Illumkuh's temple in a moment. General, make the soldiers form a free passage row between the temples so that we can get there."

"Yes, High Priestess," Tesfa nodded, admiring her composure.

No one but the queen had ever given him orders, but he always felt respect for the High Priestess of the Moon Lady, and on that day, he had no doubt that she should be listened to in this extraordinary crisis situation. "Tamrin, let your people tell those who gathered in front of the temple and those who are waiting for a feast in the city, that new wonderful times are coming, and that the old gods of Sheba are joined today by Yahweh, the god of wisdom, justice, and wealth," she passed further orders. "Priest Sethon, as everyone knows, has been ill for a long time and waited only for the return of the queen to bless her. When he did, he died happy that Illumkuh had let him fulfill his last wish."

She looked into the faces of those present, seeking confirmation that they understood the seriousness of the moment and the need for swift action.

"Handake, order to give gifts to the people now, as soon as we leave. Let's not wait until the feast. The death of the high priest will touch hearts. You have to calm them down somehow and direct people's thoughts to other things."

They nodded to show they agreed with her decisions and knew what to do. They went to their tasks.

When Sethon's body rested on a litter, the High Priestess stood under the statue of the Moon Lady, next to the queen who was sitting on the throne again, and again spoke in a great voice, "The new times are coming. They will be even better for us than those that have passed," she called, raising the cane topped with a silver scepter. "Let's be happy, let's rejoice. The golden age is coming. We have an heir sent to us by the gods. The old prophecy is coming true!"

***

Since his escape from Aksum, Den had lived in the lands that Pharaoh had assigned to him. He watched what was happening in Mariba and Aksum from a distance. He hoped that in the absence of the queen, he would be able to return to the city and conquer it, but General Tesfa staffed it with such a large army, and stayed himself there so often, that Den would stand no chance. So, he waited for the right moment, believing that it would come soon.

He often sent spies to Aksum. They met with dignitaries who not so long ago were trusted by his father. They collected news and assured people that Den would one day return because he was the rightful heir to the throne.

"I just need the right moment," Den believed. "The pharaoh will give me soldiers because he thinks ahead. He would rather have me in Aksum than the mighty Makeda, because he thinks I'm subordinate to him, while she guards Sheba's interests and doesn't let Egypt interfere with them. Thanks to me, the pharaoh will have an open path to the riches of the Dark Continent." Den had no doubt that Egypt would support him with the army, if he had a clash with Sheba.

So, months and years went by. At that time, Pharaoh Siamun, who had accepted Den in his country, departed to the gods, and Psesunnes II sat on the throne. Fortunately for Den however, Egypt's policy had not changed.

Finally, the long-awaited moment arrived. He got information about Makeda's return from Jerusalem, the planned triumphant entry into the city and the ceremonies.

"When will the better moment be for my return to Aksum if not now?" he wondered excitedly. "After all, that loser Caleb, appointed as the prince of Aksum, more important nobles and most commanders watching over the peace in the city, will definitely go to Mariba. The remaining army will be reduced. As soon as I enter Aksum, they will announce me a true prince." He had the right to think so, especially since the new pharaoh was more resolute than his predecessor, and the commander of his troops, Sheshonk, had great ambitions to extend Egypt's power to the south of the country.

The secret messengers sent to Pharaoh brought good news. The ruler of Egypt gave him two thousand Nubian soldiers, weapons, horses, and camels. There was just one caveat: Den, or anyone around him, could never reveal where the troops came from. Pharaoh did not want to get into a conflict with the influential queen. At the same time, he knew that if Den, supported by him, would win, it would mean profits for Egypt and an open road to the lands of the Dark Continent. Therefore, he decided to support him, but in such a way that the queen of Sheba could not have evidence that he was involved in it. So, Den had at his disposal a well-trained army, paid for by the pharaoh, appearing in clothes with his own signs.

The road to Aksum was difficult, it took the soldiers forty days. However, the prince's mood was very different from what it was when his father was murdered, when he fled from his kingdom in fear. Now, riding at a head of a large group of Nubians, he felt almost like a king!

In Aksum things went as he expected. He found no resistance anywhere. Prince Caleb, general Tesfa, as well as the more important commanders and nobles, went to Mariba to welcome the queen. The few troops guarding peace in the city did not expect an attack. Those who resisted, were killed. In addition, after the city surrendered almost without a fight, Den ordered his Nubians to kill every tenth soldier, so that the survivors would know what awaits them for not complying with the new ruler. With the skilled Nubian army at his disposal, he forced the army and the people of Aksum to pledge allegiance to him already on the next day after the city was seized and proclaimed himself the king of Aksum. That's how his rule began.

It happened on the day of Makeda's solemn entry into Mariba.

***

Two days later, the news of the occupation of Aksum reached Makeda. That was how long the bird sent from Aksum to Mariba flew.

"He had been preparing for it as soon as the spies informed him of the celebration being prepared for your return, lady," agitated Seshep knelt at the queen's bed.

It was morning. The ruler just woke up.

"He rightly decided that the princes of the lands subordinate to you and the commanders of the army of Aksum would want to attend the welcoming ceremony," she continued.

"He was right," Makeda jumped off the bed and pushed away the maid who wanted to take off her night gown before morning washing and anointing. "It's not time for morning rituals now," she called. "Looks like we've got a war!"

"He won Aksum with almost no fight," Seshep continued the report, following her.

She sat on a wide stool in front of the silver mirror and allowed the maid to comb her hair.

"He led the people that Pharaoh gave him into the city. Egypt has always been clever. He doesn't want to offend you, so it gave him an army secretly. If Den lost, they would deny that they supported him. If he won, Pharaoh would not take credit for himself, but he would enjoy the benefits that you would have never allowed him. Den sold himself and Aksum to Pharaoh!"

"As if I didn't have enough problems," Makeda shook her head in disbelief that Aksum was taken from her so easily. "Are the gods still testing me? I just gave birth to a child, I came back from an expedition, I am still weak...And here, Sethon is dead, Aksum is not mine anymore," she began to list, gesturing at the same time at the maid combing her to hurry up. "A war is coming, because I should, after all, go overseas as soon as possible and take back what he took from me. I wonder if the gods are planning anything else for me in the near future?"

Seshep understood her agitation, she was nervous, too. She knew however that one should not act hastily in difficult situations. First of all, you need to calm down and try to look at things as if from the outside. She did just that. She closed her eyes. She took a big breath, held it in her lungs and let it out after a long moment. She did this seven times. Makeda held the hand of the maid trying to comb her hair. She knew the hemet was trying to focus. She herself preferred to ride on horseback in difficult moments, without thinking about where the animal was carrying her, to feel the wind in her hair, and the momentum of the universe in her body. Seshep preferred to delve into herself. She was able to control her emotions quickly. So, it was also this time. When she opened her eyes, she said, "Just because something went wrong today, doesn't mean that the end of the world has come. A wise ruler, and as we all know, that's who you are, takes up the challenge only when she is ready for it and when she certain of a victory. Give yourself time, queen, give yourself time."

At these words, Makeda pushed away the hand of the maid, who was holding a tortoiseshell comb over her head, and stood up. She went to the window with a view on the Mariba gardens. She looked at the wide lane of sycamores. Their sight had a soothing effect on her.

"I should order to close my ranks and focus on what I have," she said to herself, but loud enough that both women could hear her. "I'll give myself time. I will get stronger."

She turned away from the window.

"You are right, Seshep," she looked the hemet in the face. "Now, after returning from Israel, after I was away for so long, when I have a young baby, when we have the great successes of the merchant fleet at our fingertips, we should not go to war, even a small one."

"Let Den carry on his rule in Aksum, let the mighty get reminded what it is like to live under his rule," Seshep added, entering the role of a political strategist. "It will do them good, because they neglected their defense, dulled their vigilance and maybe ceased to appreciate what a comfortable existence you provided for them. And when the right moment comes, we will move in! Today is not the time yet, you are right. Besides, and, most importantly, you've just given birth to a baby. You need to rest."

"Solomon used to say that everything has its time and place," Makeda sat down again on the stool, letting the maid know she could continue combing.

CHAPTER VIII

FINAL SOLUTIONS

Two years have passed

Makeda looked at her son playing. She was sitting with the High Priestess on a bench in the garden, to which her favorite sycamore avenue led. Its sight was not only calming down but also moving, because she remembered almost every time that her great-grandfather had planted it. In her eyes, the sycamore lane became a symbol and a lasting of a dynasty. She was thinking about the past, and now she was looking with affection at the one who would sit on the throne to replace her when her time is up.

"My ancestors built a dam and a city, built a palace, planted trees," she said. "I guaranteed the lasting of the state and prosperity and wealth for the people. What will my son do?"

Since the time Menelik appeared in her life, she had ordered to diversify her favorite place. To the right of the bench, delicate grass was sown, imported from the other side of the Mediterranean Sea, which was like a soft carpet, and allowed the prince to play safely when she was talking with guests right next to him. A small pool was built nearby, in which the boy liked to splash around. The place was sunny, but also properly shaded. It was nice to spend time there both on the cooler and hot days.

"I didn't think you could love someone that much," she confessed, looking at the boy. "I am literally enchanted by everything he does. I love him like no one else in the world. It gives me a storm of feelings I have never known. I love him absolutely. I watch how he develops, how curious he is of the world, how eager to find out new things. There is no cubit of the earth left around here that he would not thoroughly examine. When he picks up a flower, pulls out a grass or holds a fruit in his hands, he always tries to find out how they are built, what is inside, what its smell is and how it tastes."

"Children are generally curious about the world," the High Priestess remarked, without a trace of emotion.

"But he's extraordinary, you have to admit!" Makeda snapped.

"Of course," she said apologetically, knowing full well that for every mother her own child is the greatest in the world. "He has really special parents, and the gods who made him appear in the world, have special care over him."

"He looks like Solomon already. Can you see that?"

"He is born to do great deeds. It has been written in heavens."

"Time passes very quickly with him. It seems to me that he has just been born, I remember the moment when I took him in my arms for the first time. He was beautiful already then."

"And now he looks like a child of the gods."

Makeda looked at her son tenderly. He watched the two monkeys playing in front of him, kept on leashes by servants. Next to him lay a young leopard brought by the High Priestess. It was tame, obedient, and the prince met it before. Menelik, the monkeys, and the leopard looked as if they were perfect buddies and understood each other very well.

A few steps from the prince knelt two nannies, ready to respond to his slightest gesture. However, the queen's recommendation was not to limit the boy's independence in any way, so they allowed him to explore the world freely, naturally within reason.

Menelik was protected by royal guards. During the day, there were always at least four of them near him, and at night, two soldiers were on watch in his chamber, in addition to the nannies who slept there. The queen spent every spare moment with her son. She took him with her on short rides, when she was going to look after the dam in the morning, to check if the orchards and gardens closest to the palace were properly tended and watered. After all, they were, apart from trade, one of the main sources of wealth in her country. At that time, she would put the baby on the horse and explain the world to him, hugging him tightly. When he was tiny, he hugged her, trying to put his arms around her and folding his legs over her hips. It looked then as if he were glued to her. When he grew up a little, he rode facing forward and looked with delight at the passing area and people bowing to them.

At least four soldiers on horseback accompanied them on such rides. Although the country was peaceful and no attack was expected from anywhere, Ashenafi believed that the safety of the ruler was a crucial issue for the state, and he made sure that the most experienced soldiers guarded them day and night.

"When I look at him, sometimes I think about how much I lost by not having a mother," Makeda spoke to the High Priestess but kept her eyes on her son. "Not because I was not able to meet her, but because I did not know the caresses and love experienced by children whose mothers are with them."

"The queen gave you love by carrying you under her heart. I remember how eagerly she was awaiting you. She spoke to you; I have witnessed this many times. She gave you all the best she had," the priestess put as much emotions in her words, as it was possible in her case. "Later, you had nannies, until one day Seshep took care of you. She gave you the best feelings she had for the world. You were like a daughter to her, especially during your childhood."

"I love her. She is a wonderful woman. You and her taught me a lot. It is thanks to you that I know what femininity means. I am strong, I value independence, I believe I can handle any situation. You made me realize that femininity is divinity, and divinity is wisdom. You told me that the goddess is within me, you taught me to listen to the inner voice, to believe in the power of wisdom that is in my heart. Thanks to you I understand that everything in life is one, and the opposites complement each other perfectly. The only thing constant in life is a change and there is harmony in it," she spoke, calmly ordering the knowledge that she had had for a long time. "If it wasn't for you, what would I be like today?"

"You look very much like your mother. Believe me, she is proud of you."

"When I was little, I only had father, you, Seshep, and nannies. Of course, you all loved me, but only now I know what I missed. When I take Menelik in my arms, when I hug him, when I hear his little heart, or when I watch him sleep, I think about my mother. About how much I miss her. Even though I don't remember the touch of her hands, I miss her in a way that I wouldn't even dare try to describe."

"You knew her. After all, you were one once. You can be sure: the love she has given you will last for you for the rest of your life. You can give it to others without losing anything."

"I feel a hole in my heart. I didn't understand it once, but today I know that I've missed her my whole life."

"She watches you from her brightness up there, and at the same time lives in every part of you."

"Thank you for your words," Makeda stroked the priestess's hand. "Thank you for being here. I don't know what my life would be like without you and Seshep."

"You'd have a different priestess and a different hemet. But the goddess sent us to you, because we are obviously needed on the path she has marked out for you."

"I wonder where this road will lead us?"

"There is still a lot ahead of us," she answered mysteriously and patted her thigh.

Makeda remembered a similar gesture of her father. He made it often when he thought the case was over, and she did the same. However, the priestess patted her thigh for a different reason than Makeda and her father did.

At her signal, the young leopard raised his head. When she repeated the gesture, he stood up and settled himself at her feet.

"Obedient," Makeda noted appreciatively. "As long as I can remember, all your leopards, pumas, and other cats have been listening to you. How do you do that?"

"Cats are sent to us by the Moon Lady. They are at our service. They have always been and will be assigned to priestesses. It is entirely up to us to what extent they will obey us. If we subordinate a cat to us, no matter what kind, we can be sure that the rest of the world will also be ready to serve us."

"An obedient cat?" Makeda wasn't convinced. "They always walk their own paths."

"Let them walk but let them obey us at the same time."

"It is hard."

"Being a priestess is not easy..." she stood up slowly. "Can I be excused?"

Makeda nodded.

When the priestess rose, the leopard did the same. As she walked along the wide lane, he walked beside her. Steadily and obediently.

"The whole world is serving the High Priestess," the queen thought, admiring the woman walking away.

The priestess turned her head toward her and bowed with distinction and dignity, as if she were hearing her thoughts.

***

Sheba flourished under the rule of the Great Kandake. Both trade routes, by sea and by land, functioned perfectly, thanks to the contracts signed with Solomon. They were called "New Roads of Fragrances," and even the smallest child knew that the growing riches flowing into Sheba were the result of the queen's wise actions.

The dam, the great treasure of Sheba, was taken care of every day. It was maintained on an ongoing basis, because everybody remembered how valuable it was. No one had doubts about it before, but since the queen's visit to Solomon, many songs had been created to praise the water.

The people silently told each other about the night the queen had spent in the king's chamber, and how big the price she had to pay for him letting her drink water. Also, thanks to this story, which started growing into a legend more and more with each passing month since her return, it was obvious to everyone that water is the most valuable thing in the world.

Sheba had always been a wealthy country, but thanks to the riches that had been recently coming here, it had become a Croesus among its neighbors.

Along with riches coming from distant lands, and stories about the Queen's meeting with Solomon, there were also stories about Yahweh. People talked in taverns about God who created the world in seven days. It was also said that compulsory rest after six days of work was not a bad idea, and that the first man on earth, Adam, had only one wife in Paradise, and that Yahweh required his believers to do the same. Sheba had long had the tradition of having only one wife, but it was not a law. They joked about the choice God gave Adam and Eve. In taverns, oases and by campfires on trade routes, from mouth to mouth, with laughter, the story was told how God created them as the only people in the world, and then, generously, pointed to each other and said, "And now choose your spouses!"

In many places, it was said more and more often that the queen was a faithful follower of the Lady of the Moon, and even her priestess, but since her visit to Jerusalem, she also became a follower of God. No one saw anything wrong with it, since in Sheba one had freedom to choose whom to pray to for centuries. But since the faith in Illumkuh and his temples had deteriorated since the priest Sethon left, it seemed that Yahweh was gaining more and more followers.

***

Den's rule in Aksum had already lasted two years. It started off bloody, with killing of every tenth soldier serving Sheba. Although no one dared to talk about it in the city, the inhabitants remembered this cruel act. As soon as he declared himself king, he introduced new taxes to pay off the Pharaoh. It did not help his popularity with people or the nobles. Both remembered the times of Prince Caleb and the gentle supervision of Makeda. Above all, they were resentful that the trade revenues they had until recently, were used under Den's reign almost entirely to pay off the debts incurred in Egypt.

After two years of his reign, the whispers in Aksum turned into increasingly bold voices. It was said that the power, gained with the support of the Nubian army, was maintained only because of its constant presence there. There was fear in the city, and faith that one day the old rule would return, and with it the prosperity and peace.

In addition to paying off debts, Pharaoh demanded more and more tribute, and the living costs for the Nubians were high. It put Den in a bad mood. In addition, the spies he sent to Mariba brought messages about Sheba getting rich, about more great caravans traversing the world, which bypassed Aksum, out of fear of Den and not wanting to offend Makeda, about the cooperation with Israel, the new oases, a powerful commercial fleet, and finally about Makeda's son, who was already two years old and was being bred to be her heir.

"How to bring about an alliance with Makeda?" Den wondered. "How to win her over? And how to make Pharaoh cease his never-ending demands?" he kept wondering.

He had no advisers he could trust. Everyone he wanted to have on his side, fled to Mariba when he won. He was alone and it was getting to him.

"Makeda is the love of my life," he assured himself. "Together we would create an invincible empire. Why doesn't she understand this? She thinks, silly, that I revealed her virgin secret? I had to do it for Aksum's sake. Maybe one day she would understand how great her fate would be if she were with me. We would make the strongest pair of rulers in this part of the world! She never gave me a chance to prove it to her."

He believed that even if information had come to Makeda that his father was to blame for the death of her brothers - Sirah and Tomaj - she would not associate him with this matter. He knew her pure heart. He was convinced, and this thought encouraged him, that if only he could meet her and talk to her face to face, old times would come back, she would love him, and they could finally be together – and he would be able to implement his life plan.

"You have proven faithful to my family and the kingdom of Aksum many times," he looked at the man with a scar he had called into his chamber. "You are not a youngster anymore, but you are still fit, and I trust you as much as my father did."

"At your service, my lord," the assassin lowered in an awkward bow, waiting for instructions.

"I entrust to you a mission that will determine the fate of our kingdom," Den rose from his chair and stood before the man who was still half-bent.

"You will go to Mariba, get to the palace and..." he hesitated, but only for a moment "...you will kidnap the queen's son."

The man with a scar straightened up and looked into the eyes of the principal.

"Is there something you didn't understand?" Den didn't like his reaction. He found it audacious and insolent. He promised himself that as soon as the man would complete the task, he would not need his services anymore.

"I am to kidnap the heir to the throne of Sheba, I understood," the man said through his teeth.

"Exactly!" Den patted the man's shoulder, pretending not to see his displeasure. "Maybe then the queen will finally turn to me for help. And I will give him to her, saying that I have rescued him from the hands of the kidnappers. Understood?"

"You will give him to her, my lord, saying that you rescued him," the assassin repeated almost accurately, and dispassionately.

"I will earn her gratitude this way, it's obvious. Then she will finally have to start talking to me!"

"Sure thing," the man said, and Den didn't notice the mockery in his voice.

"It's a delicate mission, that's why I can entrust it only to you."

"You don't have anybody else," the assassin thought, but he didn't say a word.

He promised himself that this was the last job he would do for Den. The payment he was counting on, together with a large pile of gold accumulated over the years, was to ensure him a peaceful life in his old years in a place he had long ago chosen and reserved.

He took the purse and nodded, which was to ensure that he would not fail also this time.

***

Reaching Mariba was not a problem for him. He secretly arrived in the city and got into the palace many times before, during the times of Prince Seth and King Nikal. A network of spies, once paid by Seth, and now by Den, helped him for hiding in the city, but also in reaching the palace. The assassin knew where the royal chambers were and how the guards were set up, including the ones most important for him, that is, those watching the door of the little prince.

There was peace in the city. No enemies were expected in the palace. The task seemed simple to him - all he had to do was to get to the royal chambers without arousing suspicion and carry the prince out unnoticed by anybody.

He remembered how many years earlier, in the same palace, he had poisoned Prince Sirah. The women screams that were heard when he ran away, were still in his ears. He also remembered dropping snakes into the room of Prince Tomaj. He imagined the scream of those who had discovered them.

"Hemet, this wild cat that guards the queen, doesn't scream at all," he realized, remembering Seshep. "I don't think Makeda does either, actually," he admitted, wondering if he had ever heard the queen of Sheba raise her voice.

The abduction plan seemed good to him. Sheba, despite the painful experiences, was still a peace-loving powerful country. Nobody thought that there might be someone who would dare raise his hand at the royal descendant. Surprise gave a huge advantage in the task he undertook.

Entering the palace in the disguise of a fruit supplier was not a problem. Everyday dozens, if not hundreds of people brought fruit, fish, wine, textiles, and even rare weapons or jewels there. Getting to the guarded door of the little prince, however, required more cunning and skill.

He had to wait for the corridors he was sneaking through to become empty, and when he was close to his destination, he had to look and act in a way that the sentries would be convinced, at least at first, that he was there by accident. He succeeded in that. Years of work gave him great experience.

Everything went very fast. He killed the guards and rushed into the chamber. The nannies were also dead before any of them could make the slightest noise. They were killed by quick thrusts of the sword, and the expression of enormous surprise remained on their faces. He just had to take the child, lightly stun him, so that he was quiet while being carried out in the basket under the fruit, and get outside the palace, where a cart was waiting to take them out of the city.

Everything was going according to plan. With the child in the basket, he went out into the narrow corridor leading from the royal to the general part of the palace. He saw already a huge room in which the service received suppliers and distributed purchased goods and food. Then he noticed a woman who entered the narrow corridor. He froze. It was hemet Seshep. The most dangerous woman he knew!

He couldn't go back. Turning his face to the wall, he bowed to her and stood sideways so that she could pass him in the narrow corridor. She nodded to thank him and looked into his face. She froze, just like he had a moment before. Flames appeared in her eyes. She recognized him! She threw herself at him, simultaneously shouting to alert the guards.

He had no choice: he threw away the basket and drew his sword from under the tunic. Almost at the same time, four armed guards appeared, followed by others. The narrow corridor gave him no chance. He was surrounded on all sides; he had no escape. He knew he lost.

He felt one thrust of the sword, which hurt his side, then another. The next one made his eyes fog, and his hands drop limply, letting go of the sword. Darkness enveloped him, and his body fell senseless on the stone floor.

At the same time, one could hear crying from the abandoned fruit basket. Seshep jumped toward it. She did not have to put the fruit aside, because Menelik, who began to recover after a slight stun, got out from underneath by himself.

***

"How could he?!" agitated, Makeda hugged her son to her chest. "I will never forgive him!"

When she heard Seshep's story, she was shocked. She understood that Den was behind the attempt to abduct her son.

"I have forgiven him his past faults," she exclaimed excitedly. "How stupid I was!"

Seshep listened in silence. The maids huddled against the walls. They rarely saw their lady in such a state. If the man with a scar saw her, he would probably be surprised, because, contrary to what he thought, she could not only scream, but also use terrible curses.

"He was like an evil demon, a heartless monster, but I let go off him. He humiliated me in front of the whole kingdom, revealed my secret, made me a laughingstock, and yet I forgave him!" she yelled so that she could be heard in the furthest chambers of the palace. "I was hoping that he would change. Now, I am sure that it was not only his father behind my brothers' death, but also him. He had to know everything from the beginning! Disgusting, emotional corpse, power-hungry monster!"

Seshep understood her anger. Den didn't know what he was getting into. Makeda could forgive everything. She had good heart. However, anything that concerned her son was a separate world. She would give her life for Menelik without hesitation. She would also destroy anyone who would threaten him. She knew Den had made the biggest mistake of his life.

What he had done before always found some explanation in Makeda's eyes. She believed in his innocence and that he found himself by accident in the circumstances that meant that he could be accused of various evil acts. He was her childhood friend who had a bad father, but he himself was good. She convinced herself, and often also Seshep, that earlier problems resulted from Seth's ambitions, and Den was innocent. She even explained that he conquered Aksum with Pharaoh's army because it was the only chance for regaining the throne of his father, and she understood him.

Seshep was happy about what had happened, and that Makeda saw her earlier attempts to justify Den as groundless and even pathetic.

"How little I knew him," Makeda thought. "Seshep was right from the beginning. She has never liked him much." She remembered the suspicion with which the hemet had treated him when he was a boy.

"Lady, thank you for watching over my son," she said loudly, raising her eyes to the sky and making the triple sign of the goddess. "Lord, thank you for watching over Solomon's son," she folded her arms and bowed her head.

***

On the same day, the queen summoned the generals, Tesfa, and Ashenafi. They were outside the city at army training, but appeared quickly at her command, knowing what had happened.

"Something happened yesterday that I cannot forgive as a mother or a queen."

They were surprised by the calmness with which she said these words. They saw, however, that it was apparent. She was nervous: her jaw was clenched, and she tried to speak more slowly than usual, so as not to show how angry she was at what had happened.

"You know better than anyone how much I tried to understand and explain Den's actions," she said. "I didn't listen when more experienced people said that he was like his father. Even when he conquered Aksum, using Pharaoh's army, I tried to justify him."

"Lady, you have good heart," Tesfa said.

"A queen should be able to control reflexes of this type," she scolded him and herself, but she was grateful to him for this remark, because she believed that listening to the heart, and thus the voice of the goddess, helps in governing.

"A wise man once said that just as water is a mirror to the face, so the heart is a reflection of a man," Ashenafi reminded the words of Solomon.

She fell silent and closed her eyes. She recalled the image of her beloved. She saw him standing, beautiful, upright and shining with the light of wisdom. He was smiling at her. A question crossed her mind, what would it be like if he was with her? If they could rule together? She pushed that thought away.

The men were waiting for what she would say. The silence continued. Finally, when Solomon disappeared from her thoughts, she spoke, still without opening her eyes.

"Everything has its time. There is a time of birth and a time of dying, a time of planting and a time of collecting the planted plants. There is a time to kill and a time to heal, a time to destroy and a time to build. There is a time of crying and a time of laughter, a time of mourning and a time of joyful dance. There is a time to throw stones and a time to collect them, a time for kisses and to refrain from them. There is a time to seek and a time to lose, a time to take in and a time to reject. There is a time to tear and a time to staple, a time to be silent and a time to speak. There is a time to love and a time to hate, a time of war and a time of peace*." She paused. She opened her eyes and looked at the generals.

"Tesfa, you led the first expedition to Aksum for my father. You helped prince Caleb bring peace to Aksum after Seth's death."

The man nodded, and she looked at Ashenafi.

"And you have served me faithfully for years. I trust both of you and I know you are the best. I want Den's punishment to be a warning to others who would ever want to threaten Sheba's heir."

"Lady, it will be done according to your will," they said almost simultaneously, bowing their heads to her.

She stood up.

"The time of peace is over," she said. "The time for war has come. Let's get ready!"

***

"Queen, we have a plan on how to conquer Aksum. However, the success is contingent on an absolute secrecy," said Tesfa two days later.

They were at the council.

"Nobody should know our intentions," Ashenafi replied.

"I understand that this is not about Seshep?" the queen laughed, watching as the hemet sitting next to her stood up and intended to dutifully leave the chamber.

"It's obvious, Queen," Tesfa realized his tactlessness.

"This also doesn't apply to the High Priestess, I believe?" Seshep returned to the place, looking forgivingly at the general. "Will I be able to tell her about what I hear here? Secretly, of course," she lowered her voice.

"Hemet guesses my thoughts before they come to my mind," the general laughed, relieved to find that Seshep was joking, when trying to leave.

"Thank you." She knew that the general would never deliberately want to offend her in any way, much less the High Priestess.

For both men, the fact that the High Priestess and hemet Seshep should know all that the queen knew was obvious.

"Let us announce that the expedition will be led by General Ashenafi," Tesfa leaned down and lowered his voice as if it would make the secret even more secret. "Seven thousand soldiers will participate in it. They will cross the sea and reach Adulis. From there, there are only seventy-five miles to Aksum."

"Of course, Den will very quickly find out about this from his spies," Ashenafi interjected, "and that's what we need. We want him to cover the gorge with all his army."

"Prince Tomaj was killed in this gorge." Makeda remembered her brother.

"May the gods give him a peaceful rest in the eternal gardens," Tesfa bowed his head, still remembering that tragic event. He still felt a bit guilty.

Others did the same. After a moment devoted to the memory of Tomaj, Ashenafi looked at the queen. It was obvious that her brother's memory was still alive in her. When she made the triple gesture of worship to the Moon Lady, he decided that she could continue speaking.

"If Den reaches the gorge, it will allow us to implement the second, secret part of the plan."

The generals leaned in even more. Makeda and Seshep did the same.

"When everyone's eyes are turned to the army that is making loud preparations for the war, I will secretly go to Mocha, take a thousand soldiers from the camp there and sail the sea at night," Tesfa said. "As you know, lady, we'll be close to Asab from there. We will cross the water at night. Nobody will notice us. Then we will go not along the coast, but inland, and from there, from the south, we will get to Aksum. It's a difficult trip, over four hundred miles, but we'll take horses and camels, we'll make it. Most importantly, nobody will expect us from that side."

"Den will be in the ravine with the Nubians and the rest of his army, because he will want to defend access to the city," Tesfa continued. "Ashenafi will set off with a big and loud procession directly from Mariba two weeks after us. He will make a rumpus. In fact, we will start making it the moment you decide that our plan is good. Let all the spies know that Sheba's army, led by General Ashenafi, is going to get Aksum, and let them send reports to Den. Meanwhile, we should reach Aksum, following the southern routes, at the same time as Ashenafi will stand by the ravine."

The queen looked at Seshep.

"And how do you explain that General Tesfa doesn't lead the army?"

"Nobody expects the war to last long. Tesfa does not have to get involved in it," explained Ashenafi.

"Besides, I'm already old," the general smiled, pleased with the plan and his role. "My daughter is expecting a child, I will be a grandfather, for me it is not the time to fight. I will stay at home, especially since I am a bit under the weather," he was amused by the small lie he invented for the purpose of implementing the secret plan.

"Are you going to pretend to be sick?" hemet inquired.

"What wouldn't I do for the good of the kingdom?"

Seshep nodded, considering his explanation credible.

"Generals, that's a good plan," the queen felt that everything would go well. "May the gods be with you. Let's do it!"

She rose, which meant that the meeting was over.

"One more thing," she added. "I want you to bring Prince Den here. Alive!"

"Lady, it will happen according to your order," Tesfa respectfully put the hand on his chest, as soldiers used to do before the commander.

"I'll punish him myself," she said, as if she needed to explain her motives to anyone.

It was talked not only in the palace, but all over Sheba, that the queen announced preparations for war, causing excitement among men and anxiety among women. Everyone wanted to believe that the war would be short and victorious. Especially since Sheba was doubly protected: by the Lady of the Moon and the mighty Yahweh.

***

Sometime later, at night, Tesfa left for Mocha with a small detachment of trusted soldiers.

At that time, Ashenafi formed an army in Mariba. Soldiers were even drawn from distant garrisons, given new weapons, and commanders carried out exercises with them from morning till night. The camp was growing bigger with every day. No secret was made either of the number of soldiers or of the types of weapons, or even of the fact that the army intended to travel to Aksum by the old and tried route.

Things happened exactly as the generals had planned. Four weeks after the start of the preparations, Ashenafi's army stood in a ravine. At the same time, Tesfa and his soldiers reached the gates of Aksum. He knew from his scouts that exactly like they had anticipated, the gorge was manned by Den's soldiers. There were almost two thousand of them.

***

In the evening, after reaching the destination, General Ashenafi ordered to distribute tella, tej, and roasted beef to the soldiers. Campfires were lit. They didn't hide from the enemy, quite the opposite. The point was, after all, that Den would be sure that the whole Sheba army was in this place, so that it would not occur to him to focus on protecting the city from the direction from which General Tesfa would attack it.

The night was cool. Soldiers arranged themselves around bonfires. The tella and tej warmed them up a little, and the roasted meat filled their bellies, but the tunics and the leather covering them, protected them more from arrows than from cold. They were getting cold.

At dawn, they were awakened by a freezing cold weather. Despite the smoldering fires, the cold air made itself felt. But the shouts of the commanders quickly set them on their feet. The last weapon check and the army was ready to attack.

General Ashenafi delayed the order. He knew perfectly well something that his soldiers had no idea of: that from the south, by side roads, troops under Tesfa's command are going to get to Aksum imperceptibly and conquer the city.

Their task was to keep Den's troops in the gorge for as long as possible.

Ashenafi ordered the first attack. The gorge's entrance was narrow. It was impossible to attack it with the whole army. Despite the significantly higher number of soldiers in Sheba's troops, it seemed that the terrain, and therefore nature, was on Den's side. That was the impression the old generals counted on, when they were preparing the plan to get Aksum.

At Ashenafi's order, the fight was started by archers and slingers. They covered the enemies with a cloud of arrows and stones. This did not do much harm to the Nubians, who dodged missiles, sheltered behind rocks and single boulders. The spearmen started to attack next. However, they were overwhelmed by a hail of arrows from Den's army. Several soldiers died; the rest began to retreat. Their shields resembled hedgehogs; so many arrows were stuck in them.

At one point, Ashenafi ordered that the attack be stopped. There was silence on both sides.

In the evening, the general gathered commanders for a meeting. He still didn't tell them anything about the army coming from the other side of Aksum. He knew that the sign for him that Tesfa had taken the city would be a stir among the defenders of the gorge. This place provided Den with great conditions for defense, but upon closing it on the other side, it was certain that Den's army would be stuck in a deadly trap.

"Today our troops fought with the enemy," the general began the council. "We know that the enemy has almost two thousand Nubians, and some calculate that even two thousand of their own troops. Nubians are paid well. However, local soldiers, as well as ordinary residents, have had enough of his power, and treat him as an oppressor. We must reach them and convince them to come over to our side and attack the Nubians."

The commanders liked his words.

"Tomorrow," he continued, "we will attack the gorge with greater forces. Archers and slingers will go first, they will cover the enemies with a barrage of arrows and stones. Then they will part, and the spearmen and axmen will go to attack. This time, however, archers and slingers are to protect them for as long as they can without hurting their own. Finally, infantry with swords will move in. Horses and camels stay."

The commanders looked at each other. The general's plan was reasonable. Conquering the ravine gave free access to the capital, which was separated by a day's journey.

The meeting was over. Commanders returned to the troops. The soldiers sat by the fire and talked excitedly about the passing day. They knew that this evening could be for many of them the last one in life. But they did not talk about it, they did not want to say something that the gods could hear. Because as it is known, the spoken words easily turn into reality. Finally, tired, they lied down by the fires and fell asleep.

The morning welcomed them with cold again. Commanders quickly formed troops and moved to the designated positions. General Ashenafi stood on the hill, along with several commanders, and looked at the ravine and the field where the battle was about to begin.

Slingers and archers started. The chords growled; the slings' cords buzzed. A hail of arrows and stones covered the gorge's throat. The slingers and archers parted in two sides, creating a passage. Immediately, a column of spearmen and axmen entered the corridor. Enemies' arrows whistled, but this time also Sheba archers answered.

Busy shooting, the Nubians were unable to protect themselves behind the rocks. Many fell, but others, more cautious, immediately came in their place. A column of axmen and spearmen reached the gorge's throat. The Nubians were already waiting for them. Iron gnashed, a soldier collided with a soldier. Every now and then someone fell on one side or the other, but still nobody had the advantage. The attackers struck harder, but the Nubian ranks did not break.

Finally, Ashenafi ordered to play trumpets for a retreat. The army began to go back. The archers released the last swarm of arrows, but at that moment the fight was over.

Ashenafi gathered the commanders again.

"Seventy-three our men died today," he began. "Tomorrow, only archers and slingers with infantry will go to attack. However, this time we will only fake an attack. After reaching the first ranks of Nubians, we retreat. This is my order!"

The general knew well what he was waiting for. It was at this time that Tesfa should take the city and attack the gorge from the west on the next day. It was a shame to throw soldiers at Nubians. He could see the losses he would have suffered if he really wanted to conquer the ravine from the side they were on.

Indeed, at this time, soldiers under General Tesfa were entering Aksum. The plan that Tesfa and Ashenafi introduced to the queen, was being implemented.

Nobody had informed Den about the column travelling down the longer, difficult roads. Soldiers entered the city via the road from the south. The entrance was guarded only by a few defenders who, upon seeing Sheba's army, laid down their arms and welcomed Tesfa like a savior.

The general quickly occupied the entire city. Minor fights took place only during the taking over of the palace, where several soldiers loyal to Den stood on guard.

When Sheba's symbols began to flutter at the highest watchtower in the city, Tesfa started toward the ravine. Just a little over half a day was enough for his army on horses and camels to reach the rear ranks of the enemy defending the ravine.

Den did not expect an enemy from this side. Two days of battles reinforced his belief that even though outnumbering them, the Sheba's army would not conquer the ravine. He felt confident. He did not suspect, however, that his soldiers would suddenly find themselves in a jam.

A moment later, a messenger of general Tesfa appeared. He demanded that he surrendered immediately and unconditionally. He knew that to surrender would mean a death sentence for him. Will they kill him here, or will they take him to Mariba and put him before the queen? None of these solutions left him any hope. So, he decided to fight to the end.

However, the mercenaries, even if they were ready to defend the ravine, did not want to die in it. They knew that what had been their asset before, had now become a trap. They knew that in a few days they would run out of water and food. They did not have much food with them, because meals from Aksum were delivered to them every day. Now that the Nubian commander heard the words of Tesfa's messenger, and understood what answer Den wanted to give, he strongly opposed.

"This is a dead end. The enemy has cut off our way back. It stands in front of the ravine and closed it from behind. We won't get any meals, water, or food from Aksum. I will not let my soldiers fall from exhaustion. If you want to fight, do it. But we are coming back to Nubia."

A moment later, disregarding Den, the mercenaries commander went to Tesfa. The general told them to give up their weapons and swear an oath to their gods that they would never again attack the kingdom of Sheba. He saved their lives and allowed them to return to Nubia.

When the other soldiers of Den found out about the promise, they also went to Tesfa. They begged for the opportunity to pay tribute to Queen Makeda and to join them in the ranks of her army. As a proof of loyalty, they promised to hand Prince Den over to general Tesfa.

Tesfa agreed to their offer.

A moment later, led by his soldiers, Den stood before the general with his hands tied. The war was won. Aksum was recaptured and became a part of the Sheba kingdom again.

***

"On the queen's order, I am to personally escort prince Den to Mariba," said Seshep.

"If the queen so wishes, the captive is yours," General Tesfa was not going to argue with her. "How many soldiers do you need to escort?"

"None."

She was in a traveling outfit. She looked like a man. She had short hair, a skirt that did not cover the knees, feet and calves wrapped in canvas, and high-tied sandals. Her torso was covered with a loose shirt, over which she put on a simple leather vest, fastened at the sides with metal snaps. From under it protruded a wide, but light belt, behind which were various types of weapons.

"Hemet, I appreciate your skills, but you are, after all, just a woman," he worried sincerely, not wanting to offend her. " Forgive me for saying it, you're tall and fit, but Den has twice the weight you have. If anything unexpected happens, gods forbid, you will not be able to handle him by yourself."

"The goddess is with me," she assured. "Everything will be as it should be."

He didn't answer, so she added to calm him down:

"Believe me, I'm really big, I can fight, win and I've been tying my own sandals for years."

"Do as you wish!"

The general knew that hemet can be talked to like a man, that she was probably more fit than most of his soldiers. However, he was already old, and the fact that he had a daughter who was pregnant, meant that he had increasingly looked at women from father's perspective.

She looked at him almost tenderly. Hardly anyone cared for her. His words touched her.

"General, everything will be fine," she assured him friendly.

"May the Lady of the Moon lead you!" he finished, calmed down by the certainty in her voice.

***

They traveled on two horses. The mare which Seshep intended for bound Den, was tied to her saddle with a rope. So, she had him at her fingertips and kept an eye on him. She knew his capabilities and was sure that he would try to escape. She also knew that she would not let him. She felt exceptional strength and power. She believed that the goddess was with her.

Late in the evening, they stopped for the night. It was cold, so she lit a fire. Still tied Den was lying on the mat she laid.

"Will we eat something?" he asked.

"I will," she wasn't going to engage in a conversation with him.

"I will not?"

"No."

She took out pies and dried meat from a purse. She started to eat. He spat and turned his back on her.

"I have always said you were a bitch," he growled. "And I've always hated you."

She heard him but didn't think it appropriate to react. She thought that it was not worth to talk with a liar, cheater and someone who doesn't like people, because it was a waste of energy.

***

It was dawn when she woke him up with a slight kick.

"Stand up, you bastard!"

He didn't even twitch. She leaned down, her instincts failing her. He was waiting for it. His reaction was lightning fast. He swung his head with all his might and hit her between eyes with his forehead. She fell over and lost consciousness for a moment. That was all he needed. Despite his legs and arms being bound, he threw himself over her body, banging his head against her forehead.

"I will kill you, bitch, I will kill you!" he shouted.

She thought her end had come; she saw only darkness. After a while, however, she heard that he got silent and fell down on her senselessly.

She was surprised. She didn't know what happened. As the darkness cleared her head, she understood. Someone saved her life. But who?

Above her stood a man in black. The same one she met in Seth's bedroom a few years ago. She recognized him immediately.

He once came to the palace at Aksum for the same purpose that she was there. They had a similar task to complete. He was Almakah's priest.

When she shook unconscious Den off her, he reached his hand out to her. She stood up.

Just as when they met for the first time, he made a gesture of thanksgiving to god. She did the same, then bowed low before him, thanking him for his help. He also bowed. Without words. Then he turned away and he was gone.

She leaned over Den to assess his condition. She checked whether the bindings on the arms and legs were holding tight. She bent to see if he was breathing.

Then he did exactly the same as before: he swung his head with all his strength, trying to hit her. But this time she was faster.

"One day you will die, witch. Faster than you think! And your sweet girl with you," he hissed. "And believe me, I will kill each of you with my own hands. And before that, I will skin you! Both."

She kicked him in the stomach. He curled up in pain. She tied a rope to his bound hands, intending to lead him behind the horse.

She walked away and stood a few steps away from him. She was going to jump on a horse, but something stopped her. She returned, bent over him again, and took a knife from behind her belt.

His eyes widened in fear. He expected a fatal blow. But instead, showing her sharply filed teeth in a grin, she cut the cords that bound his legs and arms.

"Get up!"

"Not only are you a bitch and a witch, but you are also stupid," he laughed sneeringly, understanding that she had decided to fight with him. "You're going to die!"

She punched him in the face with all her strength. He staggered but did not fall. He lunged at her. She fell under his weight. They struggled and punched for a moment. He was stronger and he knew he had the advantage. It was his mistake. At one point, when with one hand he tried to take a knife from behind her belt, while holding her throat with the other, she swung with all her might and hit him in the larynx, almost simultaneously kicking him with her knee in the crotch. When he doubled in pain, she took advantage of the moment and straddled him.

"Will you give up finally?" she drawled through her teeth.

"Never!" he charged at her again.

They fought in a whirl so that it was not clear which of them had the advantage. Finally, Den stopped moving.

She stood up and spat out the blood that had accumulated in her mouth. She was looking at him. He lay still. She was sure however that he was still alive. She was right. When she let him out of her sight for a moment, she heard a soft whistle. She leaned back. It saved her. A knife flew past her ear. One of those she carried under her belt. Den had to take it out during the fight. Without thinking, she leapt towards him like a wild leopardess. She didn't think, she just acted. She craved blood. She went wild. She knew that for as long as he lived, neither Makeda nor she would ever be safe. She jumped to him and stuck the knife straight into his heart with great force. It was a reflex.

He stared at her in amazement.

"How could you..." he whispered in a fading voice. "You promised the queen would decide what would happen to me. You said you wouldn't kill me..."

"I changed my mind," she showed her sharp teeth.

She did not like the dark side of her power, but she was already mature enough to not only accept it, but also manage it perfectly.

"You can never tell with a woman," she said, pressing the knife deeper into Den's heart. "That is how the goddess created us."

CHAPTER IX

ARK OF THE COVENANT
TWENTY YEARS LATER

Kingdom of Sheba

Mariba

"I am ready to meet my father," Menelik announced solemnly, standing in front of his mother.

He was twenty-two years old. His face was covered with fresh and fairly soft facial hair, but his muscles and posture were already well shaped, thanks to daily exercise and military drills. He was handsome, and his body, eyes, shoulders, all limbs and gait resembled King Solomon*.

He was tall and slender like him, but definitely more muscular, and his shoulders were broader. Some thought he might be like his famous grandfather, the Israeli king David. The official palace version was that he inherited his mother's beauty and the strength of his grandfather, King Nikal.

"Have you thought it over?" the queen was not impressed by his idea, but she had long known that her son had to meet his father eventually.

She remembered when Menelik raised the subject for the first time. He was twelve years old then.

"Why do you ask about it? I am both your father and your mother," she was indignant at that time.

"I want to know," he replied unexpectedly calmly for the young man he was then.

His demeanor was a combination of Solomon's reflective nature and her father's impetuousness. She was also happy to see a lot of her own features in him. He was curious about the world, self-confident, he couldn't be dismissed by superficial answers. When he asked her about his father, she knew he would not give up until he got a satisfactory answer. He wasn't satisfied with what he heard from teachers, colleagues, and soldiers, who told him all kind of stories at the evening bonfires during military expeditions.

"His country is far away," she said. "The road that leads there is very difficult."

"Is my father the most powerful ruler of the modern world?"

"Yes. It is Solomon."

He was silent for a moment, enjoying the loud sound of the name that came from his mother's mouth. He had never heard her say it in front of him before. He imagined how much that meant to her. She was sitting upright, straight like a zither string, motionless as a lioness before an attack, and tried not to show her emotions. Yet they had to be enormous: she talked with him about his father for the first time in her life then.

"I want to go to him," he said.

"When you reach the right age, I will not deny you," she assured him as she stood up. "You have my word for it."

Then she kissed his forehead to seal what she said. He knew that when the time would come, she would keep her word. She never broke her promises.

Now, he decided that he was as old as necessary to go on a trip to Israel, that the right time had just come.

"Wouldn't you rather stay here**?" she tried to stop him, knowing that nothing would change his decision.

"I'll go there and look my father in the face," he promised.

"And then I will come back to Sheba," he added softly, looking into her eyes that became foggy.

"Here's the ring," she took a gift from Solomon, with which she never parted, off her finger. "You will give it to the king."

"Did you get it from him?"

"Yes."

"You still love him, don't you?"

"It's God-given love. It will last until the end of the world."

***

The queen called Tamrin. His hair was already gray, but his steps were still springy. Living with Varda, with whom he had four children, made him feel young, even though he was seventy years old. He was healthy, fulfilled, and happy.

"I know you rarely go anywhere far, my friend," she began as they sat side by side on a bench in the palace garden. "I won't feel offended if you refuse."

"Lady, my whole life is serving you," he guessed what she would ask him to do.

"Get ready for a trip to Israel and take with you the young man who torments me, claiming that he must go there," she already accepted the departure of her son.

She knew Tamrin would not refuse her.

"Please take him before the king and come back with him safely*."

"God favors you, queen," Tamrin enjoyed the thought of the travel. "He led you to Solomon to give you a son. None of us knows the intentions of the Most High, but I am sure that just like he always had a plan for you, he has one also for Menelik."

"Eh, our gods," she sighed. "They do what they want with us!"

"We can do nothing but surrender to their will," he laughed.

"Do you remember how you were scared of a relationship with Varda?"

"I was young and stupid!"

"Indeed, you were probably not even fifty years old at the time," his mood infected her "As a young man you had right to err."

"I have matured, but fortunately only a little," he waved his hand dismissively, emphasizing that he still does not feel fully grown up.

She valued his sense of humor and his joy of life. He took handfuls of it, also when he settled down and devoted himself almost entirely to his family.

"God has made you wait for her for a long time, hasn't he?"

"Apparently, it was supposed to be this way. We both had to be ready to be able to live together. It was worth it, oh so worth it!" he murmured.

"How much effort did it take for all of us to make you open your eyes," she nodded at the memory of the past tricks.

"Queen, does it mean you participated in the plot against me then?" he joked, knowing full well that it was so.

"Of course!"

"Right, that's what I have always suspected!"

"Rather, admit that you were sure!"

He nodded, trying to make an innocent face.

"Tell me, lady, could I refuse any of your requests? After all, thanks to you I am the happiest man on earth."

"We were all sure you were meant for each other. So many women could not be wrong at the same time! Also, at a time when you didn't know that you loved Varda yet, Seshep saw you when she opened the curtains of time. Varda was pregnant in this vision. With you."

Tamrin did not expect that he appeared as a hero of the priestess's visions. He smiled and that was his only comment on what he heard. They had known each other with Makeda so long that they didn't need words to understand each other.

"In this vision, I am asking because I'm just curious, she was pregnant with which of our children?"

"Would you like to have another one?"

"If God allows, I would like to, because children give sense to life, but I know that I'm already too old for that."

"What are you talking about? I don't know a man younger than you!"

"One could find a few," he answered in his style.

Makeda did not want to get into the subject more seriously, because she knew she would hear about leaving this world, that children had to be brought up by somebody, and that he was a responsible man and always tried to approach life reasonably. So, she laughed out loud, "Your spirit isn't getting old!"

"The children don't let me squander," he was glad that she redirected the conversation to a brighter topic again. "They are absorbing, but I must admit that Varda also gives me a hard time."

She patted her thigh, and Tamrin thought nostalgically that this gesture, ending a certain stage of the conversation, was done by the queen exactly the way her father had once done it. This observation made him realize that he was indeed very old, if he remembered for no reason the king who had been dead for so many years.

Maybe Nikal calls me to himself, he got scared in his thoughts.

"Take her to Jerusalem," the queen stood up.

"Do you think she would like to?" he awakened from his reverie.

"You know her. I'm sure that when you propose it to her, she won't hesitate for a moment!"

***

Solomon, king of Israel

many years passed, since I had the opportunity, joy, and honor to draw from the treasury of your heart and mind. Many years have passed since my stay in beautiful Jerusalem, and I still feel like I have just been looking into your eyes filled with divine wisdom a moment ago. The time spent by your side was invaluable to me. There is no day that I would not remember it with great affection. You gave me yourself; you opened your heart to the feeling offered to us. In your generosity, you offered many gifts to a queen from a distant land, including one priceless and special. You made the prophecy come true.

The one who will stand before you and give you my letter is a gift sent by the Lady of the Moon and the God who has long become mine, too. This young man is the fruit of the perfect love. Do you remember my visions? You ordered to write them down. As you know, they also happened outside of Jerusalem. I had them before. They were not only prophecies about the future of people who will live after us. They also concerned something else that I didn't tell you about.

Since my childhood I knew that I was going to go to a wonderful king from a distant land, sitting on a throne carried by twelve lions*. All my life, the gods have led me to You. The visions said that you would give me the most precious treasure in the world. And here he is, the greatest gift in the world I have ever received is standing in front of you. Look into his eyes. You can be mirrors to each other. The visions have come true.

God, who is wisdom, will decide his future. Great King Solomon, I have a request, I suppose most likely, the last one I will have for you in this life. It may surprise you and even offend you. I assure you, however, that it is not boldness that drives me, but a desire to humbly submit to God's will. In the name of love surrounding the world, in the name of our beautiful past and future of our son, please give us a fragment of what is priceless for you and your nation. Please give us at least a scrap, a tiny piece of the heavenly Zion, the Ark of Divine Law, which we will be able to embrace with our thoughts and prayers.

I have already received one of the most precious gifts God promised me. My heart tells me that the second one will come from the same source. We want to worship the Ark when we worship God. May the vision of a world, in which the descendants of David and Solomon sit on the thrones of the greatest kingdoms and give their people faith in the Most High, come true.

I am humbly asking you for this gesture that is so important to us. Fulfill my request and you will make me the happiest person walking the Earth. May the Song of Songs in the world continue and be fulfilled! May the Ark become forever a symbol of love. May the years to come be a continuation and consequence of the covenant. May the Song triumph forever!

In the meantime, please take care of the one who wears your ring and give him your wise affection.

Forever Yours,
Queen of Sheba
Makeda

***

Jerusalem
The Royal Palace

Three months later

"Lord, the young man at the head of the caravan has a striking resemblance to you," scouts brought intriguing news from the southern borderlands of Israel. "His eyes are full of joy, like of a man who has drunk wine, his legs are slender and graceful. They say his head has the shape of your father David's head," said the head of scouts. "He is similar to you in every way, and every limb of him looks like your own*!"

"Where is he coming from?" Solomon was intrigued by this report.

"We asked questions to his people. We are coming from the land of Great Kandake, the queen of Sheba, and we are going to Israel, the land of King Solomon," they replied. They didn't want to reveal anything more.

Solomon was sitting in a royal chair in the council hall. The most important advisers surrounded him. When the first words about the similarity of the newcomer to the king were spoken, and then, when they were strengthened by the statement that the young man was from Sheba, something strange happened to Solomon.

He closed his eyes and leaned his head against the back of the chair. With every sentence that came to him, his body shuddered. When the scout finished, the king sat still for a moment. He said nothing. He was thinking about Makeda. She appeared before his eyes as if alive, beautiful, and mysterious. With a ring on her finger. The same one he made for her. He remembered their time together and his promise that he would visit her in a flying machine. He remembered that he wanted to build wings to fly to her. However, life wrote a different scenario. Finally, he opened his eyes, sighed deeply, and looked at every one of the present advisors in turn.

"God gave grace to my father, his servant David, and assured him that one day his descendant born of a virgin would sit on the throne of Israel," he announced. "And here God's promise has a chance to be fulfilled."

Many of the dignitaries nodded. They knew the prophecy.

"During my long life you have repeatedly provided me with information about the son of the Queen of Sheba," he continued.

"However, in the years since her visit here, Great Kandake has never given me even a shadow of hope that the boy she raised was mine. Now, when I hear that the one who is heading towards us is my mirror reflection, I look forward to meeting him. You are not surprised that I want to see him as soon as possible, are you?"

On the same day, Solomon sent Benaiah to meet Menelik.

When the general and his team reached the oasis, they found a caravan resting there. The young man received Benaiah in a tent. He bowed low, gave gifts from Solomon and said, "Come with me, for our ruler's heart is full of love for you. He hopes to recognize his son in you. You are identical in appearance, behavior and speech, I can see it. Get up, Lord, because my King said, "Hurry up and bring him with the proper honors, comforts and joy."

"I thank the God of Israel that I found the grace of the king before I saw his face. I trust in the Most High that he will allow me to meet the king and then lead me safely to my mother, Queen Makeda, and my country."

Benaiah was certain that he was standing before the son of Solomon and Makeda. So, what the scouts were saying turned out to be true: the Queen of Sheba has managed to deceive the best Israeli spies all these years. For over twenty years, she claimed that her son was a gift from the Lady of the Moon. The King of Israel, knowing that God did not give him sons for some reason, suspected that Makeda had a child in order to provide Sheba with the heir to the throne, and the father was not him, but one of the priests or soldiers. If she chose a magnate or a prince, it would complicate dynastic matters, because her son's father would certainly demand participation in exercising power. And he was convinced of one thing: he thought that Makeda, having a child whom she claimed gods had given her, did not have to get entangled in the necessity of sharing the throne with a man. She could be, as she always wanted, an independent virgin queen, foretold in prophecies. And she certainly planned to hand over the throne to her son at the right moment.

Benaiah shared the king's view once. However, when he saw Menelik, he was certain that they had been wrong all these years. The young man had quite a few features of his grandfather David, and above all, he was a reflection of Solomon.

"Lord, you will find great joy in spending time with my king," he wondered how he should behave so as not to offend someone who he thought might soon be the heir to Israel. "You just said 'my mother' and 'my country.' Know that our country is more powerful than yours. I have heard that Sheba has excess sunlight and annoying heat, or is cold and covered with clouds, and even snow and ice."

"Sheba is vast,"   although he did not like the general's words, Menelik replied calmly as befitted the heir to the throne. "It stretches on two sides of the sea. You will find here everything that a human being needs. Sea and mountains, hot sun and frosty peaks. I love my country. It is beautiful."

"Israel is the Promised Land that God gave us, as promised to our fathers. It is a land flowing with milk and honey, where nobody fights for food, it is a land that breeds fruit of every species without exhausting work. My heart feels that all this can also be yours if you live with us."

At that moment, a large man entered the tent. He had gray hair, wrinkles covered his face, but he was still as straight as he once had been. Benaiah immediately recognized him as Tamrin.

"Benaiah!" cried the merchant after he bowed to Menelik. "Peace be with you!"

He approached the general briskly.

"And peace to you too, Tamrin!"

They embraced each other. It was obvious they were happy with their meeting. Menelik looked at them approvingly, then pointed to two chairs, inviting them to sit down. With the arrival of Tamrin, the atmosphere relaxed.

"General Benaiah claims that Israel is a better place to live than Sheba," Menelik succinctly introduced Tamrin to the course of their conversation. "He also thinks I'm a descendant of the kings of Israel and I should consider staying in Jerusalem. Is that right? Have I understood you well, general?"

"You understood me perfectly, my lord! Israel is the Promised Land," Benaiah confirmed firmly. "The best place in the world."

"Benaiah, with all due respect to King Solomon and without belittling Israel, believe me that our country is better," assured the merchant, understanding that Menelik did not like Benaiah's opinion on Sheba. "The climate is nice, there is no excessive scorching sun, the water is good, and it flows continuously in rivers and even on the tops of the mountains. Where currents are temporary, our ancestors erected huge dams, thanks to which we have plenty of water and we can manage it well. We don't dig deep wells searching for water sources and we don't die in the sun like you. We have such good weather that we hunt animals even at noon, wild buffaloes, gazelles, and birds. We don't starve at any time of the year. Our fruit grows on our trees, wheat and barley in the fields, our cattle graze in the fields, providing us with meat all year round. Sheba is a beautiful, prosperous country!"

"I do not deny, but it was the Queen of Sheba who went to Solomon, and not Solomon visiting Sheba. Yes or no?" Benaiah looked from Menelik to Tamrin and back.

"You know full well that the queen went on a journey to draw on the treasury of your king's wisdom," Tamrin's tone indicated that the too audacious beginning of Benaiah's argument should be cut short.

"You're right, let's not argue. What could be better than wisdom?" the general agreed with Tamrin. "Wisdom is given by God and it is his inherent quality."

"There is no doubt about that," Menelik said to end the meeting and leave old friends alone so that they could enjoy each other's company.

He assumed the pose of a friendly heir to the throne, however, demanding a quick and specific response.

"What do you expect from us, general?"

"Come with me to the king," Benaiah liked the clearly asked question. "His heart is full of love for you, sir. He asked me to bring you to him as soon as possible!"

***

Over the next few days, Menelik rode a horse, followed by fifty men accompanying him. General Benaiah on a big steed was on his one side, and Tamrin on the other. As they passed villages and towns, people bowed low to them.

He felt as if he entered a dreamland. He looked at those he passed, listened to their shouts, and it seemed to him that what he saw and heard was not really happening. The pace of life slowed down, and he decided that when he crossed the border of Israel, he entered an unreal world, existing as if behind an invisible fog.

"King, may God be with you!" people cried.

"Solomon, peace be with you," they greeted him.

"David, King David is with us!" the oldest shouted in disbelief.

Before he crossed the gates of Jerusalem, Menelik knew how much he looked like his father and grandfather, and that what would happen in the near future, for the most part would not be his call. He had the impression that the reins of his life had been taken over by the forces above him, and that what was happening had been planned for a long time, and he was only realizing the Divine plan.

He felt it even more when he found himself in the palace and stood in front of Solomon in the throne room.

At the sight of him, the king jumped to his feet and exclaimed, "Look, here is my father, David, he brought his youth back!"

There was a stir. Everyone whispered and exchanged comments with each other.

Undaunted, Menelik crossed the middle of the room and knelt down in front of Solomon. He handed him the letter. He watched the color of the king's cheeks change as he read Makeda's words. He could also clearly see the tears welling up in his eyes.

"It's him whom my mother has been pining over all her life," he thought.

"She has been longing for him on moonlit nights. She gave her heart to him. I am a son of the man that they say is the smartest man in the world. I have been waiting for so long for this meeting, I imagined it so many times. Why doesn't my heart tremble and my tears don't flow? Mother was right: she was both a mother and a father to me. She has raised me, led me to the place where I am. He didn't even know about my existence. And yet his blood flows in my veins. And I'm really like him."

Memories came to life for Solomon. The time he spent with Makeda came back. He remembered their first meeting, conversations, trips, and the riddles she asked him. She stood before his eyes young, beautiful, wise in every word and gesture, gentle, tender and sensitive. He remembered their nights together and the most beautiful verses of "Songs of songs." He read the words of the letter again and was moved more and more. "God, why did you want me to meet him so late?" he raised his eyes to heaven. "What was your idea that made you keep him so far away from me? Shouldn't a son grow up with his father? What are your plans for him?"

When he put the scroll away, he sighed so deeply that even those who stood in the remotest parts of the room could hear it.

"Here is my son," he announced proudly. "Blood from blood, bone from bone!"

He approached Menelik and held out his hands towards him. He opened his arms wide and embraced him. They hugged each other for the first time, and suddenly they both felt, almost at the same time, an extraordinary bond. They stood for a moment, saying nothing, father and son, until recently complete strangers, and yet close, because they were connected by a divine thread.

"This is the crown of Israel," Solomon took the symbol of power off his head. "It will belong to you because you are my eldest son. And you look," he said to the audience. "This is the fruit from my body that God unexpectedly gave me!"

Then the prophet Nathan stood up.

"Blessed be the mother who gave birth to this young man and blessed be the day you met her, king," he said in a loud voice. He looked at the faces of the assembled people, as if to speak to each individually, and then stated even more prominently.

"Nobody should ask his father questions, or doubt where he comes from. Indeed, he is an Israelite, a descendant of David and Solomon, shaped after his father. We are his servants because he will be our king."

Here, it turned out in one moment that Solomon had a firstborn, about whom he had not known before. This was all the more important because the one who had so many hundreds of wives and concubines, had only begotten two boys until now. And it was the king, followed by the prophet, who announced that a young man miraculously brought to their country by God, would most likely sit on the throne of Israel.

Menelik, even though he did not want to strengthen his position even more, stretched out his right hand and showed his father the ring he wore on his pinky finger.

"King, my mother, Queen of Sheba, Great Kandake Makeda asks me to give it to you."

He removed the signet ring and handed it on his open hand. Solomon took it in his trembling fingers.

"I gave it to your mother when she left Israel," his voice broke with emotion. "This sign is not necessary. You are so similar to me that I have no doubt that you are my son. I believe everyone who stands here thinks the same way?" He looked around.

"Yes, king!"

"He is your son."

"Mother assured me that when you see the ring, you will fulfill our request." Menelik wanted to present the official reason for his visit.

"What are you asking for?"

"I came here, knowing the power of the God of Israel, to beg you for at least a scrap of the Ark of the Covenant."

A murmur of surprise mixed with indignation went through the room. Nobody had ever ventured to make such a bold request. Everyone knew whom Yahweh made the chosen people and whom he entrusted with the ark! Meanwhile, a young man appeared, who not only turned out to be the son of Solomon, but also expressed such an unusual request. How many surprises God sent them on a single day!

"You don't have to ask for a scrap of our greatest treasure," Solomon replied on reflection. "As my son, you'll be the king of Israel. You will sit on the throne. You will then have the Ark at your fingertips. It will protect and strengthen you, just as it has protected and given strength to our entire nation from the very beginning."

"Lord, I came here because ever since I learned of your existence, I wanted to see you. God has taken my steps here and I trust that he too will decide when I go back to my mother."

"To mother? What work does a woman do for her son apart from the pain during childbirth, and the breastfeeding?" Solomon was indignant, noticing Menelik's tenacity. "Don't you know that a daughter belongs to the mother and a son belongs to the father? I will not give you back to Makeda but will make you the king of Israel. You are my firstborn*."

Menelik did not want to express in front of his father's subjects how much he disagreed with him. He did not intend to cause scandal, saying how great he thinks the role of mother is in how the boy grows up and becomes a man. He was raised by the greatest woman in the world, and no words, not even from the man considered to be the smartest of all the living people, could change that.

***

The unreal world to which Menelik came did not disappear. And it even became more and more fairytale-like. Solomon sent him exquisite meals every morning and evening, and gave him gifts of magnificent robes, gold and silver. He behaved like in the days when Makeda was visiting his palace. Menelik's servants were amazed at his generosity. They wondered what decision their lord would make about staying in Jerusalem. Their doubts, if they indeed had them, were quickly dispelled.

After another day, when Solomon's servants showered him with gifts again, Menelik wrote to the king.

Neither gold nor silver nor rich garments are the objects of desire in my country. I came here to hear your wisdom, see your face, greet you, pay homage to your Kingdom and you, and then return to my mother. Everyone loves their native land. Although your country is as enjoyable as a garden, my heart is not completely happy because I am far from the place that I love. I will worship the Ark of the God of Israel everywhere. I believe that it will give me glory. Please give me at least a scrap of its cover, and I, along with my mother and all my subjects, will cherish and worship it.

When Solomon received the letter, he realized with pain that Menelik was not going to take the throne of Israel. He decided to talk to him.

"Why do you want to leave me? What does your country have that isn't here?"

"I want to go back to my mother. I love her the most in the world," he emphasized with such force, as if he wanted to make up for the moment when he did not protest, when Solomon said that the only merit of a woman in raising a child is that she gives birth and feeds him. "You have a son, Roboam. He will be a good successor. In addition, your legitimate wife gave birth to him. And my mother is not, in the light of your law."

"If it were like you say, it would also mean that according to our law, I am not the son of David. After all, he married a woman of another man, who was killed in battle, and begot me with her. However, God is merciful and has forgiven him for this act. And who is wiser than him? He created me in the image of my father, and you in mine. Do not be angry, just accept what I offer you, because in the future you may not see me anymore - both you and your descendants. You're talking about Roboam. He is six years old. It is true that he is brought up in Israel and could be my successor, but you are the firstborn. You should rule the country. I have been ruling for a very long time. However, I was not able to do everything I intended to have done. That is why I am still asking God to let me remain in rule for as long as he has allowed my father."

"I wish you that with all my heart!" Menelik understood his anxieties.

"Thank you. And I would very much wish for myself that you would sit on the throne when I meet my ancestors. You will rule, elders and young people will love you. You will judge entire nations and countless families. Agree and I will organize your wedding right now, I will give you as many wives and concubines as you like. The Ark of the Covenant will belong to you and your descendants. God will hear your every word, take you under his protection and favor you."

Menelik was surprised at how much his father was pushing him to accept his offer. And Solomon felt it was the only way for his country to return to the path of splendor. For he had already felt the approaching dusk for a long time.

"King, father, I can't, and I don't want to leave my country and my mother. She made me swear that I would not stay in Jerusalem and would return as soon as possible. I also promised that I would not marry any woman here. I really believe that the Ark will bless me wherever I am. Your prayer will also reach me everywhere. God will hear me from every place on earth. Isn't it true?"

Solomon was disappointed, but he nodded.

"I wanted to see your face, hear your voice and receive your blessing," Menelik continued. "And then to come back to Sheba."

"The proud eagles don't give birth to docile pigeons," Solomon thought, knowing that further attempts of convincing his son wouldn't do anything. His and Makeda's blood flowed in his veins. He knew that if Menelik decided something, he would not change his mind. At the same time, he wondered what were God's further plans for his son.

God had not spoken to him for a long time. For years he felt left alone with his problems by him, and as he wasn't young anymore, as soon as he heard about Menelik, he hoped that the Lord himself sent him. And that it was a sign, given by god, that the end of his earthly journey is approaching, because a worthy successor is coming. God in his wisdom caused that he was brought up far from Jerusalem by the wisest woman on earth, who not only taught him how to govern, but gave him the boundless love that only a mother can give. Of course, he did not think that her only merit was giving birth and feeding him. He said this in defiance. And maybe out of regret or jealousy, when he realized how much affection Menelik had for her.

Maybe it was already then that his inner voice told him that his son would not stay with him?

He called for the most important people in the country.

"I can't convince him to stay here," he said. "My prayers are useless; gifts and promises do not affect him. Hear, therefore, what my will is."

Like the king, they have long felt that the state was not doing well. This was confirmed by reports of regional managers and everyone for whom the good of the state was important. With Menelik's arrival, new hope grew in Solomon and in them.

"God promised that our descendants would sit on the thrones of the world. I am sure that he was the one who directed Menelik's steps to Israel. And no one else but God speaks through him, when he refuses the honor of taking our throne so stubbornly. Who are we to oppose God's plans? We are but servants of the one who knows everything."

Officials, soldiers, elders and other trusted men looked at him, sometimes just nodding their heads. They felt something beyond their control was happening. For a long time, things in Israel had seemed in limbo, and the unknown hang in the air.

"Menelik will be the king of Sheba," Solomon said loudly and emphatically. "By God's will, he will rule with our blessing and bring our faith there."

"That is God's will," few voices could be heard.

Those more prudent were silent, suspecting that Solomon had not yet said everything. They were right.

"Together with my son, we will send your firstborns to Sheba. Let them rule with him, support him, promote faith and principles given to us by the Most High. In this way his will be done."

The recent years of Solomon's rule have caused that his listeners more and more abstained from voting, not wanting to reveal their views. They didn't agree with him at every matter.

Many decisions aroused their objection. And this one in particular was a decision they didn't like.

"God promised my father David that the descendants of Solomon would become the heads of three earthly kingdoms, that our priests would promote the true faith, that nations worshiping idols would make us their kings and would glorify God. Let my son thus become a king in Makeda's country, and let your children who follow him, help him in ruling, achieving the highest positions and privileges. In this way we will rule over one of the great earthly kingdoms."

"Who among us would dare to oppose God's commandments?" Priest Sadok asked with pathos, seeing that Solomon's words did not meet with enthusiasm. "Let others learn from us, let them accept our laws as their own, may the will of the Most High be fulfilled!"

"We and our sons are yours and your descendants' servants," said one of the nobles, standing up. It was the one whom the king had honored many years ago, visiting him in the company of Makeda when his son was born. The young man, who was then subjected to the brit mila ritual, as the firstborn, was soon to set off with Menelik to his country. His father was one of the few who didn't mind.

"We will respect God's will," he added. "Our sons will go on a journey and become companions of your firstborn!"

A buzz rose. The gathered realized that they would soon lose their eldest sons, whom they had been preparing for their successors for years. The buzz had not yet subsided when the father of another of the firstborn spoke.

"Your descendants will rule the three kingdoms. One of them is Israel, the other is, I understand, the kingdom of Sheba. These countries have heirs begotten by you, king. And the third one? What is this kingdom and who will rule it?"

"God works in mysterious ways," Solomon replied. "Perhaps, by his will, something will happen tomorrow that will change our thinking and open our eyes to something new? Nobody knows the future after all. Who among us had thought I had a son with the Queen of Sheba? And here he stood before me. Let us be trusting and open to God's judgments."

***

The next day, Menelik was blessed and anointed in the temple, and was given the name after his grandfather David.

"From today your only guide will be the God of Israel, and the eyes of your spirit will fall on the Ark of the Covenant, from which you will draw power," priest Sadok announced so loudly that he was heard not only in the temple, but also in the large square in front of it, where the crowds gathered that day, and in narrow streets of the city. " And let it be so forever!

"Let it be so," Menelik repeated after the priest.

"Amen," Solomon confirmed.

"Now listen to my words, David," the priest used his son's new royal name. "If you do not live in harmony with God, he will punish you, you will be crushed by your enemies. He will turn his face away from you, you will feel great anxiety and sadness in your heart, and your sleep will not heal you. Listen to the word and follow it. Do not be a servant of any other god, for all possible plagues will fall upon you, your cities, fields and your people. God will send you hunger and pestilence and will destroy everything you touch. However, if you follow his will, his blessing will come to you from all sides. You will receive eternal glory. You will be blessed in the town, in the field, at home and outside, the fruit of your body will be blessed. God will accompany you during your actions and will fulfill your will in everything you desire. If you love him, he will love you. If you keep up his commandments, he will do the will of your heart. He is good to the good, merciful to the merciful. Love justice and he will make your life flourish. Reprimand sinners, put aside cruelty, shame those who use force against their neighbor. Be righteous to the poor and orphans. Do not be partial in your judgements, do not be afraid of anyone, judge with fairness. As the son of Solomon and blood of David's blood, be a great king in your country."

"Let it be so," Menelik-David bowed his head before the priest.

"May God be blessed now and forever," the priest said the old formula.

This way, in Jerusalem, Menelik was blessed and anointed as King of Sheba. Joy reigned in the city, because prophecies were beginning to come true.

***

"The queen is asking for news, what should I write?" Varda hugged her husband.

Their bed was wide. As the most important members of Menelik's court, they were recognized as special guests of the king and received a large chamber in the palace at their disposition.

"Write the truth," he replied, stroking her back. "Describe exactly everything that happened. After all, a lot of time will pass before you can tell it in person."

"Should I also mention that what our intelligence agents said is true?"

"About what?"

"About temples of other gods still being erected here, about idolatry, and how much Solomon has changed since she was here."

"The queen knows it, but it won't hurt if you write about it, too. She should have a complete picture."

She thought that Makeda would not be delighted with the change that had taken place in Israel. Yes, Jerusalem was more beautiful than before. People lived in prosperity, the buildings dazzled with wealth, but the spirit of the eternal city withered, shriveled, got lost somewhere in the nooks of carefully paved streets. Solomon's eyes did not glow like they once did. The judgments, so famous in the world, did not take place often. Since the completion of the construction of the temple and then the palace, the king more and more often locked himself in his chamber and wrote songs or lost himself in revelries and parties with those of his wives he liked most at the moment. He seemed to have lost the joy of life. Perhaps he was waiting for something that would motivate him to pave new ways and lead the nation further? Or maybe he thought that one should take care of what is here and enjoy what one managed to have built?

"As far as I know her, she would like to know everything down to the smallest detail. I will do it as accurately as I can."

"Why do you think I took you on this trip?" Not knowing how far her thoughts went, he teased her amicably. "None of the men would describe so well the gestures, facial expressions, dresses, colors, flavors, quality of dishes, but also the appearance of the wives and Solomon's attitude towards them, and most importantly, the emotions that accompany everything we witness here. You will do it masterfully."

"Yes," she admitted. "And surely in a way that the queen will be well informed."

"None of us, no matter how hard we try, will never match you."

"I am grateful to my parents for having me learn to write."

"All in all, this skill is rarely used, but it is indeed valuable," he admitted. "I can't imagine that anyone who doesn't know how to write could think about a career or promotion nowadays."

"Seshep says that the times will come that all people will be able to write and read."

"Oh, a visionary!" he laughed. "There is no way for a simple mind to master enough characters to communicate something in writing."

"And yet she said she saw it behind the veil of time."

"What exactly?"

"That people can easily decipher the signs. Everybody. They were written on stiff, white, evenly cut cards, much thinner than parchment, and on shiny flat boards resembling silver mirrors."

"Fantasy. At the moment, one person in a thousand can read, and only on very basic level."

"Seshep saw it with her own eyes!"

"People do not change, so no matter how many years or even ages pass, those who will come after us will not be smarter than us."

"I am not sure about it!"

"Only the tools we find when coming to this world are changing."

"But it's people who invent them," she protested.

"Yes. But how many of them are creators and inventors?"

"Everyone comes on earth for a reason," she said firmly.

"Of course, but that doesn't mean everyone has to have a bright mind. To learn thousands of characters, you must be really smart."

"I believe in Seshep's visions," she persisted.

"I value them too. But, as you know, a vision is just a potential reality. It can come true, but it doesn't have to."

"Do you remember that Seshep had seen that we would be together before you could believe it?"

"I always knew that too," he assured her.

"Yeah, right!" She sat up abruptly, carefully looking into his eyes. "Although who knows, maybe you indeed did know? I was sure of it, though."

She stroked his bare torso.

"You are a man and you a wise one. Many centuries from now people will still talk about you. The greatest traveler, the richest merchant, a genius leading the largest caravans, the one thanks to whom Makeda met Solomon. Nobody will mention a word about me."

"If anyone ever remembers me, they'll definitely remember you too. After all, I don't exist without you! We are one."

"Do you really think so?" she patted him again.

"I'm sure about this. Our love will last forever. One day someone will write about how much we loved each other. I will describe how smart, beautiful and feisty you were. How much the queen trusted you, how you acted for the good of Sheba and how you always stood by your opinions. And everyone will read about it on stiff, white, evenly cut pages, thinner than parchment, and on shiny flat boards resembling silver mirrors."

"You are impossible," she nudged him with a gentle kick, pleased with what he said, but also sad that she didn't convince him. "You don't believe that all people will read?

"Even if such a simple system of signs is created that it would make it possible, how many of them will really understand the content?"

"Reading and understanding are two different things. It wasn't easy centuries ago and is not today."

"Exactly," he mused.

"Hey, are you there?" she asked when he hadn't spoken for too long.

"I'm thinking about what you said."

"And?"

"It's impossible for all people to be able to read and write. Simply impossible, honey."

"Nevertheless, I believe that such a time will come..."

***

Despite the atmosphere of excitement that God's will is being done, Jerusalem was not happy with what was happening. The first-borns of the most important inhabitants of the city were to leave it together with Menelik to support him in ruling a very distant kingdom. The elites were to leave the country, the greatest young men! Their parents were not happy about this, some even fell into despair and anger, but they did not talk about it loudly, believing that it was God's will that their sons would serve Israel elsewhere.

"Your wisdom is great," said many of them. "Thanks to you, the borders of our rule will extend to the land of Sheba. God will also unite all other kingdoms under your rule, because your mind is facing him, and you want people to serve him and destroy false gods once and for all."

Others added, "There is no doubt it was about you that God told Abraham, 'Thanks to your descendants, all earthly nations will be blessed.'"

However, they secretly complained about the king for depriving them of their firstborns and cursed him. They did it, even though they knew he was anointed by God, so it wasn't right to curse him.

Not only the behavior of dignitaries, but many other signs indicated that things were not going well in the kingdom of Israel. At night people did not sleep, as befits the righteous, during the day they looked suspiciously at each other, did not talk openly with each other and did not look into each other's eyes. Despite public joy, almost everyone felt that something really bad was going on in the soul of the city. Black clouds hung over Jerusalem, and the air turned gray.

***

One night, Azariah, the firstborn son of priest Sadok, whose belongings had already been packed for the journey to Sheba, had a dream. An angel stood before him in an unearthly glow.

"You will build a wooden chest the same size as the Ark of the Covenant. At night, you will go to the temple with the trusted firstborns, whom you will tell to make an oath. All gates will be open to you. You will take the Ark and put a similar wooden chest in its place. You will cover it with holy fabrics so that nobody would notice the change. God is angry with Israel for its sins and therefore turns back, taking his covenant sign. You will take the Ark out of Israel, for that is the Lord's will," he concluded and disappeared.

Azariah was terrified of what he was supposed to do, but he did everything as the Angel had commanded him. First, at night, he met with other first-borns who, like him, were preparing for the trip and life in distant Sheba.

"We don't want to leave Israel," one of them said when it was certain that no one was eavesdropping on them. "But what can we do? We have no choice."

"If we oppose the king's will, he can kill us," another agreed.

"We cannot act against the will of our fathers and the order of the ruler," another said.

Azariah heard them and said, "I'll tell you what to do. But first, I want us to make a covenant that will bind us all until the end of our days," he looked around their focused and strained faces. "Swear that you will not repeat any word you will hear here, whether you will be alive or dying, in captivity, under duress or completely free."

They looked at him, intrigued, and then, seeing the power in his eyes and hearing the great strength in his voice, they made their vow in turn. It was only when the last of them bowed his head after saying the oath, that Azariah told them what the Angel, who visited him in his dream, had commanded him.

"So, now that you know, let us act according to God's plan," he concluded.

Apparently, they too were under the influence of the Angel's power, because they had no doubt that he was telling the truth.

They wondered how God would help them take the Ark with them so that no one would notice. However, trusting in Yahweh's greatness and infallibility, they unanimously promised to obey Azariah, and he, still fulfilling the will of the Divine messenger, ordered, "Each of you will give ten didrachmas* and I will give it to the carpenter who will build a chest for us. When the Ark is in our hands, the Angel will tell us what to do next."

The chest was ready soon. When the young men went to the temple under the cover of the night, all its doors were open for them. They did everything as the Angel had commanded, and then, unnoticed, carried the Ark out and placed it in a pit they had dug earlier. In its place in the temple, they placed the chest.

***

When the day of departure from Jerusalem came, all able-bodied residents of the city came to the big square in front of the temple.

Menelik, who did not know about the actions of Azariah and the first-borns, bowed to Solomon.

"Bless me, father," he said.

The king held his head.

"Great is the God who blessed my father David and our father Abraham," he began solemnly. "Son, may all animals and birds of heaven, all field animals and sea fish obey you. Be full, may this abundance never leave you. Be perfect, may this perfection never leave you. Be kind, don't be stubborn. Stay in good health, don't let suffering reach you. Be generous, don't be vindictive. Be clean, don't be tainted. Be righteous, do not be a sinner. Be merciful, do not be oppressive. Be honest, don't be perverse. Be patient, don't let anger overwhelm you. Let your opponents and enemies fear you, and you crush them with your foot**."

"Let it be so," Menelik thanked, feeling his father's love.

At that time priest Sadok approached the king. He walked solemnly with his head raised and an expression of bliss on his face. In his straight arms he carried thick cloth, generously embroidered with gold thread.

"Here is the cover of the Ark of the Covenant," Solomon took the treasure from the hands of the priest and gave it to his son. "Queen of Sheba asked for a piece of Ark. Through you, I give her not only a piece, but the entire outer cover of our sacred treasure, as a sign of my love, devotion, respect and honor that I have always had for her. May the Ark's power be with you forever."

Menelik bowed low, appreciating the value of what he received. He knew how much his mother would be happy about the gift.

Nobody paid any attention to the anxious glances of the firstborns, looking at the priest. Sadok apparently did not discover the absence of the Ark, so they breathed a sigh of relief and became certain that God himself really protected them. Azariah wrote a letter to his father before leaving. He handed it over to the most trusted servant, asking him to hand it in ten days after his departure from the city. In the letter he explained what and why happened and described the Angel who visited him. Looking at his father, he thought for a moment that maybe he already knew everything. He breathed a sigh of relief. Sadok was not aware of what his son had done.

***

Solomon and Menelik hugged each other for the last time, after which the young man jumped on the horse and raised his hand. They set out. Tamrin and his wife Varda, both on horseback, rode right behind him. They both said goodbye to Jerusalem, feeling that this was their last visit to the city.

When the horns were blown for a farewell, the square in front of the temple filled with loud screams. Older people were lamenting, children were crying, widows were sobbing, virgins were wailing, because the sons of the nobles and the powerful men of Israel were leaving forever. The majesty that went with them was also mourned.

No one knew yet that along with Menelik and the sons of the nobles, the Ark of the Covenant was also leaving Jerusalem. However, people sensed that something immeasurably bad was happening, something that would weigh on the fate of the kingdom for centuries.

The king was also very anxious.

"Woe unto me," he thought, standing on the palace terrace in the evening, after the day's noise stopped. "Glory is leaving me, the crown of my splendor is falling, my time is running out! My son left me, along with him the children of the most magnificent families. I tremble thinking of what awaits Israel," he wrung his hands, then raised them to heaven in a pleading gesture. "Lord, I'm afraid of your anger. What are you preparing for us?"

***

Queen of Sheba, Lady of my life, Makeda!

You were with me many years ago, but the time we spent together is still alive for me.

I have Your beautiful figure before my eyes, I hear Your words, I can smell you. There is no day that I do not remember the touch of your hands and our kisses. I remember our conversations, laughter and our dreams. How I miss you! My heart still misses you. I believe that the time will come when our souls will unite, and we will be together forever. You'll put me like a seal on your chest again, like a seal on your shoulder! Because love is as powerful as death, and I believe it is even more powerful than it.

Beloved, when this letter reaches you, you will know that Israel's most precious treasure is now in our son's hands. By God's will, the Ark of the Covenant left our country. It was and it is still a great blow for me, but I know that it would not have happened without God's clear will. I do not know his mind, but I can do nothing but accept his decision.

I know, and you know, that our son, whom I truly loved and who received the name in Jerusalem after my great father David, did not know that the first-borns who had left the city with him, abducted the Ark. So, I don't blame him for that. However, I dare not blame them either. Because they were doing God's will.

Know that a divine messenger appeared in a dream to the son of priest Sadok and instructed him what to do to safely remove the Ark from Israel. So, it was God who decided that the Ark is now in your country. Let it serve our son and You according to the will of the Most High. When you were here years ago, I had a dream. I didn't understand its meaning then. Only now, when the brightness of the Holy Ark has left us, have I understood what God told me then.

I dreamed that I was standing in my chamber, and the great sun from heaven shone over our country with its splendor. I knew that the sun was God's blessing. But then it moved from Israel and lit the areas that are now in your possession. I didn't like it, but I was helpless.

When I told Sadok about the dream, he ran to the temple, and when he returned, he was unable to calmly tell me what had happened. Instead of the Ark, he found an ordinary wooden box in the holy place.

The servant gave him the letter that his son had written to him the day after the tragic discovery. Then everything got completely clear.

Now that our son has reached you already, I want to assure you that God's will is unpleasant for me and I find it difficult to accept it, but I also know that I have no chance to change it. I can only pray fervently and ask for forgiveness for my sins and not burdening with them the nation that he has loved and chosen. We have neglected God's commandments. We preferred to look in the faces of women rather than to listen to the words of priests. Woe to us! We have disgraced our lives voluntarily. Woe to us! We did not show repentance and mercy so loved by God. God made us wise and we voluntarily became dumber than animals. We loved fleeting things, we put forward the pleasure of eating delicious foods, which anyway turn into dung with time, rather than the foods of eternal life. We dressed up in robes that did not fit the soul, and we took off the costumes of eternal glory. Our managers and people did what God hates and hated what he loves: love of your neighbor, humbleness, mercy, pity for the poor, perseverance, patience, love of God's home.

God hates divination from birds movements, idolatry, magic, dead animal bodies, theft, oppression, adultery, jealousy, deception, drunkenness, false oaths and testimonies. We did all these things God hated. Therefore, he took the Ark from us and gave it to those who act according to his will and to the law given to us by him. He looked away from us and turned his glowing face toward you. He hated us and loved you because you live according to his laws.

Beloved, everything on this earth happens by God's will. Our actions can make us gain or lose His favor. We met each other with his will, thanks to him we conceived a son and he decided that the Ark no longer lives in Israel.

My days are going toward sunset. My twilight began. Remembering my life, I'm preparing for a long way. I thank the Most High for letting me meet You, the one whom I loved and who is closest to my heart. I am grateful to him for the son he gave us in his wisdom.

Although I suffer irreparable loss, I trust in God's plans.

I have been walking the earth for many years. I already know it is vanity over vanity and all vanity on earth*! What is the use for a man of all his possessions, which he strives for under the sun? One generation goes away, the other comes and the earth lasts forever. The sun rises and sets and hurries toward the place from which it rises again. And we also know that although all rivers flow into the sea, the sea is not getting full. We are alive now, Makeda, but as we both know well, because everyone knows it, we come to this world to leave it one day. We came here unsatisfied and we will leave unsatisfied. While living, we often forget about those who were here before us. Because everything passes. Also, human memory. Who will remember us centuries later? When I remember your loving look, I know that everything has its time. For everything that happens under the sun there is a designated time. There is a time to come to this world and a time to die, a time to plant and a time to collect. You know it as well as I did, we talked about it many times.

Now, when I feel the passage of time, I also know that for people there is no other happiness than to enjoy and use life to your heart's content while you are alive. I am also sure, although apparently there is nothing sure but death in this world, that everything God does, is everlasting. So, the fact that the Ark is now in our son's hands, is the turn of history. I am not going to rend my garments because of this, because I know that it happened by God's will, and He knows what and how to do for the world, so that it would go according to His will.

Makeda, the queen of my life, know that I have always loved you and I always will. We have placed seals on our hearts which are eternal, and their power is stronger than death. May God be with you, my beloved. May He also be with our son!

Forever Yours,
Solomon

CHAPTER X

THE DUSK
MAKEDA IS FIFTY YEARS OLD

Kingdom of Sheba

Mariba

"May it happen according to your will," Makeda looked proudly at her son.

"They will be the tallest obelisks in the world," he was excited by the vision of the construction he intended to build. "They will be made of one block of granite; they will be almost one hundred cubits* high. Do you know that they will be even higher than the Egyptian obelisks that your favorite from the past, Queen-Pharaoh Hatshepsut, had ordered to erect? Only they will be lighter in appearance, because they are slenderer and soaring. I want them to clearly show the way to God."

"In the future they will be called stelae of Aksum," she closed her eyes and spoke words that suddenly appeared in her head. "They will be considered the largest monolithic monuments of the ancient world."

"Mother, are you okay?" he noticed what was happening to her.

The visions she had in her childhood, and later when she was pregnant, disappeared after the birth of Menelik. Recently, however, they started to come back. They appeared not in the form of dream images, but as unexpected flares in her head. They happened during the day, in the evenings and at night. So, it was this time. She felt a hot flush, throbbing at her temples, and then a bright light filled her head. It lit up, obscuring everything. The senses merged into one. She was certain that God contacted her in this way. He gave her visions like he had once done in her dreams. He showed pictures from the future, indicated possible paths, suggested solutions. He did not impose, dictate or order anything. He opened her eyes to what might happen, and he hoped that his voice reached a sensitive heart.

The High Priestess believed that these states were a blessing that Makeda had been given in connection with another change in her life. As a girl, she had visions that disappeared when the Lady of the Moon gave her monthly blood. They came back when she was pregnant. She lost them again when Menelik was born. Now she was entering the next stage of her life. She became a mature woman. The goddess was slowly taking back her gift of blood, in return filling her heart with peace and balance, and her body with gentleness and wisdom of eternal duration. The priestess was certain that it was in connection with another life's turning point that the visions appeared again.

"Aksum will become a new nest for the dynasty of David's sons," she whispered, her eyes closed. Menelik's name will shine for centuries. The prophecies of the Queen of Sheba will come true. All over time, they will sing about her, about Solomon, their love, about God's covenant with people and the Ark, which is as eternal as the Song of Songs is indestructible.

Menelik knelt before his mother.

"God speaks through you, doesn't he?"

She raised her eyelids, but her eyes still didn't see anything.

He touched her hand carefully. It was completely cold. He kissed it. Then she awoke.

"My love, how good that you are here."

He put his hands around hers to warm them. Blood, which flowed into her heads at the time of vision, was coming back to them.

"Did you have a vision, mother?" he repeated when he noticed she was with him again.

"I saw the future," her voice was still weak but fully conscious. "You have made Aksum the new capital of Sheba. You erected the highest obelisks in the world, built roads, temples and a new palace. I also saw how I manage Mariba and you Aksum, after which you become the ruler of the whole kingdom. I saw your descendants on the throne. And our land embraced by God's love."

***

I had a hidden dream. I wanted to see the man, who intrigued me like no other, at least once again in my life. I met him only twice, and yet he left such a strong impression in my soul that I came back to him with my thoughts surprisingly often.

I didn't know much about him.

I met him for the first time in Seth's chamber. We were both doing our job. We arrived there, each of us separately, to forever get rid of the prince, because that was the order of those we served. We were both professionals. We understood each other without words.

Later, the Man in Black, because that's how I called him in my mind, appeared in my life again. Again, it was related to Aksum.

He appeared when I was transporting Den to Mariba after the victorious war. General Tesfa gave him to me reluctantly, not sure if I could handle someone who was much bigger and stronger than me. However, I was convinced that with my skills and experience, I would not have a problem escorting such a difficult prisoner. I was wrong. If it wasn't for the Man in Black who saved me, my exciting life, which I liked so much, would have ended right then.

So, I only met him twice, but I often thought about him.

So, when one day Makeda announced that she would like to visit Aksum and the Temple of the Lady of the Moon where Menelik was born, I felt extraordinary excitement, combined with the inexplicable conviction that I would meet him there again.

***

The three of us set out for the journey: Makeda, the High Priestess and me. We were accompanied by a small handful of those who we needed during the travel. Servants, several priestesses, and an armed group at the request of Menelik, walked with us. We traveled by horse, ship and camel.

Our first destination was the Temple of the Moon Lady. We have not visited this place even once since the queen gave birth to her son there.

The priestesses lived there in their own rhythm, praying, making sacrifices, healing people, preparing medicines, poisons, studying the sky and the constellations of stars, exploring sciences. They cultivated plants, raised animals. Most importantly, they effectively and imperceptibly cared for the security of the state. They did what the Moon Lady called them to do. For centuries, no one interfered with them. Nobody dared. Rulers and ordinary people had high regard for them, respected them, and feared their power. Nobody tried to mess with them. It was said that there was once such brave, or rather mad, man. He died in suffering, punished by the Lady of the Moon. A curse fell on his family and descendants, which lasted until the seventh generation, and no one was able to reverse it.

The priestesses lived in a separate, hermetic world, distant from reality, and yet they had a significant impact on it. They advised kings, princes, nobles, and were mediators in making sacrifices to the Moon Lady. On behalf of the petitioners, they begged the goddess for support and blessing. They knew when to start sowing and when to harvest crops, they knew everything about people's everyday life. They read the future, knew everyone's good and bad deeds. Nothing could be hidden from them.

I was one of them. In addition, I had the honorable name of a hemet. This meant that I had a narrow specialization. It was double. I could not only reveal the veil of time, but I also had the ability to fight. I was a scout, bodyguard, guardian, warrior, assassin, and at the same time, the closest of the queen's trusted people. There were not many like me in Sheba. The High Priestess said once that there are no more hemet as good as me in the whole world than there are fingers in a hand. I believed her, even though I had never met any of the others. Instead, I met my male counterpart.

When we got to the temple, the queen disappeared already on the first evening behind the gates of the most important part of the sanctuary. She was absorbed by the ceremonies prepared for her arrival: prayers, dances and songs.

I knew she was safe here like in no other place on this side of the sea.

"Lady, I would like to go somewhere further," I announced when she woke up around noon after a night filled with dances in honor of the Lady of the Moon.

"Take some servants and go," she turned to the other side.

"I won't take anyone. I want to be alone."

She sat up. She looked at me closely. She knew that I went on lonely trips only in matters of state importance, when it was necessary to sort things out without witnesses in order to restore the proper world order.

"Is something going on that I should know about?"

"I feel that maybe I will meet the man who once saved my life."

"Who is this?" she inquired.

"It seems to me that I've been waiting for him for a long time, maybe even forever," I didn't want to go into the details."

She understood that I didn't want to talk about it. At the same time, sensitivity told her that it was about something far more important than just meeting someone I owe a lot to.

"Each of us has her own Solomon," she sighed. "I wish you that yours will give you what you need." She nodded for me to come closer, and when I did, she kissed my forehead. I felt as if I was her daughter; maybe in some sense I was.

"I bless you, Seshep. I wish you the most beautiful fulfillment!"

I left the same day. I took only a horse, a gun and some provisions.

I rode without thinking about anything. The area near the temple was green, but already half a day away I entered the areas where there were almost no plants, and maroon, tall, raw rocks rose gently from the ground. Lonely trees stood here and there. I didn't like such spaces. It was hard to go unnoticed. Fortunately, in the evening I arrived at a small lake surrounded by lush vegetation. There I decided to rest.

I started a small fire. I ate. I lay on the rug close to the fire and looked at the stars. It was cold. I wrapped myself in a wool shawl, a gift from Makeda.

It was already very dark when I heard that I was not alone. At first, I thought that an animal was creeping towards me. I took a sharp knife, sat down very slowly so as not to scare it away, and looked at the darkness. I waited.

After a while, I already knew.

"You are here?" I made sure. "You made me wait for a long time."

He was standing in the light of the fire. The Man in Black. He reached out to me. I came closer. We stood facing each other without a word. I was shaking. Not only from the cold. I looked into his dark eyes. Just like the previous two times, when I saw him, his face was tightly covered. I touched the cloth in the place covering his mouth with my index finger. He knew what I wanted. He uncovered his face.

His skin was almost as black as mine. His nose was wide, and at the same time long and straight. His cheeks and forehead were wrinkled and scarred. There was sign of Almakah on his chin.

He didn't say a single word that evening or the following we spent together. We didn't need them.

I spoke very little, and in the last days before parting, I was silent like him. The closeness that united us did not require a voice. It spoke without words.

I knew men didn't talk much. I myself, although I was a woman, was not a talkative one. However, after the first few days of his silence, came the moment when I began to suspect that my chosen one was mute.

At dawn I bathed in the lake. He was still sleeping. I swam, enjoying the first rays of the sun. At one point, as I stepped ashore, I heard the whistle of a knife flying past me. On a reflex, I stepped aside. I didn't have to. The blade was not thrown at me. It was stuck in the heart of the leopard, who was lurking in the branches of the tree, just getting ready to jump at me.

"What have you done!? I could handle it," I got angry.

I noticed it before. I thought it would not dare to attack, and if that happened, even while bathing, I had behind my belt a knife, which had helped me to get out of worse oppressions many times in my life.

"It wouldn't have attacked me. You killed it unnecessarily," I rebuked him, standing over the body of the dead cat. He didn't say anything. At that time, I thought that he either didn't speak my language or he was mute. It soon turned out that I was wrong.

The moments we spent together were among the most beautiful in my life. However, I felt that they were coming to an end.

One night, when we were lying next to each other looking at the stars, he came to the fire. He stood looking at me for a moment. He reached out. I walked over to him. I knew it was a goodbye.

"You are and always will be in my heart," he said.

I shivered. Not at all from cold.

He covered his face with a black scarf. I looked into his eyes for the last time. A moment later he was gone.

During the time I spent with the Man in Black, the queen came a long way. She managed to get from the Temple of the Lady of the Moon to Aksum, where she spent ten days with her son. She visited the great waterfall at the sources of the Blue Nile. She was in the canyon where her brother died. I joined her after many weeks, only when she arrived at the port from which she was supposed to depart to Mariba.

"Seshep," she greeted me cheerfully. "Did you find him?"

I nodded my head.

"You were right, each of us has her Solomon somewhere far away."

***

According to the visions of the queen, Aksum, managed by Menelik and the first-born sons of the most eminent families of Israel, grew in power every year. Azaiah, the son of priest Sadok, became the high priest of Yahweh for the whole kingdom of Sheba. Others who came with him, over the years, took all the most important positions in the country. The old generation was slowly stepping aside.

General Tesfa and the governor Handake left for eternal rest, and General Ashenafi was already so ill that he appeared in the palace only for the most important ceremonies.

To the great sadness of the queen, Tamrin died. Not in the saddle or at the head of the caravan, as could be expected, but in the bed, next to his wife, when they were both sleeping. Varda didn't even know when it happened. It was only when she mournfully remembered every moment preceding this event, that she remembered that she probably heard his deep sigh at night. She later said that it sounded as if he had done it with relief and contentment. Perhaps he was glad that he was entering new spaces and unknown territories? That he was going on an expedition in which he did not know what awaited him? He liked traveling, so this last one might look fascinating to him.

Varda mourned her husband's loss and took over the family business. She was doing great. For some time, she even traveled with the caravan to distant lands with her eldest son. She liked to take care of everything personally. However, the time came that, although her spirit was still young, her body began to refuse to obey. Then she decided that she would take care of bills and correspondence with merchants from other countries and she would not leave Mariba unless necessary.

The trade flourished. As it had been for centuries: ivory, turtle shells, rhinoceros horns, skins of hippopotamus and other animals, gold and myrrh left Sheba on camel backs or sailed out by ships. The contracts that Makeda had once signed with Solomon, continued to bring profits. The dam, maintained and improved on regular basis, provided a constant water supply to fields and orchards, where fruit, herbs and, most importantly, incense trees of the best kind in the world, ripened. Thanks to the queen's wisdom, the next generations lived in prosperity.

The High Priestess was already old. Her hair turned white and the skin was thin like parchment. She was thin, straight as always and very strong. Not just physically. She still liked best to move around on foot, and she went on horseback for longer trips, enjoyed morning baths in cold water, ate mainly cooked vegetables and fruits, rarely diversifying her diet with an egg, fish or meat. More often than in the old days, she sat in the temple in front of the statue of the Lady of the Moon. Also, more often than required by the rite, she paid her homage by kneeling or lying with her forehead leaning against the floor. Sometimes it lasted for hours. The priestesses knew that she was with the Silver Mother then. It was enough to look at her face. It was beaming and happy. Nobody dared to interrupt her meditation, especially since Sheba had been at peace for many years and there were few matters whose resolution would require immediate decisions or actions in which she should be involved.

Things were going well in the state.

Just like in Makeda's vision, Menelik governed the western part of the kingdom and spent most of his time in Aksum, while she, still as the queen of the whole state, stayed almost permanently in Mariba and dealt mainly with matters of the eastern part of the kingdom.

***

Since her return from the trip to Mariba, Makeda spent more and more time in the Temple of the Lady of the Moon. She meditated, wrote, talked to the High Priestess.

"It's been many years since we were in Jerusalem and he is still in my heart," she liked to remember Solomon.

"Human fates follow various paths," the priestess still had the strong, crystal clear voice of a young girl. "Some of us have one partner in our lives, others many of them, and others live alone. There are different reasons for that. Sometimes it is our decision or the will of the gods, which people often call a coincidence, but it also happens sometimes that we have no choice."

"When I was young, I was sure that choice always exists."

"Did you change your opinion?" the priestess raised her eyebrows slightly in surprise.

The older she was, the more one could see emotions on her face.

"The choice is always there, but if we are decent people or just responsible ones, there are situations that there can be only single choice for us."

"You put obligations towards people, state and dynasty over the love for a man. Of the many ways, you chose the one that was written to you. But, contrary to appearances, you followed your heart."

"You think so?"

"I'm sure of it. Our inner voice is nothing else but divinity. By listening to it, we join the rhythm of the universe. When we choose according to the voice of the heart, we feel peace and harmony. If we listen to ourselves, it is as if the Absolute was speaking to us."

They went silent. For each of them, divinity meant femininity and masculinity, entwined inseparably, and complementary to each other. Just like the Egyptian tit and djed, or the ying and yang from distant lands, as well as the sign of David, in which two symbols merged into one. At the same time, both noted the power of the new God, his strength and potential.

"Yahweh will change the world," the priestess nodded, looking at her own thoughts.

"Oh, he will!" Makeda remembered her old visions. "I know it has to be this way, but somehow it is hard for me to imagine that the goddess's times will soon end."

"Will she lose her throne?"

"She won't lose it, but her kingdom will shrink. There will come times that the Absolute will want to show primarily a male face. The goddess will retreat, quiet down, but she will not be silent forever! She will live in women. She will speak through water, air, fire and wind, she will appear in springs and waterfalls, she will take various forms. She will not be lost but will be pushed into the shadows. She won't protest, she is a goddess, she knows and understands the changeability of history, because she is their constant element." Makeda made a triple gesture of thanks. "But when she is finally reborn, she will be stronger than ever."

"I know I shouldn't worry about that because this is the turn of history, but I still feel sad," the priestess placed her hands side by side on her thighs. "I feel sorry for the world going away. It's so beautiful."

"Something old goes away so that something new could arise in its place," the queen assured her, repeating the priestess's own words she had heard more than once from her.

"It's inevitable, I know. But I still feel sorry."

"Priestess, you will last forever. There will always be those who will carry the holy fire, and you will live in it. You'll also be in every woman carrying the flame. As you know, because you taught me this yourself, the altar fire will never go out*. And so, it will happen. It will burn forever."

"I know and I'm very happy about that, really. However, I like being here and now, I'm attached to my body. I like to touch, see, smell, taste, hear. The older I get, the more I appreciate that I still have such opportunities."

Makeda laughed happily and almost carefree, as when she was a little girl.

"I could say the same thing about myself!"

"I'm much older than you," she objected. "I'm even older than Solomon."

"Right," she was glad that they had returned to her favorite subject. "How is he? Do you have any fresh news? What do your hemet say?"

"You do not want to know."

"Is it that bad?"

"It has been better."

"Tell me!"

"Solomon has many enemies."

"Hadad. Who else?"

"People like him always have many enemies, and the people willing to alleviate their unpleasant fate as owners," the priestess joked. "Our hemet give exact numbers. Every year, his treasury receives six hundred and sixty-six talents of gold, and he has taxes on traveling merchants and traders, Arab rulers and administrators of the whole country. He has one thousand four hundred chariots and twelve thousand horse warriors, which he placed in various cities. For his soldiers, he had recently forged two hundred large ceremonial shields of gold, using six hundred shekels of ore for each, and three hundred smaller ones, each made with three minas of gold. All the goblets and other vessels used in the palace are made of gold**."

"He always liked that ore. What's wrong with that? The throne he gave me has been delighting us all to this day."

"Nothing wrong except the richer he is, the more envy it provokes."

"Well... Who, then, except Hadad, is after his golden goblets?"

"What I'm talking about is more serious than you think."

"So, I stop talking and am all ears."

"Among the most dangerous is Rezon, the sworn enemy of Solomon and all Israelites."

"The one from Damascus? A former servant who gathered dissatisfied people around himself?"

"This one."

"Is he really dangerous?"

"People like him should be disposed of before they get strong enough to strike. Because if they become strong, they will not know mercy."

"Is he vindictive?"

"Extremely. He thinks that he is not successful in life, he is bitter and dissatisfied. He blames the whole world for his alleged defeats. And to think that he has so many reasons to enjoy life!"

"So, Solomon should watch out for him. He probably knows it, but I will write to him anyway."

"According to our information, Jeroboam may be even more dangerous."

"Someone with that name, it seems to me, was the supervisor of works during the construction of the temple, do I remember correctly?"

"Perfectly."

"Solomon appreciated and liked him very much. What happened to make him pass to the other side?"

"Well, one day, this very Jeroboam met the prophet Achiah dressed in a beautiful new coat. Achiah took it off, divided it into twelve parts and said, claiming that God was speaking through his mouth, 'Solomon left me. He began to worship Ashtarte, the goddess of the Sidonians, Kemosh, the idol of Moabbits, and Milkom, the idol of the Ammonites. He left my path, stopped doing what was right in my eyes, and disregarded my orders. Because I liked his father David, I will not take twelve tribes from him, but only ten. I will leave one to him and one to his son, so that the light of David would always be burning in front of me in Jerusalem, the city that I chose for my name to live in. Jeroboam, you will get ten tribes. And if you obey all my words, if you walk down my paths, if you only do what is right in my eyes, obeying my instructions, I will always be with you, and I will soon entrust to you the whole nation of Israel.'"*

"It does not sound good."

"I told you so."

"Where is Jeroboam now?"

"Solomon wanted to kill him, but he managed to escape to Egypt. He found shelter with Shoshenq."

"Pharaoh often gave evidence of forethought and forward thinking."

"The rulers of Egypt often accept those who may become kings in the future."

"We both remember where Den found refuge. And who gave him soldiers. I understand Pharaoh, although I would not have done what he did. I value transparent rules."

"If others were like you, the world would be great."

"And it is anyway," Makeda made a wide gesture to show the beauty of the surroundings. "And Solomon is a wise and fair ruler," she added.

"I love you, Makeda. Your years on earth and subsequent experiences have not changed your heart."

"I love you, too. But as far as Solomon is concerned, I can see that you clearly don't share my opinion regarding his rule. Isn't it so?"

"He's changed. He's not the person you knew."

"Each of us is changing."

"Isn't the story of Jeroboam enough for you?"

"People tend to tell things that are not true as long as they are intriguing enough. Folk tales often have no basis in reality."

"Yes. But what happens with Solomon is more than the stories of the people thirsty for sensation, wanting to improve their mood by telling nonsense about those who are more powerful than them."

Makeda tried to pierce her with her eyes, even though she knew that she stood no chance with her, after all they had known each other for so long and each knew what the other one could do. The priestess held her eyes easily.

"All right, say it," Makeda surrendered, even though she did not want to hear about how her beloved deviated from the paths marked for him by God. She preferred for him to live in her memory as she knew him: immaculate, open, wise, and fulfilling the will of Yahweh.

"He lost his vigilance," the priestess began the story. "Things already started to go south when you left. He wrote songs, locked himself in chambers, suffered. With time, however, he dealt with his despair and returned to everyday matters. It is true that each year he increasingly deviated from God's laws, but it was spread over time. He paid tribute to foreign idols, broke the commandments. Things really started to go wrong when his hopes for Menelik were not fulfilled. He believed that God had sent his son to him so that Israel could last in eternal glory. He concluded that God made you raise the boy, to keep him away from his weaknesses and the things that Yahweh might not like. When he saw Menelik, he wanted to believe that God had forgiven his transgressions."

She listened carefully. Not only did she say nothing, but not a single muscle in her face twitched.

"However, when, together with Menelik and the first-borns, the Ark of the Covenant left the country as well, his final decline began. He let go completely. He ordered a temple to be built on a hill just below the city. His wives worship Kemosh there, the Moabic god, and Milkom, the Ammonites god. Other larger and smaller temples were also built. What's the worst and most offensive to God, it's not only them that pray there, but also Solomon himself! The women made his heart stick to foreign gods*."

"He turned away from God," Makeda whispered in horror.

"And God, unfortunately, turned away from him."

***

"Seshep!" I heard Makeda's scream in the middle of the night.

I jumped to my feet. For a moment I thought she was five, and I am still a young hemet. In fact, she had just turned fifty and I was seventy. I was no longer as fit as I used to be, I had felt grinding in my bones for a long time, and some of the old wounds had been bothering me more and more at the time of changing weather.

Little has changed at the palace in Mariba since Makeda's childhood. I still occupied a small room next to her bedroom, the same one that King Nikal had given me. In both rooms there was the same furniture, including the large bed, in which we spent many nights together when she was a child. I still remembered fondly her little hands covering my neck, and the small body nestled in me.

There still was the small gap between the door and the wall as well, which we once called a security window. It only came in handy once when Den tried his force on Makeda. Luckily, it was never needed again.

"Seshep!" she called again.

"I'm here, little birdie," I sat down next to her. I knew what was going on. The visions came again. I brushed her wet hair away from her forehead.

"It's okay..." I took off her wet shirt and helped her put on a fresh one.

After a while she was conscious enough to sit without my support.

"Solomon..." she began and her voice broke.

I knew that things should not be hurried. I stroked her back, and she sat still, her throat tight. Finally, she spoke.

"I said goodbye to him," she said shakily. "He's left. He's already on the other side."

"Oh, my beloved baby," I embraced her as tenderly as I could.

"He's looking for me."

"Do you want to tell me about it?"

She nodded.

We fell silent. I stroked her hands, waiting for her to be ready to share her vision. Finally, she straightened up.

"He was lying on a big bed in the palace," she began. "He knew he was leaving. There were a lot of people around him. They filled the entire chamber. They were waiting for his departure. They prayed quietly. There was a hoopoe in the window. Like Solomon, I also saw it clearly. 'Fly to her,' said my beloved in a speech that the bird understood perfectly. 'I want her to hear once again what she knows well.' 'What?' asked the hoopoe. 'That she is the woman of my life.' 'She knows it,' replied the bird. 'There are never too many words about love. Tell her that I have always loved her, I love, and I will love her. And that I will be waiting for her in a place where we will be together forever. She had heard these words from me before but pass them on exactly. Remember: I will be waiting, and when you come one day, I will hide you in my arms and will not give you back, even when the whole world asks for you.' The hoopoe repeated the king's words, nodded its little head and flew away to fulfill his last will."

Makeda fell silent.

I didn't say anything either. I felt that this was not the end of the story.

"When it flew away, Solomon closed his eyes. Sheol gates began to open before him. I don't know how it happened, but I found myself with him. I was standing by his bed and watching. Fortunately, no one else saw me except him. I was energy. I didn't have a body, but my senses worked. All of them. Hearing, and sight, and smell, and even taste and touch. They worked fully but were definitely more sharp than usual."

"I watched with tenderness as he began to free himself from his earthly shell. His soul reached out to mine. 'Come to me,' he said, just as we did when we were close. 'I need you.' I took his hands reaching out to me. The warmth of his hand spilled over my soul. I leaned in and covered his face with kisses. 'I'm with you. And I will always be,' I said. He kissed my lips. I absorbed his breath. The whole world flashed and swirled in my head. Our souls found each other, and when they fully felt the familiar closeness, they merged. We were one again. We danced, inextricably entwined. We swirled in the clouds, laughed and saw God's smile, and then the time stopped. Something broke. We were separated again. However, we were still holding hands. He looked towards the brightness. It attracted him with such force that despite the fact that I gripped his fingers with all my might, I felt that he was slipping away. He was floating away. But he was still looking at me. 'I will be waiting for you. You will recognize me by the Song,' I heard. 'I will always sing it for you.'"

She finished the story. She sat still, and I, an experienced, tough hemet, cried like a child.

***

Several months have passed since Solomon's death. Although they had not seen each other for almost thirty years, Makeda took it very hard. She still loved him. He was the only man in her life. She missed him and thought about him constantly. She never got involved with another man, but she didn't even want to think about someone who would give her pleasure, even only bodily.

She was a virgin queen. Apart from Solomon, she wasn't going to meet any man.

"The gods have joined us," she said. "It was the Lady of the Moon and Yahweh who made our paths converge. Menelik appeared thanks to them, he is God's gift to the world. After returning from Jerusalem, neither the High Priestess nor Seshep, who were closest to her, were surprised that she gave up the bodily pleasures of the world. She gave birth to a child, ruled the state, fought a war, but above all, they knew that she still loved Solomon, and as none of them was permanently associated with anyone, it was normal for them that also Makeda did not need anyone to caress her body or warm up her bed on colder nights. They thought that maybe with time, as a woman who once tasted happiness in the arms of a man, she would again look for someone who would be close to her."

However, as the years passed, and she never once looked kindly at any of the many man surrounding her, they accepted that it would always be so. Time has shown that they were right. The High Priestess communed with chosen men during the full moon, even Seshep sometimes decided on a bodily union with a warrior, but this never happened to Makeda.

When Menelik could be already completely independent as a ruler, Makeda, knowing that she would soon give him full power, almost completely forgot about the needs of the body, and began to delve deeper into spirituality. Not only did she avoid men, but she even gave up daily massages and beauty treatments for her face and body. She lived in harmony and peace. She prayed, she liked talking about God and the Moon Lady. She stopped wearing jewelry. Her only decoration was the ring she got from Solomon. She only took it off once when Menelik traveled to Israel. Since his return, the ring had never left her finger, even when she was going to take a bath or rest at night.

She did not eat much, and she could taste a cup of wine for hours, mainly smelling the bouquet, rarely touching the thick liquid with her mouth or dipping her tongue in it. She gave the impression that human affairs were becoming more distant for her.

One day she turned to Seshep.

"Full moon is approaching. The priestesses say that it will be special one because the Lady of the Moon will cover her face during it. Darkness will reign and for a moment the gates of knowledge will open more widely than usual. I want you to do something for me then."

"As always, I am at your service, queen," said the hemet.

Makeda had not given her orders, nor did she ask for anything for so long, that she had ceased to hope that she would do it again. The queen's words made her happy.

"I would like to know what Menelik's future fate will be," Makeda seemed to be apologizing for the unusual request.

"You don`t know it? Really?" Hemet was surprised. "I was convinced that you saw the future and you know exactly what will happen."

"There was a time of prophecies and visions. I had dreams. I looked into the future. It's true," she admitted. "But it was never like this that it was up to me what and when I would see. I couldn't look at what interested me the most. I was and am a tool in God's hands. He decides what images he gives me. I never had influence on what I saw. I wish it was different, but I can't direct my visions."

"So, you don't know what awaits the prince..."

"Exactly."

"You want me to open the curtain of time, right?" Hemet wanted to be sure.

"I'm getting older. I do not know whether it will be easier or harder for me when I learn his fate. However, I am going to take the risk. Yes, I want you to do this for me. I am asking you to do that."

***

That night, the moon not only shone in all its glory, but it was going to be eclipsed. Priestess of the Silver Mother said that this is very rare and that it is a special time, because the sun and moon would stay on the same line and join together to form unity. When the moon disappears, obscured for some time by the shadow of the sun, we can clearly hear what the gods say to us. If we ask the right questions, they may want to reveal their secrets to us, show us the past or the future, indicate the paths to us, or help us make decisions.

When it began to dusk, Makeda and Seshep entered the temple. The queen had earlier asked the High Priestess to be accompanied only by her and Seshep that night. Her request was granted. Even the priestesses whose duty was to constantly watch over the eternal fire, left the tabernacle as soon as the queen crossed its doorstep.

Temple of the Lady of the Moon was a place that Makeda had liked since childhood. The already slightly rounded steps leading to the interior seemed friendly and inviting. Five slender columns defined a circle forming a central sacred space. It was not roofed. The goddess hated restrictions. She was the world and an eternal element of creation, so she did not want to separate herself by walls or roofs. Places of worship could be anywhere. All that was necessary was to design a circle, surround it with five objects related to the elements, go inside and fully surrender to the power of the Silver Mother. Her priestesses liked to have contact with earth and heaven at the same time. Even in the chambers each of them had at their disposal, there always had to be an opening in the roof, even a small space that allowed to see the sky.

The only parts in the temple complex in Mariba that were roofed were those where the priestesses lived, and the places where work had to go on, regardless of whether there was rain pouring from the sky, or the scorching sun.

It was getting more and more dark outside.

The women stood in front of a wide granite table. The only objects set on it were the three silver goblets filled with specially seasoned wine, and a ritual knife with a white handle. That evening, the queen was to personally make a sacrifice. Because she was the one who was asking the Lady of the Moon to show the future. She wanted to know what awaits her son and the kingdom. She was the one who cared the most, she called the circle, so she should perform the ritual.

To complete it, she brought birds in cages. There were five of them. They came from her palace garden and were bred for special occasions just like this one. They were born in western Sheba. They were colorful, and at the same time so beautiful that no one had any doubt that the goddess created them, and they should have been sacrificed. The Moon Lady should receive a gift that would please her. Every priestess knew that the goddess reveals her secrets only to the ones she chooses, only to those whom she likes, whom she can trust or to those who she knows will fulfill her wish without hesitation. She is unstable in her sympathies, it happens that she changes her mind and what once seemed to be true and inevitable, after a while was not so anymore. She is smart. The goal of her actions is always balance and harmony. She loves, hugs, embraces in delight, she is awed by the beauty of creation. She gives and receives, lures and pushes away, seeks justice, but sometimes is also unfair, she gives out goods generously, but she is also greedy and can take away without mercy. However, when she loves someone truly, when a man fully opens his heart to her, she will always lead him down the paths of life. Because she is the mother of everyone and everything. She loves with her tender heart.

Seshep placed a cage on the altar. All three of them raised their hands and sang a song to the Lady of the Moon. They thanked her for the blessings and asked her to accept the gift. Their voices carried with a clear sound and flowed straight toward the dark sky. When they finished, the High Priestess handed silver goblets to them. She also took one herself. First, they raised them, held them up for a while, looking at the sky, then spilled a little on the floor, honoring the Lady of the Moon in this way.

"Silvery Mother, please accept this gift," Makeda took a bird taken out of a cage from Seshep's hands.

"May its presence in the heavenly palace please your senses!"

The priestess and hemet helped Makeda keep the bird on the table. Although it had been given specially prepared grain to slow down its movements, it flapped the wings and shouted loudly.

The priestess held its legs, and Seshep clenched her fingers on its beak and immobilized its head.

"Go to our lady, please her heart," Makeda took the knife in both hands and cut off the bird's head with a single move. It was still trying to break free when the High Priestess held it in an iron grip over the goblets to which its blood was dripping. When the bird stopped trembling, she laid its body on the floor.

"You're already with the Lady of the Moon," she patted it.

When she straightened up, Seshep gave Makeda another bird. The ritual was repeated.

"Go to our lady, please her heart," Makeda cut off the heads of the birds. Everyone kept fighting the same way, the priestess and Seshep held each of them down, and the blood of each of them flowed into the goblets. At the last one, the vessels were already so full of blood that it was spilling onto the table. However, the table had grooves carved along its sides, so that the lymph would flow along them into a container standing below.

When the offerings were made, the priestess took a small bottle in her hands.

It was wrapped in a leather strap and hung around her neck for the whole evening, resting between her breasts. She took the cork out from it.

"It's a gift from the Lady of the Moon," she said, pouring three drops of a green liquid into Makeda's and her own cup. "She always gives her daughters everything they need at the moment. We are grateful for that."

She poured seven drops into Seshep's goblet.

"Thank you for the special gifts you give me, Silvery Mother," seeing the liquid falling into her goblet, hemet knew that shortly after she would drink it, the period would begin during which she would be able to open the curtains of time.

They took the goblets. As before, they raised them and spilled a little on the floor. They drank all the way to the bottom. They wiped their mouths and bowed to the Silver Mother.

They walked away from the altar, heading to the center of the temple, where Seshep had previously set up five olive lamps. Now she lit them. A magical area was formed, into which they entered. They found themselves in a triple, closed circle. One was made of the temple columns, the other was a colorful floor with the symbols of the Moon, and the third was made of the burning lamps. They knew that none of them could leave this place until the end of the ritual. It was triple sanctified.

In the center, in a circle of fire, stood a silver bowl filled with spring water. Seshep was going to look at it to see the future.

They stood around the dish and took hold of their hands. They closed their eyes. Each of them turned in her thoughts to the Lady of the Moon, asking for support and permission for Seshep to look behind the veil of time.

When they were ready, the High Priestess raised her hands.

"The words we speak create shadows of what may emerge from them. When they flow from our mouths, we help them to come true."

"Lady, please give us your support!" Makeda and Seshep said simultaneously, then bowed their heads.

"Silvery Mother be with us!" the High Priestess repeated their gesture.

They looked at the sky. They saw the moon, which, as if with the touch of the invisible hand of the goddess, just showed its full face. It got brighter.

They knelt over the silver bowl. The contents of the goblets was already circulating in their bodies for good. They felt the connection with the Lady of the Moon. The mixture had much bigger effect on Seshep. She leaned over the water. She looked at it closely. She wanted to see what the goddess would like to show her. She looked into it intensely, straining her eyes. She closed her eyes, and when she opened them again a moment later, she saw a mist floating above the water. When it became so thick that the water beneath it could no longer be seen, she raised her hands.

Lady of the Moon let me open the veil of time " she asked, making a triple gesture of worship to the goddess.

She folded her hands at breast height, and then, slowly and smoothly, began to push the fog aside in two directions. When it was almost completely gone, she blew into its remains.

"What do you want to know, queen?" she asked Makeda when the mists were completely dispelled. "Ask. The Lady of the Moon will show the answer."

"What will happen to Menelik? What will happen with Sheba? What will happen to the Lady of the Moon when God takes over the world?"

Seshep said nothing for a long time. She stared at the water. Finally, her eyes became fogged.

"I can see Menelik. He is sitting on the throne," she said flatly. "There are golden lions on both sides. The throne stands solid. Nothing will shake it. There are children around him. Many. Almost all of them boys. One, two, three, four, five," she began to count. "Oh, there is a girl. Just one. Lovely. She looks like little Makeda. I see in total nine boys."

She leaned closer.

"They're in Aksum. I see them in Aksum. The throne stands in the palace right there."

"What else?" Makeda was impatient.

"I'm looking. I see the passing time. The throne is still in the same place, the kings are changing. They are Menelik's sons and grandchildren. Time goes by, I see clouds. Sheba splits into two parts separated by the sea. The Lady of the Moon has no temples anymore. God rules the world. Feminine energy is withdrawing. It is hiding. It hides from wars and rapes. The goddess is still alive, she can't be heard clearly because she speaks in a whisper. She remains silent, but she knows her time will come."

Seshep sighed, staring at the images that were passing quickly before her eyes.

"Time goes by. A lot of time. Here the goddess comes back to life. Oh, what a relief! Women dance in circles, joyfully, they are happy. I can hear them singing. They praise her. They feel her power within them."

Seshep smiled at the image she saw and then raised her head. Makeda and the High Priestess did the same.

They saw a figure before them. They thought it was in a flimsy, long, loose dress. However, they could not determine its color because it was all made of light. She was floating towards them. She seemed to be holding something in her hands. Something that they knew well, which was close to them and extremely valuable, which should be protected and nurtured in the heart - a live flame.

They heard a voice. The Lady of the Moon spoke to them.

"Here is the eternal fire. It burns and will never go out. It is in me and in your hearts. It ignites the senses, gives strength, encourages to act. It is in every man and woman who walks the world, it is in the earth, sky, sun and wind. And in all creation, because it comes from the Source. It embraces and covers everything. It lasts forever and is an eternity. I give it to you when you come into the world, you give it back to me when you return to me. Carry it the same way as those, who were before you did, and those who will come after you will. May the flame in your hands be steady and strong."

EPILOGUE

The day was waking up. The sun was just rising above the soaring columns of the Temple of the Silver Mother. Its rays, still weak, gently tickled her wrinkled face and silver hair.

She was standing by the bay window in her chamber. She was looking at the avenue of huge sycamores. She looked toward the dam and the gardens surrounding Mariba.

"It's beautiful here," tears flowed down her face. "It's sad leaving all that behind..."

She thought of Menelik. She was proud of him. He had ruled alone for almost twenty years. He was a wise king. He had a smart wife, nine sons, and a daughter. Every day he praised God and lived according to his commandments. Seshep's vision from years ago came true. As soon as Sheba became the home of the Ark of the Covenant, Yahweh became the god not only for her and her son, but for almost the entire country. People loved and worshiped him. At the same time, however, many paid tribute to Lady of the Moon, who had always been Makeda's protector. God, although he was known for demanding exclusivity, did not give impression to Makeda or the people of Sheba that the Silvery Mother was disliked by him. The first-borns who came with Menelik settled in Sheba so well that Israel became only a nostalgic memory for them, a country of childhood and early youth, which they did not intend to return to. They had families, they ruled the state together with Menelik, and they were doing well.

The country flourished. Makeda wasn't worried about its future. She looked at the sycamore lane, houses, temples, orchards and gardens. She was proud, happy and fulfilled. She felt calm. She missed the High Priestess who had left to the Lady of the Moon at the age of ninety-five, and Seshep, whom she knew that was still protecting her, but for over four years now only from the height of the heavenly gardens. She remembered Tamrin, whose memory had been so carefully cherished by Varda, thought of General Tesfa and Ashenafi, saw the figure of the administrator Hendake and priest Sethon. She even saw Den and felt that she was no longer resentful toward him. Then she saw her father, King Nikal, sitting on the throne in the company of her brothers. In the distance, she also saw a vague female figure. She knew it was her mother.

"It is so very beautiful here," she repeated and wiped away the tears that flowed abundantly as if their source was inexhaustible.

Suddenly she felt a lump in her throat. It was so strong that it cut off her air. Everyone was still asleep in the palace. It was very early. Hemet, who occupied the chamber after Seshep, had not yet woken up. Makeda wanted to scream, but she couldn't. She tried to reach for the gong but failed. Her body was weak. She sank to the floor.

She felt a powerful brightness explode in her head. It slowly filled her body, calming and soothing her. She could no longer feel her throat tightening, she did not lack air. She smiled to herself. She knew that she was safe, that she didn't need anyone's help because she was in the best hands.

"I am who I am," she heard.

She recognized whose voice it was because he had spoken to her all her life. The one who in her childhood was unknown to her, worried her and was a mystery, who gave her directions and prophecies, now brought relief, fulfillment and a promise.

"Here is the eternal fire. It is burning and will never go out," the Lady of the Moon wrapped her in the words she knew well.

She knew she was going to them: God and the Lady of the Moon. That they were waiting for her, and when she was sure that she was heading home and that the journey would not be long, someone else appeared. He stood in the distance, at the end of a bright path, in the sun's rays. Even though she couldn't see his face yet, she knew he was smiling.

"Come to me. We will go from now on together, until the infinite..." she heard.

He held out his hands to her.

She was walking on a wide, bright rainbow, and he waited to hug her. She floated to him, hovered above the ground, filled with love and awaiting for fulfillment. He was getting closer. Finally, their hands met. She felt his warmth. He hugged her tightly. So tightly that they became one again, and a song resounded. Countless choirs were singing it. You could hear it everywhere. It was floating over the world. It filled souls. It reached the furthest corners of the earth to move hearts and minds. It poured joy, goodness and beauty into them. It was reassuring, it was a relief. It carried to heights.

Put me like a seal on your chest, like a seal on your shoulder! Because love is stronger than death, it is as bright as the glow of God's flame. The water will not quench our love, vast depths will not absorb it. If someone would give away all the riches of their home for love, he would only be despised.

Their souls merged.

"Now I will finally hide you in my arms and not give you back, even when the whole world asks for you," she heard.

"I missed you so much..."

THE END

... no, it's not the end. For the story of the love of Queen of Sheba and King Solomon, just like the Song of Songs, will last forever...

FROM THE SOLOMON'S BOOK OF PROVERBS

The wise one notices evil and protects himself against it, the silly one goes on and then regrets.

Just as only iron polishes iron, so one man molds another.

Like cold water for the throat of the thirsty, so good is the news from a distant country.

It is not good to eat too much honey or to listen to too many words that flatter us.

Don't brag about tomorrow, because you don't know what's behind it yet.

Let others praise you, not you with your lips; strangers, not your own lips.

Whoever digs holes under others, falls into them himself; whoever rolls a stone up a hill, will get under it himself.

Lazy man, look at the ant, look at its work and be smart at last! After all, it has no teacher, no overseer or supervisor, and yet it gathers food during the summer, and stores supplies during the harvest. So till when, lazy man, will you lounge? When will you finally want to rise from your sleep? Sleep a little more, have a little longer nap, cross your hands idly, rest, and misery will fall upon you like on a beggar, and scarcity like on a pauper.

The father of the righteous rejoices out loud, because to have a wise son, is true happiness.

My son, when your heart is wise, my own heart rejoices.

Whoever seeks justice and goodness, finds life and fame.

ACKNOWLEDGEMENTS

I was in the Far East. Between rummaging through old and new knowledge for the next novel and yoga exercises, I read an email from my American publisher. Maria Cowen; she asked me what I thought about the female heroines of the Bible.

After Cleopatra and Nefertiti, Hatshepsut crowned my Egyptian trilogy. I haven't decided yet what to do next. I had a lot of ideas on my mind, the readers were flooding me with themes for new novels. Maria suggested that I look at the Bible, and specifically, to start with the Queen of Sheba. After exploring the subject, I felt that it was the path for me for the coming years. The Queen of Sheba spoke to me immediately. Iwona, Małgosia, Daga, Jurek, Mikołaj, Andrzej, Marek - do you remember how excited I was? You were there with me then.

I immediately received a lot of useful information from US, texts and tips on where to look for the ancient world of Sheba. In this way, Maria Cowen became the Godmother of my biblical trilogy. Maria, thank you very much for your idea and support during my literary "biblical" journey.

Before I started working on the novel, the first thing I learned was that Sheba was the name of the country, not the name of the queen. Did you know?

The queen of Sheba, Makeda, did not spare me information about herself. She appeared in my dreams, gave me signs, talked to me, revealing in various ways what was previously a mystery and an unknown space to me. I learned some of her secrets (because, obviously, she did not reveal all of them to me), I looked at the kingdom she ruled, I was honored to meet people from her surroundings, as well as those who functioned in the world of the man of her life - Solomon. So, I watched the members of the Sheba court, priestesses, priests, advisers, merchants, builders, soldiers, merchant Tamrin, but also Queen Bathsheba, King David and other characters that appear in the Bible, among other sources.

Makeda fascinated me. I became a faithful subject to her and, I hope, at least a bit of a friend, as did hemet Seshep and the High Priestess.

Makeda (or Bilkis, as she was also called) was the wisest, most beautiful, and richest queen of her times. When she decided, guided by the prophecies and her own visions from childhood, to go to distant Israel, she had to travel 1,400 miles. Her caravan had over 700 camels. The trip lasted six months. Among the gifts she brought for the ruler of Israel were 4.5 tons of gold!

Where did I get my knowledge about Makeda and Solomon? First of all, from The Old Testament. The references to the country of Sheba can be found in the books of Job, Isaiah and Jeremiah, and about the queen herself in the First Kings Book. Not much has been written about Makeda in the Bible, but it is a treasury of information about Israel and its kings of that time. In my novel, you will find many quotes coming from there, always clearly marked.

Here is the best known one:

[the English text is from this website: https://www.biblegateway.com/passage/?search=1+Kings+10&version=NIV]

When the queen of Sheba heard about the fame of Solomon and his relationship to the Lord, she came to test Solomon with hard questions. Arriving at Jerusalem with a very great caravan— with camels carrying spices, large quantities of gold, and precious stones—she came to Solomon and talked with him about all that she had on her mind. Solomon answered all her questions; nothing was too hard for the king to explain to her. When the queen of Sheba saw all the wisdom of Solomon and the palace he had built, the food on his table, the seating of his officials, the attending servants in their robes, his cupbearers, and the burnt offerings he made at the temple of the Lord, she was overwhelmed. She said to the king, "The report I heard in my own country about your achievements and your wisdom is true. But I did not believe these things until I came and saw with my own eyes. Indeed, not even half was told to me; in wisdom and wealth you have far exceeded the report I heard. How happy your people must be! How happy your officials, who continually stand before you and hear your wisdom! Praise be to the Lord your God, who has delighted in you and placed you on the throne of Israel. Because of the Lord's eternal love for Israel, he has made you king to maintain justice and righteousness." And she gave the king 120 talents of gold, large quantities of spices, and precious stones. Never again were so many spices brought in as those the queen of Sheba gave to King Solomon. Hiram's ships brought gold from Ophir; and from there they brought great cargoes of almugwood and precious stones. The king used the almugwood to make supports for the temple of the Lord and for the royal palace, and to make harps and lyres for the musicians. So much almugwood has never been imported or seen since that day. King Solomon gave the queen of Sheba all she desired and asked for, besides what he had given her out of his royal bounty. Then she left and returned with her retinue to her own country*.

I also looked into the Koran and books describing the riddles and tests that Makeda had prepared for Solomon. They were: Targum Sheni and Midrash Mishlei.

I often reached for Kebra Nagast "Glory of the Kings." It is the story of the Sheba kingdom at the times of Makeda and her son Menelik, and how the Ark of the Covenant got to Ethiopia. The book was created in the ancient language of Ge'ez, appeared in the Coptic language around 1225, and it was discovered for science and translated for the first time by the German, Carl Bezold, in 1886.

Who has not heard of the queen's prophecies? When I talk to Readers about Sheba, most have associations with this topic. It is obvious. The Book of Prophecies of the Queen of Sheba circulated the homes of our grandmothers, great-grandmothers, and great-great-grandmothers, where it was often read with flushed faces. It talked about the terrible punishments that await mankind if it doesn't obey God's laws, announced when the end of the world would be and what signs would precede it. In my novel I have not omitted these terrible visions.

In my search I have reached many people dealing with biblical subjects. I am grateful to Father Professor Jan Klinkowski not only for his books (including: Ark of the Covenant. From Sinai to Aksum), but also for patience, openness, and advice regarding, among others, naming and geography of Sheba. Also Fr. prof. Andrzej Demitrow showed me extensive literature on the subject and gave many tips on where to look for the queen's trails.

Professor Andrzej Ćwiek, an Egyptologist, drew my attention not only to what was in my novel about ancient Egypt, but also to the characteristic throne of Solomon, so often depicted by artists. I described it in detail in the book.

While preparing for writing, I read a lot of professional literature, watched a lot of movies, visited not only libraries, but also museums. Particularly useful in writing, in addition to the already mentioned Bible and Koran, were the Old Testament Apocrypha edited by Fr. Ryszard Rubinkiewicz, The History of Jews by Simon Schama, The History of Religious Ideas, written by Mircea Eliade, Talmud in the edition of Abraham Cohen, Ark of the Covenant by Roderick Grierson and Stuart Munro-Hay, From the Country of Queen of Sheba by Sylvia Pankhurst, and Alan Moorehead's The Blue Nile and The White Nile. I also looked into Fashion in the Bible and Biblical Geography by Barbara Szczepanowicz. I am grateful to all the authors whose works I could use.

In the novel, the name of the city of Kassala appears in the footnotes. The only son of Makeda and Solomon, Menelik, was born there, in the temple of the priestesses of the Lady of the Moon. Today, Kassala is located in northeastern Sudan. It belonged once to the kingdom of Sheba. Interesting, isn't it?

While writing, I got support from many people, as always. I am grateful to my father, Bonifacy, for the joy of life, sense of humor and the breakfasts he prepared, making sure that I ate everything. To my husband Jerzy, for kindness, forbearance, patience, and support, not only in the matters about military expeditions and wars (I am more and more convinced that men perceive the world differently from women), but also for champagne for breakfast on important family celebrations. My son Mikołaj made sure that the Song of Songs sounded properly in the book, consulting it with Hebrew professor Miri Beck - thank you, Professor, thank you Mikołaj. Besides, Mikołaj, your singing of Leonard Cohen's Allelujah, accompanied by guitar, has been invariably touching and moving me for years.

To my sister Sylwia, who is a psychotherapist, and is rarely at my fingertips - I know that we are close regardless of on which continent each of us is at the moment.

Henry Hermann, or Enri Her - the incomparable master chef for all my Egyptian queens - was also so kind to prepare dishes for the Queen of Sheba. It is his artistry that made... oh, if you have already finished reading, you know that the right dishes can change the fate of the world.

I also thank all my invaluable girl friends who support me in writing. For conversations, coffees, teas, telephones, gifts, often very long, profound conversations, including night and secret ones. Thank you for your vast knowledge, professionalism, life experience, sensitivity, and above all, for your vision of the world.

Iwona Woźniak-Bagińska, Ewa Piaskowska, Maja Zawała, Izabela Migocz, Jola Kurecka, Agnieszka Brzezińska - I don't know what Makeda would be like if you weren't with me, with your support, not only spiritual. Thank you for the opportunity to talk with those who got to know the areas I wrote about in the novel. I am grateful for the constant presence of fairies from around the world, the seeing, priestesses and other people dealing with spirituality.

I am very happy that life has come full circle, and after twenty years, I came to Videograf again. It was here that my novel Portrait of a Woman of the Age of Perdition was published some time ago. Now our paths have converged again. I thank the director Franciszek Leki for the warm, professional reception, and the whole team, especially Anna Seweryn and Magdalena Paluch, who edited my Sheba with great skill and sensitivity.

I also thank the Readers who visit my ewakassala.com page and my author page on Facebook, for their comments, letters, discussions about the book covers, tips, inspiration, opinions and reflections, not only on literary topics; and for the fact that you not only read my books but come in large numbers to author meetings. Your energy gives me strength, and the reactions to subsequent novels encourage me to meet more queens and transfer their fate to the pages of a novel.

First of all, I thank Queen Makeda for letting me write about her. It is an honor and privilege for me.

Ewa Kassala